THE STAR WITNESS

Andy Hamilton

Unbound

First published by Unbound in 2016

This paperback edition published in 2017

Unbound

6th Floor Mutual House, 70 Conduit Street, London W1S 2GF

www.unbound.com

© Andy Hamilton, 2016

Text Design by PDQ

Art direction by Mark Ecob

A CIP record for this book is available from the British Library

ISBN 978-1-78352-298-9 (trade hbk)
ISBN 978-1-78352-299-6 (ebook)
ISBN 978-1-78352-297-2 (limited edition)
ISBN 978-1-78352-396-2 (paperback edition)

Printed in Great Britain by Clays Ltd, St Ives Plc

1 3 5 7 9 8 6 4 2

Andy Hamilton is a comedy scriptwriter and performer. He regularly appears on *QI* and *Have I Got News for You*. His writing credits include *Outnumbered, Drop the Dead Donkey, Not the Nine O'Clock News, Trevor's World of Sport, What We Did On Our Holiday* and many others. He plays Satan in the Radio 4 comedy *Old Harry's Game*, which he also writes.

For Libby

DEAR READER,

The book you are holding came about in a rather different way to most others. It was funded directly by readers through a new website: Unbound. Unbound is the creation of three writers. We started the company because we believed there had to be a better deal for both writers and readers. On the Unbound website, authors share the ideas for the books they want to write directly with readers. If enough of you support the book by pledging for it in advance, we produce a beautifully bound special subscribers' edition and distribute a regular edition and e-book wherever books are sold, in shops and online.

This new way of publishing is actually a very old idea (Samuel Johnson funded his dictionary this way). We're just using the internet to build each writer a network of patrons. Here, at the back of this book, you'll find the names of all the people who made it happen.

Publishing in this way means readers are no longer just passive consumers of the books they buy, and authors are free to write the books they really want. They get a much fairer return too – half the profits their books generate, rather than a tiny percentage of the cover price.

If you're not yet a subscriber, we hope that you'll want to join our publishing revolution and have your name listed in one of our books in the future. To get you started, here is a £5 discount on your first pledge. Just visit unbound.com, make your pledge and type **witness** in the promo code box when you check out.

Thank you for your support,

Dan, Justin and John
Founders, Unbound

1

THE MISTAKE

If you know me at all, you will know me as a liar.

That is almost certainly the perception you will have of me. There's absolutely nothing I can do about that. I lied, that is public knowledge. But the lying is only one small part of my story – a story that needs telling, if only so I can come to understand it better myself. So I'm going to present myself to you, warts and all, or as my friend Mac describes me, ninety-five per cent warts. And I'm going to tell the story as I lived it, in the here and now, stumbling from moment to moment, with my heart in my mouth.

So, where to begin? With my character? Maybe. Maybe I should start in my childhood, or the rapids of adolescence, but there was nothing exceptional about my upbringing; so I think that this story begins more recently, at a critical choice, at a tipping point.

It begins with a fork.

I am sitting in a restaurant with a beautiful young woman with impossibly blue eyes and there is a forkful of lamb suspended in mid-air a few inches from my mouth. And that's where it will stay. I can see myself now, a frozen frame, the first bad decision. I should have kept eating, it was just a crass remark, I should have let it go. If only I had let it go.

She is waiting for a response to her latest observation, and I could ignore it, God knows I've ignored all the others. She's already come out with several potential fork-stoppers. Almost as soon as we arrived – as the head waiter led us to our "special guest table" – she hit me with the first one.

"Irony is dead," she announced, flicking her hair back out of her eyes. "That's what my mate Keir says, he says audiences aren't interested in ideas any more, they want emotions, he's doing an article about it – 'Sincerity is the New Irony'."

I let that one go.

I'd known many beautiful women who talked rubbish; having to listen to them was the price you had to pay.

And so I had let her babble on. There was the occasional diner, I noticed, who was staring at us, but that was normal.

All through the evening, she kept them coming. As we finished our minuscule entrées, she had told me that fashion was basically just literature written in clothing.

I waved that one through.

When she had said that if Sophocles were alive today he would be writing for Hollyoaks, again, I gave no response – not the barest flicker.

But slowly, as the meal wore on, something deep, deep down inside me had begun to recoil. I had been listening to this kind of drivel for months now, trying not to wince whenever she expressed an opinion. So why the hell was I still seeing her?

At one level, the answer was simple. She was stunning. Also, she was twenty-four and I was fifty-two, so do the maths. My ego – fairly swollen to begin with – had grown to the size of a cathedral because this beautiful young woman found me attractive, even though I was old enough to be her considerably older brother. But our conversations had become…well, I knew that my passivity was demeaning and that was making me angry, I suppose, deep down.

Looking back, I see that now.

But, at the time, I think I told myself – heigh-ho, she was what she was. We were what we were. So, the evening would probably have passed without incident if she hadn't finally come out with an absolute belter.

She looks up from her plate and says: "Of course, many people feel that the black community in South Africa was better off under apartheid."

That's the one.

The one that stops the fork.

I have a choice. I could eat my lamb, or I could change the subject, but instead, after quite a pause, and with an edge of disdain, I hear myself say that fateful word.

"What?"

I put down my fork, unaware that I'm stepping towards an abyss.

"Many people feel the black community was better off then," she recaps, with a breezy smile.

"Many people?" I echo, flatly.

"Yeh."

"Many people…as in who?"

"Well, y'know, commentators…observers." She pauses for a moment, losing confidence. "Commentators," she repeats, a little too loudly. "Y'know, Africa-watchers."

"Africa-watchers like…?"

"Well, like my friend, Janine."

"Right, Janine's a journalist, is she?"

"No, she's an estate agent."

"An estate agent." There is a coldness creeping into my voice that I can do nothing about.

"In Putney," she adds, as if that fact was significant.

"And where does she get her detailed knowledge of South African history from?"

"She's from Johannesburg."

I pause to gather my thoughts; my head now jangling with irritation.

"She's a white South African."

"Yes."

"In Putney?"

"That's right."

"So she's not really an 'Africa-watcher', is she? She's more of an Africa-leaver."

Her cheeks are starting to redden as she chases a lentil around her plate.

"I don't quite get the point you're trying to make, Kevin, perhaps I'm being thick."

I try to smile. "All I'm saying," I begin, carefully, "is that maybe your friend, Janine, is not the best qualified person to—"

Bang! In she comes! "Well, Janine happens to be a very bright woman, actually."

"Well, she can't be that bright if she's an estate agent, I mean, all the really clever South Africans get to be dental hygienists."

Her lovely mouth hangs open for a few seconds, then she goldfishes for a few more, before straightening her shoulders and telling me that I am a racist.

I laugh, a lot. I can't help it, this is like shooting fish in a barrel and, shamefully, I am starting to enjoy myself. She leans forward in an attempt to keep the conversation private.

"It is very racist of you to write her off just because of where she's from."

"Yeh, yeh, OK," I sigh, dabbing at my eyes with a napkin. "But if God had intended us to like South Africans, he wouldn't have made them sound like that."

Cheap, flip and easy, but it feels so good. Her voice has a little crack in it now and she is starting to sound like a ten-year-old.

"You are *so* prejudiced."

"All right, Jade, lighten up, it was just—" And then, suddenly, up they pop, from nowhere, two of them, a man and a woman, middle-aged, sort of drab.

4

"You're him, aren't you," says the man, pointing at me like I'm an exhibit.

"Yes." I give him the standard smile. "I'm him."

"I said you were him, we're sitting over there, my wife said you weren't him, but I said you were him. I knew you were him."

He turns to Jade. "And you're her."

"That's right, yes."

"The new one. That was a good cat-fight you had with his ex. She had it coming."

Before Jade can answer, he's turning back to me. "So what have you got planned for this one, eh? Are you going to do the dirty on her like you have with all the others, you dirty monkey, eh?"

His wife is trying to intervene now.

"Leave them alone, Barry." (It might have been Gary or Harry.) She tugs gently at his elbow, but he is still leering at me.

"So what have you got planned, eh? What's going to happen?"

"I'm afraid that, contractually, we're not allowed to divulge the storylines of future episodes."

"Oh, go on, you can tell me."

"Well yes, but then I'd have to kill you."

"What, and stick me under the patio along with that drug baron who tried to frame you for the raid on Bobby's health spa?" He swivels back to Jade. "You're too good for him, er... what's your name again?"

"Jade."

"No, no, no," he says, with a dismissive flap of a hand, "not *your* name, *her* name."

"Melanie."

"Yeh," he chuckles, "Melanie's too good for you." He's aiming his finger at me again now. "You bad dog. She's got morals. And a kiddie."

"Leave them be," sighs the wife.

"A kiddie with a life-threatening illness."

"They're having their dinner. I'm sorry, he's being annoying, isn't he?"

"No, not at all." My smile is starting to hurt now. He sets off again.

"All I'm saying, Joan –" (Jean? Jane?) "– is that he won't run rings around *her*, like he did with all the others. Especially the last one, she just cried all the time and shouted at her gay brother. But this one, she's clever and independent-minded."

"Well, her character is," I say, fast, a reflex. He stares at me for a moment, blinking slowly, like a character out of the Simpsons.

"Sorry?"

"Well, her character…Melanie…is clever and independent-minded, but in real life she gets all her opinions off estate agents."

Silence.

The wife is looking at the floor, embarrassed, and Jade is staring at me with her jaw hanging slack. It was just a moment of casual cruelty, the kind of smartarse remark that I must have made hundreds, even thousands of times.

I shouldn't have said it. If it all began with that first "what?", then this was the next nail in my coffin. And I am sitting there with a smug grin, oblivious and empty.

The man's wife is the first to speak.

"Right…well, nice meeting you both, come along, love." She leads him away. He calls over his shoulder to Jade: "Keep your eye on him, Melanie! And stay away from the canal!"

"Bye!" calls the wife.

I give her a playschool wave. "By-e."

Jade is still staring at me, her big blue eyes filming over with tears. I feel awkward. I try to lighten the mood.

"Well, that's our audience. Hanging on to reality by their fingernails. Makes your blood run cold, doesn't it, eh?"

She's still staring.

"This wine's not bad…"

Still staring.

"…for house plonk."

Finally, she half-croaks the word, "Why?"

"Sorry?"

"Why? Why did you feel the need to say that about me just now?"

A bloody good question, as it happens. After all, if you're going out with someone and you feel the urge to humiliate them in front of total strangers, then that's probably a bad sign, isn't it? True, some relationships thrive on routine humiliation but that's usually inside marriage.

Anyway, the depressing, inescapable truth was that this relationship wasn't thriving. It was no fun any more. And yet it had started out as a lot of fun, seven months ago, when we first met in make-up.

It was a Monday in August sometime, or it could have been September. I know it was warm, because I can see the sweat on Polly's face as she powders my forehead.

Nigel, the first assistant, is bustling around behind me talking anxiously into a mouthpiece and coughing intermittently, a lung-scraping cough that makes everyone wince. I can hear the sparks shouting at each other – ripe jokes about Wayne Rooney – and the clang-and-rattle of moving lights. The runner, Avril (or is it Alice?), charges past, breathlessly looking for a lost actor and I'm about to take my first aspirin of the day when suddenly Pam arrives with a continuity Polaroid. Within moments, Pam and Polly are primping and preening me.

"Leave me alone, you pair of harpies."

"Behave," says Pam, whacking me on the back of the head with a comb.

"What are you doing?"

"My job. Shut up and keep still."

Now Simone from wardrobe has arrived and they're all consulting the Polaroid.

"You know my theory about women who work in make-up and wardrobe..."

"Not interested," Pam mutters.

"I reckon they're all girls who didn't get given any dolls to play with as kids. I'm just an adult doll."

"You're not an adult anything."

They giggle as Simone gets out a different set of Polaroids.

"Scene 38B? He should be in the blue shirt. OK, shirt off, Kevin. That one's wrong."

Nigel trundles back, still shouting at someone down his mouthpiece.

"What do you mean his car didn't pick him up? He's due on set now."

"Morning, Nige," I say quietly.

"He wasn't home? Well where the fuck is he?"

"Morning, Kevin, how are you," I reply on his behalf.

"Eh? What? Oh, yeh, sorry, morning, Kevin." Then he coughs, long and hard.

"Can you die somewhere else, Nige? We don't want your germs."

But he doesn't respond. He's listening to something he doesn't want to hear through his earpiece, his forehead folding into yet more creases.

"What...? You are joking. Tell me you're joking...he said he was going to Spain?" His head drops forward in defeat.

"Gavin?" I ask, knowing the answer.

"Yeh, totally AWOL. I dunno, it was a lot easier before he went into rehab, least you knew where he was...blacked out on his bathroom floor."

Then he's shouting down his mouthpiece again. "Have you

rung his moby? I really don't need this. He's in five scenes today, without him we are totally upgefucked."

The shouting triggers his cough again. Pam and Polly shake their heads. A passing stagehand mutters: "If he were a horse, they'd put him down."

A different runner beetles past, a work-experience girl, out of breath, looking for the caterers because there are no plastic cups. A sound man (Del? Mel?), who has the beginnings of Nigel's cough, arrives to mic me up. But Simone is pulling me out of my shirt and Pam and Polly are moaning that everything's being done in the wrong order this morning and the Health and Safety man is shouting something about some cables and amid all this mayhem I slowly become aware of a beautiful young woman standing nervously on the fringe of the make-up area. She has enormous, blue Disney eyes, long, naturally blonde hair and a smile that carries a hint of apology.

"Hi," I say, as Simone rams me into a new shirt.

"Oh, sorry, sorry," Nigel flusters, "this is Jade. Everyone? This is Jade. Jade's playing Melanie, the new character."

"Hi, everyone," she says with a little-me wave.

"Welcome," I say, as Simone tugs at my collar.

"Hi."

"Nervous?"

"Terrified."

"That's normal. On my first day, I threw up in the dressing room."

"Well, you still do that," sighs Simone. Pam and Polly cackle.

"Ignore this lot, Jade," I say, "they're full of hate."

A couple of crew step forward to shake Jade's hand, but everything is drowned out by Nigel's coughing. In between coughs, as he fights for air, he is imploring the producer down the phone: "You have to do something, Louise, you have to lay it on the line for Gavin, a final warning or something."

9

The sound guy starts coughing as well. I can see Jade is looking thrown.

"The crews on soaps are always ill, I'm afraid. It's the schedule, it's relentless, long hours, up at five, not home till ten, it kicks the crap out of the immune system."

Her face has dropped.

"But the actors are OK. It's the performing, means we've got enough adrenalin to see off the bugs. Well, till we stop filming, then we're sick as dogs."

"Right," she says, raising perfectly arched eyebrows.

Then Nigel ups his volume. "Look, Louise, Gavin *has* to be put on notice...Well, I dunno, can't you have a word with the writers? They could put him in a coma or something...drop a bit of viaduct on him...again."

I step closer to Jade. She smells of apples.

"Have they told you where your storyline's headed?" I ask her.

"Um, well, as far as I know, I, um, I sleep with you...obviously."

"Yeh, that's compulsory for all the female characters."

"And then my kid's going to get sick with some disease."

"Oh, what fun."

We talk for a bit. She laughs at all my jokes, although it's too early to tell whether she's a woman who always laughs at men's jokes. After a few minutes, Nigel starts clapping his hands.

"Listen up, everyone, be quiet, listen...LISTEN...thank you so much. OK, so Gavin's a no-show, stop groaning, Gavin's a no-show, so my lovingly crafted schedule gets flushed down the bog, and we're pulling forward scene 21, Melanie's first encounter with Lenny, sexual chemistry, bla-blah-blah, up until she storms out, everyone got that?"

Jade puffs out her cheeks. "Straight in at the deep end, then. Crikey."

"You'll be fine," I tell her.

"Yeh, I'll be OK once we start to rehearse."

The make-up girls giggle. "Rehearse?" says Simone.

"Oh, bless," sighs Nigel. "OK, so it's scene 21 final checks, we'll be going straight for a take."

* * *

When the lunch break arrives (only fifteen minutes late) I head for the canteen and grab a table by the window, waiting for the new girl to appear. But instead, Gavin appears from nowhere and slumps into the chair opposite me. He has no plate of food, just a pot of yoghurt.

"Where were you?" I ask. "You were supposed to be in every scene this morning. It's been pandemonium. They said you were in Spain."

Gavin mumbles into his yoghurt. Something about nobody understanding; his eyes flicker around, like those of a small, cornered mammal.

"Are you alright?" I ask, though I don't really care.

"I can't handle this new schedule, Kevin. It's too much. They've added twelve hours to the filming week, I can't function like that." He pushes the yoghurt carton away. "It's making me ill."

"Then get a doctor's note. Get signed off."

"Not that kind of ill," he says, bleakly.

We sit in silence for a few moments. Some sparks suddenly burst out laughing on the table behind us, which makes Gavin jump. Then he lets out a deep, long, attention-seeking sigh.

Where is Jade? Perhaps she brought sandwiches.

"I'm going to make a formal complaint about this new schedule, because it is ridiculous, isn't it?"

"Yes, Gavin, it is ridiculous."

She might be eating in the make-up truck with the harpies.

"If I make a written complaint, will you sign it as well?

Perhaps you could persuade the rest of the cast. No one will listen to me."

He's right, they won't.

"If we said we felt it was in the best interests of the show, then Louise couldn't just ignore us, could she? Especially if you...y'know..."

Oh God, he's casting me as Spartacus.

"...I mean, if people get exhausted emotionally...how are we supposed to act? It's self-defeating. They at least owe us some input. No artist can work in this kind of environment."

Alright, that's it. I put down my knife and fork and stare directly into those hunted-looking eyes.

"OK, Gavin, listen...what we do here is not art. This is fundamentally a sausage-making factory and we are the mechanically retrieved meat that goes into the sausage-making machine. All that they are interested in is banging out more sausages for the buck. So, please, don't use the word 'artist' again, or I may just throw up. All anyone wants from you is for you to turn up, on time if at all possible, say the lines, collect your cheque and bugger off. No one wants your input, nobody *owes* anyone anything, you are just a piece of sausage."

Suddenly she's there, tray in hand.

"Can I join you?"

"Be my guest," says Gavin, as he picks up his yoghurt pot.

"I'm not interrupting anything, am I?"

"No," he replies, with a half laugh, then he rises and leaves.

I call after him. "Gavin, this is Jade." But he doesn't turn.

"Oh dear...was it me?" she asks.

"'Course not. You're perfect," I tell her, and her whole face lights up.

For the next few days, I did not come on too strong, I just engineered as many friendly chats with Jade as possible. And, as part of that charm offensive, I am fetching tea from the big urn in the corner of the studio, when I feel a familiar chill at my shoulder.

"Making tea for two, Kevin?"

"Yes, Louise, I'm getting Jade a cup."

"That's nice," she says, with a thin twitch of a smile. "It's lovely how you always make the new actresses feel at home…actually –" (here we go. I recognise that pause) "– I've been meaning to have a chat with you." (Yes I knew it. This will probably be about the waiting time on my cars.) "I…um…I was watching a first cut of the scene you filmed on Monday – the one where Lenny finds out that Gary's gone to the police…" (Eh? Where's she going with this?) "And I felt…" (Yes?) "I felt…well, nothing really, not a thing…and that was the problem."

"And did you expect to feel something, Louise?"

"Yes, of course. I mean Lenny's just discovered his brother's betraying him. I wanted to experience his rage."

"Really? That doesn't sound very healthy."

A micro-frown. Good. I'm getting to her. She steadies herself.

"You know perfectly well what I mean…I want to see him feel the anger."

I start pouring the second cup of tea. "Lenny's anger is inside…where no one can see it."

"Well that's not much use to the viewer, is it, Kevin?"

The urn coughs out hot water in fits and starts.

Louise takes a breath and ploughs on. "It's your job to make us feel what his emotions are."

"But Lenny never shows his emotions. That's what makes him so interesting. I've always played him…internalised."

"Yes, well there's a difference between internalised and autistic."

She's pleased with that, I can tell, but I'm not prepared to give her the satisfaction of seeing me fray. So I decide to be frivolous, because I know she hates that.

"Perhaps he *is* autistic, Louise. Perhaps that's been his problem all along."

"*Très drôle.*" (Ooh, French, she's really narked, bullseye.) "The thing is, Kevin," (come on, baby, give it your best shot) "we pay you a lot of money," (debatable) "...and for that money we expect you to deliver," (yeh, deliver, like groceries) "and that isn't happening."

As Louise drones on, I find myself wondering how much mental energy I expend heckling her like this. And it's not just her. These days it feels like I'm watching everyone from the back of the stalls. She's wearing a pained smile now, while she assesses my performance in the Christmas episode. What a waste – for such a highly intelligent woman to be overseeing a show like this. There are so many worthwhile things she might be doing, instead of trying to constantly win more and more viewers at less unit cost.

"Am I boring you, Kevin?"

"No, not at all, Louise. I'm just surprised that there are any concerns over my performance. None of the many directors you employ have mentioned anything."

"They're too busy staying on schedule. I...I'm just saying that I think you could give it a bit more."

Should I let that go? Probably. But I'm not going to.

"I give it as much as it needs, or deserves." She straightens slightly. Time for me to leave. "Now, if you'll excuse me, Jade's tea is getting cold."

As I shape to move past her, she steps closer and lowers her voice. "I want to see more emotion on screen, Kevin."

"Fine, just ask the writers to indicate which emotion you want in the stage instructions at the top of the scene...in that helpful way of theirs."

"When did you get so cynical, Kevin? (Oh this is rich, from the most cynical person on planet Earth.) The writers are giving it one hundred per cent. (No they're not. What would be the point?) I'd expect a little more solidarity from you. You used to write, yourself, didn't you? Once upon a time."

There is a twinkle behind the eyes that tells me she feels she has drawn blood. But I'm not going to show her anything.

"That was a million years ago, Louise. In a previous existence."

I start to move away with the teas. She's got nothing left. She can't fire me and she knows it.

So why is she walking alongside me?

"This...schtick of yours, Kevin. You need to be careful. Because sooner or later...it will all catch up with you."

"What exactly will catch up with me?" She doesn't reply. She just gives me a short, cryptic smile.

"Well, I hope you've taken my observations on board."

Across the studio, I can see Jade leaving the set, heading towards me, luminous and expectant. Louise turns away and starts to glide towards the scene dock. I call after her.

"It's duly noted, Louise. You think I'm phoning in my performance."

"Darling," she calls back, without a glance. "I think you're phoning in your life."

But it hardly registers, because Jade is taking the tea from me and telling me, wide-eyed, that I'm a lifesaver.

I liked Jade then, in the early days, I liked her a lot. I liked the nervousness in her. The way she would pull a face and say "Crikey". There's something very attractive about a woman who's permanently bewildered.

In the first few weeks, Jade and I had to do a lot of kissing scenes, as Melanie and Lenny began their on/off, love/hate relationship. Kissing someone on a hot, brightly lit set while being watched by lots of fat technicians is not remotely arousing. It's very un-sexy, you ask any actor, that's what they'll tell you.

And they're all lying bastards. Of course it's arousing, we're not made of stone. Yes, you're trained and professional but your hormones aren't. And, as for the stuff about it being impossible to get sexually excited kissing someone you don't really know in front of dozens of people…two words: "office" and "party".

So, pretty soon, Jade and I were a couple, of sorts. Admittedly, on my side, the relationship was a little bit penis-led, but that's how many relationships begin, isn't it? Well, most of mine. All bar one, in fact. I can't actually remember what we talked about in those first weeks, but I don't recall any conversations about feelings or families or the dreaded "where is this going?". Just a lot of sex and conspiratorial intimacy; sly glances and brushing fingers. She was fresh and she was fun, and most important of all, she stopped me from feeling bored. On set, we were discreet and professional and we did a very good job of keeping everything quiet, until the Daily Star printed photos of us snogging in a lay-by.

They weren't very good photos, they were taken from a long way away. On a mobile phone. By a twelve-year-old girl.

So, accepting the inevitable, Jade and I went public. The programme's publicity department had a multiple orgasm. To begin with, I refused all their requests for us to do joint interviews, but Jade argued that we might as well do one and get it out of the way.

Looking back, it surprises me that I gave in to her. Why did I do that? It wasn't like me. Perhaps I felt more for her than I realised.

So one morning, we find ourselves waiting nervously in a green room lined with large photos of toothy presenters.

"Crikey," she says, "this is scary."

"Hey, come on." I squeeze her hand. "How bad can it be?"

Half an hour later we're sitting side by side on a sofa, live, on daytime TV, being interviewed by a shiny two-headed creature called NickandWendy.

Wendy trills like a budgie: "And we're very excited now, yes, we are, aren't we?"

"Well, you're excited," simpers Nick.

"Well, you're excited too."

'Yes, I'm excited too, but I'm not bouncing around like a two-year-old, missy."

We have to sit there like lemons while these two fuckwits continue this display of sexless flirting until Wendy gives him a playful presenter's whack on the shoulder and hisses: "Stop it, you!"

She turns to camera two. "He is awful, isn't he, no but seriously though, we are very excited because joining us now are soapland's hottest couple, Melanie and Lenny, also known as actors Jade Pope and Kevin Carver. Welcome to you both."

We mumble our thank-yous.

"Now let's cut to the chase," bobs Wendy, "because we understand that, like Melanie and Lenny, in real life, you are an item, is that right?"

"An item?" I reply, with a professional twinkle. "You make us sound like something in a supermarket."

Nick and Wendy laugh, way too much.

"Two for the price of one," Jade adds. They laugh, we laugh, everyone's laughing, this is horrible. Already I'm regretting it, every fibre of my being is screaming "Get out now! While you can," but I just keep laughing.

"Seriously though," says Wendy, as if those two words had some transforming power, "you are together, aren't you?"

"Yes," I reply, "we are together." Although for some reason the word together comes out sounding like it's in quotation marks.

Nick leans forward, aiming for "earnest".

"Is that difficult? Y'know, having a romance which is sort of mirror-imaging the romance you're having in the show's storyline—"

17

"Which is great, by the way—"

"Oh yes – we're all—"

"Totally hooked."

"Totally, but is it a problem? The mirror-imaging thing?"

I breathe deep, to buy myself a moment where I can suppress my irritation.

"Well it's not really a problem, because, y'know, the show is just acting, whereas me and Jade…"

"…we're not acting," says Jade.

"No, that's right."

"The two of us –" she leans against my shoulder, "– that's real."

"Yeh, keep it real, man."

Nick and Wendy laugh like idiots. I laugh though inside I'm wondering why the fuck I just said that. Nick echoes "keep it real" with an attempt at a black-power, clenched-fist salute and Wendy giggles some more, but stops suddenly when she spots the Floor Manager, in mime, cutting his throat. For a moment, I get an urge to mime cutting my throat as well. Suddenly, Wendy sits up straight.

"Well, don't go away, you two, because after the break we've got Britain's Bravest Child. He's undergone fourteen major operations and I know he'd love to meet you."

* * *

I had sat on the sofa of death many times before. As Louise the producer was prone to pointing out, it was a contractual obligation. But I'd never had to fake quite that hard. Somewhere, in the dark at the back of my brain, I could hear the faint tinkle of an alarm bell.

As we ride back in the taxi, the bell gets louder.

"I thought that went quite well," she says.

A beat. Was that irony? Not sure. "Did you?" I reply.

"Yes. Didn't you?"

"No, it felt like torture."

Her shoulders stiffen. "Oh...I see...well, it was good for profile."

"Profile?"

"Yeh."

"Whose profile?"

She turns away to look out of the window.

"Everyone's."

"Everyone's?"

"Yes, you, me, the show...everyone's."

I look out of my window and watch the ant-heap of the rush hour. For a minute or so, I sit there feeling a growing sense of discomfort. Eventually, I can't take it any longer, it has to be said.

"What the fuck is 'profile', anyway?"

She looks at me as if I'm an idiot.

"Profile," she says, slowly, "is buzz."

"Profile is buzz?"

"Yes, buzz, it's important...it's why I did that photo session."

"Oh...right."

"What?"

"Nothing."

"I've got a good body, why should I hide it?"

"Did I say you should hide it?"

"It's what you didn't say."

"Oh, so now I'm also being held responsible for the things that I'm *not* saying. That leaves me a bit wide open, doesn't it?"

Jade then launches into an over-detailed justification of how the photoshoot will be "empowering" and, as she chatters, I begin to realise that this is a very different girl from the one that I had met a few months ago on the set.

This girl has acquired a strategy.

If I had had any guts I would have pulled the plug on

our relationship there and then; and none of this would have happened.

But, instead, I wait four months.

Until the moment when we are sitting in that restaurant and she hits me with that unanswerable question.

"Why did you feel the need to say that about me just now? About the estate agents…in front of that couple." Her eyes are cloudy and tears are brimming at the lids. "You showed me up, completely, in front of them, why?"

"I'm sorry," I shrug, limply.

"You're not an easy man to be with sometimes, Kevin, do you know that?"

"Yeh, I know."

She starts to ferret inside her bag for a Kleenex and I decide that this – now – is the moment.

"Listen, Jade." I reach across the table to take her hand, but I can see she's already alarmed by the new tenderness in my tone. "Erm…look, there's no easy way to tell you this…"

"You've found someone else?" she blurts.

"Good grief, no, no, there's no one else, it's just that, y'know, we've had a great time, but I feel…well, it's just this isn't working, is it? Not really, not if we're honest, maybe it's the age gap…"

"That's not bothered you before." She holds the Kleenex against her eyes.

"W-ell, I dunno it's…it just feels like we're going through the motions, I mean, at times, it feels like we don't even like each other that much any more."

What happens next is truly awful. She seems to physically shrink before my eyes; shrink and fade away, like I have pierced her. Her voice becomes hollow and tiny.

"…I like you."

"Oh…right." I can't think of what the hell to say. "Well," I falter. "…Maybe you shouldn't."

Her head drops, then she mutters: "But I do."

I feel my face flush as I stumble over my words. "Well, it's just too...too difficult, it's...y'know, I just think it'd be the best for us, y'know, 'cos, 'cos it's very difficult coping with this...mirror-imaging thing."

I know. Pathetic.

All right, yes, I could have handled it a little better. But it's never easy to avoid being trite in these situations because they are trite situations.

She doesn't say much during the rest of the meal. I can't eat. So that forkful of lamb just sits on the plate. She drinks. She drinks a lot. Very fast. I offer her a lift home and we head, in silence, towards the car park.

When we get to my car, she turns and fixes me with bleary intent; her head wobbling, loosened from her neck by the wine.

"So, when did you start pretending?"

I pretend not to understand the question. She totters forward and then catches herself. She straightens up, trying for an effect of dignity, as if the totter had never happened.

"When...when did you start pretending," she over-enunciates. "When did you start to be-gin ly-ing...that you liked me...last week? Three months ago? From day one?"

"Don't be silly. Jade, I—"

"Tell me when!" She starts shouting in my face. "When?! WHEN?!"

Suddenly, she gives me a slap. Across my face. Now this was not the first time I'd been hit by a woman, because my wife – ex-wife – once broke my nose in a tea-room in Bexhill. But this was the first time I'd been hit by a woman and half-expected it. Because if humans are divided into two sub-species, dumpers and dumpees, then I suspect Jade had always been the former. From her reaction in the restaurant, I sensed that she'd never been on the receiving end. Beautiful women rarely are. She was clearly very hurt and very raw.

So the slap is not a surprise.

The second one is, though. And the third, fourth and fifth. Now it's a problem, she's raining slaps on me faster than I can think, she's screaming, she's out of control, think, think, the slaps are getting faster and harder, I try to grab her hands and now she's kicking, kicking my shins, once, twice, so I push her and crack, her head has hit the kerb!

That's how fast it happened, in a blink. I didn't push her hard, I swear, I just pushed her away. I didn't expect her to fall, but she dropped so fast. She didn't even put her hands out to save herself, at least I don't think she did. It was so quick, so fast, one push, then she's on the ground, like there's a bit missed out, like a bad edit.

For a moment, she lies there, groaning, and the thought flashes across my mind that she might have fractured her skull. I bend down and pull her up into a sitting position, which is not what you're supposed to do, I know, but I can't think straight, I just want her to be OK.

"My God, that was one hell of a clout, are you all right?"

"I'm OK," she mumbles.

"You might have broken something."

"I'm fine, don't worry about me."

"You could be concussed."

"I'm fine."

"I could take you up the hospital."

I look to see if there's anyone else around, but the car park seems empty. Shakily, she pulls herself up on to her knees, her head slumped forward.

"We should get you looked at."

"I'm fine."

"I'm taking you up the hospital."

"No, it's OK, you've done enough, thanks."

Oddly, I find the sarcasm reassuring, it suggests that she is going to be all right.

"I...never meant for you to...I was just trying to stop you hitting me. I'm so sorry. Let me take you up the hospital, you can't be too careful with bangs on the head."

"I said I'm fine." Suddenly her voice has a metallic cut to it. "Just take me home...please."

So I did.

Nothing more was said. She seemed OK. Silent but OK. I watched her as far as her front door. She went inside. The lights went on. I went home. That was it.

When I got home the answerphone's red light was flashing and, for some reason, I remember hoping that the message would be from my ex-wife. I pressed play.

"It's me, you old bastard, give me a ring, doesn't matter how late, I'll still be up."

It was Mac. He's my oldest and best friend for reasons that I've never really been able to comprehend. We first met in the late 80s in a left-wing theatre group that toured the country performing agitprop musicals about capitalism that, for some reason, always involved juggling. Mac wrote the lyrics for the songs.

"Thatcher, Thatcher, Thatcher, Thatcher,
Wait until the people catch yer,
Your crimes will come to haunt you.
Hey, hey, Maggie, your time will come.
Bye, bye, Maggie, imperialist scum
Maggie, Maggie, Maggie
Good-byyeeee."

That was one. Well, we were young and we didn't embarrass easily. Mac still doesn't. After a couple of years, I packed it in. Somehow we hadn't managed to overthrow Mrs Thatcher and I was sick of waking up stiff-necked on someone's floor. I started hankering after a few luxuries, like an income.

But Mac keeps rolling along, perpetually joining socialist theatre groups until the inevitable happens and they fall out over money.

I ring his number.

"Hello," answers a voice so Glasgow you can smell the sticky pub carpet.

"Is that the HQ of the Scottish terror group Mac-Quaeda?"

"Hey, about time, tosspot, where have you been?"

"Oh…out."

"I was watching you earlier."

"Really, what was I doing?"

"You were setting fire to your restaurant for the insurance. Then you were telling that wee girlie with the sick kiddie that you were 'there for her'. The dialogue was ex-cre-ment-al. I couldn't bear to listen to it."

"Yeh, well, I just say it, I don't have to listen to it."

Down the line, I hear the tearing of a ring-pull.

"So, are you still going out with the wee girlie actress?"

"Um…as of tonight, no."

"She dumped you?"

"No."

"Oh, I see…were there tears?"

"Yeh, and bruises."

"Bruises?"

"Long story, it's all fine. Are you working?"

"Aye. I'm touring with a musical about asbestosis."

"Right."

"Listen, I've got some good news."

"Good ne— oh no, you're not getting married again?"

"This one's the one."

"So were the last three."

"I want you to be best man."

"Fine. Can I use the same material?"

"Everything except the anecdote about the Amsterdam transvestite and the Hoover."

We hadn't been in contact for the best part of a year, so we had a good chat. We did all the old favourites.

How the Labour Party was going down the toilet.

How the England football team were a bunch of overpaid tossers.

What pointless arseholes critics were.

How the BBC was going down the toilet.

How all comedians now had to be gay and/or Welsh.

How there are no *real* footballers any more.

How useless producers were.

How useless directors were.

How everything was now dominated by marketing.

How unengaged young people had become.

How Twitter was a form of masturbation.

How Simon Cowell now owned everyone.

How the Murdoch Empire owned everyone.

How arrogant cyclists were.

How various presenters should be taken out and shot.

Once we had finished our playlist of topics, I told him the joke I'd just heard about the skeleton who walked into a pub and asked for a pint of lager and a mop, and then he told me a dirty joke about Superman, Catwoman and the Invisible Man, which I realised I knew just as he reached the punchline.

Then we dredged through our list of mutual friends, skimming over their successes and relishing their setbacks. Then Mac spent fifteen minutes or so telling me how unbelievably fantastic his new woman was. Then he put me on the spot.

"So why were there bruises?"

"Eh?"

"You and the wee girlie – when you broke up – why bruises?"

"Oh, she had an accident, a fall, banged her head, it's OK, she's fine."

Then we did one more round of who should be shot and said goodnight.

I love Mac. He never changes. His wives change but he's always the same. Permanent. He's more than a friend, he's a geographical feature, like Arthur's Seat. To my surprise, I find I have been chatting with Mac for nearly two hours and now I am gripped by this overpowering impulse.

Her voice sounds foggy.

"Hi," I say, apologetically.

"Je-sus, Kevin, what time is this to ring for Christ's sa— Jesus, it's quarter past two."

"Sorry."

"Are you pissed?"

"No. Sorry."

"Bloody hell, Kevin, the main reason we got divorced was so you wouldn't wake me up in the middle of the night to have stupid conversations."

"What makes you think this is going to be a stupid conversation?"

"Experience."

There is the clatter of something being knocked over, followed by some swearing.

"Mac's getting married," I say. She gives her throaty chuckle.

"And this one's 'the one'?"

"Oh yes."

More throaty chuckle. "Right. When's the wedding?"

"Two weeks' time."

"Two weeks!"

"The eleventh. He said you'll be getting an invite."

"Right, the eleventh, yeh, I can do that. Will it be plus one?"

"Dunno." Should I ask? I had to. "Are...are you plus one then?"

"Might be...what about you?"

"No, no. I just became a minus one."

"Ah."

"Don't give that 'ah', I hate that 'ah'."

She laughs her full laugh, the one that sounds like a child being tickled.

"I'm sorry, Kevin, but it is sort of funny. I saw you both being interviewed on that morning show. Your body language was hilarious. Was that sofa made of barbed wire?"

She laughs some more and I find myself laughing as well. My God, how long since we did this?

"Has Mac asked you to be his best man?"

"But of course."

"Don't do the Amsterdam stuff."

I must have chatted with Sandra for about twenty minutes and afterwards, as was often the case, I found that I felt calmer. I made myself a peppermint tea – rock-and-roll – and headed for bed.

I felt sorry about how I'd handled things with Jade, but deep down I was relieved. That little knot in my stomach had gone missing. Work was probably going to be a little awkward, but work was work and everyone would be professional.

As I settle down to sleep, my thoughts drift back to Sandra.

Before I know it, I'm reliving the night I first set eyes on her.

It's August, 1994.

Mac is leading me in through the door of a converted lighthouse (yes, that's right, a lighthouse). It's the last week of the Edinburgh Fringe Festival and we are gatecrashing a party full of know-nothing students who have yet to crash into the shit-mountain that is life (Mac's words, not mine).

We're both already very pissed and the problem with the

lighthouse is that it is mostly steps: windy, uneven steps. As a result, Mac is ricocheting around the staircase as he tries to climb, spilling people's drinks, and belligerently banging into stone walls.

I, on the other hand, am amiably drunk and, I feel sure, only mildly impaired. I have found a niche on the ground floor and have wedged myself into a corner with a bottle of Riesling and a paper cup, and I am dispensing bon mots to luminous young women, all of whom (I can see) are entranced by me. I start quoting Camus. Then W. B. Yeats. Then Groucho Marx. How metropolitan I am. Met-ro-pol-it-an. I'm on fire tonight. On fire.

Mac comes tumbling backwards down the stairs, giggling.

"Whoops-a-fucking daisy," he cries. "Don't know what happened there."

He levers himself to his feet and lurches towards the young ladies I am in the process of fascinating.

"Whoa! La-deez, form a queue," he exclaims. "I only have the one cock."

The women scatter like startled deer.

I remonstrate with Mac but all he can say is: "Heigh-ho, it's off to pastures new." Then he meanders away looking for a refill (he doesn't like Riesling) while I lean against the wall and start to wonder how I will be getting home.

And then I see her.

Quite simply, one of the most beautiful women I have seen, floating, at the bottom of the stairwell, like an angel. An an-gel. That's what she's like. She's like – I tell you who she's like – she looks uncannily like Catherine Deneuve.

I glide through the crowd towards her. She is talking to a young man in a leather jacket, but I can see he is boring her. As I arrive, they are talking about the plays of Racine, so I regale her with a few quotes from Phèdre. I have surprised her, so the advantage is mine.

The young man in the leather jacket fails to realise that he is now wasting his time and insists on trying to chip in to our conversation – although most of what he says is boring stuff like "You're spilling your drink, mate."

She, I can tell, is hanging on my every word. I am bewitching her. Now she is gazing at the floor, in an attempt to hide how attracted she is. At last, leather-jacket boy gets the hint and moves off. I step towards her, so that we are close, ve-ry close.

I ask her if anyone has ever told her that she looks like Catherine Deneuve. She replies that they have. Well they are right, I tell her.

"My name is Kevin," I say, suavely. "Kevin Carver. I am an actor-slash-writer-slash-director."

She goes to tell me her name, but I interrupt her with a raffish wave of my hand.

"No, no need to tell me, I already know who you are."

Of course, she is intrigued.

"You," I proclaim, "are the future Mrs Carver."

We talk some more. She is shy and needs some prising out of her shell, but I will take my time, because I am a craftsman. Her ambition is to work in theatre, so I am able to give her the benefit of my experience. In detail.

But I don't want to intimidate her, no, no, no, no, no. So I start telling jokes. Then I admire the shiny watch she is glancing at. It's from her boyfriend, she says, but he is not here right now. Besides, he is her ex-boyfriend. I tell her again, because she doesn't seem to have heard the joke-slash-truth.

"He is your ex-boyfriend?" I reiterate.

"Why do you say that?" she asks.

"Because he just is," I quip.

The repartee carries on for a while, with me setting the pace. Suddenly, Mac looms into view.

"Who's this?"

"Mrs Carver," I inform him.

He sniggers and rocks around a bit.

"Be careful of this one," he tells her, jabbing his forefinger in front of my nose, "because he is promiscuous."

"That's not true," I reassure her.

"Yes, it is," Mac persists. "He is so promiscuous that he's got a cauliflower penis."

This is an old line of Mac's and I can see that she is offended by his vulgarity, so I give him his marching orders, and he totters away, via more walls. What a state to get himself in! I apologise to Mrs Carver and attempt to lighten the atmosphere with a very funny joke about an Irish labourer but apparently I have told her this joke some minutes earlier.

This surprises me, but I don't let it affect my stride. I start a discussion about children, to show my softer side, which I can tell is— hang on, leather-jacket-boy is back! What's he doing here? He's leading her away. What the— that's not the— that's, whoa, my head suddenly feels very light and the room is beginning to move and I – oh no – head for the door, the front door, where the fuck is the front door? What kind of moron holds a party in a lighthouse?! The front door! I've spotted the front door. I plough through the throng, buffeting and bouncing – oh God, I've got about ten seconds – out of my way – there's that feeling in my throat – a matter of seconds – the door, I've made it, I'm through the door, the cold night air smacks me in the face and I am violently sick onto a gravel path.

Oh God, I hate being sick. I can hear people laughing. There is stuff going up my nose. I hate myself.

After several painful heaves, I am bent double, knees trembling and soaked through with sweat. My eyes are streaming and snot is hanging from my nose. And I am breathing deep, long and hard, like an old man struggling on a winter's day.

Then I hear a soft voice.

"Here's a glass of water."

I look up. A young woman with a pageboy haircut and NHS glasses is offering me the glass.

"Thanks," I rasp, before gulping it down. "What's your name?"

"Sandra," she replies.

And then she smiles. She actually smiles. Presented with a glass-eyed idiot, standing in his own puke, she smiles.

Why on earth did she smile?

What did she see?

2

THE VISIT

Next morning, on the set, it feels like business as usual. Big men are carrying lights, prop-handlers are moving furniture and there is the babble of productive chaos.

Nigel, the first – the chaos controller – is shouting down his phone at the third.

"What do you mean Gavin's learnt the wrong scenes? Why the fuck has he done that? Eh…? He's not dyslexic, that's just what he tells people when he's frightened he's going to get a bollocking."

I'm keeping an eye out for Jade, but then I look at the schedule and realise she's not due in till the afternoon. Slowly, I become aware of Louise, hovering at my shoulder.

"Morning, Kevin, how are you?"

"Mystified." I show her my script. "How do I say that first line, while at the same time sounding like a sentient human being?"

"Oh, I'm sure you'll manage it, you nearly always do."

You've got to hand it to Louise, she's never stuck for an answer. Simone starts brushing the shoulders of my jacket, muttering darkly about something getting on her tits – could be the make-up department – I decide not to ask. Nigel is now hunched in the corner by the fire buckets. "I'm getting some cue cards made up, just drag the wanker down on to set now."

Louise glides silently through the chaos. Everyone is a bit scared of her: she's the shark in the lagoon.

"Why aren't we turning over yet, Nigel?" she sighs. "It's seven minutes past eight."

"Yes, yes, we're about to, Louise, OK?"

Then he is bent double by a coughing fit. Louise watches, impassively. Simone mutters something about everyone dying from consumption. Eventually Nigel straightens up, his eyes watering, claps his hands and croaks out his orders.

"OK, listen up. Scene 38, everyone, bit of a delay because of King Gavin, so we're shooting out of order. Kevin, are you cool with that? You've learnt 38, yeh?"

I start thumbing through my script. "I'm not sure, Nige, 38, um…OK remind me what I've just done in 37."

"You've lamped Freddie and you've just reminded Jess that she's family."

Nigel raises his hand to his earpiece; someone is trying to talk to him. "Repeat that, I didn't get it."

I'm flicking through the script trying to piece together the jigsaw of storylines, thinking out loud.

"OK, right", I begin. "And she's just heard about Freddie and wants to know if I had anything to do with it…blah-blah-blah…"

"What?" barks Nigel, his assistant's voice still crackling in his ear.

"So she's cornered me outside the restaurant…"

Nigel turns away from me. "Uh-huh."

"…and I'm saying I know nothing about it…then she doesn't believe me, and then I repeat that it's nothing to do with me and then…"

"…the police want to speak to you."

"Oh, right. Is that 38 B, then?" I shuffle through the pages. "I'm not sure I've got that."

I glance up to see that Nigel is looking directly at me. "No… Kevin…the police want to speak to *you*."

Louise fixes me with a penetrative stare. I become aware of

an unsettling ripple of murmurs. Nigel steps forward and places a hand on my elbow.

"There's two of them in reception, mate. OK, everyone, we'll take a break, everybody back in twenty."

My first thought was "someone's dead". Natural, I suppose, we all fear the policeman at the door, don't we? I thought "car crash" – maybe Sandra, I don't know – I just never imagined for one moment that it would be about…they are very polite. To begin with.

"Mr Carver, I'm DS Pates, this is Detective Sergeant Hooper. Sorry for any inconvenience." She smiles in a procedural way.

"Has something happened?"

A glance sparks between the two of them. Hooper (or maybe it was Cooper) rubs his forehead for a few moments. "Well, it's like this, um, a complaint…has been made against you."

"A complaint?"

"Of assault…by Jade Pope."

My mouth falls open, like a piece of very bad acting. I shake my head and then try to make my answer sound as firm and as final as possible.

"I did not…assault…Jade Pope."

"She claims you did."

"She fell!…She'd been drinking and she fell, like a stone, she was hitting and kicking me and I was holding her off and I gave her a bit of a push."

Pates repeats my last words back to me, weighing each one. "'A bit of a push'?"

"I did *not* assault her."

"Well, look, I'm sure we can sort this out, Mr Carver," she says, giving me the same smile as before. "But I'm afraid it will involve you coming to the station and making a statement."

"Fine," I say, a bit too quickly, "fine, fine, that's fine. I'm very happy to do that, very happy, more than happy."

So I rustle up my solicitor, Graham – who warns me not to say anything before he gets there – and we go to the police station to sort out this ridiculous misunderstanding. (Louise had expressed some concern – producer's concern, not real concern – and I told her that it was nonsense and that I wouldn't be gone long.) On arrival at the station, I tell the desk sergeant how absurd the complaint is and he sympathises and shows us into a room with just a table and four chairs. Graham and I sit there for twenty minutes writing my statement. The sergeant brings us some tea and biscuits.

And then DS Pates comes in, only this time with a female colleague. Pates starts the tape machine. I give them my statement. They peruse it for a few moments, not long. Then Pates reads out a section of Jade's statement.

"During the meal, we decided to terminate our relationship…"

I laugh scornfully and I feel Graham's hand touch my elbow.

"…and at first he seemed to accept the decision…"

"That's bollocks."

"…but later, in the car park, he became abusive and punched me in the face…"

"So's that."

"…knocking me to the ground. I asked him to drive me to the hospital…"

"And that."

"…but he refused."

"All bollocks."

I sit for a moment with my hands clasped behind my head, trying to fake nonchalance, but it's all too much. I can't contain myself.

"Listen, if you act on this garbage you're going to embarrass yourselves. It's not what happened. I dumped her. Then she turned violent."

Pates notes something down.

"You dumped her?"

"Yes."

The other one leans back in her chair.

"How old are you, Mr Carver?"

"Fifty-two. Why?"

She smiles. "Just doing the maths."

By the time they finish questioning me, it is dark.

* * *

Flash! Pop, Pop! Flash!

"Kevin! Kevin! Did you hit her, Kevin?"

Pop! Pop!

I can feel Graham's arm in the small of my back as he tries to helm me through the barrage of flashbulbs and questions. There must be forty of them at least, swarming over the steps of the police station. Camera drives whirr. A microphone is shoved in front of my face.

"Have you been charged, Kevin?"

Pop! Whirr!

"Any comment, Kevin?"

"Kevin, are you guilty?"

The paparazzi are all shouting: "Look this way, Kevin," exactly as they do when you're walking the red carpet at an awards ceremony. Stupidly, I hesitate, dazed, and the questions come even faster.

"Are you guilty, Kevin?" Pop!

"Did you hit her?" Whirr!

"Kevin! Just a comment!"

"Cat got your tongue, Kevin?"

"Come on, Kevin, play the game."

"Kevin! Over here!"

Pop!

"Did you hit Jade?" Pop! Whirr! Pop! Pop!

"Keep going," hisses Graham, propelling me hard towards his car. A hack steps in front of us but we just plough right through him.

A voice shouts: "Hey, that's assault!"

"Over here, Kevin, this way!"

Pop! Pop!

"Whoa, watch it!"

"You fucking watch it!"

Now we're being squeezed against the side of Graham's car, a camera gets knocked to the ground, elbows start to fly and somehow Graham manages to brace his back and create enough room to open the passenger door. We tumble inside and, after several attempts, ram the door shut behind us. Faces are pressed against the windows, still shouting the same questions. A photographer sprawls himself across the bonnet and starts shooting. Pop! Pop! Pop! Pop!

"Jesus Christ!" I look at Graham as he fumbles with his keys. "How the fucking hell did they know I was here?"

"That'll be a policeman supplementing his income," he replies with a half-chuckle and a shake of the head.

"Kevin!! Have they charged you?" Pop! Pop! Pop!

Graham is opening the automatic window. A flash goes off right in my face. That will be a shot of me looking pale and hunted. The shouting gets louder and Graham is holding up his hand in midair with the patient, weary smile of a primary school teacher.

"Gentlemen...gen-tle-men..."

Slowly, the cacophony begins to die down. I find myself wondering how we can be right outside the police station and yet not see a single policeman.

"Gentlemen...I would appreciate it if you could get off my car. Thank you."

"Kevin, did you hit her?"

Now all the others are shouting again. Pop! Pop! Another barrage of light from all sides. I cover my face and hear Graham's voice, calm and clear, cresting over the hubbub.

"Gentlemen! My client has no comment to make at this stage, other than that he is innocent of any wrongdoing."

"Innocent."

It's a word that always carries a little echo of desperation, doesn't it? At least, it does if you're innocent. That night I did not sleep one single second. I had entered that febrile daze of shock where you think everything and nothing at one and the same time. I tried all the ploys I usually tried whenever I couldn't sleep. I read a dull book – a biography of Olivier – and I got up and watched some dull TV – fat people playing poker, golf highlights and celebrity chefs judging ex-reality TV stars as they cooked for obscure comedians. From time to time, I got up and drifted around my kitchen like a ghost. It was one of the longest nights of my life.

Eventually, I saw the first fingers of daylight sneaking round the curtains and ran myself a bath. As I lay in the hot water, I tried to control the panic induced by an ominous sense of something that I could not control. I had not been this frightened since my first day at big school, or the day that Mum got her diagnosis.

I felt ashamed at going to pieces like this. Unmanned. Child-like. The truth would out, I told myself. It was a misunderstanding. Panicking would not solve anything. Come on, Kevin, grow up. Trust the process.

The following morning Graham collected me in his car and we headed straight to his office in Pimlico, where we were met by someone called Nina Patel who was, he explained, very experienced in cases involving celebrities.

She is brisk, bright and capable, and I soon begin to feel I am in safe hands.

"First things first, Kevin, tell me exactly what happened," she says. "I know it's upsetting for you, but I need to get it clear in my head. Tell me what you told the police." She makes notes on her tablet as I detail the events in the car park and, as I take her through it, I wonder if this is the story I will be telling for the rest of my life.

Nina Patel seems to register my despondency because she places her hand on mine.

"Alright, Kevin, I know this is awful, but the first thing to remember is that it is quite possible that the police won't follow up and press charges."

Graham weighs in. "That's right. Sometimes they just bring someone in to see if it encourages any other women to come forward."

I cannot believe he has said that.

"There will be no other women. I don't hit women. I didn't hit *this* woman."

"No, no, 'course not," he stammers. "I'm just saying that's sometimes what they do."

"That's more in cases of alleged sexual offences," Nina smoothes. "It's probably more a PR thing. The police like to look as if they take violence against women seriously these days."

My mouth has turned dry so I ask for water. She fetches me a bottle of Evian from the fridge.

"The wheels might turn quite slowly, I'm afraid, Kevin. They'll be nervous about whether to prosecute. Especially if she's a bit of a flake. How many drinks had you had?"

"I wasn't drunk."

"That's not what I asked you. Never give more information than was asked for. So, how many drinks?"

I make a guess.

"Two…three glasses of wine?"

"Red or white?"

"Red."

"O-kay…and was she on red?"

"No…white."

She touch-types on her tablet for a few moments.

"Good. Now, in the short term, you'll need a top PR person to come up with a strategy."

"I don't need a 'strategy'. I'm innocent."

Graham smiles ruefully. "You're trending on Twitter."

"I don't care."

"Some very nasty stuff's getting put about."

"I don't care, and even if I did I couldn't stop it."

Nina Patel lays another reassuring hand on mine.

"Kevin, it's important that we keep your version out there. Do you have a Twitter account?"

"No."

"Then we'll start one up for you."

Graham opens his laptop.

"Also, we need to release a full statement from you. About your shock and outrage et cetera. I've got the beginnings of a draft here."

A dizziness comes over me. Some terrible, inexorable story is beginning, and I am just a helpless spectator.

"There's going to be a war of words," I hear Graham say. "And you need to protect yourself. Regardless of whether it goes to trial."

Nina Patel is leaning over me now. She seems concerned. "You've gone a bit grey, Kevin, are you ok?"

I'm not OK.

She leads me into her office, draws the blinds and lays me out on the sofa. The sofa becomes my shell. I curl my body up and half-sleep in the semi-darkness, like a creature trying to cease to exist.

* * *

Two days after the media scrum, I'm summoned to the studio for a meeting. I had a pretty good idea what it would be about. I'd been on the show for sixteen years and had seen many cast members run into serious "personal difficulties". Invariably, a convenient storyline is cooked up to explain their character's sudden absence.

The PA with the mole on her cheek (Jenny?) shows me into a room that I've never seen before. It has a long shiny table and glass cabinets full of twisted chrome awards. This is clearly an important meeting because all the producers are there: the two executive producers, the consultant producers, the series producers, the three associate producers, the assistant producers, and the producer.

Louise begins by asking me for my "take" on recent events. I tell the room that, at some point, I expect sanity to prevail and the accusation to be dropped.

Nobody says anything. Very few of them are looking at me and I feel my breathing start to grow shallow. At last, Louise speaks.

"OK, Kevin. We've looked at the problem from a production viewpoint, an editorial viewpoint, um…a legal viewpoint and, of course, the human viewpoint."

"Really? Who would have provided that?"

She twiddles a pencil between her fingers, as she chooses her response. Her voice gets softer. "We're trying to help, Kevin."

I feel stupid. Why am I being aggressive? I need these people on my side.

"I'm sorry," I say, raising my palms, "that was…I'm a bit edgy, I'm sorry."

She smiles prettily. "That is perfectly understandable. Now, of course, the simple answer is to send Lenny on a bit of a sabbatical."

"That's fine with me."

"However, it's not that simple."

What does she mean? It *is* that simple, it's very simple. What is she saying? I scan all the faces, but nobody is giving anything away.

I start to laugh, nervously. "Yes, it is, it's easy, just have a word with the writers, they can put me in a coma or something. Or they can send me to Australia. Or they can put me in a coma in Australia. They can—"

"And what sort of signal would that be, eh? If we took you off the nation's TV screens? What would that imply? Wouldn't that suggest an assumption of guilt by us...about you? Wouldn't that play into the hands of the 'no smoke without fire' brigade?"

I try to think. Why can't I think?

"Well, um, possib...um...yes, I suppose it might but..."

"Ex-actly. And the same applies to Jade."

"...sorry?"

"If Melanie disappeared that would look like a vote of no confidence in Jade. So, as we don't want to be seen to be passing any kind of judgement, you both stay in the show."

A terrible premonition starts to shadow me.

"Right, but, um...we don't have to do scenes together, do we?"

Louise is smiling emptily now, like an air hostess.

"Don't be silly, darling, Lenny and Melanie are lovers, of course you'll be doing scenes together."

"But...how do we do that?"

"Professionally."

I feel my pulse quicken, but pause to try and contain the rage that I know is creeping into my voice. "So, the viewers will be watching us…kissing, while at the same time knowing that, in real life, she could be sending me to jail?"

The various producers all stare at the floor or into their coffee cups. Only Louise is prepared to look at me direct. "Well, for some of them, possibly, there might be an element of subtext."

"You're turning us into a freak show," I say, falling hard on the work "freak".

"Kevin, don't be a drama queen."

"It's a freak show!"

She leans back in her chair and sighs. "Well…Jade says she's cool with the idea. She's being much more grown-up about it."

This is grotesque, obscene. I desperately need a moment to clear my head. I find a quiet corner in the props bay and ring Graham for legal advice. But I only get to speak to his voice-mail. I leave a tangled, garbled message and then I ring Mac. His advice is straightforward: "Tell them to stick it up their arse with a broomstick."

"You mean, resign?"

"Yes, but with specific reference to broomsticks."

I go into a tailspin of anxiety.

"She's right though, isn't she? If I suddenly disappear off air, it does give the impression that I'm guilty."

"They're using you for cheap publicity. They're a bunch of deviants. Just walk, man."

"But, if I walk…"

"Just walk. You know you want to. You've wanted to for years."

That was only half true. Part of me had wanted to walk for years; but it was the weaker part. After several attempts, I manage to get through to Sandra who tells me to act normal; I've done nothing wrong, so have nothing to hide.

"Just go into work as normal," she says, "hold your head high, look Jade straight in the eye and say 'I'm not scared, you lying bitch'...Though not out loud, obviously."

So, over the ensuing weeks, that is what I did. I did my best to behave normally. It wasn't easy. I was attracting a lot of comment. In theory, I had not been charged with anything, but that didn't seem to inhibit the newspapers. The Daily Mail said: "Clearly, it would be inappropriate to comment on the details of this tawdry case, but given the drunken antics of these so-called stars, we have to question whether it is wise to pay such ridiculous sums to infantile debauchees."

And a columnist in the Sun wrote: "Whilst not wishing to comment on the case itself, it is obvious that Kevin Carver is a very arrogant man."

And the Star ran an interview with a waitress I'd screwed in Preston: "Kevin was a very unimaginative lover. He took no interest in my pleasure. After he'd drunk several tequila slammers, we performed a sexual act and then he fell asleep. I was gutted."

I have no recollection of this woman whatsoever.

I vaguely remember a waitress, but I thought that was in Burnley. Also, that was at least nine years ago. Sandra and I had just broken up and...well, let's just say that it was not my finest hour.

As the days crawled by, more and more column inches were written, every paragraph twitching with innuendo. And a lot of the great British public seemed to have made up their minds about me.

One night, at about eleven o'clock, I am shopping in Tesco's, wearing my baseball cap and trying to be invisible. I am reading the label on a ready-cooked chicken when this old boy, in his seventies at least, comes alongside and as he reaches across me for some salami, he quietly says "cunt" and then walks off.

This man had never met me, didn't know anything about me, apart from the fact that I was a cunt. Over the last sixteen years, many obscenities had been shouted across the street at me – mostly by scaffolders – and I had walked away from many foul-mouthed drunks who wanted to pick fights with Lenny, but the quiet, casual brutality of that old man left me stunned. For several minutes I stood, solitary and frozen, in the interrogating light of the supermarket, with a ready-cooked chicken in my hand.

* * *

The weeks dragged by with still no word from the police as to whether I would be charged.

Somewhere in the middle of all this madness came Mac's wedding. I offered to drop out, because I knew I would attract the vultures and I did not want to destroy the happy couple's day. But Mac would have none of it. He insisted that he still wanted me as his best man, which was a mistake.

His new bride, Julie, seemed very pleasant, probably too good for him, to be honest. Sandra was there with some bloke Ivan. He seemed decent enough, if a little bland. It's possible I might have told her that; which would be another mistake.

By the time I got to my feet to deliver my best man's speech, the world had turned blurry and bendy. Much, much drink had loosened my tongue and decommissioned my brain.

Sadly, from my point of view, I was being filmed. The following night Mac and Julie came round to play me the DVD to, as Mac put it, "give me a laugh". I watched through my fingers as I told my audience, repeatedly, that I was "as proud as punch" to be Mac's best man "yet again". Solemnly, I informed them that I had had a few drinks so they might have to bear with me. Momentarily, I blanked mid-sentence, unable to remember the bride's name. I then blethered on about how stressful a time this had been for me and how touched I was that Mac had shown this faith in me, although I did notice he had issued the bridesmaids with headguards. I laughed. Alone.

Unfortunately this ill-judged gag found its way on to page 5 of the Daily Mail thanks, Mac suspects, to one of the catering staff.

The rest of the DVD made no easier viewing. The speech just got more and more embarrassing. And I did do the Amsterdam anecdote, but in completely the wrong order.

"Sorry, mate," was all that I could think to say, as Mac removed the DVD from the machine.

"Hey, listen," he chuckled, "that speech was memorable."

"Sorry, Julie."

"Forget about it, Kevin. It's OK," she said. But I'm not sure that she meant it.

During these months of anxious uncertainty there were various meetings in Graham's office, where he and Nina Patel updated me. As I recall, the content was always the same. They were badgering the police to make up their minds about whether I would be charged. The police were being uncommunicative. Nina Patel's view was that the evidence they had was minimal, but there was probably some internal, political reason why they had not dropped the case. The court of public opinion seemed to have decided I was guilty, so perhaps the Director of Public Prosecutions was nervous about the flak he might get if he walked away. Graham usually ended the meetings by reiterating his view that the indications were that it was highly unlikely that I would go to trial.

On February the 12th, uniformed men took away my laptop and various documents, all of which they returned a week later. Once again, the paparazzi seemed remarkably well informed and gathered in numbers outside my house on each occasion. By now I was losing weight and was infected with the slow poison of fear.

Much of the fear hinged around one incident. It had happened a few weeks earlier, on set, and I could not help playing it over and over in my mind. In fact, even now I can relive it instantly.

I am on set preparing to do a love scene with Jade. We had already managed to get through quite a few of these, both approaching it the same way. It was easy, in a sense. We made no eye contact, nor even spoke to each other, until we heard the word "action".

It's the usual bedlam. I am sitting in a chair as Polly prunes my eyebrows and Simone complains about my dandruff. But the crew are different around me now. The men are less blokesy and none of the women flirt with me any more. Nigel's still the same. He is bellowing into his headset.

"What do you mean, Gavin's crying?...Eh?...Well, what's his problem?...'low self-esteem?'...No, Sigmund fucking Freud, I mean, what's the literal problem that's stopping him from coming on set now like he's supposed to?"

The second assistant's voice limps through Nigel's earpiece.

"Right," says Nigel, calmer now. "OK, I see."

Next thing I know Nigel is standing next to me with his head in his hands.

"Gavin's mother's had a stroke. Just my fucking luck."

Polly lets out a gasp. I ask Nigel to calm down. He pouts for a moment, then coughs violently for a good fifteen seconds before the phlegm shifts and he can shout at his second assistant again.

"All right, give Gavin twenty minutes to compose himself, we'll crack on with the rest of the scene."

I notice Jade ghost across the back of the set.

"OK everyone, listen up, first positions."

Wearily, I rise from my chair.

"We're going as far as the moment when Gav...Jasper enters."

I breathe in, deeply, through my nose, consciously lifting my ribcage.

"Last checks, OK? Roll tape…"

"Speed," says the camera operator.

"And act-ion."

Suddenly Lenny is imploring in a hushed, low voice: "Melanie, I love you. Don't you understand? You've totally changed my life."

"I love you too, Lenny," sobs Melanie.

"I want to be with you for the rest of my life, Mel," says Lenny. "I've never felt this way before…"

"I just need time."

"But there is no time…I…Jasper? What are you doing here?"

"A-n-d cut!" calls Nigel. I walk away, so does Jade. Louise's drawl drifts out from the wings.

"Are we going for another one, Nige?"

"Just waiting to hear from the gallery…why?"

"Well it's just I thought it might be nice on the line 'But there is no time', if Lenny sort of grabbed Melanie and shook her…hard."

I fix Louise with a glare and tell her, firmly, that her idea is not going to happen.

"Why not?" she asks, with apparent innocence. "It'd be in character…for him."

The crew seem uneasy. Micro-glances fly around the set. For a split second, a faint shimmer seems to flit across Jade's eyes. Is she enjoying this?

"Tell you what, Louise," I say, spreading my arms expansively, as if I'm relaxed, "I've got a better idea. On that line you identified, why doesn't Lenny suddenly give Melanie a whopping great bunch of flowers?"

Louise pulls a face. "Flowers?"

"Yeh, tulips. I think Lenny is a tulips man."

She shifts her weight on to her heels, weighing up the pros and cons of having a confrontation over this. The moment is punctured by another horrific bout of coughing from Nigel.

"Send him home, for Christ's sake," mumbles Simone.

A tinny voice rattles down Nigel's earpiece. "OK, listen up," he splutters, "Gavin's coming down on to set now, he's bound to be a bit fragile, so steer clear of anything to do with mums, strokes or death. And just remember, if he goes to pieces, nobody is on overtime. Thank you, everyone."

It is crystal clear what Louise is up to. She is milking an opportunity. For the past few weeks, the ratings have been creeping up nicely thanks, presumably, to the public's rancid interest in my real-life subplot. Our figures are out-gunning the other soaps and we are comfortably outperforming the sensationalist new reality show on C4. We even beat the episode where the bi-polar surfer drunk bleach. Our show is, to use that hateful little word, "hot". So, Louise is cashing in.

Next thing I know I am heading back to make-up. Suddenly, I bump into Jade in the corner. She had so far made sure that she was never alone with me since she filed the complaint, while my legal team had stressed to me, again and again, that under no circumstances was I to try to speak to her. But now, here we are, face-to-face, with no onlookers, and I can't help myself; it feels like a last, desperate chance.

"Jade, listen—"

"Will you let me pass, please?"

"This is madness."

"I said, let me pass."

"But—"

"Please."

"Why are you doing this, Jade?"

"This is not on."

"Why are you lying?"

"I am not lying."

"You know I didn't hit you."

"You did hit me!" she yells, her eyes blazing. "You hit me, that's the truth! And you're a lying bastard, Kevin!"

Then she runs down the corridor, sobbing, quivering with anger.

There is no mistaking what I had just witnessed. She meant it. Totally. Sincerely. She's not that good an actress.

It's hard for me to describe how chilling that encounter was. It made me question what sort of chance I would stand if our case went to trial. The conviction in those wounded blue eyes filled me with dread.

* * *

Eventually, Nina Patel came up trumps. She wrote a succession of increasingly intimidating letters pointing out how unreasonable it was to continue to make me perform alongside Jade. She argued that it was causing me considerable stress and that my employers were failing in their duty of care. So, the legal department put pressure on Louise until she agreed that Lenny and Melanie should take a sudden mystery trip to Australia. Jade and I no longer had to endure the indignity of being a freakshow.

I thought I would be relieved at not having the tension of pretending to work as normal, but, in fact, it was worse to be at home, alone with my thoughts. I grew a beard. It came out grey and straggly but I had stopped caring about my appearance. Besides, it made me look less recognisable at a time when I didn't want to be recognised, though I didn't go out. I sat in my house, quiet and still, like some hibernating mammal. I had only moved into the house eight months before and I'd barely spent any time in it, so I took comfort in the idea that I could just bunker down in my new home and let the busy world pass by.

But even the house turned on me.

Several of the radiators started to leak. Taps started to drip. The bathroom door warped in the damp weather to the point where it was impossible to close. The garden pond began to drain slowly into the lawn. The dishwasher broke. The extractor fan in the toilet started making a sound like a demented cricket. The pump in the loft kept surging and thumping. Yet I ignored it all. I didn't care. I wasn't prepared to call out workmen because that would mean having strangers in the house.

There was the occasional visitor. Nina Patel drove by to get me to sign some paperwork.

She is wearing perfume. She is sitting next to me, very close, leaning across me as she presents documents for signature and I notice, for the first time, my total loss of libido. An attractive woman is millimetres away and I feel nothing. What is even odder is that the nothingness doesn't disturb me. Something that once seemed so important – that defined me – has disappeared and yet I can't even muster a shrug. In fact, it might be a relief to no longer be dragged round by the idiot in my trousers.

I am still pondering all this when I realize that she is asking me a question.

"How do you feel about the trial? If there is one. Mentally, are you feeling prepared?"

"Well, I'm hoping there won't be one."

"Yes, but we need to prepare you, just in case."

"Right."

"We'd need to do some sessions, y'know, pretend cross examination, to get you used to being knocked about a bit. Their barrister's bound to play pretty rough."

"If there's a trial."

"Of course. You're not thinking of keeping that beard, are you?"

"No that's just…I…it's not going to stay."

"Good. You look like a hobo."

"Cheers."

She starts putting documents away in her briefcase, brisk, business-like.

"We might have to do some work on you." She flashes a short smile. "You're going to have to lose the arrogance thing."

"Arrogance thing?"

"Oh, come on, Kevin, you know what I'm talking about. That sort of general air of 'fuck it. I can't be bothered with you'."

She is amused by the look on my face. "I'm not criticising you, I'm just saying, you have a manner. And it's very handy for when you're playing Lenny, but if you end up facing a jury, then…"

"I don't think I'm arrogant," I say, limply.

"OK, whatever, it's—"

"It's…I'm…well, I'd accept that I'm…self-contained."

"Self-contained, exactly, people hate that. Me? I quite like it, but juries like you to open up."

She heads for the door. "Just a bit of vulnerability, Kevin. That's what they'll want. Take it easy."

The door closes and I'm alone again with the clicking radiators and the rattle of the extractor fan. I switch on the TV and blip through the channels, emptying my brain.

3

THE ESCAPE

One Saturday night during this half-life, as I sat watching Match of the Day, I heard the doorbell ring. At that time of night, I thought it was probably kids or pissheads, so I stayed put in my chair.

But then the bell sounds again, long and piercing, like it's an emergency.

So, muttering curses, I drag myself out of the chair and shuffle down the hall. Now the doorbell is one continuous jarring ring.

"Who is it?" I call.

"It's Scarlett Johansson," comes a muffled, Scottish growl.

I open the door and Mac sweeps past me carrying a suitcase.

"Oh right, are you coming to stay then?"

"This suitcase is for you," he says, as he heads for the kitchen. "I'll make a cup of tea while you pack."

"Pack?"

"Yeh, you need a break. Look at the state of you, what's with the beard?"

"It stops people recognising me."

"Oh, OK, I thought you were auditioning for Robinson Crusoe. Go on, just a few days' stuff is all you need."

He clanks the cupboard doors open and shut as he hunts for the tea.

"You've lost weight," he says. "You look like a very ugly, hairy supermodel. Come on, don't just stand there like a fucking statue, let's hit the road."

"And where are we going?"

"That's a surprise."

"Well, maybe I don't want to go anywhere."

"Why not? What, you want to stay here?" His eyes drift to the television in the kitchen. "Oh God no, Chelsea—Man City, two teams I loathe equally."

Then he picks up the remote, turns off the TV.

"What the fuck do you think you're doing?" I exclaim.

"I'm being a friend. Come on, move, pack something warm."

"I'm happy where I am."

"Oh p-lease."

"I don't want to go anywhere…there'll be people and…"

"Don't worry, I've thought of that. This milk is on the turn."

He stops sniffing the bottle and pours the contents down the sink.

"Come on, Kev, don't be a tosser."

I stand stock still, making a point.

"What? You'd rather sit around in here, picking away at all the wee scabs of self-pity?"

"You've no idea what it's like."

"I don't care what it's like, you don't stop answering people's calls. Now stop being such a girlie and let's get moving."

"It's half-past eleven at night," I point out.

His face lights with mischief.

"I know, exciting, isn't it? It's a full moon as well." Then he howls like a werewolf as he fills the kettle. I head for the bedroom to pack.

We drove north, or rather he drove north, fast, treating most of the road marking as bourgeois suggestions. It took an hour or two to escape the outer tentacles of the suburbs, and then we travelled along dark motorways, following a river of red brake lights, as a river of white lights flowed towards us. I tried to stay awake, tried to keep chatting, to help him stay lively, but my heart wasn't in it. I didn't have enough to say, or the will to make small talk. So, eventually, I drifted off into a sleep of sorts.

When I woke up it was light. Mac turned down my offer to take over the driving – he said I wasn't in a fit state to operate heavy machinery – so we hurtled on at full throttle until we decided we needed a pee and some food.

The roadside café was empty and basic, to put it at its kindest. Every surface was protected by plastic that was tacky to the touch. I had a light breakfast; Mac had almost every item on the sun-faded menu. We were somewhere near Berwick, but Mac refused to tell me our destination because he was enjoying being an arsehole. I kept asking and he kept cackling with amusement.

As the morning wore on, we continued through the borders, skimming Edinburgh, then north-west through the glens, where gleaming quilts of snow still lay in any dents near the peaks. I was quite enjoying being driven, watching the landscape unfold itself around us. I became a bundle of matter being transported to God-knows-where. Mac didn't seem to mind that I was in no mood to talk.

Eventually, we arrived, in light, misty rain, at Ullapool, where Mac followed the signs to the ferry port.

"Wait a second, you've brought me to the back of beyond... and now that turns out to be phase one?"

"Well you said you didn't want to see people so—"

"Bloo-dy hell, Mac."

"And you've often said you'd like to visit the Outer Hebrides."

"I've never said that."

"You have."

"Yeh, but it's fucking freezing."

"It's a little brisk."

"It's freezing."

"To a wee southern fairy-boy."

"Look at the temperature, there, on the display."

"You're going to love it, nae sweat."

"Look! Four degrees!"

"What are you? An orchid?"

"*Four* degrees."

A man in a high-vis tabard (and an overcoat and gloves) taps on the window. Mac presents a pair of tickets. The cold air starts filling the car.

"We'll load in a few minutes," says the high-vis tabard. "Don't go wandering off anywhere."

Once he is gone, Mac starts giving me the hard sell on how good the food is in the ro-ro ferries.

"Also, they're really stable. I've sailed through a force seven and not spilt a drop."

"So will you tell me now?"

"We're going to Harris. It's stunning."

"Harris?"

"Yeh...joins on with Lewis. Lewis is bleak. Moonscape. No trees. I think the Wee Free chopped them all down because they were green." He chuckles at having stumbled on a joke. "Yeh, fucking bastard decadent trees...always rustling their leaves on the Sabbath. But Harris is beautiful and magnificent."

The car in front of us starts its engine and the queue edges forward. Mac turns the key in the ignition.

"Wagons roll," he cries, before humming the theme from Lonesome Dove.

"And what about your new love – 'the one' – how come you've abandoned her?"

"I made it clear at the outset that our relationship might involve unexplained absences. Besides, she's in Munich on a course."

The high-vis tabard motions for us to proceed up the ramp. There is an unsettling clunk as we lurch forward into the gaping maw of the car-deck. Another high-vis figure points to the lane nearest the side of the ship.

"What's the weather forecast?" I ask.

Mac brings the car to a halt.

"Mixed," he says.

"I don't want to be recognised, Mac."

"Well, you're not allowed to stay in the car."

"I don't want to be gawped at."

"There's hardly anyone here. Come on, we'll find a nice quiet corner."

As we climb out of the car, I put on my woolly hat and pull my coat up around my ears. Mac tells me that my attempt to look inconspicuous just comes across as attention-seeking. I tell him to shut up.

As I squeeze my way between the parked cars a small yapping white dog throws itself against a window.

"Juno! Be quiet!" screams its owner. As she struggles to clamber out of the driver's door, she apologises for the dog's behaviour, but I ignore her and keep on walking.

We found a quiet corner, by the toilets – a seated area where I could sit with my back to everyone without it looking odd. I slept most of the way, not because I felt especially tired, more because I couldn't be bothered to be awake. Mac went up on deck, briefly, to see if he could spot some whales, but the cold drove him back inside.

After three hours or so, an announcement asked us to please return to our cars. There was a momentary confusion when we went to the wrong vehicle deck, but then we managed to spot Mac's car and were weaving between the bumpers when the small white dog threw himself against the glass again, barking at me as if I was Satan himself. It was startling enough to make me jump. Once more, the woman made her flustered apologies and, again, I ignored her. This time, Mac told her not to worry. Why did he feel the need to do that? Was it some kind of criticism of me?

We climb inside the car.

A klaxon sounds.

Some grey sky starts to appear, as the ferry's visor slowly lifts, revealing the low stone frontages of Stornoway. Gulls surf the wind. A tattered Saltire flaps, lonely, on a flagpole next to a portakabin.

"Welcome to the Hebrides," I mumble sourly.

Mac starts the engine and we follow a travelling home out of the ship's belly on to the quayside.

"I'd forgotten just how miserable a fucker you can be," he chirps. "You'll see, this place is like Paradise, only windy."

We join a one-way system as I adjust the settings on the heater.

"And where exactly are we staying?"

"My cousin's got a place at the southern end of the island. Not far. An hour at most."

"Your cousin? Is—"

"Don't worry, he's away, it's empty. And it's nice and secluded. There's no mobile signal. No TV. Nothing. It's perfect. Like stepping back in time."

"Are you all right to drive? You've had no sleep."

"Ach, I'll sleep when I'm dead."

I ease back in my seat and close my eyes. The dog thing? Was that criticism? For a moment, I consider asking him, but then I decide it doesn't matter enough. You're a passenger, Kevin. Just sit back and let it happen.

Getting to his cousin's place took longer than Mac had predicted because we got stuck behind a herd of sheep. He seemed to regard it as quaint and rustic, but I was hungry, tired and pissed off, regally pissed off. Why had I been so passive? Now look where I was. Stuck in a car, looking out on a land shrouded in rain, being dictated to by sheep. I told him, several times, to honk on the horn, but he just laughed and said I had to get off "city-boy time".

Eventually, we find ourselves bouncing up a steep, rutted track towards an off-white bungalow, with black clouds gathering behind it.

Mac gets out of the car with his face illuminated. I try to get out, but because I am on the windward side, I have to wait for a gap between the gusts before I can open my door. When I step out, the wind knifes me.

"They call this 'a lazy wind'," shouts Mac.

"'Lazy'?"

"Yeh, 'cos it can't be bothered to go round you."

He heads for the doorstep where he finds the key beneath a flower pot. As we enter, Mac feels for a light switch.

"Ta-ra!"

The light comes on, watery and insipid.

"Home sweet home for the next few days."

I look around me. It feels like I've stepped into the 1950s. There are swirling nylon carpets, straight-backed plastic chairs, a pouffe of indeterminate colour.

"You're not impressed."

"How long do you imagine us staying here?"

"I have to be back by the end of the week."

"A week? Are you mad?"

But I'm talking to myself; he's set off to fetch the suitcases out of the boot. There is a radio – a museum piece. I half-expect to hear the Goons coming out of it. Mac re-enters with the suitcases.

"We'd best decide who has which bedroom."

"Mac...what the fuck are we going to do here?"

He plonks the suitcases on the ground.

"You are such a snob."

"It's...depressing."

"Well, I'm sorry, Lady Penelope, but Balmoral was fully booked."

"Seriously, Mac, what are we going to do?"

"We can go for nice walks."

"If we can get out of the door."

"There's lots around here. And there's a very good chance of seeing an otter." He knows what I am about to say. "Once the weather eases off."

"And if it doesn't?"

"We put our feet up, read some books, get nice and cosy. Look, see, there's a chess set. And we can chat, spend some time together, when did we last do that, eh? Just the two of us. It'll be like old times, only without the moments of degeneracy."

His shoulders droop slightly.

"Come on, Kevin. It's a change of scenery. It'll do you good. You were..." His voice fades away beneath the frustration.

"What was that with the dog-lady?" I ask.

"Eh?"

"You were all nice to her when her stupid dog barked at me."

"I was just being polite."

"What, and I wasn't?"

"No, you were fucking rude if you must know. But you're having a bad time of it, so..."

"Don't apologise for me, OK?

I can hear a tremble in my voice. Mac stands very still.

"I have to say, Kevin, that if you're thinking of starting a fist-fight, I don't think that you're in very good shape."

He's right. I'm being moody and absurd and the realisation makes me laugh.

"Let's go see the bedrooms, wee man!"

Both bedrooms turn out to be extremely small, as are the beds.

"Well," pronounces Mac, "if we pull any women, they'll have to be midgets. This one's slightly bigger, you can have it. You'll need more room for your head."

He laughs at his own joke as he bustles into the other room with his suitcase. Then he charges down the hall shouting that he's going to buy some provisions. The front door slams and he's gone.

I turn up the tiny radiator in my room. Thank fuck there's central heating, a small concession to the march of progress. The wind starts to whistle through a weakness it has found. I head for the tiny lounge, get out the chess set and start laying out the pieces.

Come the next morning, the world could not look more different. The clouds have given way to a blaze of colour and as we sit in the tiny kitchen, eating a fried breakfast, we take in a panorama of blue sky, gleaming sands, lush green dunes and distant purple mountains.

"What's this bay called?" I ask.

"Scarista. How did you sleep?"

"Surprisingly well. I had to curl up like a hedgehog, but..."

"Yeh, me too. I slept like a baby...woke with my pyjamas full of shit." He laughs like a drain. "Sorry, that just came to me... maybe it's funnier with 'pyjamas soaked in piss'."

"No," I tell him, "it isn't."

Mac starts crunching through his toast. I had forgotten what a noisy eater he is.

"I'm sorry about yesterday, Mac...I was a bit wound up."

"Forget about it."

We eat on in silence – not awkward silence, but the silence

where you know each other well enough not to have to speak. Down below us in the bay, breakers are rolling up the beach with steady grandeur. He was right. It is very beautiful here.

"That headland jutting out on the left there?" he says, sawing at some bacon. "That's called Toe Head. We can walk to the end of that."

"You know the area well then?"

"Been here a couple of times. Mostly when I was younger. Didn't appreciate it then. You're not easily impressed when you're a kid, are you. Nature's just something people drag you round. But now...well, you've got to admit, that's a world-class view. Not seen much better than that. In New Zealand, maybe. Have you been to New Zealand?"

"No."

"It's like Scotland on steroids. Magnificent vistas in every direction. So magnificent, in fact, that it gets a bit boring. Perfection dulls the mind."

"Is that a quote?"

"No, that's me being poncy. The New Zealanders have this funny accent. Instead of 'six' they say 'sex'."

"Right."

"Yeh...it can cause confusion when you're trying to buy eggs."

He then launches into a rambling, tangled anecdote involving a misunderstanding with a female shop assistant in Auckland. Like a lot of his stories, it is a maze of tangents and detail, although it does end with the two of them having sex in a cupboard. I am not totally sure if I believe it, but it's a story, and he is trying to raise my morale.

"OK then," he announces, wiping egg from his chin with the back of his hand, "shall we go walkies?"

"Um...yeh...all right."

"Good, good, good." He starts clearing plates and dumping them in the sink.

"I haven't got boots," I tell him.

"Neither have I. Come on, let's get cracking before the weather changes."

The shoes and coats go on and we head out the door, down the steep, loose-stoned track towards the honey-gold curve of the beach.

The wind feels like it is blowing every thought out of my head, buffeting and slapping my face, drumming on my ears. The colours seem to intensify by the minute in the slanting northern light. The blue of the water blends towards green, then back to brilliant blue again, then a mottled silver as some clouds hurry past. About twenty yards out, a squad of gannets arrow into the waves, white darts, catching the sun. We stop and watch them for a while, watch them circling into the wind before folding their wings to become missiles, piercing the water.

"They go blind in the end," Mac shouts above the wind. "They've got this membrane-thing that protects the eye from the impact. But eventually it wears away, so…"

"That's them finished, I suppose."

"Well you can't give one a guide dog."

A gannet hits the water, smack, right in front of us.

"Whoa!" exclaims Mac. "That looks like fun, doesn't it? It feels like they should be calling 'wheeee' on the way down."

Mac's face is lit up as he watches them. I had no idea he loved birds as much. When did that happen? Now he is pointing out some smaller birds, swooping in shorter, stabbier flights, further out above a foaming reef.

"Arctic Terns. But those two brown things over there, the ones that are sort of half-buzzard, half-gull, they're skuas. They just steal fish from other birds. They're opportunists. If they can catch a gannet when it's still on the water, they'll try and murder it. I've seen them do it. It's horrific."

Then he starts laughing. "Just like people, eh? Two types. One lot who work really hard just to survive, and the other bastards who steal it."

That's more like the Mac I know, the man who can turn any topic into a socialist commentary.

We turn and walk along the beach with the wind at our backs. The head of a seal pops out of a heaving wave and it tracks us, disappearing occasionally, but always resurfacing nearby, curious and watchful.

After a while, I decide now is the time to broach something.

"Why have you never asked me, Mac?"

"Asked you what?"

"You know perfectly well...why have you never asked me whether I hit her."

"Well, I kind of assumed...from your demeanour, that you didn't."

"But you've never specifically asked."

He stops to poke his toe into a dried-out jellyfish.

"Would you like me to specifically ask?"

"Were you frightened you might get the wrong answer?"

He tips his head back and laughs.

"God, you always have to torture yourself, don't you?"

A few steps brings his face right in front of mine.

"OK now, pay attention. I assumed...that you would assume... that I had assumed...that you didn't hit her...I took it as read."

"And...supposing I had hit her?"

"Then I would feel you'd behaved like a total shit, but you would still be my friend. I'm lumbered with you now. That's what friends are, lumber."

The seal bobs up in front of us.

"They're like marine Labradors, aren't they," he chuckles. "Who are you staring at, pal?"

There is a volley of screeches as the gannets escort a loitering skua off the premises. I stand and watch the aerial dogfight as Mac walks on ahead, calling back over his shoulder, "You need to get over yourself. All this angsty crap…waste of time and energy."

He scurries to his right, as a longer wave chases him up the beach.

"And I tell you something else. If you want people to accept that you're an innocent man, you'd best start behaving like one."

Of course, that is what friends are for – to give you patronising advice that you resent. So I let Mac walk well ahead of me, while I hang back to watch the seal. What the fuck did he mean by that?

I let the rhythm of the waves take me over. There is a kind of slow melody to them. But, every now and then, an incoming wave meets the gentle ripples of a receding one and creates a lateral explosive charge, accelerating across the shallows. I become hypnotised by this effect. One dying wave meets another fading one and produces this electrifying slash. How is that happening? And why not every time the waves meet? What energises it?

Mac is now a distant speck, so I set off to catch him up, jogging towards the looming form of Toe Head.

The walk was extremely enjoyable and perfectly timed. We spent a couple of hours walking through the machair, then round the back of Toe Head, past many small sandy coves to a ruined chapel, where we sat for a while as Mac pointed out curlews, redshanks and, at a very high altitude, a huge white-tailed sea eagle, sailing with barely a flap of its wings.

Then a few grey clouds began to sneak over the hills, so we headed back and by the time we reached the bungalow, the sky was a low ceiling of leaden cloud and the first fat raindrops were spotting the paving stones. As Mac shoved open the front door, the clouds burst and the bungalow was suddenly turned into a percussion instrument. We laughed at how lucky we had been and settled down, snug in our little bolt-hole as the storm raged around us. There was something very comforting about sitting quietly reading while rain and hail were thrown against the windows. This was something mankind had been doing since we were monkeys, waiting in a cave for Nature's rage to pass. The various pitches of whistle we could hear, as the wind forced its way through cracks in the building's fabric, somehow made the experience even cosier.

As evening arrived we started playing chess. The set was missing a few pieces, so Mac had a small pepper pot for a king and I had a matchbox for a rook and two pawns that were dice. The games tended to be short because Mac's game was based on all-out attack with never a thought for any consequences.

"Are you sure you want to do that?" I ask him.

"Don't patronise me."

"Very well then." I move my bishop. "Checkmate."

"Oh f—! Why didn't I see that?"

"Because you don't stop and think."

"I like to play off the cuff. You play the boring way."

"The successful way."

He starts laying out the pieces again.

"Come on then, one more, I'm getting the hang of this now."

"I don't think so."

Soon, Mac is sending his first pawn on another suicide mission.

"So when did you go to New Zealand?" I ask.

"About eight years back. Touring a show about the Suffragettes."

"Was it any good?"

"The material was good. The execution was abysmal."

I feel a little embarrassed that there are big chunks of Mac's professional life that I know nothing about. Obviously the periods where we had drifted out of touch were longer than I had realised.

Already, two of his pawns are back in the box. "What's up next for you?" I ask.

"Well, there was supposed to be a gig doing Victorian factory work songs, but the money buggered off, so..."

"How can you stand it?"

"Eh?"

"Well...y'know, all the setbacks...the shows that collapse or–"

"I can't give in to the disappointment. That'd be a victory for the Man."

"Yeh, I know, but the – you can't go there you're moving into check – the vast majority of what you do is...well, no offence, but it's crap, isn't it, be honest."

"When was the last time you saw a show I was in?"

"I saw the one about the sugar trade, at that place in Aldershot."

"That was badly directed. He was a choreographer, had no stagecraft."

"The piece was shit."

Mac moves his rook the length of the board and I take it immediately.

"Well," he mutters, "it may have been shit...but at least it was *original* shit. Everything I do is original."

"And short-lived."

"It's better than just doing the same old shit over and over again, year after year."

Mac gives me a smile, waiting to see if I'll pick up the grenade he has lobbed. I smile back.

"Millions of people watch that shit."

"Yeah, like you care about them."

He taps away, looking for a nerve. "When was the last time you took a risk, professionally, well no, a risk of *any* kind?"

"When I sat in your passenger seat yesterday", I reply, calmly.

"Seriously, you used to write stuff and be all experimental and you'd commit, you'd really commit and..."

"Jesus, Mac, that's over twenty years ago. We grow up."

Suddenly he lets rip with a maniacal laugh.

"You have walked into my little trap, Mr Bond."

I move my Queen one square.

"Checkmate."

"What? Oh for— you jammy fucker. This is a stupid game, anyway. The one with the most power and freedom is the woman! How's that an accurate picture of society, eh? Politically, it's a nonsense."

Mac starts to yawn, long and slow, like a lion, so I start to pack the chess pieces away.

"Yup, bedtime for me. Could be a big day tomorrow", he says, through the yawn.

"Big day?"

"Yup, depending on the weather."

"Why, what are we doing?"

"*That*, Kevvy-boy," he proclaims with a wolfish grin, "will be a lovely surprise."

Then he heads off to make alarming noises in the toilet. A squall batters on the windowpanes. We are safe in our cave. And London seems a million miles away.

The following morning I woke up feeling genuinely rested, a feeling I had almost forgotten. I lay curled in my bed for ten minutes or so, listening to the calls of the gulls. Why did I find them comforting? Perhaps they were a reminder of early holidays in B&Bs in Lowestoft and Yarmouth, back when the furniture looked huge, before I realised that Mum and Dad were unhappy. Eventually, I dragged myself out of my own thoughts and headed for the kitchen.

There is a note on the kitchen table from Mac – "Back in a Minute". A wave of panic ripples through me. Nobody knows where I am. I ought to let someone know. It is Monday, the working week, I need to let them know.

The front door flies open and Mac blows in like a gale.

"Man, it is one beautiful day out there."

"I need to let my solicitor know where I am. In case something comes up."

Mac looks exasperated. "If you go to the end of the point there –" he gestures out of the window "– up there by that cairn, I found a signal up there."

So I get dressed and haul myself up the steep rise, where rabbit holes lay hidden in the grass like traps, until, eventually, after much moving around, there are enough bars on my phone to contact the outside world.

I ring Graham, but he does not pick up. So I ring Nina Patel. I make a conscious attempt to sound casual.

"Hey, it's Kevin, how's things?"

"Graham just rang, he said your place is all locked up, where are you? We've been trying to contact you."

"Sorry, I didn't mean to frighten anyone. I'm with a friend. We're on the island of Harris."

Nina laughs. "Harris? Je-sus, Kevin. Oh well, 'least you're still on UK soil, Graham was worried you'd fled the country, joined the Foreign Legion or something."

"I'll be back in a few days, that's OK, isn't it?"

There is a slight delay and I hear my last few words being repeated back to me. She goes quiet for a few moments.

"Are you sure you're all right, Kevin? You're having a rough time, you need to take care of yourself."

The kindness in her voice – even down a crackling line – makes me suddenly feel weepy. Where did that come from? Am I so fragile now that it only takes a few kind words to make my chin start to tremble? For Christ's sake, Kev, get a grip.

"I'm fine," I tell her, nice and loud.

"Who's with you?"

"My friend Mac."

"All right…well, take it easy."

I could end the conversation right there, but the anxiety inside me jabs out a question.

"Any developments?"

Why is she hesitating? She doesn't usually hesitate.

"Well, you'll probably get to hear about it, so I might as well tell you." My mind starts to race. New witnesses? More accusations?

"Don't worry, Kevin", she soothes, "we'll get on top of it, but…um…some idiot has put up something on YouTube. It's infantile nonsense, we're getting them to take it down."

Carefully and calmly, she describes the piece to me.

It seems some cybernerd-type has cut together lots of clips of me in character as Lenny. He has grabbed individual words from dozens of different episodes to create a monologue.

"What sort of monologue?" I ask.

"I think it's supposed to be comic, but it isn't."

"And what do I – what does Lenny – say in this monologue?"

Another hesitation. I feel my stomach lighten in the few seconds it takes for her to answer.

"…he confesses to hitting women."

"What?!"

"It's a stupid piece, and we're getting it taken down."

"How many people have seen it?"

"Not that many. 'Least by YouTube standards."

She talks me through the legal steps they've set in motion, but my mind is seething with half-completed thoughts, so I struggle to take any of it in. I'm spinning around, mentally and physically, trying not to be overwhelmed by a growing sense of impotent rage.

"That's got to be defamatory, surely."

"Yes, of course it is," replies Nina Patel, "it's outrageous."

"So we can sue the bastard."

"Well, if we can identify him, or her."

"So, we identify…and then we sue."

Yet another hesitation. "I'm not sure that would be my advice, Kevin. If we take legal action we just turn it into a much bigger story that will play out for a lot longer. Let us deal with it and we'll make it go away quickly."

For a few minutes, she allows me to let off steam. I rail and rant and swear about the sheer injustice of it all. She listens, patient and sympathetic, before convincing me that they have the situation under control.

"Do I need to come back?" I ask.

"No, no point," she says. "We just need YouTube to accept it needs to be taken down. We'll win that argument, trust me."

Do I trust her? Do I trust anyone now? In the end, a kind of exhaustion sets in and I agree that she should handle it however she sees fit. I think I trust her.

I have to trust someone.

On returning to the cottage, I replay the whole conversation for Mac. He agrees with Nina Patel's strategy. If you get too worked up, you start to look more guilty.

"Besides," he says, "it's YouTube, nobody takes anything they see on YouTube seriously."

"You think so?"

"Definitely. Don't waste any more brain-space worrying about something dreamt up by some sad wanker in his bedroom. You cannot let these people drag you down."

I appreciate his efforts to buoy up my morale, but I can't help feeling that the YouTube piece is just one more insidious accusation. The world seems to have made up its mind about me already, so what will happen if and when I get to court? Mac urges me to tackle things one step at a time.

"And the next-most-immediate step is...the surprise I promised."

He starts breaking eggs into the frying pan.

"Make yourself useful, Kev, we'll need to make ourselves some sandwiches for later. Come on, chop, chop. Stop moping."

"I'm not moping," I protest.

"Good, then get a move on. I promised the boatman we'd be there for ten-thirty."

"Boatman?"

"Yeh, Calum he's called. He said they're expecting a bit of a swell, but we're OK for the trip, so get some breakfast down you and we'll head off."

"Where's this boat trip to? And if you say 'it's a surprise' you're getting this fork up your arse."

Mac pauses for dramatic effect. "It's to St. Kilda."

"...St. Kilda...the island?"

"Aye, how cool is that?"

"The abandoned island?"

"Yeh. Well, I think the RAF might be there and possibly some scientists but—"

"How long is this boat-trip?"

"Just three hours or so."

"Three hours!"

"Three and a bit."

"What, three hours out, three hours back?"

"Well, obviously, but—"

"Going west?"

"Yeh, but—"

"Three hours off the west coast off the Outer Hebrides? That's the middle of the fucking Atlantic Ocean, Mac."

"Well it's hardly the middle, it—"

"What sort of boat is it?"

"A sturdy one. Calum does the trip all the time. He takes tourists to—"

"Tourists? I'm not spending hours being gawped at by tourists, that's not—"

"Will you calm down, man." He flaps his arms in exasperation. "There'll be no-one else. I got chatting to Calum yesterday when I was getting the provisions. He's running some supplies to the RAF boys, 'cos the helicopter's kaput, and he wants to give the boat a wee run before the tourist season starts so…you won't get recognised, I promise. You'll not be bothered. And it's a great chance to see something extraordinary."

He steps towards me. "Come on, Kevin…you always used to be up for extraordinary. You've been holed up for ages, let's get some air in your lungs."

I glance out of the window. The sea does not look too rough, although there are the occasional flecks of white horses.

"Come on, man, there's no need to be so anxious, it's—"

"I'm not anxious."

"What? You've marinated yourself in anxiety. Come on, let's go have a bit of an adventure, eh? A three-hour boat-trip, what can be more fun than a boat trip?"

He's right. I'm sick and tired of feeling anxious. Fuck it, why not? Three hours on a boat, that hardly turns us into buccaneers, what's the matter with me? I refuse to be ruled by the knot in my stomach. A bit of an adventure, perhaps that's just what I need.

After wolfing down a hearty breakfast, we drove for about fifteen minutes through a scraped, rock-littered moonscape, past a succession of narrow bays until we reached Leverburgh, a small port protected by an archipelago of low islands.

"How big is this boat?" I ask as Mac parks the car at a jaunty angle.

"Reasonably big. It's a tourist boat."

"How many people does it hold?"

"I dunno, I think Calum said ten, twelve."

"That's not a big boat, Mac."

"It'll be powerful."

Then Mac opens the car door, which kicks a little in the wind.

"We should probably put on a few layers," he says. So we put on our jumpers and jackets and go looking for the jetty, past some stinking lobster pots, beyond some empty skips. The jetty has one boat bobbing alongside it, not that small, but not massive either. But it has an enclosed cabin and looks reasonably modern. A young lad is winding ropes at the stern. He is tall, slender and his face suggests that he hasn't seen a vitamin in years.

Mac walks towards the boat, giving the lad an over-cheery wave. For a moment, I'm standing alone at the edge of the jetty, staring down into the dark water. With a shudder, I catch myself thinking how easy it would be to take just one step forward and end all the chatter.

I hear Mac call "Calum!" and turn to see a leather-faced man emerging from inside the cabin. He is wearing waterproof over-trousers and a blue donkey jacket. He gestures for us to step aboard. Mac introduces us and Calum gives me the faintest of nods. He points at the pasty-faced lad.

"Fergus," he informs us.

"Hi, Fergus," says Mac.

Fergus gives a thumbs-up, then carries on rope-winding. They clearly have no idea who I am, so I relax a little.

"Safety briefing," announces Calum. "Life-jackets down there." He points at a pile in the corner of the cabin. "Mind your head on this. You're safer sitting down. Don't wander around. Obey instructions. Don't fall into the sea."

So we sit down, just inside the entrance to the cabin, while Calum fires up the engine. He glances over his shoulder and gives Fergus a tiny nod, which is apparently the signal to cast off.

I lean closer to Mac. "A man of few words."

"He loosens up after a bit," whispers Mac. "Just don't mention Alex Salmond."

We start to chug out through the archipelago, where seals

are reclining on rocks like sultans and cormorants sit drying their greeny-black wings. Then the boat starts to bounce a little as we head out into the open sea.

The first thirty minutes or so are moderately enjoyable. We watch the coastline of Harris retreat, with sunshine and shadow chasing each other across the hills. But then the sea grows livelier beneath us. Soon we are plunging into troughs and rising on the swell. From time to time, we hit the top of a wave and become airborne, hanging for a moment above the water, before coming down with a jolt. A jarring jolt. We start anticipating it, the weightless sensation of being in mid-air, followed by the spine-rattling crunch. It is a relentless and bruising repetition and, after a while, I start wondering how thick the hull is. Mac – who had been so full of the joys of spring – now sits quietly, with his gaze focused firmly on the distant horizon. Is he feeling sea-sick? Oh I do hope so.

To make matters even more uncomfortable, the sea has no real rhythm to it. It is a dirty mess of swells and cross-winds, a sprawl of lurches, pitches and rolls. Lurch, pitch, roll, pitch, lurch, lurch, roll, pitch, lurch. Am I going to be sick? I can feel a light-headedness creeping up on me. I slide from seat to seat towards the open back of the cabin where there is more fresh air. I really do not want to be sick. It's a feeling I have dreaded ever since I was a child. I lean out into the elements and gulp down as much oxygen as I can. The sickly, sweet fumes from the diesel are not helping, but after a few minutes I feel my head clearing and my thoughts sharpen and I know that I'm going to be all right.

Fergus comes and stands behind me, bracing himself in the doorframe.

"Are you OK there?" he asks. I give the best smile I can manage in the circumstances.

"This is the choppiest bit. Well, apart from the bit around the island."

"Right…so what is this, force four?"

He studies the churning of the waves for a second, grimacing as he peers beyond the stern.

"Maybe a five, possibly a six."

Then a ve-ry big wave slaps us side-on and the boat rolls, and rolls, and keeps rolling, I am thrown on to the next seat, still we're rolling, shit, are we going over?

A glance at Fergus's impassive face tells me that we're not. The boat rocks back towards an even keel and I feel ashamed of my fear. Did he see it? If he did, he has probably seen the same panic on the faces of countless tourists. Get over yourself, Kevin.

"How far is it to St. Kilda?"

Fergus puffs his pale cheeks. "From port? Ooh, about fifty-ish miles."

"How long to go?"

"We've done about, er…just under half of it."

Great.

He glances over his shoulder deeper into the cabin, drawn by a straining, mechanical, ratcheting grunt that I know is the sound of Mac being sick.

During the next hour and a half St. Kilda gradually took shape in front of us. It began as a ghostly, thrusting outline and then hardened into a grey-green tooth of a rock, with more teeth to either side. Then a second mass appeared from behind it. As we got closer, it started to look a little less relentlessly sheer and vertical. Shoulders of rock, long ledges and ragged promontories fell into focus. Vertical, brutal stacks stood guard, with foam boiling at their base. And, in the middle, a pyramid of rock, larger than the rest, rising out of the sea like a lost world of myth and monsters. St. Kilda.

Calum had given a tattered tourist guide to Mac, who kept trying to shout statistics and facts over the din of the wind, the sea and the seabirds thickening in the air around the rocks. A hundred miles from the mainland, he shouted. Tallest sea-cliffs in the British Isles! Thousand feet! Humans have lived here for three thousand years! Evacuated in 1930! The colour had returned to his face, now that he had got rid of his breakfast.

The closer we drew to St. Kilda the more intimidating it became. At least, that was how I felt, but Mac seemed enchanted, standing at the back of the boat with his jaw hanging open in wonder. Fergus suggested he close his mouth, with so many seabirds flying over our heads. The sea was becoming calmer as we rounded a jutting outthrust of rock and entered a small bay. Mac read more text out of the guidebook. We were looking at the remains of a volcano. The bowl-shaped bay in front of us – Village Bay – was part of a semi-submerged caldera. A little disappointingly, the first structure you noticed on the shore was a small, very functional-looking, squat, square power-generator. But to the right of that, at the foot of a steep slope, you could see the ghosts of settlement, small, ruined, roofless cottages, lined up in a short street, with a couple of restored ones in the middle.

Peppered randomly over the hills were hundreds of round stone storehouses – which Mac announced were called cleits – and which, at a glance, could pass for natural features of rock.

Calum slowly edged the boat into the bay and anchored about forty yards offshore. Then a small rib was lowered to ferry us to the stone pier. Apparently, the boat was not allowed to moor alongside the pier in case there were rats aboard, who might escape and decimate the seabird colonies. Gingerly, Mac and I clambered down to the bouncing rib, followed by Fergus, then Calum, who steered us steadily towards the stone pier. As we approached it, I noticed an exchange of apprehensive looks between the two crewmen. Rather solemnly, like some Presbyterian preacher, Calum announced that the swell was higher than had been forecast and we would have to do exactly as he instructed. Watching the waves, with intense concentration, he manoeuvred the rib till we were alongside the ledge of the pier. But then the swell would billow beneath us and carry us ten, fifteen yards too far.

There was another exchange of looks and Fergus was no longer so slow-pulsed, his movements quick, sharpened by adrenalin. Mac and I sat, poised, nervously waiting for our orders. After a few attempts, Fergus managed to hook a rope through a rusty, metal ring and tug us closer to the jetty. Now it was getting to be a question of timing. Calum looked over his shoulder at the surges of water rolling in, as he waited for a pause. He told me to get ready. When he said "jump" I was to jump.

I moved to the side of the rib. A wave grew beneath us, then faded, the rib settled for a beat, Fergus pulled the rope harder, the gap closed and I heard "jump", so I put one foot on the rib's edge and propelled myself on to the jetty.

I felt so pleased with myself. Why? It was hardly commando training. Now Mac was poised to jump. Calum told him to wait, and wait, and wait, and jump. With a tiny stumble, Mac scrambled on to the pier, clutching the backpack containing the sandwiches.

Then Calum gave us clear instructions that we should all meet back here at four and we set off, along the pier toward the corpse of the village.

We spent about two hours exploring the ruins. The only people we spoke to were a couple of academics – indomitable ladies in their fifties, the kind who built the empire – who were there studying rare plants. If they recognised me they didn't let on. We saw a couple of uniformed figures, briefly, down by the little power station, but otherwise it felt like we had the place to ourselves. We strolled around the stone skeletons of dykes and pens behind the village and then we explored the ruined houses, with occasional commentary from Mac and the guidebook, trying to work out what the living arrangements would have been.

One of the tiny, restored cottages turned out to be a museum with displays describing how the St. Kildans survived for centuries against what, to modern eyes, seem like impossible odds.

When we come out of the gloom of the museum we are met by brilliant sunshine, so we sit and eat our sandwiches.

Mac's empty stomach means he is bolting down his food like a prisoner-of-war. I can't bear to watch.

"Did you read the display about the missionaries?" he asks, his cheeks bulging.

"Yup."

"What bastards, eh? The poor fuckers survive perfectly well for centuries, eating puffins and playing their fiddles through the long, dark winters and along come some puritan fuckwits who say no dancing, you spend all your free time on your knees, in churches, crippled with fear, guilt and self-loathing."

He starts to demolish a ham bap.

"Tell me, is there any culture in the entire world that has not eventually been fucked up by religious wankers?"

"And that was 'Thought for the Day'."

"Even out here, on the edge of nowhere."

He exhales with annoyance. I feel a pang of envy at how fired up he can get.

"After this, we go up," he says, offering me a Kit-Kat.

So, once lunch is devoured, we climb the curving ever-steepening slope behind the village. It is not a problem to start with, but the last hundred yards or so turns into a real struggle and I have to keep stopping to get my breath back. Have I really got so badly out of condition? Or is it anxiety? To my relief, Mac is also struggling.

"Je-sus, this is deceptive!"

He stops, with his hands on his knees. We both look like old men, which makes us laugh wheezy old-man laughs.

"One last push," he gasps.

As we slog to the top, we slowly realise that this cliff has been eaten in half by the elements. It has no back; and instead of a cliff-top ledge there is a nothingness, just an astonishing drop to the crawling waves. In fact, the razor's edge is so intimidating that our bodies instinctively tell us to lie flat on our bellies so that we can look over the edge in safety. A thousand feet below us, gannets and fulmars float like tiny scraps of white paper. At least, Mac says they're gannets and fulmars; they could be anything.

"Jesus, look at that," he says, with a whistle.

"Imagine this place in winter." I look to my right, to another towering crag. "People have lived here for thousands of years, you say?"

"The book says there are Neolithic remains all over it."

"Who in their right mind would opt to live here? Why did they come here?"

"I think it was attached to the mainland at one point."

"Yeh but once it was an island."

"Pretty in summer, I expect."

"But a hell-hole most of the year, why would primitive human beings sail across miles of terrifying sea, in boats with no engines, to settle here?"

Mac gives it some thought.

"Fear. It has to be fear."

"Fear?"

"Aye, fear and greed are the two great impelling forces and it is not going to be greed, there's nothing here and it's tiny…so it has to be fear. Look at Venice, right, that was malarial marshland, right, no one wanted to live there, but the tribes were running away from…the Lombards, was it? They thought, fuck it, we'll go live out there, in Nature's arsehole, they won't follow us there."

On a very clear day, I suppose, you probably can see St. Kilda from Harris, so he might be right. Frightened people might have thought – that weird little island, right out there, maybe there we'll get to live in peace.

"Let's face it, if it wasn't for fear of our fellow human beings, we'd probably all still be living in Mesopotamia." Mac ends his observation by spitting over the cliff like a schoolboy, but the wind whisks it sideways. "Fear...can drive us to great deeds, Kev...or it can make us curl up in a fucking ball."

The journey back was memorable. The wind had dropped slightly so Calum headed out from the island and pottered around the base of the sea stacks, which loomed over us like dark skyscrapers. As we rocked in the troughs, seabirds swirled around us, some strafing the surf, others floating directly above our heads as if suspended on wires. Gannet after gannet moved in for a close-up, posing at head-height alongside us, catching the intermittent bursts of sunlight. When they glowed we could see the elegance of their lines, the perfect design of their long beaks, the tapered, black-tipped wings, the subtlety of their colouring as the white of their bodies shaded into a honeyed yellow around the head. On several occasions, they started feeding around us and torpedoed down into the water at startling speeds. Fulmars escorted us as well. Smaller, prim, almost ladylike. Less streamlined than the gannets, almost chubby in comparison, but still perfect and effortless in flight. It is hard to describe how exhilarated I felt, how thrilled I was to be bobbing around engulfed by wildness and ignored by Nature.

From time to time, Fergus pointed out features of the geology, or wave-lashed platforms of rock where the St. Kildans would land when they came to climb the stacks, hunting for birds. All the rock faces looked unclimbable to my eyes, but I suppose if you grow up climbing cliffs then you see every available hand-hold. All Mac and I saw was precipices and certain death.

The last rock is called Stac an Armin. It soars above us, as the boat edges closer.

Fergus shuffles across the deck to point something out.

Disconcertingly, I notice that, in several places, the water seems to be bulging higher than we are.

"See right at the top there? That little dark patch?"

Mac squints and shakes his head.

"I see it. Is it a cave?" I ask.

"Sort of. It's a shelter the fowlers hollowed out. A bothy. That's where they'd sleep every night for a fortnight while they were catching birds." A gannet spears into the water a few feet in front of us.

"In the early 1700s," continues Fergus, "the boat dropped off twelve men. For two weeks, they caught birds…only the boat never came back. Virtually everyone on St. Kilda had died of smallpox inside a fortnight, so there was no one who could row the boat out to fetch them."

Mac grimaces. "So they died?"

"No, they survived, nine months, I think, all through the winter, twelve of them in that wee cave. Until the rent collector from McLeod of McLeod came to fetch the rent, was told about the stranded men, and organised a rescue party."

We both peer at the small, dark patch that looks like no more than a crack.

"Fuck me," says Mac. "They must have been tough wee bastards."

"What did they eat?" I ask.

"Birds. But they couldn't drink the water off the rocks 'cos it would have been polluted with bird-shit, so they drank puffin-blood."

"Jesus, I've drunk some horrible stuff in my time but…"

"We're heading back now," calls Calum.

The boat is turned towards Harris and the engine is freed to full throttle.

The trip back to Harris was much more comfortable. The wind was still high, but it was mostly behind us so we ploughed a clean furrow through the waves and the rolls were slow and steady. It sent me into a kind of trance.

I watched the grey peaks of St. Kilda fading slowly away into the ocean for over an hour. Somehow it seemed more beautiful than on our approach. Was that the light? Or was it me? Maybe something becomes more beautiful once you know it.

"Wasn't that amazing?" says Mac as he slides in alongside me. He hands me a mug of hot tea. "Fergus made it. I've been thinking about those fellas in that hole for nine months...not knowing why no one had come for them...not knowing if anyone would ever come for them...all through the darkness of the winter and the storms..."

"Yeh, it's incredible."

"Just goes to show how adaptable people are, doesn't it? How they can survive anything...even when the future's scary and uncertain...they just hang on in there and wait for things to turn their way."

"OK, Mac." I look him in the eye. "I get the message."

He sips his tea. "There is no message." Then he puts on an American accent, "Messages are for Western Union." He's crap at accents.

As we pulled into the harbour, I felt calmer than I had felt for months. I knew the realities that were waiting for me in London, and my stomach still turned a little if I thought about them, but Mac's highland adventure had given me some emotional distance – a sense that all things pass. Most of life is chatter, so don't panic. That was how I felt as I stepped on to the quay at Leverburgh. It would be all right. Just drink up your puffin-blood. I was renewed.

4

THE WAIT

The day after I returned to London, I was charged, and my sense of renewal disappeared in an instant. Inevitably, the photographers had prior warning of my appearance at the police station. One of them broke his ankle in the scrum. I was deemed not to be a "flight risk"; bail was set at a minimal two thousand pounds, and the trial date was set for August 21st. Four months. Four more months.

So, like a crab, I retreated back into my hole in the mud. I grew the beard even longer, and I sat for hours, unfeeling and unthinking, watching images flicker across the TV screen. I tried to read some books, but the mental focus was not there, so I found myself re-reading the same paragraph over and over. Looking back at that period, I find it very hard to separate out any real memories. Life defocused into a blur. One episode, though, does manage to poke through, like the outline of rocks in a fog.

My solicitor, Graham, came to my house for a meeting, stayed for a drink, and then another and another, and then started telling me things that I didn't want to know. The first was the break-up of his marriage. All his fault, apparently. He had been too clingy, so she had left for Australia. Then he moves on to my case.

"The thing is, Kevin," he says, tapping me affectionately on the knee, "the thing is – and don't tell Nina I said this – but there

is another option you should keep open for yourself…y'know…
in the great scheme of options."

"Another option?"

"Yuh…a very valid option." He puts his whisky glass down on
the table with exaggerated care and then looks me hard in the
eyes. "You could cop a plea. Plead guilty to assault. Accept the
sentence, it'll be short, might even be suspended, and then move
on, and get on with the rest of your life." He leans back in his
chair. "I'm just throwing that out there."

"Oh fuck off, Graham."

"Fair enough."

"I'm not pleading guilty to something I didn't do. Why the
fuck should I do that?"

"Just laying out the options." He picks up his whisky again.
"Just examining the realities."

I know Graham is pissed so I shouldn't take him too seriously,
but the word "realities" buzzes in my mind.

"Realities? What realities?"

He leans forward conspiratorially. "The reality…that we have
to work with…which is that juries no longer like celebrities. They
used to. In the good old days, you used to go to court with a
celebrity and the jury would go 'oh that's old so-and-so off that
TV thing set in the hospital, we like him, he can't be guilty. He
swims things for charity!' Always. Celebrities. People believed
in them. Juries believed them. But then…" He pauses to burp.
His voice gets louder: "But then…along comes Mister Jimmy-
fucking-Savile and now if you're a celebrity you're guilty – guilty
as sin – from day one. Juries think all showbiz people are kiddy-
fiddling, tax-avoiding rapists or worse. So, one option open to you
is not to risk getting in front of a jury…I'm just saying…don't
mention this to Nina. She hates defeatism."

At this point, I decide to call Graham a taxi. But he hasn't
finished his observations.

"We're living through a witch-hunt. And once someone points at you and shouts 'witch', that's it...on the bonfire with him, whoosh! The justice system...out of the window."

"Graham, are you seriously suggesting that I can't get a fair trial because of Jimmy Savile?"

"And Rolf Harris...and Stuart Hall...and that disc jockey... and the other one, with the hair."

I steer him back on to the subject of his failed marriage just to shut him up until, at last, I hear the toot of a car horn and I lead him out into the rainy night and fold him into the back seat of a taxi. As the cab starts to pull away he leans out of the window and hisses: "Ignore me, I'm a bit pissed."

And then I sit in the darkness thinking about what he said. Savile was a devious psychopath – an exceptional, obscene monster – he had nothing to do with my case. Only an idiot would lump me in with him. The public weren't idiots, even if some of them did occasionally confuse me with a fictional character. No, I had to believe in people; I had to believe in the law; I had to remember the ones who had been vindicated – Paul Gambaccini, Jim Davidson. There were others, but I couldn't remember them. No, the whisky in Graham had made him exaggerate and generalise. Don't fret over the words of a drunk.

The next time I see Graham no reference is made to our conversation. We are in a meeting with my barrister, who looks like a barrister, rotund, with slicked-back hair. He even wears a waistcoat, for Christ's sake. His name is Seymour and he has a rich, deep voice which he seems rather proud of.

"Now then, Kevin, I'm afraid I'm about to ask you a lot of questions which may strike you as rather tedious, but they'll prove very useful for me when I have to paint a picture of you to the jury."

In the corner of the room, Nina Patel starts tapping notes into her tablet.

"Why do you need to paint a picture of me?"

"Well…" he gives me a smile that drips with condescension, "that's because, to help their deliberations, I'll need to give them a sense…a fully rounded sense of what kind of a chap you are."

"Will they need that? The case is about the facts, isn't it? The facts speak for themselves."

A look shoots between Graham and Nina. They think I am being difficult.

"The facts," Seymour booms, "of course the facts will be our guiding stars, but, in my experience, people also like to understand the people in a case, so part of my task is to give a favourable impression of your character and, if possible, taint the character of your accuser." He glances at some notes. "Tawdry, I know, but this isn't tiddlywinks. Now then, you were born in…?"

"Stoke Newington."

"OK, and your parents are…?"

"Both gone."

"I see…Father's occupation?"

"Postal worker."

"Did your mother work?"

"She was a dinner lady."

He pauses, as if to picture them.

"So…working-class, then."

"Yes. Is that good?"

He ignores the edge in my question.

"So how were things for them financially?"

"Tough, I suppose…I think they put pretty much every penny towards me."

"Only child?"

"Yes."

"Any childhood illnesses?"

"Are you serious?"

He doesn't even bother to look up.

"Any childhood illnesses?"

"Yes, I lost an arm in some factory machinery."

Nina Patel leans across to tell me to stop being a dickhead when people are trying to help.

"I'm looking for an element of heroism, Kevin," Seymour intones. "I'm looking for a way of presenting you as the little guy who battled through, even though the odds were stacked against him."

"But they weren't."

He lets out a sigh.

"I'm not going to turn you into a Barbara Taylor Bradford novel, I am merely looking for something people can connect with...When did your parents die?"

"Erm...Dad in '89...Mum six years ago."

"Natural causes?"

"Dad, liver failure...Mum, cancer."

"You've been married."

"Yes, Sandra, didn't work out, but we remain friends."

"And she is testifying on your behalf."

"That's right, yes."

"She'll say nice things about you?"

"She'll say true things."

He peers at me for a few moments. "I think it would be worth a meeting with her," he says to Graham and Nina, casually. "Now then, Kevin, we're going to practise thickening up that skin of yours. Do you think you're up for that?"

"Is this necessary?"

"First off, I think it'd be really useful if you could unlearn this habit of answering every question with a question. That won't play well, I'm afraid. Second off, I'm presuming that the beard is going to go soon...?"

"Yes...the beard will come off."

"Splendid. A plain suit on the day, please. Something you'd

wear to your granny's funeral. Now then, imagine you're in the witness box and that I'm the prosecuting counsel...are you ready?"

The rehearsal lasted about forty-five minutes. It reminded me a little of being on set as they gave me various playing notes. Part of me wondered whether it was dangerous to prepare an actor in this way. What if the jury started to feel I was giving some kind of performance?

There was only one of these sessions, thank God, so the weeks limped past me in my mud-hole until, at last, the big day arrived. August 21st. My Mum's birthday.

5

THE TRIAL

My legal team gave me a final pep talk a few minutes before we entered the courtroom. Don't get angry. Don't wave your arms around. Do look at the jury, but not too often. I had shaved and was wearing a sober blue suit.

The first morning of the first day is largely procedural. Then, in the afternoon the jury are shown police photographs of Jade's face the morning after the incident. In lurid close-up, the varnished blue bruises around her cheekbones do make you wince a little, but then she did hit the kerb pretty hard. After that, Jade takes the stand, wearing a dark blue, sombre trouser suit. She starts giving her evidence – all of it totally believable – because she believes it. In her memory, I hit her, pure and simple. As I sit in the dock, listening to her terrifying certainty, I begin to sweat, which I know will look like guilt.

Seymour questions her all afternoon, without leaving a mark on her. Every time I glance up to the gallery, Sandra gives me a brave smile.

Next into the witness box is a young woman called Tracey Martin. Apparently she is an eye-witness and there is a bit of a swagger in her answers. The counsel for the prosecution – a shambolic-looking man with feral eyebrows and a mass of mad-professor hair – guides her gently through her evidence. Then it is Seymour's turn. He takes her back to the beginning of her account.

"And you were getting out of your car, which was parked in the position marked on the diagram?"

She glances at the diagram. "'S right, yeh."

"And as you got out of your car, you heard raised voices. And when you looked you saw Mr Carver and Miss Pope having an argument."

"Yeh."

"And what happened next?"

"Well, I hear a thump, like, and then she's lying on the ground, and he's, like, leaning over her."

Seymour pauses. He shuffles his notes with a slightly distracted air.

"Did Mr Carver seem concerned?"

"Yeh...sort of."

Their barrister shifts in his seat as if he is about to object, but then thinks better of it. My barrister ups his volume slightly.

"And what did you do next, Miss Martin?"

"I walked out of the car park...towards the shopping centre."

"Right. Nothing else?"

"No, no, sorry, no. I *did* do something else..."

The prosecution team look slightly thrown.

"I, um...I texted my mate Karen that I'd just seen Lenny and Melanie having a barney in a car park."

Someone titters quietly near the back of the courtroom. Seymour gives a sly grin and goes in for the kill.

I ought to have gone home feeling confident. He had torn Tracey Martin to shreds, exposing her as silly and unreliable. As we adjourned, my legal team clustered round to tell me we had had a good day. But it did not feel that way to me, I still felt shrouded in dread.

At home, curled in the corner of my sofa, I watched the news. Ludicrously, I was the second item, ahead of an earthquake that had killed several hundred people in Guatemala, two suicide bombs in Kabul, a lethal mudslide in the Philippines, a murder in Guildford and a possible cure for Parkinson's disease. The report itself contained very little, just some footage of my arrival, the ITN correspondent shouting platitudes down a microphone and an artist's impression of me standing in the dock looking extremely shifty.

I felt hunted.

Mac rang to tell me that TV News was now run by "limp-dicked wankers" and I wasn't to let them get to me. Sandra phoned and offered to come round. I wanted to say yes but for some reason I didn't. Shame, I suppose. She told me that she thought things had gone well for me in court and that I could face tomorrow with confidence.

"And don't forget to breathe."

"Don't forget to breathe?"

"Yuh."

"Yeh, that'd be a pretty basic error, wouldn't it?"

"I mean it, Kevin, when you get tense you do that shallow-breathing thing, and then you get anxious."

"That's rubbish, I'm an actor, I'm trained, I breathe properly."

"Only when you're being someone else."

6

THE DOCK

Morning came, eventually, and Graham picked me up in his car. As we arrived at the courthouse, a group of about thirty paparazzi avalanched towards the car. Two policemen muscled in and forced them back so we could scuttle inside.

There is time for a cup of tea and yet one more pep talk before proceedings begin. My first hour in the witness box is nowhere near as bad as I had feared. Their barrister's line of questioning is not particularly aggressive; he restricts himself to establishing the sequence of events, my relationship with Jade, the dinner, the argument. He barely questions my account of how I had pushed Jade away to protect myself. It has all been very matter-of-fact, business-like.

Then he stops and shakes his head. He seems to have got his notes in a tangle. For a good thirty seconds, he shuffles his papers around in silence before looking up at the ceiling and puffing his cheeks.

"Tell me, Mr Carver, when you first approach the portrayal of a character, where do you start from?"

"I'm sorry, I…"

"Well some actors like to start with the shoes, don't they?"

What? Where the hell is he going with this?

"Other actors like to nail the way a character walks or—"

Seymour is on his feet. "Your honour, I—"

The judge is ahead of him. "Mr Sims, I trust this is going somewhere pertinent."

"I think so, m'lud. So, Mr Carver, as an actor, where do you start?"

"I start with the text."

"Right, and when you're shaping a character, do you draw on your own personality and experience?"

"Well, to a certain extent…you have to bring it from somewhere."

"From somewhere, so you draw on your own psyche, as it were."

The judge steps in. "Perhaps you might like to move beyond theories about acting."

"I am happy to leave that avenue, m'lud."

"Thank you."

"Mr Carver…have you ever struck a woman?"

"No, never," I reply, quickly, firmly, definitively.

"That's…um…" he pauses to read some notes. "…that's not strictly true, is it? You've struck many women and what's more, millions of people have seen you do it. In fact, as Lenny, you've hit three women in the last year."

I concentrate on remaining calm, and breathing. "Lenny isn't real. That's what we call pretend."

"Of course, yes, absolutely, but purely on a practical level, and please excuse my ignorance here, but when you do those violent scenes, do you actually strike the actress, or…"

The judge interrupts loudly, losing his patience. "Once again, Mr Sims, I feel we're going off on a rather luxurious tangent."

"I do apologise, m'lud, I'll move on. If you'll just bear with me a moment."

He's shuffling through his papers again. Is this some kind of tactic? Now some have dropped on to the floor and he's scrabbling incompetently to pick them up.

"Sorry, sorry. Sorry about that. Mr Carver, do you read reviews about yourself?"

"Only the good ones."

He laughs. "Well then, perhaps you saw this very complimentary one you got from the TV critic of the Daily Telegraph."

Seymour looks concerned and gets to his feet. "M'lud, I confess, I'm bewildered by—"

"I'll allow it for now, Mr Sims," the judge intones, with the suggestion of a warning.

The prosecution starts to read out the newspaper clipping: "'In a gallery of otherwise vegetoid characters, one performance stands out. Kevin Carver, who plays "sexy bad-boy" Lenny, convinces the viewer that beneath the character's wisecracks there is a dark, ever-present suggestion of potentially explosive violence.' Where do you think you bring that from?"

I hesitate, I can feel ice cracking beneath my feet.

"Earlier, Mr Carver, you said 'you have to bring it from somewhere', so that on-screen violence against women, where's the 'somewhere' that you bring that from?"

I can't marshal an answer. Seymour is on his feet protesting, but their man is shouting over him: "Perhaps from the same somewhere that led you to punch Miss Pope in the car park, is that where it comes from?"

Now my man is protesting more loudly and the judge steps in to instruct the jury that they are to disregard any questions that were to do with the character I play on TV. But the damage is done, I can read it in the jury's faces. I am him. I play a man who treats women cruelly, often brutally. How can I do that? Where do I bring that stuff from, if not somewhere deep inside?

A bloody good question, as it happens.

The next two hours are a nightmare. Every question is an accusation, sometimes snarled, sometimes slid in, sly, like a stiletto. Every answer I give he labels a lie. My brief is up and down like a jack-in-the-box, but this man keeps coming for me; he has sunk his teeth in and he is going to bring me down.

The judge warns him every now and then but fundamentally, I am on my own. He destroys me. He makes me feel pathetic and stupid and, for the first time in decades, I am working-class again, one step behind, out of place, the boy in the wrong kind of shoes.

"You say she kicked you and she hit you, Mr Carver."

I must be decisive. "Yes." Loud and clear.

"Hit you how many times?"

"I can't remember exactly."

"Once, more than once, several, many, dozens?"

"Um…several."

"With her fist? Or just slaps?"

"Bit of both."

"How many fists, percentage-wise?"

"I can't remember, it was—"

"More slaps than fists?"

"Not sure, probably, yes, I—"

"So it didn't really hurt, then?"

"No, not really, it was more disorientating, I—"

"And you pushed her away, you say, in order to defend yourself?"

"Yes."

"To defend yourself from what? You just said it didn't hurt."

Stay calm, Kevin. Think.

"Mr Carver?"

Choose your words.

"You're a strong man, could you not have just restrained her by holding her by the arms?"

Yes, that's what I should have done, but I must choose my words.

"Possibly, that's how I should have reacted, but it all happened so fast, I wasn't thinking straight."

"You hit her, Mr Carver, didn't you?"

"No, categorically not."

"You're certain?"

"One hundred per cent certain."

"You're one hundred per cent certain on that point...and yet so very *un*certain about everything else."

He starts to shuffle his notes, as I hang, turning, silk-wrapped.

Inevitably, I could not sleep that night. I just lay on the bed, hollowed out with mental exhaustion. I took a sleeping pill, but it didn't work. And I was frightened to take another in case it dulled my mental processes in the morning. How long was this trial going to last? How much could I take?

The following day, probably as a defence, I find my brain has slipped into neutral. Luckily, all I have to do is sit and watch. I have become a member of the audience, watching my story being acted out in front of me. Sandra appears as a character witness. Mr Sims is clinical, but civil.

"And did you ever experience Mr Carver being physically abusive?"

"To me?"

"To anyone?"

"No."

"And what about verbal abuse? Was he ever verbally abusive to you?"

"We were married. The abuse was mutual."

My barrister looks pleased. She is holding her own.

"You divorced Mr Carver on the grounds of his unreasonable behaviour, is that correct?"

"Yes..."

"Did that involve other women?"

"To an extent, yes."

"How would you describe his attitude to women?"

Sandra hesitates, flummoxed by the general nature of the question. He presses on. "Do you think he treats them as people?"

"Yes," she replies with an upward tilt of her head. "As much as any man does."

Mr Sims rearranges his notes. "No further questions, m'lud."

It was a battling performance from Sandra but I knew it would not be enough. The prosecution was skilfully piecing together the argument that I was clearly the kind of man who hits women.

At the end of a gruelling day, while leaving the courthouse, I heard a voice behind me – probably one of the journalists – mutter "dead man walking".

As the trial wore on, my legal team started to look more and more round-shouldered. Even Nina Patel looked downcast. Oh, and the Home Secretary had announced a big crackdown on crimes of violence against women. So that boded well.

But then, a stroke of luck. The judge got knocked down by a van. His injuries weren't serious – a few cracked ribs – but it meant the trial was adjourned for a week.

I just stayed inside the house, wearing my pyjamas like a uniform. I didn't want to do anything, didn't want to see anyone or go anywhere. That's what happens with depression, I suppose. You take yourself hostage. My cleaning lady stopped coming. I couldn't be bothered to find out why.

Then I had another stroke of luck. Some England footballers were caught having sex with underage girls in a health spa. There were four players involved, so the two photographers who had been permanently parked outside my house suddenly disappeared, presumably to stake out some Tudor mansions in Cobham.

But I still didn't venture out.

I measured my day in the sounds of the street. The eight a.m. electric whine of the milkfloat. The three p.m. clunk-clunk-clunk of car doors, as the mums' army mobilised to collect kids from school. The midnight wails of sirens drifting up from the High Street, half a mile away.

Sometime after midnight on the Thursday when all seems quiet, I take the wheelie bins down to my gate. A fox is watching from the other side of the street. He knows it's bin night. The contents of several bin-bags are already strewn down the street. Suddenly, a voice comes out of the darkness.

"Little buggers, aren't they?"

Shit, a photographer. But a man steps forward under the streetlight and I can see that he has no camera. "Sprinkle pepper over your bins, that's the answer." His tone of jovial familiarity is unnerving.

"Sorry, um, do I know you?"

He chuckles. "You probably think you do. People always think they know me. It comes from having such a bland face, I think. When you look like nobody in particular, you look like everybody in general."

I get it now. He just wants someone to talk to. One of the innumerable lonely, harmless semi-nutters.

"Right, well, goodnight."

I turn and head back towards my front door.

"I need to talk to you, Mr Carver."

"I'm sorry, it's late, I—"

"It's not right, what's happening to you."

Oh no, a fan.

"Well, that's very kind and thank you for your support but—"

"She's lying."

I have reached my door. "Well—"

"She's lying, Mr Carver. And I'm prepared to say that in court. Tell them how I saw everything."

I wheel slowly, not quite sure what I've heard. "You saw everything?"

"Everything."

"Are you...are you saying...that you're a witness?"

"Yes, I'm sorry. If I'd known about your plight I would have come forward sooner but—"

"No, no, that's fine." I hurry back towards him, my arms outstretched as I try to organise my galloping thoughts. "But let me get this clear in my head, you're saying you saw everything, and that you want to give evidence on my behalf now, is that right?"

"Absolutely. To prevent a miscarriage of justice. You're an innocent man, Kevin."

And I start to weep. Uncontrollably. For so long I'd clung to the hope that somehow the truth would out, because the truth always does out in the end, doesn't it? In every great play or novel the truth finds a way through, like water. And now here it was. Here he was. I was saved. And so I weep, sobbing like a child, swallowing great gulps of air.

"My name's Derek," he says.

7

THE TRUTH

In exceptional circumstances, fate has sent me a wholly unexceptional man. Derek is average height, average build, with a forgettable face crowned by a flop of sandy-coloured hair. His voice is flat and neutral. He would never turn a single head and yet, as he sits on my sofa, drinking beer, to my eyes, he is an angel.

"So," he pauses to take in the room, "this is how TV stars live. Cheers."

He toasts me with his can of Becks.

"Cheers. Listen…Derek, I'm sorry about the waterworks just now…only it's been a hell of a time for me."

"I can imagine."

I feel an overpowering urge to cross-question him in order to check, one more time, that there hasn't been a misunderstanding.

"So, Derek, just to be one hundred per cent clear…you were in the car park."

"Yes."

"And you saw Jade hitting me."

"Yes."

"And you saw her fall and—"

"Bang her head, yes."

"Right, good."

"It was an accident."

"Yes."

"I'm prepared to say all of—"

"You're prepared to testify."

"I'm happy to stand up in court and say that I saw her hit you, fall, and crack her head."

"And did you hear me offer to take her to hospital?"

"If you like."

This stops me in my tracks. "Sorry, Derek, I…"

"I can say that if you want me to."

"No. No, no, you must only…y'know…you can only say what you saw. So…you're saying you didn't hear me say that, about the hospital? "

"No, I didn't."

"OK, no problem, that's fine, no problem at all…what, were you too far away to hear what I said?"

Derek looks at me blankly.

"Y'know…in the car park…were you too far away in the car park? Whereabouts were you in the car park, Derek? I mean, which bit of the car park? Were you on the other side of the car park? You weren't in the car park, were you, Derek?"

"Not physically, no."

I let out a suppressed, frustrated roar. How could I be so stupid? I had been ignoring alarm bells in my mind for the last ten minutes. God, this is cruel! To be offered salvation and then – hang on, what did he just say?

"Not physically? Wait, I get it, Derek, you saw it all on security cameras, didn't you?"

"No."

My head is spinning now. There's a wave of nausea. Remember to breathe.

"Then…with respect, Derek…*how* did you witness all this?"

"I witnessed it all…emotionally."

My voice deadens. "You witnessed it…emotionally."

"Through my emotions, yes," nods Derek.

"Right…how does that work exactly?"

He puts his beer down on the table. "Well…it's like this…y'see, Kevin, like you I was once falsely accused – also by a lady-friend, as it happens – so I've experienced your sense of helplessness. Your story resonates with me as being emotionally true. Instinctively, I can tell you're innocent, and I want to help you."

"…Help me?"

"By setting you free."

He beams at me triumphantly. I press my hands against my pounding temples.

"You're…you're offering to stand up in court…and tell lies on my behalf?"

"No."

"No?"

"No, I'm offering to tell the truth…the events are true, it's only my perspective that's theoretical."

I try to shape an answer, dumbfounded by his deformed logic. And I know, in my bones, that this is a defining moment. It's a perfectly straightforward situation. A stranger – probably a nutjob – is proposing that he and I collude in a criminal act. All I have to do is calmly show him the door – which is what I start to do.

"No, I'm sorry, Derek, it's not on. Now if you wouldn't mind lea— you can take the beer – but I'd really like you to just—"

"No, listen, Kevin, please, they'll send you to jail."

"I'll get longer for perjury."

"I'm the one who'd be doing the perjuring."

"Please go. I'll take my chances in court." I usher him to his feet.

"I think you're being foolish," he says.

"I'll be OK. The truth will out."

"And I'd be facilitating that…outage."

I start to guide him, gently but firmly, by the elbow in the direction of the door.

"Think of me as a kind of midwife," he pronounces.

"...a midwife?"

"Yes, helping to birth the truth...y'know, inducing it."

I'm getting the measure of him now, he's an obsessive, a fantasist and a New-Age bullshitter.

"We'd get years, Derek. It's called conspiracy."

"Yes 'Conspiracy to Ensure the Course of Justice'."

For some reason, momentarily, he reminds me of Ross from Friends. Isn't that odd? As I reach for the latch on my door, his grey voice acquires an edge.

"You are innocent, aren't you?"

"Yes," I snap. "I'm innocent."

"Then why should the innocent be punished?"

How that question hung in the air.

There was no escaping it. There was a very good chance that I'd be sent to prison for something I didn't do. Even if I only got a suspended sentence, I would still be publicly branded as a woman-hitter. But perhaps I was being pessimistic. Perhaps the legal system would win through, if only I could trust it. I was fearful, confused. I didn't know what to think. But I didn't turn the latch.

"It probably would make no difference, Derek, the jury could still convict me."

"No, no—"

"Well—"

"No, I'd be too convincing. I once trained as an actor."

An actor? Hard to believe. He cuts no shape at all.

"...What do you do now?" I mumble.

"I phone people and ask them if they're happy with their electricity supply. I don't usually get any further than that. But I'm good at handling rejection, which is just as well really."

Derek witters on in his featureless drone for a few more minutes about how he sees the call centre as "one more island in the odyssey of his life". I am trying to herd the thoughts stampeding around inside my head and then, as if from out of thin air, as if I was somebody else, a third party, I hear myself say: "How much?"

"Sorry?"

"If I agreed…how much are we talking about?"

"I don't want money."

"No money?"

"No."

"Right…but, well…sorry, but what do you get out of it?"

"I get to help a fellow human being in pain."

Yes, I know. More alarm bells. But the thundering in my head was drowning them out. "This whole idea is…it's madness."

"It'd be madness not to."

"But—"

"Have you thought what your life will be like if you're found guilty? It's a big step, I know."

"Too big."

"Just think about it…think about the alternative. Why don't you sleep on it?"

I didn't sleep on it because I didn't sleep. It felt like I would never sleep again. My brain boiled with possibilities. It was too reckless, I'd be placing myself at the mercy of a total stranger – and they didn't come much stranger. On the other hand, what chance did I stand in court? It was my word against hers. And she made a much more convincing victim than I did.

And the jury was eight women, four men.

And I didn't like the way they were declining to look at me. Irrational? What's rational in an insane situation? The bottom line is the truth; the truth is the truth is the truth. Does it matter who tells it? Or how? I could picture my face on millions of front pages in countless homes; that would be obscenely unjust, to be publicly reviled. Didn't I have the right to prevent that? And how big was the risk? Even if Derek turned out to be an unconvincing witness, as long as no one knew we had met, then—no, it was all too much, it wasn't me. I shouldn't panic. The jury aren't idiots. But juries make mistakes. Could I just run away? Or am I going mad? Should I take some more sleeping tablets? Perhaps I'm already mad.

At last, light began to creep into my bedroom. I got up, made myself some breakfast and listened to the radio. John Humphrys was interviewing a psychologist about how the human brain was being changed by new technologies. Another cricketer had been accused of taking bribes. A banker had received a bonus. Someone had been stabbed in Hammersmith.

At nine o'clock, the phone rang: like a question.

"It's me. If the supervisor comes across I may have to start asking you about your electricity supply."

"Where did you get my number?"

"There are ways. Nothing is private any more, Kevin."

"Blood-y hell, how did—"

"So, have you decided?" he asks, talking over me. "Have you? I mean, if you've decided to play it all by the book and just take your chance in court, I'd understand, Kevin. I can see you're a pretty principled kind of guy...y'know, I'd respect that choice... totally. Are you still there?"

"Yes, I'm here, Derek...and the answer is I'm not interested."

8

THE EVIDENCE

In the days after that conversation, I kept telling myself I'd made the right decision. It'd be insane to commit a criminal act in order to prove my innocence, wouldn't it? Of course it would.

Derek left a few messages on my answerphone. Was I sure? Perhaps I should think about it some more. He left me his number. I meant to erase the calls, but somehow I never got round to it.

It's very hard to be certain about what might have been. I don't like hindsight, it's such a know-all. But I'm quietly confident that nothing more would have happened as regards Derek's offer, if it had not been for my next stupid, imbecilic mistake.

I went on Twitter.

God knows what made me do it. I can only put it down to morbid curiosity. I had been thinking about it for ages but now, with the trial about to resume, I got this overpowering urge to find out what people were saying about me.

I search my name and brace myself.

I know it might be bad, but I am not prepared for what comes next. There are hundreds, hundreds of tweets, nearly all of them dripping with vitriol about me. It's terrifying to realise how despised I have become. I scroll and scroll in the hope that I'll find someone who doesn't think I am scum, but it's a lost cause.

Every now and then I happen on one that is condemning the

trial as a circus – and a few misogynists are getting stuck into Jade – but overwhelmingly, it is pure hatred directed at me. Many of them want me sent to prison for ten years, plus. That phrase – 'dead man walking' – appears on a regular basis.

Like an idiot, I read them all, transfixed by the horror of the procession. Eventually, shaken to the core and weak-limbed, I switch off my phone and lie out on the sofa. All the panic that I thought I had mastered comes flooding back and I am utterly and indescribably alone.

I stand no chance.

I feel like I am crouched in front of a firing squad.

After a few minutes, with my heart still pounding in my chest, I rise a little groggily to my feet, fetch a pen and paper and head for the answerphone.

We meet in a very quiet corner of a local park. I kid myself that I am still undecided.

We conduct a little exercise. I play the part of that assassin of a barrister and cross-question Derek relentlessly, manoeuvring him, berating him, ambushing him. But he holds up very well. His version of my version never falters. He seems in control; which, with hindsight, he was.

"We mustn't meet again, Kevin. If we were seen together, then…"

"No, 'course, absolutely."

"I'll go to the police, offer to make a statement etcetera, they'll put me in touch with your legal team."

"Why now?"

"What?"

"Why now? Why have you left it so late? To help me?"

"Well, I had the idea a while back, but I thought I'd wait and see how things panned out…see if the case against you collapsed. No point committing a criminal offence unless it's necessary, that's what I always say."

Always? What's the word "always" doing in that sentence? "Have you done this before?"

He smiles. "Not this, no, not as such."

"Not as such'? What does that—"

"I'll be off then."

He shapes to leave, but I have one big question left.

"What makes you so certain I'm innocent? You don't even know me."

"Yes, I do. I can read people." He can read people. I wish I could read him.

The next day the police contact my solicitor, who calls me in for a meeting. As I'm shown into Graham's office the first sight that greets me is Derek sitting straight-backed in a worn, dark blue Sunday-best M&S suit. Across the desk sits a very excited Graham and to the side, perched on a sofa, absorbed in the text of Derek's statement to the police, is Nina Patel.

Graham rises quickly to his feet.

"Kevin! Some good news at last. This gentleman is called Derek Tapscott. And he's come forward to vindicate your version of events. He was in the car park, he saw everything!"

I pretend to be stunned. Don't do too much, Kevin. Less is more. Derek stands and greets me as if we have never met and I feel sure that we must look like a pair of total fakes. But my solicitor clearly hasn't registered that anything is amiss, he is beaming at me, while Nina Patel is still poring over the details of Derek's statement.

"The tide has turned, Kevin," chuckles Graham. "The cavalry is here, have a seat, make yourself comfy, tea?"

I nod, still doing "stunned".

Nina Patel looks up from the documents with a reassuring smile.

"Well this is very timely," she says. "Our barrister is going to be very pleased."

I ask where my barrister is. Nina Patel explains that he's in court, but that she will brief him. But, all the time that she is talking to me, she is looking at Derek, weighing him up. She's too bright for us, this isn't going to work.

"You do understand what will happen, don't you, Derek?" she begins. "You'll be put in the witness box and their barrister will set about trying to destroy your credibility. It'll probably get quite rough. Have you ever been to court?"

"Only once," he responds breezily, "over an unfair traffic fine."

"Right, well this will be a lot more…invasive. He's bound to ask you lots of unsettling questions, he'll want to explore your background. Just for our info, what is your background?"

For the next twenty-five minutes, Derek fills us in on his background. Nina Patel smiles at him and says, "Well, we probably won't want as much background as that. But it's useful to have such a full picture, so thank you."

She then does some role-playing, asking the kind of aggressive questions that Derek can expect in court, but he seems unfazed. His answers are clear and calm and, unlike me, he only answers the question, not the insinuation.

After about twenty minutes of this, she congratulates Derek and thanks him for his time. We all stand and shake hands and I concentrate hard on not arousing suspicion. But, to me, my acting feels dismal.

Once Derek has left the room, my solicitor breaks into a little jig. "A surprise witness! I've always wanted one of those. Like in a movie." But his tone dampens when he sees Nina Patel looking pensive. "What? Oh come on, Nina, he's a game-changer, isn't he? You've got to be pleased about that, surely."

"I am pleased."

"Well then, tell your face."

She screws up her nose and shakes her head slightly. Oh God, this isn't going to work.

"I don't know," she mutters, "he worries me."

Graham spreads his arms wide in frustration. "Why?"

"There's...he's...he's not quite...he's not...of this world."

"Oh for Christ's—"

"I can't put my finger on it. I just worry about him in the witness box. What do you make of him, Kevin?"

I take a moment to appear calm.

"Erm...he seems reasonably ordinary to me."

"Ordinary," agrees Graham. "Exactly. Very ordinary. In fact, pretty bloody boring, which is perfect."

Nina Patel tilts back her head and stares at the ceiling for a few moments. Graham looks at me and shrugs. We sit and wait in the silence. The suspense is torture, as the tick of their office clock counts down the seconds before Nina Patel sees through this sham. She's spotted something. Of course she has. What was I thinking of?

Suddenly, she returns to us. "Oh, I dunno, I'm probably over-thinking."

Graham laughs, relieved. "We don't look gift-horses in the mouth, Nina. Not when..." He tails off. Nina flashes him a look.

"Not when what?" I ask.

He shuffles in his seat. "Erm...well, y'know...it's not been going as well as we might have hoped...it's what I told you about earlier...the jury...there's a climate...it's unfortunate."

"I know...Jimmy Savile."

"Yeh, it's..."

"You're saying they don't believe me?"

"That's my fear...yes."

He turns to address Nina Patel. "I think your doubts are a bit of a luxury in this situation. We have to use Derek. Or else..." His voice tails off again. She gets to her feet with a new urgency.

"You're right. I'm just being a scaredy-cat. He's a game-changer."
Then, with sudden resolve, she says: "We'll unleash Derek."

"Unleash the Derek," echoes Graham.

And they laugh. So I laugh too.

Four days later, I'm back in court watching Derek take the stand. The prosecution barrister attacks hard from the off, but Derek is a consistent performer. He comes across as steady, reliable; his monochrome appearance and neutral voice give him an air of objectivity, a whiff of detached authority that slowly frustrates his interrogator.

"So, Mr Tapscott, you are totally confident that you saw the incident unfold in *exactly* the…the ve-ry detailed way that you have described?"

"Yes, I'm confident."

Their barrister chuckles. I don't like that. "You're a very observant chap, aren't you? Not like most of us who wander around…head in the clouds. If I'm ever attacked, I hope you're there to witness it."

"Um…she wasn't attacked." Derek corrects politely. "She hit him."

Seymour raises his eyebrows. He's impressed. Their barrister is picking at a small piece of fluff on his gown.

"This case has regrettably attracted much tabloid 'excitement'. It's been headline news for a couple of months now, and yet you only came forward as a witness three days ago, is that right?"

"Yes."

"How do you account for that delay?"

"I don't have a television."

"Go on."

"So I didn't know what 'Lenny' or, um…"

What a skilful pause.

"Melanie?" prompts the barrister.

"Yes, I didn't know what they looked like...because I'd never seen their programme, so I didn't connect them with the incident I'd witnessed in the car park. Well, not until I saw their photos in the paper last week."

"But their photos have been in the papers for months, Mr Tapscott."

"I take the Telegraph...and not every day."

Their man is starting to look worn down.

"You watch no TV...and you take the Telegraph."

"Yes, sorry, I'm a bit of an oddity, aren't I?"

"Not at all, Mr Tapscott, you'd make a very fine judge," says m'lud, with a twinkle.

Laughter. The judge's joke is met with a warm ripple of laughter, genuine laughter, not the polite laughter that had greeted his previous jokes. The atmosphere is starting to change. The jury are making eye-contact with me.

Derek continues to give a pitch-perfect performance. Great actors are defined by the choices they make. He seems to know, instinctively, when to pause and when to quicken as he effortlessly replicates sincerity. In fact, it *is* a form of sincerity, because all truly gifted liars begin by believing their own lies.

The prosecuting counsel is looking beaten now. But then he starts fumbling with his notes, shuffling them around. And I feel sweat trickling down inside my collar.

"Sorry, m'lud..." More paper shuffling. Something is coming. "Bear with me a moment...ah, yes...one more question, Mr Tapscott."

Now he is fiddling with the back of his wig. "Have you ever spoken with the accused?"

Derek looks thrown. Is that acting?

"What I mean, Mr Tapscott, is, prior to this trial, have you ever met Mr Carver?...Do you know him? Have you ever spoken to him?"

"No," Derek replies, totally relaxed.

The barrister looks at him for a few moments, but to me it feels like an age. Does he know? Is there an attack coming? "No further questions, m'lud."

He sits down. You feel him admit defeat. It's tangible. He knows Derek's version is the most credible that the court has heard. Seymour takes a long, satisfied intake of breath. One hour later, the jury retire to consider their verdict. For twenty minutes.

"First reactions, Kevin?" Pop, pop!

"Kevin! Kevin! Over here!" Pop! Whirr!

"Kevin, how do you feel?" Pop! Pop! Pop!

"Kevin, this way!" Pop!

"Kevin!" "Kevin!" "Kevin!"

Two paparazzi square up to each other. As Graham tries to steer me through the crowd, several microphones are thrust under my nose, a TV cameraman is knocked off his stepladder. I find myself laughing at the mayhem.

"How do you feel, Kevin?"

"Give us a quote, Kevin?"

I raise my hand, like Charlton Heston playing Moses. "My main feeling, obviously, is one of relief. This has been a gruelling ordeal. But justice has been done in the end. As I always believed it would. Now I just want to get on with my life. It's time to move on."

Funny how the clichés tumble out when the emotions get too big and formless. In the big scenes, life's very badly written.

Pop! Pop! Pop! Pop!

"What are your plans, Kevin?"

"My immediate plans are to celebrate with the friends who've supported me through this whole, grim…soap opera."

"What about the show, Kevin?" Pop! Pop! "Are you going to leave?"

"Hey! Careful!"

"Who are you pushing, you prick?"

"My client has no more comments to make right now, gentlemen," Graham shouts above the swearing, as we bounce through the shoulders and elbows.

I didn't thank Derek.

I thought thanking a witness could have looked inappropriate somehow. But I smiled at him. As he hovered on the courtroom steps. And then, as we made our escape, a few of the press approached him and I could just about hear him, fielding their barked questions.

"Please, please, this is not my day, this is Kevin Carver's day. I'm just glad that I could help an innocent man go free, that's all."

In the evening, we go to a restaurant and get pissed. Me, Mac, Mac's new wife and my old wife. A discreet corner table, away from prying eyes. After a few looseners, I claim centre stage.

"And my defence team said 'Try not to look arrogant'. Yeh, can you believe that? They said that my face, at rest, looked arrogant, so I said: 'What can I do about that, wear a fucking balaclava?'"

Through the laughter, Sandra is trying to say something. "They've got a point though. There is an arrogance...and a sort of innocence."

"Arrogance and innocence?"

"The two can go together. But mostly it's arrogance."

"But...that's probably just the set of my features, isn't it? The way my face is arranged, I can't help that."

"No, it's more than that. Something about the way you carry yourself, the way you look at people. You don't know you're doing it."

"OK, Sandra. Balaclava it is."

"For Christ's sake," bellows Mac, shaking the last drops from a bottle of wine, "can we not talk about something other than Kevin's facial features, which are, if truth be told, those of a girlie-man."

"Girlie-man?"

"Aye, you use moisturiser, don't deny it, pal."

"I suffer from dry skin."

"It's pouffiness incarnate!"

"Piss off! When are you pissing off, by the way?"

"Tomorrow. Touring the Midlands with a new show. An improvised piece about the potato famine."

"Quick, get Cameron Mackintosh on the phone!"

Mac gets me in an over-affectionate headlock and because I'm trapped in his armpit, it takes me a while to realise that Derek is standing a few feet away, smiling.

"Oh…hi, Derek."

"Hi." His smile widens.

"Oh, sorry, um, Derek, this is Mac, Sandra, Julie."

There is an awkward round of hi's. "Are you eating here, then?"

"Oh no…no, no." He holds up a self-effacing hand. "No, I just happened to be passing, on my way home, spotted you and um… well, just thought I'd pop in and say hi."

"Right, listen…thank you so much for today, I…I was going to write to you."

"Oh, not necessary."

"No, it is. I just…well, I don't know where I'd be without you."

"Yes, you do," Mac shouts, "Wormwood Scrubs!"

Above Mac's raucous laughter, I thank Derek again.

"No thanks needed, honestly. All I did was tell the truth."

"Well…I'm eternally grateful."

This is so awkward. The conversation is going nowhere. Derek hovers for a few moments more.

"Well…erm…bye then."

"Bye."

I reach across and shake his hand. There is a staggered chorus of goodbyes from the others as Derek exits, in nervous English instalments. Once he has left, Sandra punches me on the arm.

"Ow!"

"Why didn't you ask him to join us? He was obviously waiting for you to ask."

"No, he wasn't. He was on his way home, he said."

"Oh for—"

"…just passing through, he said."

"It's just common courtesy."

"Besides, it wouldn't have looked very good, would it? After a 'not guilty' verdict, for me to be seen knocking back the vino with the key witness."

"Aye, fair point, girlie-man."

"Wouldn't look good."

Sandra shrugs. "You're talking like someone who's guilty."

My voice rises in volume and pitch. "It just wouldn't look very good. What if there were photographers? There weren't photographers, were there?"

"Didn't see any," says Julie, the words echoing in her glass as she drinks.

"Let's hope the bloody jury don't suddenly turn up, that would look bad."

I can feel my cheeks reddening, but people would assume that's the drink, that's what they would assume, it's the drink doing that.

"It just felt like he was waiting for an invitation," Sandra says quietly. "Didn't you sense that?"

"I don't know what he was thinking," I snap, "I don't know the man."

Sandra probably suspected something after that evening. I've never quite had the guts to ask her. As we say goodnight, she whispers: "Take care, and don't do anything stupid."

It would be a lie if I said that the prospect of blackmail had not crossed my mind. But Derek didn't seem the blackmailing type – whatever that might be. The only blackmailers I had ever met were producers.

His appearance in the restaurant had unnerved me. It was a bit of a coincidence. And how could he have spotted us? We were miles away from a window. My elation at the verdict was already clouded by questions. I felt cheated out of my moment. When I got home, I dug out one more bottle of wine and drank myself to sleep.

The morning papers made enjoyable reading. The Daily Mail was unequivocal: "Clearly, the terrible ordeal that Kevin Carver has experienced is the direct result of a feeding frenzy among the more irresponsible sections of our press."

A female columnist in the Sun spoke for the sisters: "Jade Pope is a lying cow, as many women had always suspected."

And the Star found a waiter she'd once screwed in Basingstoke: "Jade was a very cold lover, and a very mean tipper."

In every paper, kind things were now being said about me. I had been cruelly wronged, my reputation was instantly returned to me. Of course, there would always be the whisperers, but I could do nothing about those. That damage had been incurred from the moment Jade had accused me.

I felt calmer, but strangely flat. Perhaps I had imagined this day too often.

Come Monday morning, I find myself back on familiar territory. The crew greet me with slaps on the back, hugs, and the girls start flirting again. Various actors tell me how they have stuck up for me at dinner parties. Nigel gives me a matey wink as he shouts down his mouthpiece: "Well, how long has he been in the toilet?... Twenty minutes? Well, go and check up on him, we don't want him self-harming again, that put us nine scenes behind schedule. Just stick your head over the partition thing, OK?"

He is briefly bent double by a coughing fit, then he spreads his arms to embrace me.

"Kevin! Is this a social visit?"

"I've been summoned for a meeting."

"They've got plans for Lenny," says Simone, "that's what we've heard."

"And plans for Melanie," adds Pam, with a giggle.

"Yeh, shark attack," says Nigel. "In Australia. Great white shark eats her, the kid and half the boat. We won't see any of that, of course, the whole story's read out by Denzil the priest in a letter from her Nan."

"Right...bit ignominious for Jade."

"The cow deserves it," says Pam.

"In spades." Simone repeats it for emphasis. "In – spades."

A small voice crackles down Nigel's earpiece. Nigel listens, his brow furrowing to the point where his eyes disappear. "What do you mean, he's praying?" He exhales long and hard and stares at the ceiling.

"Gavin?" I ask.

"Yeh, he turned Muslim last week. See that arrow painted on the wall there? That's pointing to Mecca. He put that there, although strictly speaking, that's pointing north-east, towards Seven Sisters but we haven't got the heart to tell him."

Nigel starts laughing, till the cough takes hold.

"You need to get that seen to."

"I'm fine," he splutters.

"Nice to have you back, Kevin."

I turn. It's Louise. Though there is something different about her. Simone mouths the word "botox" behind her back.

"We're ready for you in the meeting room."

I had no idea how I felt about returning to the show. Part of me wanted to just walk away. But then I had felt that way for years. I was forever fantasising about making a grand exit while denouncing the programme as shit-based baby food – Mac's description.

But I am interested to hear what the producers have to say, if only out of mischief. Louise opens proceedings by saying how pleased everyone is about my vindication and praising my mental strength. She tries to smile, but her face won't let her.

"We've had some editorial brainstorm sessions," she announces, "vis-à-vis Lenny, and we've come up with some exciting new ideas."

"Really? I very much doubt that, Louise."

Oh yes, this is going to be fun. Louise takes a deep breath. The other producers wait expectantly.

"We are sorry about what Jade put you through. It was unacceptable. Her contract has been terminated. Melanie is going to be—"

"Shark food, yes I heard."

"No, no, that's just the decoy story we're putting out to snow-blind the press. No, she's going to be killed by terrorists."

"Terrorists?"

One of the young assistant producers pitches in. Martin? Marcus? Matthew? "Suicide bomber," he says. "Topical and edgy."

A wave of approval crosses the room; edgy, we like edgy. Louise jabs a pencil towards me. "We're keeping that under wraps, of course, in case those bastards from Emmerdale try and jump in with a beheading or something. We won't see the actual suicide bombing, obviously."

"Right."

"No, it all gets read out in a letter from her Nan. But we've got some great ideas for Lenny."

Martin/Marcus/Matthew dives in again: "We envisage Lenny becoming even more central. Central, *and* more layered."

"More layered?"

"Yuh, yuh…we think Lenny should be less of a git." He says the word "git" as if it were in italics. "And start behaving with more nobility."

"Why?" I ask, flat and fast. Martin/Marcus/Matthew looks flustered.

"Kelly did some audience research."

Kelly? Which one's Kelly? Oh right, the one with the folder. She looks eleven.

"In the light of the trial outcome," she begins nervously, "it seems there's now a widespread audience perception of you as a victim...who bore his ordeal with nobility."

"A 'widespread audience perception'?"

"Yes," asserts Kelly.

"You mean a focus group."

"Yes."

"Of how many?"

"Twenty."

I laugh heartily, can't help myself.

"They are an accurate cross-section," croaks Kelly.

Hang on, I remember her, she was a runner.

"You're going to have to get used to it, Kevin," drawls Louise. "In a totally unexpected turn of events, people now like you."

Where are they going with this?

"So we need to reflect this new reality. We want to make Lenny more nuanced..." Nuanced? On this show? "We need to give him more varied scenes. No more 'shut it, you slag' stuff. No more socks full of billiard balls. We want viewers to get a chance to see what a good actor you are..."

This is bullshit of the highest order.

"...and for you it could be the springboard to bigger things."

Well, I knew she was trying to manipulate me, of course I did, but I thought it was worth considering at least. My agent agreed. And Mac had a view.

"Tell them to shove it up their arse with a barbed-wire broomstick."

"A *barbed-wire* broomstick? That's a development."

"They cashed in on your predicament big-time, now they want to cash in on your vindication. They're scum, just walk."

"It might lead to better things."

Mac lets rip with a quick burst of unintelligible Glaswegian before telling me that I am away with the fairies.

"It might, y'know…if I get better storylines."

"Listen, pal, the moment ratings start to dip, they'll have you back strangling coppers and biffing wee girlies."

"Well, maybe so, but…"

"What are you scared of?"

Good question. One that Sandra asks me when I phone her with my dilemma.

"Are you scared of obscurity? Is that it? People forgetting you, no longer recognising you?"

"No, I think it'd be very nice not to be recognised."

"Nearly convincing, but I'd try for another take, if I was you."

She laughs that laugh and for a moment I'm younger and stronger.

"…Are you 'plus one' at the moment?" I ask.

"Mind your own business. Are you plus one?"

"No."

"Oh…right…heigh-ho."

"Yeah…heigh-ho."

There are no inhibitions quite like the inhibitions between two people who know each other too well, are there? Socking great razor-wired fences of the unspoken.

She was right about my fear, of course she was. I liked being recognised, especially now that I had been recast as the hero.

At a garage, I am shouted at by a white kid who wants to be black: "You're the man! Hear what I'm sayin'? You're the man!" He flicks his fingers at me.

"Thanks."

"That bitch will burn in Hell, man."

"Well, I don't—"

"No, she will, man, she's gonna burn, after what she tried to do to you, she deserves a good slap. You give her a slap, man, a slap. Like you did before."

"Well, no, actually that's Lenny who—"

"They should put her in prison, sick kiddie or no sick kiddie."

"N...no, she...she doesn't have a child, not in real life, see she's—"

He speeds away on his bike, calling over his shoulder: "You're the man!"

"...Cheers."

Not everyone who expressed their support was like him. Some of them had a brain. Mostly, people gave me a wan smile, and maybe a nod, as they passed me in the street. It felt a bit like being a vicar.

But, with every smile I saw, I couldn't help wondering if a few weeks earlier that same person would have called me a cunt. The whole experience – Jade's accusation, the trial, the press campaign – had sluiced the last drops of trust out of me. I was wary now, all the time, ears permanently pricked.

It took me a while to make up my mind but, in the end, I decided to return to the show. Why? Probably because I didn't have the guts to say no. An unmapped alternative was too daunting. Where would I start? What if I disappeared?

But the decision brought me no real satisfaction and, as a sop to my self-esteem, I told them that I would only accept a three month contract to be going on with, to see if Louise's promises were kept. I also told them that, before I would resume filming, I required six weeks paid holiday. Louise said she understood perfectly, although I could see a small muscle twitching behind her jaw.

I rented a cottage on the Isle of Skye. For the first weeks I did virtually nothing but sleep. Even when I wasn't sleeping, I felt leaden and bone-tired, like you do after a bereavement. But then, gradually, I began to embrace the change. It was liberating just to wake up each morning, at whatever time I pleased, and know that my day wasn't spoken for, wasn't already calibrated in deadlines – lines of death – that had been decided by outside forces.

That felt good.

And yet. And yet. Somehow, nothing felt as good as I had anticipated. Even though my waking hours were illuminated by deep blue skies and blinding surf-pounded beaches, I could not shake off a sense of anti-climax. What was wrong with me? This place was perfect.

To try and lift my spirits, I threw myself at activities. I went on long wind-battling hikes. I tried fly-fishing, kayaking; I went out in boats and saw sea-eagles and dolphins. I black-and-blued my shoulders on rocks while white-water rafting. I even jumped off the side of a mountain and hang-glided in curving, lazy spirals down into a field of scattering sheep. I overloaded my senses as much as I could, but still nothing.

From time to time, I ventured into the nearest village. Some stared, a few asked for selfies, but by and large, I was left alone. They could probably see the wariness in me.

Increasingly, my favourite pastime was to sit by the stream which ran through the bottom of the cottage's garden and simply stare into the perpetuating shapes of the water, letting my brain empty. I could do that for hours, till it felt like there was nothing left in my mind at all; not even the smallest shard of memory.

Then, one golden evening, when the sun is refusing to go down, I find myself sitting by a salmon stream, feeling calm and unimportant, when I suddenly hear my name: "Kevin? Is that you?"

I turn to see a man wearing a kagoul, even though there's not a cloud to be seen. For a moment, I can't recognise him – he's silhouetted – but as he walks towards me I feel my stomach turn light and head towards my throat.

"Kevin? I don't believe it! What are you doing here? Well I'll be jiggered."

My God, no. I try to paint a smile: "Derek…hi."

"How the devil are you, Kevin?"

"I'm fine, yeh…and yourself?"

"Oh, mustn't grumble, y'know. Not when there are people dying from starvation."

A crow flies past, cackling. I'm struggling to think straight.

"Are you up here on holiday then, Derek?"

"Yeh, staying at Dunvegan, I come here every year. Are you on your own?"

"Um…yeh."

"Me too. We both like our own company the best, eh?"

He picks up a stone and walks to the water's edge.

"This is a lovely spot, isn't it?"

"Stunning," I reply.

"Fancy bumping into each other up here. What a coincidence, eh?"

"It's not a coincidence, you lying bastard, so don't insult my intelligence," I say, but only inside my head. The truth is, I am horribly rattled. As I watch Derek skim his stone across the water, my brain spools through countless possibilities. Hang on, he's saying something, what's he saying?

"Stalking's great fun."

Is this some kind of confession? He sees my knotted expression.

"Stalking," he repeats. "The deer. Only with cameras, mind. You should try it. I did it the other day. There's a place just along this road, they take you out on the hills – 'the Wildlife Safari… something'. Saw some stags fighting. Magnificent sight."

"Right, I'll, erm – I'll look into that…thanks."

Derek is smiling at me and I am smiling back at him. Why

doesn't he say something? In the woods behind us a pigeon takes off with a clumsy crack of its wings. He is still smiling at me. I hear myself speak.

"Well, we should go out for a meal, you and I."

"Good idea. I'm free tonight."

I had panicked. It was the silence that spooked me. But, on reflection, I was glad I had panicked, because I needed to spend some time with him to straighten things out. It would have to be handled sensitively. It was important not to upset him.

To create the right mood, I take him to a very exclusive restaurant – one that doesn't demean itself by having its name visible on the outside, menus chalked on small squares of slate, that kind of thing. Derek is very taken with it, and soon becomes expansive.

"The thing is, and this is going to sound funny, but I've always felt a kinship with you, y'know, whenever I've seen you playing Lenny, I've always thought to myself: 'I bet if we met, he and I could be mates'."

I watch Derek lay into his prawn cocktail.

"...You told the court you didn't have a TV."

"Well," he chuckles, "I told the court a lot of things." He wipes mayonnaise from his chin. "Are you going back into the show?"

"Um...yeh...for a while anyway."

His face brightens. "Oh great. We can meet up for a regular beverage down in London then, 'cos I live not far from the studios."

"...Right."

"We can go out together on the pull."

"...Right. Look, Derek—"

"We'll make quite a team."

"Yuh, look, Derek—"

"Actually I'm thinking of going back into acting."

"Really, look, Der—"

"'Cos I trained as an actor. At drama school. In Ipswich. Did two months till…well, the tutors complained I was taking up too much of their time. But I think they couldn't handle my quest for perfection, y'know. Anyway, the past is another country – the thing is, I was wondering if maybe you could give me a little bit of coaching, y'know, maybe have a few sessions, and then maybe a meal afterwards."

It is now that the full horror of my situation finally strikes home. I have been targeted by an attention-seeking missile. He has locked on to me, hard, and I need to take evasive action. I interrupt him as he starts to tell me about how he was once nearly cast as Coriolanus.

"Look, Derek, I have to be honest with you…what you're asking for…the coaching thing…well, it isn't…" I search for the softest adjective, "…realistic."

"…Realistic?"

"Yes."

"…Isn't 'realistic' in what sense?"

"In the sense of…being connected to reality. I…I'm not a drama coach and…well, I'm not sure it's…viable –" Viable? Not a great choice. "– for us to be…mates."

Derek blinks. His bland, regular features give nothing away. "Why not?"

I make a conscious effort to make my voice as kind and gentle as possible.

"Because…we're not mates, are we?"

"We can be if we want to. We can be whatever we want to be."

"No, no, we can only be what we are. We are two very different people…with very different lives…and different personalities."

He goes to say something but I head him off. "Al-so – and this is a very big also – it would be bad news for us if we were seen around together a lot, y'know, after the trial…if we seemed… connected, especially if I was seen to be helping you, people might start asking questions."

I clasp his hand for emphasis. This has to be a big finish.

"Now, I will always, *always*, be extremely grateful for your very kind...intervention...you got me justice and I will never forget that...and I will always appreciate it...but I don't think it should go any further than that."

He takes his hand away – and stares into the table.

"I'm sorry, Derek. I'm just being honest."

He nods. But he looks shaken and I misjudge the moment.

"Are you OK for money?"

Slowly, he looks up. "I don't need your money. It was never about money."

"No, fine, sorry, I didn't mean – I just, well, I dunno I was – look, I was just trying to express my gratitude. Sorry, I didn't mean to...y'know, imply..."

He reaches for the inside pocket of his corduroy jacket.

"Well...if you really feel the need," he begins, with a hint of a tremor in his voice, "you can make a donation to this charity."

A card is offered, I take it.

"They run hospices...and they've lost some grants."

"Right, OK. Will do."

His chair scrapes back and Derek is on his feet, smiling limply. "Well, I'd better go. There's nothing more to say really, is there? I'm sorry if I've embarrassed you."

"No, it's fine, you haven't, of course you haven't. Please, stay and finish the meal."

"No...best not."

He offers his hand. "Well...goodbye then, Kevin."

I shake his hand, warmly, perhaps too warmly? Too big, doesn't fit the moment.

"Goodbye, Derek. And, again, many thanks."

"Think nothing of it," he says. And then he walks out of the restaurant.

At the time, I convinced myself that I had handled the

situation quite well, on balance. It was a very tricky and delicate conversation and, yes, he was a little hurt, but he seemed to understand. I couldn't see any other way I could have managed it, without stringing him along or raising false expectations.

I returned from Skye partially refreshed, and as the weeks rolled by, Derek gradually faded from my thoughts. I went back to the studio and started to lose myself in the reassuring rituals of work. As promised, there was a change. Bigger scenes, less shouting, more telling people I was there for them.

Mac split up with his wife. Inevitable really, once she got to know him.

Autumn came and went. Winter stripped the trees bare. Snow arrived with no warning. Initially, the TV channels greeted it with photos that viewers had taken of cheery snowmen. But then people started dying on icy roads and so the bulletins led with newsreaders shouting things like "Britain's Winter Wonderland Turns Lethal." Almost every snow-dusted stranger seemed to say, "So much for global warming, eh?" as if they had coined that thought themselves.

The show's figures remained stable. Around mid-January they dipped a little, so Lenny killed two low-lifes. Four cast members left the show. One died, one was written out and two had to leave because they got drunk at an awards ceremony and told a revolting joke about a necrophiliac trying to have sex with the late Queen Mother.

Louise couldn't finesse that one.

My life dribbled on pretty much as it had before all the madness of the trial. I was neither happy nor unhappy. The only oddity was that I caught myself increasingly thinking about Sandra. She rang less nowadays. She had found a man. His name was Pete. Decent bloke. A photographer. Lies in the bushes all night to get a shot of a badger.

Then, one rainy evening in April, she rings. "Kevin, you've—"

"Hey! I was just thinking about you, and not in a sordid way, how's things?"

"Switch on the television," she says rapidly.

"Eh?"

"ITV. Switch it on, now, I'll ring you back."

So I turn on ITV and there is Derek, sitting in a moody pool of light and being interviewed by one of those compassionate presenters whose head is permanently tilted to one side. She is putting a question to him in a low, soothing voice: "And it was at this stage that Kevin Carver suggested to you that you commit perjury on his behalf?"

Derek nods sorrowfully. "Yes."

"And did you feel comfortable with that?"

"No."

"So why did you go along with it?"

"I felt sorry for him, I suppose. I personally believed his version of events – that he'd been wrongly accused – and he seemed to be in a lot of pain…I wanted to ease his pain."

There is a stretched span of several moments before I start to take in what is happening. It is – cliché coming – like a bad dream. That is the only way to describe the experience of watching this man spew his lurid perversion of the truth into millions of people's living rooms.

"Have you stopped to ask yourself why you felt this need to try and ease his pain?" she asks; she's a nurse at his bedside.

"Oh, many times, yes." He is instinctively pitching his voice at the same note as hers. "And that's not easy to answer, but I think it dates back to my having an alcoholic and abusive father…which meant that I grew up with an exaggerated sense of responsibility for other people's feelings, a kind of guilt that means I'm always trying to make people happy."

"You're a people-pleaser."

"I suppose so, yes."

His eyes are welling up now. God, this is terrible acting. Surely everyone will see through this pantomime? They've got to, haven't they? The public aren't that stupid. They can see when something is grotesque. Suddenly the room starts to recede from me and I dash to the toilet to throw up. I hurry back to find Derek is telling the world how much he liked me.

"And did Kevin Carver like you?"

"Oh yes."

"But he used you."

Derek bows his head, like a saint about to be martyred. "Yes... yes he did."

I am watching my whole life unravel. Everything I have is was being destroyed, in high-definition slow motion, by Derek and this woman.

"And did he offer you money to commit this perjury?"

"Yes, yes he did."

Oh God, no.

"But I didn't want any money, so I asked him to make a donation to my favourite charity. It supports hospices."

Oh Jesus Christ. I wrote a cheque.

"We should perhaps point out that you're not being paid for this interview."

"That's right."

"Knowing what you know now, Derek, do you think Kevin Carver did or did not...assault Jade Pope?"

Derek puffs his cheeks. "I don't know...I mean...if their relationship was in trouble...well, I'm not sure that Kevin finds rejection easy to cope with. But, y'know, it's really not for me to speculate."

"You just did!" I scream at the television. My body starts to heave with wracking, gulping sobs and, even though no one can see me, I feel humiliated.

"Finally, Derek –" she leans forward and spreads her hands "–

the question that a lot of our viewers will be asking, namely, why now? Why have you waited to come forward and admit your crime...because it is a very serious offence you've committed."

On the screen, with misting eyes, Derek is slowly choosing his words: "Yes...yes it is a serious offence. And I'm not proud of the mistake I made. Not at all. So I've chosen to come forward because basically, I couldn't go on living a lie. I take full responsibility."

Everybody takes full responsibility now, have you noticed? It's funny that. We must be getting more honest.

For a moment, a fast-fading moment, I cling to the hope that they won't believe him; all the millions of people with their suppers on their laps. Then I know that they will. Why wouldn't they believe him? He is creating a moment of mass intimacy with them; they love that.

It's over for me, that's inescapable. I've been placed in the national pantheon of liars. Somewhere between Jonathan Aitken and Jeffrey Archer. In the eyes of millions, I am now arrogant, corrupt, violent, and ridiculous.

I feel stupid and shamed; which is why I don't answer when Sandra rings back.

9

THE NEW HOME

My cell-mate's name is Dougie. His body is mostly tattoos, but he's alright once you get to know him – and as long as you stay off the topic of race. Funnily enough, the other night he came out with the same observation as Jade did at our disastrous dinner – the one about black South Africans having been better off under apartheid.

I didn't pick him up on it.

He's in for GBH. Self-defence, he says. He beat a man senseless with a wheeljack, which I did once as Lenny. Although I don't suppose Dougie needed four takes to get it right.

There's no point my dwelling on the details of the trial, because it was a foregone conclusion. Even though I had lied to them, my legal team stuck with me. I felt acutely embarrassed by their loyalty because I knew I wasn't worthy of it. They tried to argue that Derek's TV interview made it impossible for me to receive a fair hearing. There was a day and a half's discussion on various points of law before the judge decided that the trial could continue, provided that none of the jury had seen the programme.

I gave my evidence and told the truth, the whole truth and nothing but the truth; and the more truthful I was, the more absurd it sounded. The prosecuting barrister spent most of his time just repeating my words back at me.

My counsel did his best to explain that, yes, I was guilty of lying to a court, but not guilty of the offence I had been lying about. It was laughably futile.

Derek gave Queen's evidence and got a suspended sentence. I was found guilty on both counts and sentenced to five years. They tell me I'll probably serve a minimum of two.

The prison came as a shock to me, as in my mind's eye I had been picturing a modern, clinical facility where inmates sat around watching DVDs – the kind of prison you read about in the Daily Mail. Instead, they put me in a van and delivered me to this rotting Victorian relic that smells of damp and cabbage.

In his summing-up, the judge had highlighted my "deviousness and contempt for the law", so perhaps that marked me down for special treatment – who knows? The newspapers had been unanimous that an example should be made of me. 'Lock Lenny up and throw away the key!' said the Star, as ever, struggling to cling on to where reality starts and ends.

As we approached the prison, the walls seemed to lean over me. We drove in and the main gate closed behind me with a heavy clang, like it would in a movie. How could this be happening to me? It was only the last tattered shreds of pride that stopped me from curling up into a ball and whimpering like a beaten animal. But that's what I wanted to do.

That's what I felt like.

A beaten animal.

The staff greeted me with civility, no more, no less. I tried to crack a couple of jokes, but a watery smile was the most I got. My clothes and belongings were logged. I filled out some medical forms. I won't bore you with it all.

About an hour after my arrival, I am sitting, in pale blue shirt and dark blue trousers, outside the office of the prison governor, trying to ignore the random flickers of a faulty strip-light.

A voice calls me into the governor's office. I am expecting to meet my idea of a prison governor; some grey mediocrity who has been moved sideways into the post, but this one is quick and sharp.

"Kevin, come in, sit down, sorry about that light out there. They do that when they're about to go, bloody annoying. I'm Malcolm."

He thrusts a hand towards me. I shake it, weakly. He smiles. He is surprisingly young. Late, maybe mid-thirties. And there is a crackle of energy about him.

"Feeling pretty dazed I expect, yes?"

I nod.

"Totally normal, one hundred per cent normal. You'll probably feel like that for a while. It's like going into shock. You'll be fine. Cup of tea?"

"Please."

He reaches for a pot on his desk.

"Sugar?"

"No, thanks."

"Sorry about the cups. They look dirty, but they're just stained…I hope."

He gives a mischievous little chuckle, which, for some reason, reminds me of Harry Secombe.

"We'll be putting you in with a chap called Dougie," he tells me as he pours. "He does have a slight history of violence, but he's a talker, and we think that'd be best. Initially. For you. Given that you're new to this."

He hands me the cup of tea, which, once in my hand, starts to rattle in the saucer.

"Most of them in here have had lots of experience…"

He smiles at me and I try to smile back, but I'm just moving my mouth.

"You're not our first 'face'. No, no, we've had an MP who got done for fraud, a former Big Brother housemate who liked setting fire to things...a drug-pushing disc jockey." He lets out the Goon-ish giggle again. "All sorts. No one as big as you, though. It's not easy being a celeb in prison. Some do OK. It's an alien world. I mean, someone like Jeffrey Archer did fine, because he lives in his own world and just carries it around with him, but...um... well, for a sensitive person, it's...are you a sensitive person, would you say, Kevin?"

It's an impossible question. Do I feel things more or less than other people? How would I know?

"I don't know, Malcolm," I mumble.

"Indeed, indeed. People react to prison in all sorts of unexpected ways. Some of them discover they've got minds. They throw themselves into books and start devouring ideas. It's good to see. We've turned out three sociologists."

"Right."

"And an urban poet. Although he's just been done for criminal damage. Some chaps find a kind of comfort in the routine of the place, y'know, the little daily rituals. The games room. The meals. The chat. Some lose themselves in new hobbies, y'know, like Burt Lancaster in The Birdman of Alcatraz. Do you like birds? We've got a kestrel that hovers over the yard sometimes. That's the upside of having mice."

He pulls an embarrassed face. It would be easy to mistake him for a clown, but he's sounding me out.

"The ones I worry about are the ones who don't talk...who don't engage...that never works." His eyes drop for a moment, as if he's visiting an ugly memory. Then he starts up again, louder and more emphatic.

"But you, Kevin, are a man of talent and resource, so you'll be fine, I'm sure. Do you feel sorry for what you did?"

The question has taken me by surprise.

"Um...sorry for which thing that I did, only—"

"You know what I mean," he interrupts, "do you feel –

sincerely feel – and acknowledge that you did something wrong?"

"I…acknowledge…that I made mistakes."

"Ah, yes," he chuckles, "that old favourite."

"Why does it matter? My thinking I've done something wrong?"

He sips his tea as he considers.

"It's of no huge significance…just a starting point."

We talk a little longer, small talk mostly, the occasional question about my background; then, suddenly he's on his feet ushering me towards the door.

"Well, let's get you settled in. We're not part of the private sector…not yet anyway. So we still try to treat inmates as people, not units. But the rules are the rules and apply to everyone. So I'd advise against trying to take any liberties. Prison officers don't like that."

I bristle at this change of tone.

"I don't expect star treatment."

"Good. I've only two objectives here, Kevin. The first is the safety of prisoners and staff, obviously, and the other is rehabilitation."

"I don't need rehabilitating. I'm only here because…because of the actions of two delusional people."

"Just the two?"

He gives me a cryptic smile, which irritates me intensely, and then guides me out of the door towards a waiting officer.

"Give Kevin the tour, please, Frank."

My cell turned out to be far less depressing than I had feared. I had steeled myself for some bleak hole straight out of Midnight Express, but instead I was presented with something that could have passed for student accommodation at a third-rate university. There were bunks, quite new (and surprisingly comfortable), a small desk, two knee-high cupboards with sharp corners, and a door that opened into an extremely compact toilet with a tiny plastic washbasin. All very basic, but I had stayed in worse places touring as a young actor.

And the Governor was right about my cellmate. From the outset it was clear that, despite his Magwitch-like appearance and piercing stare, he was a sociable individual whose conversation ranged freely, in urgent, jabbing rhythms, across a wide variety of topics. He does have certain ground rules, though, which he laid out for me in our very first conversation, a few moments after an alarmingly firm handshake that felt like some kind of test.

"Listen, Kevin, I hope you don't mind but there's some basics you need to be aware of. (Oh-oh) I know that you are from the world of showbiz and I know that the world of showbiz is full of bullshitters and I don't like bullshitters. Hate 'em. (Don't say anything.) Just wanted that on record. OK? I also don't like whingers. I don't like finger-pointers, timewasters or naysayers. ("Naysayers"?) I don't like queue-jumpers, scroungers, ponces and people who criticise her Majesty the Queen, because she can't answer back. I don't like Wayne Rooney – he's an embarrassment – Richard Dawkins – too smug – any of the Brontë sisters, (What?) Jeremy Clarkson, musicals based on films, and rudeness. Erm…also…I don't like rap, Channel Five, the metric system, lazy use of Americanisms, wanky ringtones, panel shows and vegans. Everything else I like."

It was not the most promising of starts, but within a day or two we were putting the world to rights and identifying who is to blame for everything. Or as Dougie puts it: "which fuck-up has been fucked up by which fucker-upper."

In many ways, my conversations with him remind me of talking to Mac. We tend to run through the same index of grievances. The only difference is that when Dougie concludes (as Mac often does) that those responsible should be taken out and shot, you sense he may not be talking metaphorically.

Now and then, just occasionally, Dougie does manage to get on my nerves (though I choose not to let it show). One night, a few weeks into my stretch, sticks in my memory.

A hot night. We are lying on our bunks, Dougie is listening to Radio Four through earpieces. I am just staring into space, thinking about how I am probably two thirds of the way through my life – possibly three-quarters even, or worse. Contemporaries of mine are regularly appearing in the obit pages.

This gloomy line of thought is punctured by Dougie's voice.

"What's it like being famous?"

"How do you mean?"

"Is it nice? Or is it a pain in the jacksie?"

"Both."

"Must be weird though. Having strangers come up to you and that, wanting to photograph you?"

"It's OK…most people are very nice…they never seem to know how their cameras work, but most of them are pleasant enough."

Dougie makes approving noises. "Really? That's good to hear. 'Cos manners are important. As I had to point out to someone yesterday."

"Yeh, I heard about that."

"Well, queues are there for a reason…I don't think he'll do it again."

"No, I'm sure he won't."

The springs creak above me, as he shifts his weight.

"I bet some people take liberties, though, don't they? What's the worst that's happened to you?"

"Oh, I dunno…I've had the occasional drunk who wanted to fight me…"

"That's predictable."

"Some old boy called me a cunt once."

"Why?"

"He believed the papers. Thought I was the kind of man who beats up women."

"Well if you were, then you *would* be a cunt."

"I suppose so…if I were…but I'm not."

"You didn't hit her, or manhandle her in any way, then?"

What sort of a question is that? Why doesn't he just listen to his radio? I retreat into silence.

"Not even a gentle clip?"

"Listen, Dougie, we've been over this. She was deluded, emotional. I was totally innocent."

The springs dance for a moment as he gets more comfortable.

"Well, maybe not *totally* innocent," he mutters.

"Sorry?"

"Well, y'know, Kevin, no disrespect, but you did invent an alibi, didn't you?"

"I didn't invent it."

"Didn't you?"

"No. Someone…presented it to me. Someone who was a—"

"Nutter."

"Yes."

"But you still availed yourself of the nutter's services, didn't you? I know you had your reasons, which made sense at the time, you've explained that, but…let's face it, Kevin…you made some very bad choices, didn't you?"

"Yes, but the accusation that started it is—"

"I know, it's—"

"It's false, Dougie."

"I know but—"

"Completely false."

"Yeh, but that doesn't make you 'innocent', does it? You knew you were doing something wrong…but you went ahead and did it…just like the rest of us."

God Almighty, is he seriously bracketing me with all the lowlife in here?

"We're all responsible for our actions, Kevin. That's the basis of civilisation..."

Please, spare me the pearls of wisdom.

"You're an educated man, Kevin, you know how it works."

Right, I'm ending this conversation.

"I'm tired, Dougie. G'night."

"I haven't upset you, have I?"

"No."

"Does this light bother you?"

"No."

"Are you sure?"

"Yes."

In the distance I can hear a growing chorus of car horns. Lots of them, blaring incessantly. What I wouldn't give to be sitting in that traffic jam.

"I'm sort of famous," says Dougie, quietly, "in Dagenham."

I know that some people have written entire books about their experience of prison, but frankly, there is not much to tell. Prison life is exactly as you would imagine it, a grind of tedium and routine punctuated by the occasional moment of terror. The first few weeks were the hardest. I felt alone, disorientated, scared, etcetera, but it is surprising how quickly you can get used to an environment, even a very weird one. I went to a ClubMed once and, within days, I was doing the water aerobics and singing the club song. It's shocking how passive you can be, isn't it? If you just go with the flow.

The one pleasant surprise was the attitude of the other prisoners. They accepted me almost immediately. As a joke – at least I think it's a joke – they nearly all call me Lenny. One prisoner called Toby took an immediate shine to me. (He's not here any more.) He followed me around telling me how big a fan he was and, on one occasion, he took me to one side in the computer room and expressed the view that Derek was scum and could meet with an "accident", if I wanted him to arrange it.

I was touched; as, indeed, was he.

To begin with, the nights were the worst part. Most nights I barely slept. I just listened to the babble of thoughts inside my head.

And in those first few weeks, there were depressingly few visitors. Mac, inevitably, was the first to come and see me.

I can see him now, the big, open face, I can hear that smoked, whisky laugh.

"So, then, bollockbrain, how's the tunnel coming along?"

"Yeh, no, fine, just waiting for a full moon."

"Are they treating you OK?" he asks, taking in the bareness of the Visitors Room.

"Yeh, fine."

"No funny business?"

"Funny business?"

"Yeh, y'know, in the—"

"Oh, no, no, nobody's made me their bitch."

He laughs. That's a good sound.

"Too ugly, that's why." He laughs some more. A few of the other visitors glance our way. Mac lowers his voice. "Have you befriended any wee sparrows?"

"No, and I haven't stabbed anyone through the eye with a spoon."

After a few more jokey film references, Mac takes his voice down to a whisper.

"Can I ask you a question?"

"Yeh, sure."

"What the fuck were you thinking of?"

I stare at the floor. He ducks down a little, to find my eye-line.

"I mean, I know the wee toe-rag approached you with the idea, but, in that case, why didn't you just tell him to—"

"This is going to involve a broomstick, isn't it?"

Mac looks at me, unamused. Suddenly he's not up for jokes.

"Well? Why didn't you?"

I slump forward and cradle my head in my hands. "If you'd been in my position, Mac, back then, if you'd felt that…hunted, that desperate, and you'd been presented with that…possibility, a way out, risky, but a way out…if you'd been presented with that dilemma…can you honestly say what you would have done?"

He goes quiet. Then he flaps a hand in the air. "Listen, pal, what I would have done is irrelevant because I've got appalling judgement. I'm touring Wales with an opera about the Tonypandy Massacre. The little weasel's a celeb now. Keeps popping up on daytime crap, emoting."

I laugh at the inevitability of this.

"He was on this morning, sitting next to Louie Spence. And I see your wee girlie, Jade, has gone back into that shite-fest of a show."

"I heard, yeh. I thought Louise might explore that possibility."

"You don't watch the show in here, then?"

"I've never really watched it, to be honest."

Mac shakes his head and chuckles. "You cynical bastard."

"Hang on, how did they get round the fact that Melanie got eaten by a shark?"

"Oh, Jade's not playing Melanie. No, no…she's now her long-lost twin—"

"– sister, of course she is. They just went to the old 'previously-unmentioned-twin-sister' cupboard. That's priceless."

In the remaining minutes Mac and I start to go through the playlist of old favourites. But we only get as far as how the BBC is going down the toilet before the bell sounds to end visiting hours.

Friends. That's all you're left with in the end.

If you're lucky.

They're the gold standard.

You can always rely on friends. Although I wouldn't rely on Mac for anything important, no, the man's a nightmare, but I know we'll always be bound by an invisible contract.

Unless we fall out.

The second person to come and visit me, a few days later, is Sandra. She looks worried, so I try to keep things light.

"Have you heard about Mac's show?"

"An opera about the Tonypandy Massacre."

"Yeh, well, you know Mac. If a show doesn't have at least one massacre in it, he won't do it."

She fiddles with her hair. Has she lost weight? Or is it the lighting? Her face looks drawn.

"Is it very boring in here?"

"We make our own entertainment. Yesterday it was earwig-racing and synchronised buggery."

"I'm being serious."

"I'm fine, don't worry…"

"Are you sure?"

"Yes…it's fine. They all call me Lenny and treat me like minor royalty."

She looks like she needs more reassurance.

"My cellmate's a good laugh…complete lunatic, but a good laugh."

She snorts, we giggle, but then the laughter dies away into a silence. I feel a stinging at the back of my eyes and my voice develops a quaver. "I'm glad Mum isn't around to see me in here."

"Your mum wouldn't have blamed you, you could do no wrong in her eyes."

"No, I know. 'What's that, son? You've murdered someone? Well, I expect he ran on to your knife.'"

She nods in recognition. "Yup."

The silence returns for a while. I find myself thinking back, a long way back.

"My dad used to knock her about a bit...y'know...on the quiet."

"Mine was the same."

There's lots more I would like to say to Sandra, but there are only a few minutes left. Maybe next time. She is smiling nervously at me.

"I'm getting married," she says.

I am still trying to take in Sandra's revelation as I do my best to down some lunch in the canteen. Dougie is sitting opposite me, having nearly cleared his plate.

"So, that was the missus, then?"

"Ex-missus."

"Ah, right."

His fork chases a pea around his plate.

"She's got a lovely smile. My wife, Judy...she's got a fantastic smile. It's like the sun coming out. I'm powerless against it. Can never say 'no' to her, never managed it, not once."

I try to picture Dougie as an acquiescent husband, but it's not easy.

"Do you think everyone has a special someone, y'know, *the* one?"

Oh, no, he's feeling sentimental.

"I'm not sure," I reply.

"I am."

"Well, you're a romantic."

"I am, Kevin. Always have been. The moment I clapped eyes on Judy I thought, 'that's her'. Never a moment's doubt in my mind. So I pursued her. Romantically. It wasn't easy, 'cos she was married to a policeman. Luckily, he got done for corruption."

He spots a look on my face.

"Nothing to do with me," he adds.

"How long have you been together?"

"Twenty-one years. Isn't that amazing? I've spent ten of those years inside. The woman's a saint. Love her to bits."

I begin to wonder whether he is piling it on a bit thick, but then his eyes start to film with tears.

"Love's an incredible thing, isn't it?"

"I suppose so."

"Do you know that song from My Fair Lady? Rex Harrison…"

With no warning, Dougie starts to sing in a voice that is surprisingly delicate and melodious.

"'…I've grown accustomed to her face.'"

Quite a few inmates look up from their lunches. Clearly, they have not heard him sing before.

"'…Like breathing out and breathing in.'" Dougie stops and lets out a sigh. "That is so on the money, isn't it, eh? 'Like breathing out and breathing in', that's exactly what love is like. Imagine being able to write something like that."

Inwardly, I debate whether or not to tell Dougie how much I've always hated that song. But it's a very short debate.

"So, what do you reckon? Has every one of us got a special someone out there?"

He watches me intensely, waiting for an answer. I start to shake my head.

"Life's too chaotic for that, isn't it?"

"Is it?"

"Well, mine is," I shrug.

"So there's been no one special in your life? Up till now."

"There's someone who's special, but whether she's *the* one… that's impossible to know, isn't it? Unless you met all the women in the world."

This idea makes Dougie chuckle.

"Well, there's a project for you, Kevin, eh?"

As he saws at a sausage, his plastic knife snaps in half.

"I hate this fucking toy cutlery."

That night, as I lay sleepless, in my bunk, I found myself picking away at Dougie's view of love. How could anyone be *destined* for someone? That made no rational sense. And what about change? People are changing all the time, aren't they, so you're never really connecting with *one* person, are you? You're linked to successive versions of that person, you are both waves interacting and interfering with each other, creating effects and turbulences. So a predestined lover would have to be fluid, not permanent – or maybe fluid *and* permanent, like a river.

Though even rivers can disappear.

10

THE CONSULTATION

As my early months in prison dragged by, the only serious problem I had was insomnia. At first, the difficulty was simply getting my brain to clock off at the end of the day. It would ricochet from one half-formed thought to another, like some manic puppy. So I tried to expend more physical energy during the day to wear myself out. In my gym-time, I jogged as far and as fast as I could on the treadmill. In my yard-time, I ran till my legs ached. But none of that seemed to help. So I started on the crosswords and Sudoku and the video games and the online chess and the difficult books about obscure science and philosophy, but the simple act of dropping off remained elusive. With a dead libido, sexual fantasies were no longer a way of thinking less, so I would try boring my brain into submission. I would lie there trying to compose England cricket elevens whose surnames all began with F (not easy). Or a Welsh rugby side full of W's. (Easier, because of all the players called Williams.)

These mental games proved surprisingly absorbing and the obsessive streak in me meant I had to keep going until I'd reached the pointless target that I'd set myself.

One night, at about 3 a.m., I wake Dougie with a triumphant shout of "Shearer!"

"What the f'!" he growls. "What did you say?"

"Shearer."

"Shearer," he repeats, with a deadness in his voice.

"I'm really very sorry. I'm, um…I can't sleep, so…I'm trying to think of an England football team made up entirely of players whose names are…jobs."

Dougie doesn't respond, but his breathing is heavy.

"Y'know, like Butcher," I continue. "Or Baker, or Cooper…I've got seven so far."

Still silence, apart from the breathing.

"I'm sorry I woke you…it won't happen again."

"If it does, it'll be the last time," comes the response. Then I hear the rustle of blankets as he rolls over.

"Really sorry, Dougie…I don't mean to disturb you."

"Just ask them for some sleeping pills," he mutters.

"Right," I reply, quietly trying to work out if a Lineker is a kind of job.

The following morning I find myself sitting across from the prison doctor (Dr Harris? Harrison?), who also looks like he is starved of sleep.

"We've got a new baby," he explains, hunting for his pen, which he eventually finds in his top pocket. "So, what's the problem?"

"I'd like something to help me sleep, but I don't want sleeping pills."

"Well, I can't make you sleep without sleeping pills, I'm a doctor not a bloody wizard. What have you got against sleeping pills? Half the prison takes them…I use them."

He buries his face in his hands for a moment, as if he's shutting the world out.

"Have you ever tried sleeping pills?" he asks.

"Yeah, but…" I hesitate. This is none of his business. "…once, during a difficult time. And I found it hard to come off them. Extremely hard."

"What sort of difficult time?"

"I'd had a bereavement." (That's as much as you're getting, pal.)

"Have you tried all the obvious things? Y'know, counting sheep…masturbating?" (I'm definitely not telling him about my ex-libido.)

"I just don't think that me and sleeping pills are a good idea."

He shakes his head in exasperation. "I don't do magic potions."

"I just thought maybe you'd have a suggestion that—"

"Yes, my suggestion is don't come asking for help and then reject the help."

He rubs his face for a few moments.

"I'll make an appointment for you to see the psychiatrist."

"No, thanks, I don't need that."

"It's not optional."

It was somewhere around this time that the fat, rather slow-blooded warder (Mr Hughes? Mr Hewitt?) came and fetched me from the yard where a half-hearted kickabout was under way.

"Lenny?" he calls, jerking his thumb. "Visitor."

That's odd, I think to myself, Sandra came yesterday and Mac's on tour in Shetland. I follow the warder through overlit corridors, towards the Visitors Room. As he walks he produces a book.

"Can you autograph this for my wife?"

"It's a Delia Smith recipe book."

"Yeh, doesn't matter."

When we get to the Visitors Room, there is only one visitor sitting there.

Derek.

Oh fuck.

Derek.

"Hi…how's things?" he asks.

I turn to the warder.

"Can you get rid of this man, please? And maybe bounce him down the steps on the way out."

The warder grins. "We're not allowed to do that to the visitors."

Derek stands up, spreading his palms apologetically.

"I won't be staying long."

"No, you won't."

"I expected aggression."

"Good."

"That's understandable."

"Why are you here, Derek?"

"Please –" He gestures towards the empty chair. "– just for a moment."

The warder backs off and leans against a wall. Oh, what the hell, I'm here now. I sit down opposite Derek, quietly weighing up whether I should run the risk of punching him in the face.

"I am here," he begins, in a voice dripping with self-importance, "to show solidarity."

"What?"

"I wanted to show support for you because, y'know, it's important we don't give up on people just because of a mistake. That's what I say whenever people start slagging you off, I say 'you don't know what he was going through,' it's not for anyone to judge you."

"I'm in prison, Derek. That usually involves a judging element. And we both know who put me here, don't we?"

I wait to see if this causes him any discomfort. Not a flicker. He leans forward.

"All I'm saying is that I don't judge my friends."

"I'm not your friend."

"All right, you're not my friend."

"Right."

"But *I'm* still *your* friend."

I take a deep breath to give myself time to calm down.

"Can you leave now, please?"

"March 5th, 1999," he announces.

"What?"

"That's when you became my friend."

He flares his eyes and raises his eyebrows, in an attempt at drama. "You were filming Roscoe's wedding to Stacey and I was one of the supporting artists."

"You were an extra?"

He stiffens slightly.

"I was a supporting artist. Invisible to the stars and crew, as per usual, it was freezing cold, but as I was queuing at the tea wagon, you were two in front of me and you asked me if I wanted tea and I said yes, and you poured me a cup of tea from the urn, and I said thank you, and you said 'no problem'."

Good God. Is that where this nightmare began? With a cup of tea?

"Do you remember that?" asks Derek, as if we had once been lovers. "Do you remember me?"

"No." I reply, with as cruel an emphasis as possible. But Derek doesn't notice, he's off again.

"I was only on set for one day. The assistant director got rid of me because he said I was asking too many questions. But I never forgot your act of kindness, which is why I lied for you in court."

"And then you lied about me...to millions of TV viewers."

He pauses for a moment, before frowning slightly.

"No, I believe I told the truth."

I look into his eyes and see total conviction.

"Just go," I tell him, "before I rip your freakish head off."

Again, not a flicker, he just smiles and gets to his feet.

"You know Jade's back on the show?"

"Yes."

"And, as of next month, I'm in it."

He flares his eyes once more. My money says he's been practising that in a mirror.

"You're in the show?"

"Louise cast me...I made a showreel."

"You are a showreel."

No response. Is he deaf?

"I'm playing Howard, gay dentist and best friend of Deborah, twin sister of the late Melanie, played by Jade. She's cool with the idea of acting opposite me. We cleared the air about my giving evidence against her in court."

"False evidence."

"Well, she's big enough to accept that people make mistakes," he says, with just the faintest suggestion of a dig. "Louise says that casting me is..."

"Edgy?" I interrupt.

He seems surprised that I guessed.

"Yes, and subversive, because we're 'operating in the cracks between soap and reality'."

Involuntarily, I let out a contemptuous snort, which just spurs Derek on.

"And a friend of hers has interviewed me for the Guardian. He says I 'highlight the fissile interconnectivity of popular culture'."

"OK, I've had enough now. Are there photographers outside? I bet there are, eh? To photograph Princess Derek, the angel of compassion?"

He offers his hand, then realises there will be no handshake and turns to head for the door.

"This...cynicism thing of yours, Kevin, I know it's a mask. I can see the real you. And he's much nicer than this, and that's the truth."

I follow him, talking to his back.

"I'm not sure the truth is really your area, Derek, I'd stick with the delusional egoism, that's your strong suit."

I'm rather pleased with that, usually when I'm angry I don't think of that kind of line till half an hour afterwards. The warder moves to open the door for Derek, who is offering me his hand again.

"I just wanted you to know that I am sorry that you're going through this pain."

He gives me a soft, sorrowful smile. I punch him in the face.

Derek went straight to the newspapers.

The Mirror put his shiny, cosmetically-enhanced black eye on the front page, beneath the headline "Lenny Did This". The Sun went with "Carver Hits Man For a Change". The Express published an interview with Derek where he explained that he would not be pressing charges against me because it felt wrong to punish someone who is "spiritually in a bad place".

The governor, Malcolm, had no choice but to be seen to discipline me. So I lost some privileges, though he kept the loss to a minimum because, as he put it, Derek has a face that is asking to be punched.

The guards all seemed to think it was a huge laugh. So did most of the inmates.

It's only in the psychiatrist's office that it is treated it as a matter of any significance.

This psychiatrist is new. The one who assessed me on my arrival was short, stout and bald. This one is late-thirties, lean, and he doesn't like me. He says "take a seat" after I have sat down.

He has over-lustrous black hair, which he runs his hand through at every opportunity.

"You know why you're here, don't you, Kevin? You were referred to me because you are complaining of sleeplessness but are disinclined to take sleeping pills…have I got that right?"

"Yes. I don't like taking pills."

He leans forward a little. "Why is that?"

Here we go.

"I just don't like taking pills."

No response.

"...like a lot of people," I add.

A quick note is made. I can see the bulge of his tongue inside his cheek.

"Now, since you were referred to me you have, of course – infamously – punched a visitor. Any thoughts about that?"

"Not really."

"Any regrets?"

I can't be bothered to answer that.

"Why did you punch him?"

"Have you met him?"

This gets a languid half smile and a ruffle of the hair.

"How is your hand?"

"Still pretty sore."

"I'd have thought you would know how to throw a punch."

"Yeh, well, when I throw a punch at a stuntman he rolls away. He doesn't stand there like a brick."

"Do...you...regret..." He teases out the words as he leans back and stares at the ceiling. "...that you gave this man exactly what he wanted? Clearly he lives for attention, and you presented him with acres of newsprint, front-page photos and a huge interview in the Express."

I don't bother answering this either, because I know he's right.

"An-y-way," he drawls, "the insomnia. How much sleep per night would you say you are getting?"

"None."

"None at all?"

"Well...maybe twenty minutes...I dunno...but, basically none."

"We could film you if you like. Install a camera in your cell."

"I'm not sure my cellmate would be very keen on that. Also, I don't need to be filmed, why can't you just take my word for it?"

He bounces his fingertips against each other for a few moments. He does like to keep you waiting.

"In my experience, patients who claim to be getting no sleep are invariably getting more sleep than they realise. It's perfectly understandable. We remember the anxiety of not being able to sleep, rather than the fact of sleep."

This really gets under my skin and, for the next few minutes, I give him a large piece of my mind about how I don't like being patronised and how I can't see any scientific basis for him knowing more about my insomnia than I do.

"Alrighty," he says, "let's change tack a bit. There were some riots in Manchester last night. Did you see that?"

"I heard it on the news."

"There was a lot of looting." The half smile puts in another appearance. "Why do you suppose that was? Why did so many people come out on the streets? Was it opportunism? Greed?"

"Something was happening."

"How do you mean?"

"Lots of people live their lives waiting for something – anything – to happen…when it does, they all pile in and go nuts. Life throws you a brief moment of apparent power and you OD on it."

"And do you ever feel like that?"

"No." I sigh – just to let him know that it's a predictable question. "I have lived a very prosperous, very privileged life… until now."

"What I was getting at –" He rakes his hand through that ludicrous hair "– is…emotionally, do you get bored? Do you find yourself desperately craving for something to happen? Is that how you ended up here?"

I take my time and choose my words.

"I ended up here because I took the wrong way out of what looked like a hopeless situation."

"The trial was only halfway through."

"The trial was clearly not fair."

"Most of life isn't fair, Kevin. Does that provide an excuse for anti-social behaviour?"

"I was about to be found guilty of a—"

"What's your attitude to women?" he interjects.

Exasperation takes over, so I shout: "I don't have an attitude to women!"

He makes a note and mutters something about an interesting turn of phrase. I raise a hand.

"Excuse me, but I thought you were supposed to be addressing my sleep problems."

"Well, Kevin…something is obviously stopping you from sleeping as you would like, and I'm looking for clues as to what that something might be, so that hopefully, by explaining it and understanding it, you can come to terms with it."

"The 'talking cure'?"

"If you like. Is there a woman in your life?"

"Can I go? I don't really believe in this stuff."

"What do you believe in? Are you religious?"

"I'm an atheist who likes Christmas."

"Why do you like Christmas?"

"Just do."

"Is it a family thing? The getting together?"

"I don't have any family to speak of. Mum and Dad are gone. A smattering of cousins."

"But you think family is important?"

"Of course family is important. If it wasn't for family, we'd have to fight with strangers."

"Kevin, it does seem to me that whenever the conversation tends towards something that makes you uncomfortable, your default setting is to crack a joke."

"That sounds about right."

He makes notes, while stroking his hair. I would like to set fire to it.

"Well, Kevin, what's your theory? Why can't you sleep? You seem to know everything else?"

I was right. He definitely doesn't like me.

"I'd really like to go now."

"Why? Are you scared?"

"Yeh, I'm scared you might bore me to death."

"Perhaps that's why you can't fall asleep. You're too scared to."

"Why would I be scared to fall asleep?"

"I dunno. Perhaps you're frightened of your dreams. Where they might take you."

"I don't dream."

"You mean you don't remember your dreams."

"No, I don't dream." I do really, but I just want to close this conversation.

He writes something down.

Dougie thinks I made a mistake with the psychiatrist. As we lie on our bunks listening to 'Just A Minute', he explains where I went wrong.

"By saying that, y'know, you never dream, you have basically identified yourself as someone who is a bit different. Y'know, maybe a bit unfeeling, a bit shutdown. You have to be careful about that, otherwise they can mark you down as a psychopath. Next thing you know it's 'hello, Broadmoor'."

He lolls an arm over the side of his bunk so that it floats in space above me. Graham Norton is buzzed for hesitation.

"See these tattoos?"

"...Yeh."

"The psychiatrist was really interested in these in Pentonville. And I know why, 'cos, y'know, I've read stuff about it. See, apparently, psychopaths have a higher pain threshold, less physical fear, so, like, they're not bothered by the idea of needles, ergo, a psychopath is more likely to have lots of tattoos."

"...Right."

This is not a comforting conversation, I think to myself, as I gaze at the skull on Dougie's upper arm and the cobra coiling up from his wrist.

"Yeh, no, the shrink in Pentonville used to interview me for hours to see if I was psychopathic. He's dead now." He pauses (for effect?). "Heart attack. Then lots of shrinks interviewed me."

"So...what was the outcome?" I fish. "Did they classify you...as..."

"No, luckily they decided I wasn't intelligent enough to be a psychopath."

"OK...well, that's good."

"Yeh, so if you get shrinked again, don't come across as bright. And don't say you don't dream, 'cos I read that a lot of psychopaths reckon they don't dream, and the ones that do have some dreams they reckon they dream in black and white."

"Right...so psychopaths only have arthouse dreams."

"That," Dougie chuckles, "is the sort of crack not to make, unless you want to wake up sharing with a serial killer."

Paul Merton starts to talk for a minute on the subject of Feet. He says that feet are a vital part of the human body because if we didn't have feet then the ends of our legs would fray.

"I like that," laughs Dougie. "Yeh, no, that's good, frayed legs."

"Why would not dreaming be the...the sign of a psychopath?"

"Well, from memory, I think it's, y'know, it's because dreams are part of your sort of emotional life. I think the theory is that there's a bit of the brain that gives us emotions and makes us sensitive to others. And that in psychopaths that bit isn't sort of working properly...or maybe not even at all."

Sue Perkins buzzes Paul Merton for repetition.

"In this article I read," continues Dougie, "there was, like, a list of, y'know, ways to spot a psychopath. Manipulating people, that was a biggie…cruelty to animals during childhood, that was another one. I mean, I ask you, what little boy hasn't pulled the wings off an insect, eh?"

"Yeh."

"Or lobbed bricks at a cat."

Fortunately, Dougie can't see my face.

"Promiscuity. That's another symptom," he informs me.

"…Right."

"Lack of, um…empathy."

"Yeh, you've covered that," I say, a little irritable. "Anyway, all this bollocks about empathy, how can they possibly know the correct level of feeling towards others? What's the standard unit of empathy? The world's full of posers who go around constantly empathising, how do we know any of that empathy's genuine? It could all be narcissism."

"That's what I am," he remembers.

"Eh?"

"The shrink at Pentonville…that's what he decided I was. A narcissist. We should have a 'Just A Minute' competition here, shouldn't we, eh? The whole prison. Yeh, I'll suggest that. It'll be a nice diversion."

'The Minute Waltz' plays as I launch into a tirade.

"People just wallow in their emotions now…incontinently… blabber about their feelings…tell their Facebook 'friends' about whether they're in a relationship…give interviews about their struggles with their demons. All that used to be personal. None of that stuff matters to anyone else. Who the fuck do these people think they are?"

"Spoken like a true psychopath," chuckles Dougie, as his illustrated legs swing over the side of his bunk. "Time for supper by my reckoning."

A thought strikes me.

"By their definition…"

"Jesus, Kevin, give it a rest."

No, I will not give it a rest.

"By their definition, I reckon we're all psychopaths. Or half psychopaths. Because when it comes down to it, deep down, none of us really care about anyone else, do we?"

Dougie jumps down on to the floor.

"You're upsetting me now," he says, "because I love my wife and my mum."

Then he shows me the tattoos to that effect.

11

THE DEATH

A few days after Dougie's little lecture on psychosis (it could have been a week) Malcolm called me to his office to tell me that he was worried about me. The psychiatrist had told him that my manner had been prickly and uncooperative. Malcolm said he found that disappointing. He also expressed the view that I needed to engage more with the activities the prison had to offer. Five-a-side football, perhaps? Or zumba? Or I could start some activity group of my own? I told Malcolm that I was prepared to take part in more activities, provided I did not have to attend any more sessions with the psychiatrist. Then Malcolm asked if I was trying to manipulate him, so I backed off.

The second session with the psychiatrist did not go much better. We seemed to go around in circles, with me trying *not* to sound like a smartarse.

Suddenly, from nowhere, he ambushes me with Sandra.

"Now, you were married." He pauses to sweep back his mane. God, this man is annoying. "Am I correct?"

"You are."

"And are you on good terms with your ex-wife?"

"Yes, we're friends."

"'Friends'," he parenthesises. (Get your hair cut, you look pathetic.) "She gave evidence on your behalf at the trial – your first trial."

"Yes."

"And she comes to visit you."

"Yes."

"Sandra."

"That's right."

He waits. He wants me to fill the silence and start talking about Sandra. I don't want to, but I will be out of here quicker if I do.

"She's probably my best friend," I begin, "although we didn't really become friends until after our marriage ended. Somehow things became easier between us."

"Why do you think that was?"

"I don't know...maybe, when you're with someone... everything can become...over-nuanced."

He's taking a lot of notes now.

"Maybe...the...steering gets too sensitive," I add.

"And why do you think the marriage broke down?"

"My fault."

"In what way?"

"I was a prick...there's no need to write that down."

One of his eyebrows rises.

"Interestingly, Kevin, that is the first time in either of our conversations where you have taken responsibility for anything. Usually, something is always somebody else's fault."

He smiles, knowingly, at me.

"And is Sandra still single?"

"She's about to re-marry."

"Ah," he says (like he's some kind of genius detective) "and does that bother you?"

"I'd just like her to be happy."

"Yes, but does it bother you?"

"If I said it doesn't bother me...would that mean I was unfeeling?"

"You haven't said that it doesn't bother you."

"All right then, it doesn't bother me."

There is a hiatus as he stares thoughtfully at the wall.

"Very well, let's move on."

Should I have said that? I'm not even sure it's the truth.

"How's the sleeplessness, Kevin? Worse? Better? Any dreams yet?"

"Listen, I know where you're going with this."

He straightens up in his chair. Shit, that was clumsy, why didn't I just keep my trap shut?

"Go on."

"Well, all I'm saying is…just because a man doesn't seem to feel things very much…or as much as people think he should… that doesn't make him…y'know…a psychopath."

He chuckles to himself. "Have I said I think you're a psychopath?"

"No…do you think I'm a psychopath?"

"Do you?"

"No, certainly not."

"Good. Although, of course, that is exactly the answer a psychopath would give."

He laughs at his little joke. "Shades of Catch-22, eh?"

"Do you think there's something wrong with me?" I blurt out. Where did that come from?

He sucks in air, like a shady plumber.

"Well…you're here."

After a few more months inside, I stopped taking any notice of the outside world. I no longer bothered to read newspapers and if the TV news was on in one of the recreation areas, I would just let it wash over me. I was dimly aware of markets imploding, rebellions being crushed, politicians talking about tough choices, journalists getting arrested, but it was only background music.

Then, one morning, as I am playing Dougie at chess, the con with the beaky nose (Boyd? Boyle?) calls across the room.

"Shame about your mate, eh?"

He's reading the Sun.

"What mate?" I ask, not really interested.

"Your mate…from the show." He crosses the room to give me the paper. "There. Your mate – messy business."

I take the paper, secretly hoping that something horrible and final has happened to Derek, but it isn't Derek.

"What's happened?" asks Dougie.

"It's an actor I used to work with…Gavin…" I scan the text. "He's thrown himself off a bridge."

"Poor sod."

"Yeh."

"Was he a friend?"

"No…no, he was a colleague."

In my mind, I start hunting for memories of Gavin, but all I can find are the moments when we took the piss out of him for being such a flake. We found it funny, the way he was forever bursting into tears, locking himself in his dressing room, converting to some new religion. He was our little comic soap opera inside a soap opera. Everyone cracked jokes about him. All of us; but especially me.

"Terrible thing, isn't it," says Dougie solemnly. "To do something like that…to be that desperate. Was he a nice bloke?"

"He was quite…um…emotional…a bit hard to take seriously sometimes…but I never imagined for one moment that he might do something like this."

"Yeh, well, people are weird, aren't they?" says Boyd/Boyle as he walks away. "…you can hang on to the paper."

I read on. There are three pages about Gavin, mostly tributes from people who couldn't stand him. If the truth were told, he wasn't that good an actor. When you were playing a scene opposite him, it always felt as if he had decided exactly what he was going to do in advance. Even if you changed your delivery during a retake, he kept his performance precisely the same, beat for beat. That's what someone does when they're scared. And he was always scared.

"You could ask to go to the funeral."

"Not appropriate, Dougie…we…we weren't mates…besides if I turned up, the reptiles would turn it into a circus."

"Oh yeh, hadn't thought of that. You'll have to just send flowers then."

"Yeh."

"How old was he?"

I search through the tributes.

"Um…forty-seven."

"God, that's no age, is it?"

Poor Gavin. All these kind words about him, but none when he needed them. How hard we all were. Dougie moves his rook. I am about to put the paper down when my eye lands on a quote from Derek. Derek! Who has only been on the show a matter of weeks!

"This is repulsive," I mutter.

Derek's words are mawkish, self-regarding, grief-porn. I sling the paper away in disgust.

"Are you OK?" asks Dougie.

"Yeh…just got a bad taste in my mouth."

"It's your move."

When someone close to you dies, you always feel that you let them down. No matter what your objective, rational self tries to tell you, somehow you feel you should have saved them; you should have done more. It's an understandable response, people we love are taken from us and we are helpless bystanders. Eye-witnesses. Shocked, angry and guilty. That's how you feel when someone close is stolen. But why the hell was I having those kind of feelings about Gavin? Why were my eyes filling with tears? We were not even friends and yet that night – the night after I read the newspaper article – my mind would not let me rest. Try as I might, I could not get the image of Gavin out of my head; he was standing on the parapet of that bridge, alone and beaten. I tried to conjure up other images of him – memories of him enjoying himself on set – but there were none to be found. The only other picture of him I could recall was his taut, anxious face when we had our little confrontation in the canteen, the one about the sausage-factory. For a moment, I wished I'd made the effort to get to know him better but, deep down, I knew that in a few weeks' time that thought would have faded into nothing.

So, if he meant so little to me, why was I feeling this disturbed? Perhaps it wasn't about him, perhaps this was about the others. Perhaps he was just the stick that was stirring up the mud. Whatever the truth, waves of indefinable emotion kept breaking over me until I realised that I had to get some kind of control to give myself any hope of sleeping. For a few minutes, I concentrated on breathing deeply through my nose to try to restore calm. Then I began compiling mind-clearing, pointless lists.

By about two in the morning, I had moved on to famous Belgians and actors who had played Sherlock Holmes. The prison's night-time soundscape was the usual emptiness, with the occasional melancholy of a guard's slow, echoing footsteps.

Tedium. Same old, same old.

Then, suddenly, from a distant cell, comes the most spine-scraping sound. First, a long scream, then a series of staccato shrieks that sound more like a fox caught in a trap than a human being. Sweat starts trickling down the back of my neck. The shrieking gets louder. What can be happening in there? I get out of my bunk.

"Dougie...what's going on? Who is that?"

Dougie is fast asleep.

I can hear many footsteps now, people hurrying, boots click-clacking along floors.

I get back into bed and press the pillow hard against my head but the shrieking cuts right through. Why doesn't he stop? Just make him stop. More feet clank rapidly down staircases and now the screaming is mixed in with indistinct shouts.

I lie rigid in my bed like a child fighting the urge to yell for Mum, and I don't know which is the more terrifying: the piercing, bestial screams, or the suddenness with which they stop.

I decided to send flowers to Gavin's funeral, without really understanding why. Mentally, I didn't feel up to organising it myself, so I used my allocated phone call to ring my agent's office. They could contact a florist for me. True, they had kept a considerable distance from me during my personal difficulties, but I was still on their books and they were collecting commission, so they could earn their keep.

The receptionist sounds bright-eyed and keen. I wonder if she is being paid.

"Good afternoon, Jackman International."

A fog shrouds my thoughts for a moment. Should I ask her to sort out the flowers for me? That will require a lot of explanation to a total stranger. "Jackman International," she repeats.

"Oh...hi, erm...could I speak to Roland, please?"

"Roland? Roland Abbot?"

"Yuh."

"I'm afraid he's left the company."

What? When the fuck did that happen?

"Erm...right...um...so who's dealing with his clients?"

"I'll put you through to someone."

"Only I'm one of Roland's..."

"Who shall I say is calling?"

"Kevin Carver."

"OK, Kevin."

Not a flicker of recognition. Why should I be so surprised? The world forgets about you, that's to be expected. Now I'm being played "Mandy" by Barry Manilow. Then a voice cuts him short.

"Hi Kevin, it's Kara."

Kara? She hears my hesitation.

"We met a few years ago...at the Christmas party."

Oh Christ, Kara! Now I remember. Oh well, she was as blind drunk as I was. We were just two pissheads who ended up in a cupboard. Or was it a toilet?

"Oh hi, Kara...how are you?"

"Good, thanks. And you?"

"Erm...I've been better."

No laugh.

"I'm sorry to hear that," she says. "Are you calling me from...?"

"Prison, yuh."

"Right...so how can I help you, Kevin?"

"Well, um...when did Roland leave?"

"Ooh, three or four months ago."

"Why?"

She sounds slightly amused by the question.

"Well...he sort of retired. Y'know, the agency has been getting a lot bigger, the client list's a lot longer, the business is a lot more full-on and, um, Roland's been having some health issues, so..."

"Serious health issues?"

There is a pause as she reaches for the right words.

"Health issues...relating to his lifestyle."

Oh right, that'll be drinking, Roland always liked a drink. When he took me on, as a young actor, we would spend a few minutes in their tiny, shambolic offices chewing the fat and then adjourn to the Blue Posts. The office isn't in a Soho backstreet any more, it's a big glass and chrome job in Victoria.

"What can I do for you?" she asks.

I remember now, it was definitely a cupboard.

"Erm...I need some flowers sent...to a funeral. Gavin Plunkett."

"Oh I know, wasn't that sad."

"I don't know exactly where the funeral is happening."

"Leave it with me, Kevin. That's no problem. Was there anything else?"

Suddenly, a decision bursts upon me.

"Yeah, actually, Kara, I think I'd like to come off the books."

"Sorry, I..."

"I don't think I need the agency to represent me."

"Oh...right." She sounds surprised. I feel very surprised. Thirty seconds ago this thought had not even entered my head.

"I'm not dissatisfied or...y'know, I'm not...there's not another...sorry, I'm not expressing myself very...I've not been getting much sleep, so...I don't need an agent, let's be honest... when I get out of here...I'm going to be poison so..."

"Well I wouldn't go that far."

"I won't be an actor again, that...that part of my life is over, isn't it?"

"Again, not necessarily."

"No one will employ me."

She falls silent. Other inmates are queuing for the phone.

"I don't *want* to be an actor again," I tell her.

"There's still the occasional residual payment coming in."

"OK, can you process those for me and..."

"Sure."

"If anyone asks, I've quit the business."

"Understood."

I feel a light tap on my shoulder.

"What's the message?" she asks. "On the card, with the flowers."

"Oh, erm...'In fond memory'." No, Kevin, that sounds ridiculous. "No, scrub that Kara...erm...'in loving remembr...' – actually, you know what, forget the flowers, they were a stupid idea. Sorry."

"OK. No problem."

"Sorry, Kara."

"No, it's fine."

There's a firmer, more final tap on my shoulder, so I apologise one last time and then hang up.

It's amazing how little sleep you can get by on, provided you don't have to achieve anything. The weeks continued to slouch past and the insomnia remained constant, but it hardly mattered.

Conversations became hard work. On many occasions, I would find that even though I had been talking to people for a while, I had barely taken in a single word.

Watching TV was OK. In one ear and out the other. A sequence of pictures that asked nothing of me.

I fought the passivity a little.

I took Malcolm's advice and signed up for the five-a-side. Mildly therapeutic. I would charge around the gymnasium like a man possessed, losing myself in the angles of the passes and the pointless pursuit of victory. For one hour, I was a kid again and, apart from being elbowed in the face by an embezzler, it was fun. I pushed myself to the limit, chasing every lost cause in a conscious effort to exhaust myself. I emptied the tank.

And it worked. I began to get some sleep – but only in the daytime. I started nodding off in the TV room, the games room, the canteen, the toilet but, come the night time, once again, my brain would fizz with chaos.

The lack of sleep created a new problem – clumsiness. To

begin with, I would scrape or graze myself, or catch a finger in something, or pour liquids down my front, but soon I was routinely walking into stationary objects, or dropping trays to ironic cheers.

Finally, I was coming down some metal stairs and my brain told me the steps had finished when there were still two more. Next thing I knew my head hit the floor, followed by more ironic cheers. The guard who took me to hospital for the X-ray said that it was the best pratfall he'd seen since Norman Wisdom. Pratfall. Yeh, the right word.

Nothing was broken, but I did lose a tooth.

So, all things considered, I am in a pretty bad way when Sandra pays me her first visit in several months.

It doesn't start well.

"You look like shit," she says. "What's happened?"

I push the tiredness away and put on a brave face.

"I'm fine really. Just a bit short of sleep, that's all."

"You're not on drugs, are you?"

"No."

"Are there drugs in here?"

I give her a look.

"Sandra, it's a prison."

"Are you eating all right?"

"Yeh."

"What's the food like?"

"Basic."

"You've lost weight."

"Well, I was carrying a bit, wasn't I?"

She looks upset.

"The love handles have gone," I tell her.

She's chewing her lip with tension.

"Don't forget to breathe," I remind her.

She seems to be scanning my face, looking for clues. I don't like seeing her so anxious.

"How are the wedding plans going?" I ask, trying to up the energy.

"Yeh, no, good thanks, yeh...good."

"How long now?"

"Five weeks..."

"Church wedding?"

"No. Has Mac been to visit you recently?"

"No, well, he's still touring with that show, isn't he? The... um...musical about...the Tonypandy massacre."

"Oh God, yeh."

At last, a laugh, she's laughing, that's a relief.

"Limits him a bit, doesn't it," she giggles. "In terms of bums on seats, doing shows about massacres."

"He'll be OK once Lloyd Webber writes Culloden."

We kick around the notion of an Andrew Lloyd Webber musical about the annihilation of the clans, starring Michael Crawford as the butcher Cumberland, and for a few minutes it is like the old days, before all the nonsense.

"So it's a registry office job?" I ask.

"Yeh."

"...Are you excited?"

God, this is like pulling teeth.

"Is he excited? He should be, he's a very lucky lad."

She shifts in her seat slightly. Am I making her uncomfortable?

"Alright, I'll stop the interrogation."

"Pete's lovely...he's very caring."

A terrible thought starts to take form.

"And you love him?"

"Totally."

She's being so defensive that I can't help myself.

"It's just...y'know...I'd hate to think...somehow...you were..."

A pair of brown eyes are drilling into me. It's very disconcerting and my addled brain hunts for the right word.

"…settling."

I don't think that was the right word.

"I'm not settling, you arrogant shit. What the fuck gives you the right to say that?"

"I'm sorry. I'm…knackered, I…can't—"

"Pete is wonderful."

"Good, that's brilliant, and, I'm sorry, I'm not thinking straight."

She flops back in the chair and exhales, hard. This is a disaster. I reach for a joke.

"That's why I got thrown out of the Diplomatic Corps."

She's not playing. Behind her, a guard glances at his watch.

"With Pete," she begins, haltingly, "I…I'm going to have a crack at the stuff we never managed…I want to just…sit with someone curled up in front of the telly, like that's the only place in the whole world…I want to hear a key in the door and think 'oh great, he's home' and not 'where the hell has he been?' I want to take our kid to the zoo, and don't make that face."

I wasn't aware of making a face, but she obviously spotted something. She gets louder.

"My friend Natalie's just had her first and she's two years older than me…so why the hell not? Lots of women have babies in their forties now. And if necessary, we can adopt. I'm going to do it, Kevin."

This is the first time since we separated that she has got angry with me. There are tears in her eyes.

"There are some things you don't have the right to ask me any more," she murmurs.

Damn this exhaustion, I can't think. Think! There is a feeling I want to – but the words are – everything is scuttling away from me.

"Listen…the…there's…I'm sorry, how things turned out… and I know that was down to me…and I really regret that…

because I know that if I hadn't played around, then…"

"That wasn't the worst part," she interrupts.

"Oh…what…what was the worst part, then?"

"…You hide."

"Hide?"

"I probably know you better than anyone and yet I hardly know you at all."

"…Well, everyone hides a bit…don't they?"

She laughs.

"A bit, maybe. But you hide inside yourself – or rather yourselves. You're like a Russian doll."

What does this – this accusation – what does this amount to? Is love about surrendering up every innermost thought to someone else? What is she talking about? Does this…this Pete person…does he come home and spill his guts every night? Is that what she wants? Never mind, concentrate on the apology, that's all that matters right now.

"I'm sorry if that's…the signal I give off."

"It's not a signal, it's the substance."

"…Maybe so…" I rub my face to try and clear my head. "I just want you to know, that you are the only woman I have ever felt… truly comfortable with…" She mutters the word "comfortable" "…and I will always regret the fact that my behaviour meant… that it didn't work out between us, and that—"

"It would never have worked out between you and me, Kevin. To be perfectly honest, I'm not sure it could ever work out between you and anyone."

There is a tremor in her voice now.

"The walls are just too high."

It is a moment or two before I can take in what she has said. I am still processing it as she scrapes back her chair and starts putting on her jacket.

"I'd better go."

"But the bell hasn't gone."

"We don't need the bell," she says.

* * *

My immediate reaction was to dismiss Sandra's comments as simplistic sentimental rubbish. Relationships are far more complex than that and besides, she puts up walls, so does everyone, it was all bollocks. Self-absorbed tosh.

But a few days after her visit, my psychological and physical well-being started to plummet dramatically. The first major change was that I stopped eating. I stopped *wanting* to eat. I stopped wanting to talk. Or move. I even stopped looking at people. I wanted no form of contact whatsoever. Even Dougie got locked out.

Ideally, I would have just stayed in my cell, but that would have triggered dialogues with the guards – negotiations, pleadings – so instead I shuffled robotically, passively, from place to place, trying to think, feel and experience nothing, in an attempt to un-person myself.

There is probably a name for this mental state. Whether it was depression, or Depression, I really couldn't tell you. I vaguely remember being visited by the psychiatrist in my cell, but my memory (unreliable) is that the visit was…I don't think it was productive.

All I can tell you for certain is that a gauze had been placed between me and the world. There had been a spell, briefly, a few weeks before that visit from Sandra, when the opposite had been the case; when I had been feeling the world too keenly. All my senses were intensified, every colour enhanced and every clatter and jangle of prison life seemed to travel the length of my spine. Then, the world felt too live. Now, it was dead. My body no longer felt like it belonged to me. It had become a conveyance.

At one point, I developed the conviction that the prison had secretly dosed me up with Largactil. (I have since received assurances that I was given no medication.) Another time, in the middle of the night, I felt I could hear the whole of London – literally, the whole of London, every beep of every car horn, the chatter from every restaurant, the shouts of every drunk, all mixed together in a dissonant soup of noise. It felt like millions of thoughts were trying, second by second, to push and jostle their way through a narrowing gateway in my brain. But, by morning, the mania had subsided and my mind was re-emptying.

I have no idea how long I was this hollowed-out version of myself. A couple of weeks? Perhaps a month? Time had no meaning as I trudged through the minutes. Nothing stood out. Nothing had significance. Because nothing mattered. Nothing was king.

Then, one day, oddly, I become aware that I am staring at my own name on a poster written in huge, squared-off red letters, like the top billing in a movie epic.

"Kevin Carver: Drama Workshop. Games Room. 3 p.m. Today."

Today? What does that mean? Is it an order for me to attend? Or am I supposed to be running this workshop? Could it be a joke?

A familiar voice stops the questions.

"Sorry to ambush you, Kevin," says Malcolm. "But we've been meaning to start up something like this for a while. And I know you're the ideal man to put in charge. As our resident thespian."

What the hell is he on about?

"I think you need something to take you out of yourself."

Slowly, I begin to understand. I start mumbling that I can't face it and that he'd better look elsewhere. But Malcolm isn't budging.

"It's this or medication," he states cheerily. "You started out doing workshops and stuff, didn't you? All those years ago.

In that socialist theatre collective that helped put an end to Mrs Thatcher."

He gives his little Seagoon laugh. "I googled you. This'll take you back to your roots. Roots are important, stop us blowing around like tumbleweed. You might want to have a shave."

I look at my reflection in the glass of a partition. Can that be me?

"You'll be fine," says Malcolm, gripping my shoulder. I mumble more protests.

"No, no, let's have none of that, fella, the show must go on."

He gives another little laugh as he strides off up the corridor.

"Come on, Kevin," he calls over his shoulder. "You've done self-pity, time to move on."

12

THE WORKSHOP

To be honest, I was looking for the first opportunity I could find to bin the drama group. Thank you and goodnight. All I needed was a pretext. A lack of numbers would do. Most of the prisoners were blue-collar, under-educated, they were unlikely to sign up. Anything less than five people and I would tell the governor that the workshop was not worthwhile and hope that he would get out of my face. Besides, could I run any kind of workshop in my mental state? You need to be able to think straight, look like you know what you're doing; talk. Talk sense. It was a stupid idea. Stupid. Stoo-pid.

So when I push open the door to the Games Room, I am half-expecting it to be empty.

Shit.

There must be at least ten of the bastards. All looking at me, all with different expressions; some friendly, some challenging, some empty. It feels like a moment from one of those dreams; the ones where you're due on stage and you don't even know what the play is, or where you're sitting your driving test stark naked, but nobody seems to be commenting on it.

"Hi," I croak.

How the hell do I begin? Keep it simple.

"My name's Kevin."

"We know," says a voice.

"Yes, of course…sorry."

I scan the faces. They are all familiar, to a greater or lesser degree, but I can only put names to a couple of them. So, as an opener, I ask each of them to say their name; but I am only buying myself thinking time. Once they have finished giving their names I realise, in the ensuing silence, that I have not retained a single word.

"Alrighty, I'll be honest. This has been sprung on me a bit…so I haven't really had time to prep anything…Let's find out what you each…erm…want to get out of this experience."

I head for the one face that's smiling.

"Dougie…what do you hope to get out of this?"

"I thought it'd be a laugh," he says. "But I could be wrong."

There's a ripple of dry laughter, which I join in with. Scanning the faces, there don't seem to be any receptive ones, so I don't know who to involve next. The Jamaican guy (did he say his name was Pulse?) seems to be looking straight through me and out the other side, like I'm an X-ray.

In fact, most of them are looking at me like that. The bald bloke with the missing eyebrow (what's that about?) is picking at his teeth. The tall Irishman (Kieron?) is drumming his fingers on his knee. I can hear myself flannelling and padding and faffing and I feel embarrassed. I should be able to improvise something better than this. What is wrong with me? I used to have a talent for spouting empty bullshit, but that's gone now. Now I can't even manage to be a convincing fake.

I'm not sure what that leaves.

One by one, I go round the group, trying to find some possible starting points for a discussion, but nobody seems up for that. They can probably sense that my heart's not really in it. You get out what you put in, that's what Mum always said.

Suddenly, out of the blue, a hand pops into the air; it's the one who looks like an insurance salesman.

"Yes? Sorry, it's, um..."

"Gerald."

"Sorry, Gerald, yes...you've got a question?"

"Yes, will we be looking at set texts? Or are we going to prance around pretending to be butterflies?"

Right. So, Gerald is different.

"Well, Gerald, I, um...I think the sessions can be whatever you all want them to be. Drama is a...well, it can cover pretty much everything really. Basically, it's just stories, y'know, and we all have stories and, y'know, stories can take so many forms, y'know, um, plays, films, novels..."

"Alibis," adds the Irishman.

A few of them laugh, partly out of deference. The Irishman scares people, even Dougie.

"Stories," I repeat, sounding lame. "That's all it's about. Stories."

I wait to see if anyone wants to add anything, but there is only silence and a bit of shuffling.

It is then that I notice a man who is trying not to be seen. He is standing in the corner of the room, flattened against the wall, as if attempting to merge into the masonry. He is painfully thin, and his features are striking; tufty, white hair, white eyelashes, very pale skin. It is hard not to stare.

"Excuse me," I begin. "Sorry...um, in the corner there...I'm not sure if I caught your name."

He looks up, startled. His hand flicks something away from his cheek. What is he doing? There's nothing there.

"I...I..." He clears his throat (although he's forcing it, it doesn't sound like it needs clearing). "I...erm...I didn't give you my name."

"Oh, I see...right...well, can you tell me it? Mind you, I'm not promising I'll remember. My head's all over the place today, as you've probably noticed."

My attempts to place him at his ease are failing. He looks like he could bolt at any second.

"My name is Paul," he says softly, "…but everyone calls me Albie."

"Why Albie?" I ask. He hesitates.

"Short for albino," says a gruff voice to my left.

"I'm not an albino," he stutters, flicking at his cheek again. "I don't have the eyes. I'm…I'm just extremely pale."

He certainly is. Beneath the harsh strip-lighting, he looks like he has been dipped in bleach. Why hadn't I noticed him around? I know I've not been taking much in, but even so, he is hard not to notice – which must be agony for him.

"Are you new here?" I ask.

He glances away. "No…I've just been a bit poorly."

"So, which would you rather? Albie or Paul?"

He stares at the floor for a few moments.

"Albie is fine…no one's called me Paul for years."

"OK then, Albie…what would you like to get out of these sessions?"

He keeps staring at the floor.

"…Albie?"

There is a faint snigger from the bald man with the eyebrow.

"Albie? What brings you here?"

"The governor told me to come," he replies, still looking down. "Said it would help."

"Help what?"

Out of the corner of my eye, I catch sight of Dougie rolling his eyes.

"My confidence." Albie looks up, with just a hint of a flinch. "I'm due for release. In a couple of months…he says I need to work on my confidence."

Christ, I'm a therapist now, am I? Albie stands there, blinking, and I reach for a smile.

"Okeydokey." ("Okeydokey"? When have I ever said "Okeydokey"?) "Well, um…today was only ever going to be about…y'know…thinking about what our expectations might be, so…in that sense…"

The fat warder (George? Geoff?) appears at the door and taps his watch. Thank you, God. I declare the session over and head for the door.

"When's the next session?" asks the Jamaican.

"It says 'daily' on the poster" says the warder.

Jesus, does it? I didn't see that. Daily? That's fucking ridiculous.

"I…um…I think that could be a mistake."

"That's what it says on the poster," repeats the warder. Is he grinning? "Says it down in the corner."

The tall Irishman rises wearily from his chair. "Well, I don't give a flying fuck when the next session is," he says. "That was shite."

A few voices mutter their agreement.

I feel my spirits lift. It looks like there may be no one at tomorrow's session. As everyone shuffles towards the door, I turn to the fat warder.

"Is there any chance of a quick chat with the governor?" I ask, trying to sound as casual as possible. But he just chuckles and walks away.

I went to the second session desperately hoping that the room would only contain empty chairs. But no, there they were, sitting, waiting. The good news was that the numbers had dwindled to six. The tall Irishman was gone and so was Mono-Eyebrow. Just six left. Almost the point where I could justify shutting the group down.

"All right, um…so, the chosen few, eh? Um, now I know you all told me yesterday, so, if you can bear it, can we just quickly run through the names again? Erm, Dougie, I know, and Albie… Albie, why don't you pull your chair more into the middle of the room?" Hesitantly, he scrapes his chair forwards. "OK, perhaps, um…perhaps you could go first."

I nod at the Jamaican, who smiles and says, "My name is Pulse."

"That's an unusual name."

"I gave it myself."

"What's…what's its significance?"

He shakes his head in amusement.

"It ain't got no 'sig-nif-ic-ance'. It's just a cool name."

"Uh-huh…can I ask…what was your original name?"

"No."

"OK, fine, yup, and you…sir?"

"Gerald."

"Oh yeh, 'course, sorry."

"I'm Simo," says the young man sitting behind him.

"Is that short for Simon or something?"

He gives a dark, dirty laugh. "Simon? Oh yeh – like – there's just millions of Simons in— what the f- Simon? Do I— nobody's called Simon any— are you taking the— is he taking the pi— Simon? No it's not short for anything, it's like, fuck me – innit, like – Simon? What are you—"

He carries on like this for several minutes, with every sentence breaking into fragments and spinning through the air. To my relief, I am not the only one looking perplexed. Gradually, Simo becomes aware that he is bewildering people and dribbles self-consciously to a halt, before quietly muttering "My mum named me after a dolphin."

Several faces turn to look at him.

"It's a long story," he shrugs.

The last member of the group, I realise, is a new face. Asian. Bearded. Don't make assumptions, Kevin.

"You weren't here yesterday."

"Is that a problem?" he counters.

"No…no, no, not at all."

"My name is Mohammad."

"Has it always been Mohammad?" drawls Gerald.

"That's none of your business."

They immediately start arguing, talking over each other and, judging from the reactions of the others, this is not an unusual occurrence. My mental tiredness stops me from thinking clearly enough to intervene, so I stand there like a dazed tourist, which is sort of what I am. Dougie steps between the two of them with his shoulders squared.

"Alright, girls, don't get menstrual."

The argument stops and I mumble a few thank yous.

Albie is dabbing at that invisible something on his cheek again, but he controls the tic once he notices me looking at him.

"Have you done any prep this time?" enquires Gerald. His voice contains a constant undertow of disdain.

"Sort of…I thought we'd start with some storytelling. We all know stories. We all have stories. So I thought, what might be an easy, but interesting, start is…um…if we just told stories from our own lives…y'know…funny or sad…or both, doesn't matter. Who wants to start?"

Dougie looks as if he is about to volunteer, but then loses confidence. Simo looks appalled by the idea, as does Albie. Pulse has his eyes closed and Gerald is wearing a smile that is really a challenge.

"Alright then" I say, "I'll start, just to get things rolling. Erm… why don't I tell you the story of exactly how I ended up here – apologies to Dougie, he's heard this all before – and some of you may know bits of it, probably inaccurate bits – so here it is, chapter and verse, from the horse's mouth."

For the next twenty minutes or so, I tell them my story, from meeting Jade, through the trial, Derek's intervention, my acquittal, Derek baring his diseased soul on television, the second trial, and ending with my conviction and the Judge's observations about my "manipulative cowardice".

As I finish, Pulse is nodding sagely.

"Man, that is a story an' no mistake."

"Yeh, but what kind of story is it?"

Mohammad can't contain himself.

"It's a story about what happens when everybody tells lies all the time. The girl lied, this Derek-character lied, you lied, that's 'cos everyone lies here, innit? That is the West for you. You're obsessed with the wrong things. And you're willing to lie and cheat for them and you forget that God sees everything."

Gerald yawns, loudly and provocatively.

Then Simo bursts into life.

"That story is— your sto— it's a fu— yeh, that's just total fu— it's— God, man, that's— it's a fucking tragedy, isn't it... yeh...isn't it?"

"Well that's a very good question, Simo. Is my story a tragedy? What do we think? Albie, any thoughts?"

"I doubt it," mutters Gerald.

"Albie? Anything you'd like to ask, or say?" Albie looks upwards and blinks, like a startled ghost.

"I think it's very sad," he says, quietly. "Why did that girl make that stuff up?...blame you like that? And now you're inside... that's sad."

"So, group," I spread my hands to try to get their focus, "is it a tragedy? What do we think?"

"There's nothing tragic about it," Gerald sniffs. "You brought it all on yourself. You allowed yourself to be at the mercy of other people. You failed to control events because your fear got the better of you. So no, not a tragedy. There's an element of farce, possibly."

For a moment, Gerald and I lock eyes. He is extremely bright and he knows it.

"Dougie thinks there's an element of comedy in it, don't you, Dougie?" I prompt.

"Well…sort of…in a sick-joke sort of way."

"It's interesting though, isn't it? One story. And everybody's got a different take on it."

I get up off my chair and start walking around the room. For the first time in I don't know how long, I get the vague sensation that maybe I know what I'm doing. They seem to be listening. Or are they just there killing time?

"Ambiguity. What your different views of my story add up to is called 'ambiguity'. And you'll find it at the heart of every great story."

"Course, we only heard your version of events," Gerald snipes. "How do we know that was the truth?"

"You are absolutely right, Gerald." (Don't overuse his name, he'll feel patronised.) "You only heard my version. You can't be sure that is the truth. And *that* is another layer of ambiguity."

"I believe you," says Albie, almost inaudibly.

"Yeh, why would you lie?" nods Pulse.

"OK, well, that's enough of my story, who wants to tell the next one?"

Dougie is instantly on his feet.

"It can be about anything at all?" he asks.

"As long as it's from personal experience."

He launches into what begins as a picaresque story about his Sunday league football team getting stranded in Frankfurt, but then it slowly turns into a disgusting tale about a prostitute who sets fire to a client.

Dougie sits down to shocked silence.

"Not a lot of ambiguity there," says Gerald.

The night after the second workshop I am laying on my bunk trying to usher in sleep.

I think about rivers, my newest escape strategy. I try to summon up memories of rivers that I have experienced; try to recapture the peace of being on water, with the landscape slowly unfurling itself around me.

And I am drifting slowly up the Tweed, with the old arched bridge at Berwick receding behind me, and white swans escorting me in smooth flotillas, when the spell is broken.

Dougie's voice.

"You're very quiet."

"I was on a river."

"Nice. What do you make of your workshop group then?"

"Erm...dunno...don't really know them yet, what do you make of them?"

Dougie gives out a knowing chuckle. "What, honestly?"

"Yes."

"Well..." he pauses, as if he's deliberating – but he isn't.

"Personally...in my opinion...I can't see you achieving anything with that bunch of cunts."

"I'm not out to achieve anything."

"Well that's just as well, isn't it."

There's a thump as he jumps down on to the floor. "Mind you, I'm not sure I believe you. Have you seen my headphones?"

"No, sorry. Why don't you believe me?"

"'Cos I think you're just enough of an arrogant fucker to believe that you can ed-u-cate them. Y'know, like My Fair Lady – only with ignorant cunts for Audrey Hepburn."

I am amused, and intrigued, by Dougie's analysis. Can he be right? Have I made them my project?

Dougie is fishing beneath my bunk, muttering dark oaths about his missing headphones.

"That's the trouble with this place...full of thieves."

I laugh, but then Dougie's head bobs up and the frown tells me that no irony was intended.

"It's not funny, Kevin. They have no respect for other people's personal property."

"Didn't you rob a bank once?"

"That's different, that's a bank." His head disappears beneath my bunk again. "And it was more than once."

"I'm not aiming to educate anyone. Those workshops, at best, are just a way of...I dunno, filling time...keeping the madness at bay."

Dougie is burrowing into his locker now.

"Oh, right. Ah, found the bastards! My memory, eh? It's this place, turns your brain into mush. That's why I'm going to your sessions, to give my brain a work-out."

"Right, well, that's as good a reason as any, I suppose."

"I am trying to save my brain."

"Right."

"But some brains are beyond saving."

He is giving me a mischievous grin. I know what's coming.

"You're about to slag people off, aren't you?"

"All I'm saying is that Pulse has probably smoked his brain away and Mohammad's is awash with Islamic sewage. You're talking about two broken brains, and that's not racist, that's fact. And as for Simo...and Albie...dear oh dear."

I feel a flush of defensiveness.

"Listen, my expectations are...realistic, OK? I will consider it a major achievement if I can get Simo to finish a sentence and get Albie to...not jump at his own shadow...but, to be honest, I don't expect either of those things to happen."

Dougie clambers back up on to his bunk, gripping the headphones in his teeth. The springs bounce and squeak above me.

"Here, Kevin...how old do you reckon that Albie is?"

That's a difficult question. He feels like he's about fifteen, but physically he's – well, the paleness means that he lacks definition.

"Twenty-five?"

"Thirty-four," replies Dougie, with slow relish.

"You're joking."

"He's thirty-four."

"But…he's just a kid…isn't he?"

"Mentally, yeh…but he's thirty-four."

"Christ."

"He's spent seventeen years inside, apparently. Half his life."

"Did he murder someone?"

"No, no, not one long stretch, lots of little ones, in different prisons."

"Where did you get all this?"

"The old jungle telegraph…plus, I asked him."

"Oh…right."

"He didn't want to chat, but I just hung in there. Winkled it out of him. It's a gift."

Thirty-four? That's a real surprise.

Oh well. That shows how much I know.

My thoughts drift back to the Tweed; to the lapping of the water as it nudges my boat. The soft whisper of the breeze. Next thing I know, I can hear feet clattering on walkways. I glance at my watch. It's seven fifteen. I have slept, uninterrupted, for nearly nine hours.

13

THE LETTER

The realisation that I had enjoyed a proper night's sleep filled me with elation and trepidation in equal measure. On the one hand I was experiencing, for the first time in many months, that sense of rested well-being; that relaxation of muscle and mind, but on the other hand, there was a small, frightened voice in the back of my head which was asking what if it had been a fluke? What if the waking hell returned tonight?

Well, there was no point fretting over an unknown and as I was experiencing a return of mental clarity, I decided to sit down and do something difficult that I had been putting off for weeks.

I composed a letter to Sandra – in pencil. In pencil, because I knew it would take me several drafts. How long had it been since I last wrote a letter to her? Or to anyone, for that matter? In fact, I wasn't sure I had *ever* written a letter to Sandra. So this might be the first and it was going to be an abject apology. How sad was that?

I could vaguely remember writing a letter to Mum when I was touring with Mac. Nearly thirty years ago! I couldn't remember what I said, although I had a vague recollection of asking for money. Jesus, I was not much of a son.

I must have written to friends, mustn't I? If I did, I obviously didn't see it as important, otherwise I would remember, wouldn't I? It's such a puzzle, when and why your brain hits "record".

It took a few goes to get the first paragraph right. Basically, I just wanted to apologise to Sandra for the things I had said during her last visit. But I found that repeatedly using the word "sorry" didn't make it sound any more sincere.

Less is more, Kevin.

So I pruned the number of "sorrys" back to just the one. In the end, I decided that was as sincere as it was possible for me to sound.

The final sentence proved to be a massive hurdle. I was desperate to capture the right note, but every choice I made felt trite. Initially, I signed off with "All I want is for you to be happy." On re-reading, however, I did not like the sound of "All I want". It felt too egocentric. This was about my acknowledging – no, accepting – that I was no longer relevant to her future.

So I reworked it to read "All that matters is that you should seize the chance for happiness, however you see fit." Was "seize the chance" right? Was there a risk that she might see that as a suggestion that her forthcoming marriage was a gamble? Of course, every marriage is a gamble, but it's not something you want to see written down. Especially from your ex-husband.

And what was "however you see fit" doing there? Hanging off the end, like shit on a sheep's tail? What I had been trying to convey was, again, my irrelevance, her autonomy, but somehow, the more I looked at it, the more I saw an inference that she might be deluding herself. "However you see fit"!?

What the fuck had made me write that? It made me sound like some smug barrister, with my thumbs in my lapels. But it didn't matter how it made me sound, did it? This was about making Sandra feel good about the future, and free of our past.

In the end, after much rubbing out, I finalised the wording.

"You have known a lot of pain (much of it because of me) but all that matters now is that you should get the happiness you deserve."

I read it back over and over. It felt slightly formal, but I quite liked that. The bracket felt right. An acknowledgement of my behaviour, but on this occasion, only as a sidebar, finished, incidental now. And I liked the idea of her receiving the happiness that she was owed. Even if, deep down, I didn't believe that was how life worked, I still liked the *idea* of it. It was the right final chord.

I then spent the best part of an hour trying to choose between "Yours, as ever", "Yours, as always" (both too presumptuous/possessive?) and "Yours affectionately" – which just looked ridiculous. Eventually, I decided to opt for just "Kevin". Then I found a biro and wrote the whole letter out in the neatest italics I could manage. Finally, with my head thumping from mental exhaustion, I checked over my handiwork one last time. I was about to fold it and place it in the envelope when I heard Dougie behind my shoulder.

"You've forgotten to put your prisoner number," he said.

"Thanks for the reminder."

"My pleasure."

The sleeping turned out to be no fluke. For successive nights I got at least eight hours of profound, restorative sleep. My thinking continued to sharpen up and I began to prepare more and more effectively for the workshops, which gradually became productive.

For the first few sessions, I had just let people tell stories and then we would discuss them, rather haphazardly. It seemed best not to intimidate anyone with anything too structured. But then I decided to attempt a few basic acting exercises. I had no expectations. The likelihood was that they would all be crippled by self-consciousness. However, I could not have been more wrong.

Four of them, Dougie, Gerald, Pulse and Mohammad threw

themselves into the improvisations heart and soul. Dougie was a born performer (which, deep down, I suppose I already knew), fearlessly plunging into any set-up I lobbed his way, (apart from one, when I asked him to play the victim of a theft.)

Gerald, too, quickly revealed a talent for characterisation. He seemed able to instantly shape himself into someone else. And his characters all had a coherence to them, voice, mannerism, movement, language – everything seemed to fit together. In fact, it was depressing to realise that, purely by instinct, he was a much more accomplished actor than I could ever be.

He had a real flair for comedy, too. Time and again, in mid-improvisation, he would conjure up a line that was both killingly funny and yet still perfectly in character.

Pulse, also, had some talent. He could not think on his feet with Gerald's speed, but he had genuine stage presence. Even when he was doing very little in a scene, you could not tear your eyes away from him. And his bassy, rum-soaked voice seemed to give him extra substance. The man had charisma.

Mohammad, on the other hand, had no ability at all. What he did have in abundance, however, was commitment. Whatever situation he was supposed to be acting out, he attacked it as if his whole life depended on it. The result was that, usually, once Mohammad joined an improvisation, it was doomed to break down. I tried casting him in comic downbeat roles, but nothing worked. When he was the Funeral Director trying to explain to a bereaved relative that the deceased had been eaten by foxes, he somehow ended up ranting about the CIA. When everyone had to turn up at a party portraying a single characteristic I gave him "reasonableness". Five minutes later, he was shouting about compromise being Satan's gateway drug. He was pre-set for aggression and conflict, although mostly he just seemed at war with himself.

Quite often – both during improvisations and discussion – he would try to drag us towards the eternal truths of Islam. But he was invariably made to back off, either by Dougie's hardening stare or a withering put-down by Gerald. At all times, I did my best to stay neutral and steer us towards calmer waters.

The other two, Simo and Albie, watched from the sidelines. Simo, you sensed, wanted to join in but knew that he lacked the basic equipment. It is almost impossible to act, or to do anything for that matter, if you can't string any words together. So, mostly, he watched, waiting, desperately trying to manage his frustration; like some chaotic Labrador on a leash. But that's not to say he was getting nothing out of it. He got quite involved watching the improvisations develop and, every now and then, he would intervene in the discussions, and jagged splinters of sentences would fly around our ears like shrapnel.

The only real success I had with Simo, in those early weeks, was when I asked people to pair off and try to create a dialogue consisting entirely of animal noises. They each had to select which creature they were going to be. Simo chose to be a hyena, who spoke in loud yaps and screeches. Very convincingly. Even long after the improvisation had ended.

I had absolutely no success, however, with Albie. The only times he spoke were when he gave a quiet "no" in response to my questions. He wasn't surly, or sullen; most of the time he wore an awkward little smile. Occasionally, very occasionally, he would give a thin, breathy laugh when someone said something funny, although only if he saw others laughing first. For the vast majority of the time he sat, silent, in the corner, flicking phantom specks from his cheek.

Yet he was there for every session. Something was working for him. So who was I to question it? Provided it didn't affect the group – who seemed happy to tolerate him as a spectator – then there wasn't a problem, was there?

No, there wasn't a problem.

I had been running the drama workshop for about a month when I received an invitation to take tea with the governor.

"Greetings, Kevin," chirps Malcolm. "Look! In your honour, new china."

He is looking fit and tanned and seems more full of enthusiasm than ever.

"Been away?" I ask, as he pours.

"Costa Rica. Just a week. Amazing place. Wildlife everywhere. Lovely people, all highly educated. In 1948 they decided to scrap the army and plough all that money into education. And the upshot is that they're the only country in Central America that isn't a basket case, isn't that brilliant? Radical thinking, y'see."

"And have they been invaded?"

"Not yet." He lets out one of his trademark chuckles. "If anyone does invade they'll just have to chuck books at them. Ever been down that way yourself?"

"Nearest I've been is Cuba."

He widens his eyes. "Viva Castro."

"Yeah, I went there with my wife."

"Was it nice?"

"We drank in the bars Hemingway drank in. Which seemed to be all of them."

Malcolm laughs. "Drinking, bullfighting and swordfishing...he liked his hobbies, didn't he, eh?"

A rain shower starts to patter against the windows, so he glances up and gazes at the speckled pane, like a poet searching for inspiration.

"Now then, Kevin...it's like this...my wife works in publishing and she was glancing through a trade mag and she happened to spot a little piece about your old friend, Derek."

I feel my stomach clench. Jesus, what am I? One of Pavlov's dogs?

"What's he up to now?"

"Well...erm...it would seem that Derek is writing his autobiography."

I take in this news for a moment, but then I find I can't stop myself from laughing. Of course he is, why wouldn't he? Malcolm is laughing as well, shaking his head.

"I know, I know, what a ridiculous world, eh? Try the biscuits, they're homemade."

"Well, there's nothing I can do."

"Doesn't it bother you, then?"

"It'll be shit."

"That's beyond dispute."

"Full of the same old lies about me."

"But what if he makes up some new ones?"

Malcolm holds the plate of biscuits in front of me. I take one, as I try and work out what I feel about the possibility he's just raised. In fact, it's more like a certainty.

"Same problem," I say, "I can't stop him."

"W-e-ll, not strictly true...erm...legally you could demand to see the manuscript to ensure you're not being misrepresented..." He bites into his biscuit with a ludicrously loud crunch. It sounds like his teeth are being broken down into dust.

"...and then you'd be within your rights to ask for all the inaccurate passages to be removed."

"'Inaccurate passages'? That'll be the whole book."

"Well then you could take out an injunction. Sabotage the whole thing. That'd be fun." He giggles impishly. "Think how angry you'd make him."

I tip my head back and sigh most of the air out of my lungs.

"Yeh...but...well, it'd just be my version against his, wouldn't it...mostly..."

"And?"

"Well nobody's going to believe me. I'm the celebrity perjurer."

Malcolm furrows his brow.

"So...you just let Derek get away with as much as he wants? That's defeatism, Kevin...I didn't have you down as someone who throws the towel in."

What's he up to? Is he trying to manipulate me?

"Derek's screwed you over several times already. Are you going to let him do it again? And make money out of it?"

"I'd kind of promised myself that I'd never let that man back inside my head again...and this feels like letting him in."

"I understand that...look...take your time...mull it over."

He proffers the plate of biscuits again.

"Please, take some, or I'll end up eating them all. And they're full of butter, so, please, for the sake of my arteries..."

So I take one. He leans back and plonks his stockinged feet on the desk, as the squall chucks volleys of rain at the window.

"We've got a hosepipe ban where I am...my wife sneaks out in the middle of the night to water the garden."

He seagoons to himself for a few moments. Why am I still here?

"How's the drama workshop coming along?" he asks, breezily.

"Um...yeh, not bad, thanks."

"Any Laurence Oliviers?"

"Well, actually, Gerald is a surprisingly good actor."

"Not that surprising, he's a con-man. Takes considerable acting skill to convince three banks that you've got the ear of the Sultan of Brunei."

"Is that what he—?"

"On one occasion, yes."

"Right."

"I didn't tell you that, of course...I'm not supposed to discuss prisoners' criminal records with other prisoners."

"No, 'course not."

"What about the others?" he asks, brushing crumbs off his shirt, "Are they OK?"

"Well, I've got two who are a bit of a problem. There's Simo..."

"The lad who never finishes what he's saying?"

"Yes, he's challenging..."

Malcolm nods and smiles at the euphemism.

"...and then of course there's Albie...Paul."

"Oh yeh, how's he getting on?"

"Well, to be honest, he's just a presence, really. He makes no contribution."

Malcolm stares pensively at the desk. I sense an opportunity.

"Look, what exactly is the deal with Albie?"

He looks up, he's miles away. "Sorry?"

"Well, Albie said, at an early session, that he was participating in the workshop because you told him he had to, to boost his confidence prior to his release."

"That's right, yes. I'm not forcing him to attend though. You must be doing something right."

"I...I think he just likes the company."

"Uh-huh." He nods, his thoughts still elsewhere, somewhere full of shadows.

"So what's Albie's story? What's he in for? I know you're not supposed to discuss it but—"

"Housebreaking. He, er...he broke into a house, um, set off the burglar alarm and was still inside the house when the police arrived."

"Right...so, he's an incompetent burglar."

"Oh he knew what he was doing."

"I'm sorry, how do you mean, he knew what he—"

"He wanted to get caught. Just like the dozen or so previous releases where he got done for housebreaking."

"But why?"

"Albie prefers prison. Life outside scares him too much. Not uncommon. He's just a particularly chronic example. He's been re-incarcerating himself for the last seventeen years."

"Bloody hell."

"Bloody hell indeed. It would be brilliant if he could set himself free somehow, wouldn't it."

This conversation is beginning to worry me. Am I being co-opted on to some kind of Escape Committee? Malcolm sits forward, with that zealot's gleam in his eye.

"He just needs some help. To conquer his fears."

"Oh, I dunno." I shrug. "If that's the choice he's made then—"

"But he's never had a choice, Kevin. Not a real choice. Not since he was a boy – And, in many ways, that's what he still is."

He sits back in his chair in exasperation. "I mean if he ends up spending his whole life in prison, that's...well that's just a total waste...waste of his life...taxpayer's money...and I don't like waste, Kevin, I really don't."

I find myself wondering if it is a waste for someone with Malcolm's energy to be managing some shabby two-bit jailhouse. Oh no, here he comes again with the biscuits.

"Come on, Kevin, they need finishing."

He is a hard man to say no to. "All that we need is to give Albie...Alb— Paul...Paul...the confidence to face the outside."

"Oh, is that all?"

"It's worth a go, surely."

"Why's he so terrified?"

His expression darkens, and he starts to pick his way through an answer.

"Well, he was extremely unlucky. Fate ganged up on him...in a big way."

"Go on."

"See, Albie...Paul...is what used to be called ESN."

"Educationally sub-normal?"

"Yuh, and so life was always going to be a bit of an obstacle course for him but...well, his first crime...the one he got sent down for..."

"What did he do?"

Malcolm looks at me intensely for a few moments and I start to experience a tremor of foreboding.

"I...I really can't tell you, Kevin...that would be...I can't take the risk...for his sake and...well, for everyone's sake..."

My God, this is starting to sound grim.

"...all I'll say is that...he was only sixteen and there were millions of mitigating factors that the judge took into account, which is why he gave a comparatively light sentence for an offence...of that seriousness."

My imagination starts to run away with me.

"You might as well tell me. I can always ask one of the prisoners, they're bound to know."

"No, no, I'm pretty sure they don't...not yet at least. The original case was dealt with using great discretion; Paul pleaded guilty, and it was done and dusted before the media could go to town so...and it was seventeen years ago."

"Well, what if they find out?"

"...Then he'd have to move prisons. He's seen lots of prisons already."

In the silence that follows, sunlight starts to illuminate the rain-streaked windows.

"And this...crime," I begin, "is the reason he's so terrified of everything?"

Malcolm thrusts the plate forward one more time. "Last biccy. Take it, go on."

"You'd make a great Jewish mother."

His shoulders heave as he giggles.

"Yes, I would...Do you remember the Furies?"

"Rock band?"

"No, Greek mythology. They harried their victims every day, as a punishment, for transgressing against divine law, driving them mad in the process. That's what Paul's up against – he's trying to hide from the Furies. I think he needs help to turn and face them."

For the first time I realise how dangerous a man Malcolm might be. He's a romantic, and they can wreak more havoc than hurricanes.

"I'm not a social worker," I tell him, as I polish off one last biscuit.

14

THE SCOTTISH PLAY

One of my trips to the library triggered a brainwave. I found a DVD of Polanski's film of Macbeth, so I checked it out and showed it to the group. It's far from being a masterpiece and, at first, it prompted quite a lot of lewd heckling. But, gradually, the story took hold and they fell quiet.

As the final credits spool past, I ask them for any first impressions.

Pulse laughs and shakes his head. "Man, those old bitches saw him coming. They burnt his arse good."

Simo wades in, agreeing with Pulse. It's a bit hard to follow his argument as it's expressed in a machine-gun fire of fractured obscenities, but his gist seems to be that the whole tragedy was the fault of the old hags and that Macbeth had a knife so he should have just shanked them.

"But what about Macbeth?" I ask. "The blame lies with him, doesn't it? He's the master of his own destiny, surely?"

"Abso-fucking-lutely," nods Dougie. "It annoyed me when he started whingeing about all the blood and the ghost coming to dinner and everything. If you can't do the time, don't do the crime."

I try to prise an observation out of Albie, but the only critique he offers is that the wife isn't a very nice person.

"Tasty, though," adds Pulse. "Ve-ry tasty."

I start to explain the various theories about tragedy, probing them for what they think is Macbeth's fatal flaw. Mohammad says Macbeth's weakness is that he turns away from God, so God destroys him, just as he will destroy the Americans.

"Is it ambition?" I ask. "Is that the aspect of his character that destroys him?"

"Yup, definitely," says Dougie. "I mean we've all been there, haven't we? We all want to be top dog. That's just human nature. But there's a line, isn't there. A line you don't cross. Y'know, I mean, you don't go around stabbing kings while they're asleep, that's just mental."

Pulse argues that it's sex that powers Macbeth. Clearly, him and Lady Macbeth have got some heavy sex-vibe going and she uses it to manipulate him. Simo starts shouting about evil, e-vil, the old bitches are e-vil and Macbeth should def-initely have shanked them.

"End of story. End of— no old bitches— no story."

Pulse weighs back in and soon the three of them, Pulse, Simo and Dougie are talking animatedly over each other, until I have to step in and ask them to keep the volume down. Then I find myself waxing lyrical about Shakespeare.

"What is so fantastic is that you have all watched this story and you've all taken something different from it. It's touched you in different ways. Even though it's written in verse, in an old kind of English, it still reaches us. And it's exciting, and dynamic and gripping, but it's also ambiguous and complex...and dense..."

I continue to talk in this vein and, as I talk, a different part of my brain starts to monitor what I'm saying. After a few moments, I realise I'm experiencing a feeling that I had assumed was long dead. This is enthusiasm. I am being enthusiastic. How long since that happened? There's no trace of irony, there's energy in my voice as I try to convey the wonders and the plasticity of language that make Shakespeare a genius. It feels invigorating. And I seem to be cutting through – they all look interested and engaged, apart from Gerald, who is peeling flaky paint off a windowsill.

"Gerald, what's your take on Macbeth?"

He gazes at the ceiling for a few moments. "My take is the only take."

"Well I think we've already seen that Shakespeare's tragedy is subtle enough to support lots of interpretations."

Gerald sighs. "There is no tragedy. It's all pre-ordained."

"Yeh, by Allah," adds Mohammad.

Gerald gives him a pained smile. "Duncan is doomed from the start."

"Once the witches trick Macbeth." Now Pulse receives the same smile as Mohammad.

"Duncan's doomed from before that. From before page one," says Gerald, very matter-of-fact.

"How come?" asks Simo.

"Because Macbeth's a killer," Gerald replies. "Pure and simple. He's a killer. He's decided to kill Duncan from before the play even begins."

Dougie takes issue with this. "Nah, nah, look at how he reacts, he's got a conscience, there's tons of guilt."

"There's tons of self-dramatisation and sentimentality," counters Gerald, flicking some flakes of paint to the floor. "No, the witches are an irrelevance. So is the wife."

I point out how, in Shakespeare's time, there was a genuine belief in witches being sent from Hell to entrap and destroy people.

"Then why doesn't he 'shank' them, as Simo so eloquently suggested? If they're such a danger. No, he listens because they tell him what deep down he's already decided. Duncan is kaput. Macbeth is a killer. Shakespeare understands that. It's just that most of his audience are too stupid to." He gives us all a little smile. "There is no tragedy. Just banal inevitability. Sorry, folks."

"So, let me just check I've got this right, Gerald." I pause to see if he'll stop picking at the paint. He doesn't. "You're saying that we are all pre-programmed. That nobody is capable of change."

"I think this place proves that."

"…and that Shakespeare knew that, and you know it, but the rest of us are too mired in stupidity to understand it."

Gerald gives a chuckle and flares his eyes. "Give that man a coconut," he sniggers.

I think Gerald may be a psychopath.

"Lady Macbeth changes," Dougie points out, "she's a bitch without a conscience, then, hey presto, she's a bitch who can't sleep 'cos her conscience is sending her doollally."

"That's a very good point." Dougie looks pleased with my compliment. "Lady Macbeth demonstrates that people can surprise you."

Gerald stares at the ceiling for a few moments as he weighs up this counter-argument.

"Shakespeare probably wrote that bit just so that she got punished. Bad women always have to be punished, don't they? First rule of our culture."

"You're saying Shakespeare wrote something he didn't believe?" I ask.

"He was just delivering what society expected of him. Most people do that."

A thin smile twitches across Gerald's lips. Pulse starts another branch of discussion about the link between tragedy and hot women, but time is up, so I end the session and we fold the chairs away as Pulse reminisces about a stripper who led to his downfall in Montego Bay.

One morning – it might have been a week later, maybe more – I received a letter from a TV company that called itself Going Forward Productions. I know, my reaction as well. I nearly didn't bother reading any further. They said they had heard about my drama group (how?) and that they felt it would make a fascinating documentary. They stressed that the documentary would be a serious study of how people in the darkest circumstances can still embody the human spirit. They used the word "narrative" several times. And "uplifting". And "synergy". I scanned the letter once more to check I had understood it and then I threw it in the bin.

Then I picked it out of the bin, tore it into tiny pieces and threw them back in the bin. I didn't want Dougie to read that.

I showed the group a succession of DVDs of Shakespeare plays. They were riveted by Julius Caesar, Coriolanus, Hamlet, but they struggled with King Lear, who they felt was irritating and deserved everything he got.

One morning, with the stink of stewing cabbage filling the room, we are halfway through watching Othello – which Gerald claims should be called Iago – when the very skinny warden, Stewart (strange, how much better I've become at remembering names) slides into the room and raises his arm to get my attention.

"Yes, Stewart, can we help you?"

"The governor wants to see you."

"OK, we're nearly finished."

"No, I think he wants to see you now."

When I step into Malcolm's office he is on the phone, sounding stressed. I sit quietly and wait for a few minutes while he argues with someone about the difference between investment and overspend. Eventually, he hangs up and gives me a tense smile.

"Welcome to my world," he says. "I'm all out of biscuits, I'm afraid."

He stretches his arms and folds them behind his head.

"I got a phone call from Going Forward Productions. You didn't respond to their letter."

"Well I did respond to it, actually. I chucked it in the bin. It was bullshit."

"Yes I know." He sees that I'm puzzled. "I got virtually the same letter. Lots of 'synergy'." He flourishes the letter for a moment, with a weary sigh.

"Like I said, it's bullshit," I say, falling on the word "bullshit".

"Yes it is bullshit, but it could be helpful bullshit."

"What?"

"A programme like this could show the prison in a positive light. Good PR could help us. If we become a showcase prison, then it's easier to ask for a showcase budget. A bigger budget means everyone's lives – prisoners', staff's, everyone's lives get a little easier."

"Oh come on, you know why they're interested. They're not interested in my drama group, they just want to gawp at me."

"Oh, so it's your drama group, is it?"

"No, that's not what I—"

"It's all about you."

"I didn't say that I—"

"Don't you feel that maybe you should put the offer to the group, see what they think?" I get a strong impression that Malcolm is playing me, although he is very hard to read.

"I don't want to be…gazed at by the public any more, they've had enough pieces of me. I'm done with that circus. I just want to be left in peace."

"Are you sure? I think you could come out of it very well. It could show the real you."

"Isn't the 'real' me a woman-hitter and a perjurer?"

He tosses his arms up in exasperation. "Well, what about the others? They might get something out of the experience."

"I very much doubt it."

"Well, I think it's sad you're not even giving it any considered thought, it's – you're starting to achieve something – a small something, possibly – but…well, you can't just go on assuming that the whole world is trying to stitch you up."

He is rubbing his forehead now, as if he's trying to stir his brain into finding some magic compromise. I decide to put him out of his misery.

"Can I go now?"

It took a few weeks for me to pluck up the courage; but in the end, I decided I would just blurt out my idea and see what happened.

They are all clustered round the tea urn, laughing at a joke Dougie's just told about a parrot that is rescued from a brothel. Even Albie is laughing. The atmosphere feels good; this seems like the right moment.

"How about we do a performance?"

The chatter stops and they are all staring at me, so I feel obliged to carry on. "A show. Not a big one, something small-scale. Something simple." They are still staring. "I just thought it would be nice for us to have a goal. Something to work towards."

"What kind of performance?" asks Pulse, with a challenging bob of the head.

"Well, that's for the group to decide, obviously, we'd all have to agree."

"With an audience," checks Dougie.

"Yeh, but the audience can be small. Very small if you like."

I notice that Albie is getting fidgety. Simo also seems a little agitated.

"Like— y'know, the— I mean— what…"

"What could we do?" I prompt.

"Yeh."

"Whatever we can agree on."

"No plays," says Mohammad. "And no Christian shit."

"We can keep religion out of it. We could write a piece of our own if you like."

There is a rapid ripple of head-shaking, "that sounds like a lot of work" seems to be the consensus.

"Alright then, we can do excerpts from things."

"Not Shakespeare," says Dougie. "Too much to learn."

I begin to wonder if I should have started down this road. I had forgotten how lazy criminals are. That's how most of them end up as criminals, they can't resist a short-cut.

Gerald, languid as ever, raises a finger.

"Small point. I think it's futile for us to attempt anything that involves too much co-operation."

"A show made up of solo pieces, then. Y'know, Dougie, you could do that song from My Fair Lady that you like, and maybe even a bit of a scene from it. Pulse, you could do a rap or—"

"Oh right, I'm black, so I do a rap, is that it?"

"No, I—"

"The black boy better not attempt nothing that's not black."

"That was just an ex—"

"Maybe I'll do some Pinter."

"Pinter?"

"Yuh, why not? I can do pausing, there's a lot of pausing, isn't there, I can do that."

"Which Pinter piece do you think you'd like to do, Pulse?"

"I dunno, I'll have to read some first."

I back off. Mohammad wades in.

"I could act out the story of how the Israelis faked 9/11."

Dougie mutters something ominous.

"Historical's good," I say, trying not to sound patronising, "but maybe that's a little...y'know..."

"It's anti-Semitic," says Gerald.

"And bollocks," adds Dougie.

"Or schmollocks, as you Jews say." Mohammad giggles, he's pleased with that.

"I'm not Jewish, you little cunt." Dougie takes a step towards

Mohammad and I yell the first thing that comes into my head.

"Dance! There's always dance! It's a good medium…for people who can move. Simo, I've seen you throwing some shapes."

He sets off around the room, kick-boxing invisible opponents.

"What about some pieces based on personal experience? Stories from people's childhoods, stuff like that."

Albie is staring at the floor, looking paler than ever.

"Albie? Are you in?"

"None of us are 'in'," drawls Gerald, "we haven't taken a vote on it yet, beloved leader. Or hadn't you noticed yet?"

I sense that now is not the time to force it. "Why don't we all take a day or two to think it over?" I propose.

"I'm not doing no rap," mutters Pulse.

When we take the vote a few days later, the mood has swung significantly in favour of doing some kind of performance. There are a few provisos. Nobody wants an audience of more than forty prisoners and Dougie insists that it can't include any terrorists or paedos.

The only person who makes no contribution to the discussion is Albie, who sits to one side, flicking imaginary nuisances away from his face.

"You're very quiet, Paul."

He just shrugs.

"Do you fancy doing a show?" I ask.

"If people want to, that's fine. I'll watch."

"That seems a shame."

"I'm…I'm not…I can't perform…not in front of…sorry."

"I could do something with you, maybe…if that's any help."

"I'm no good at acting." He is pulling at one of his eyebrows now, as if it is annoying him.

"Can you sing?"

He leaves his eyebrow alone and looks at me. Well, nearly at me.

"...Erm...I used to."

"Used to?"

"Before—" He stops himself. "Before all this. I was in the church choir."

"Oh...right."

Mohammad says something about how churches will all be gone soon, but nobody bothers to listen.

"Well you could sing in the show, that'd be fine."

"I...I don't sing now."

"Why not?"

"...I never feel like it."

He is clamming shut again, so I take a gamble.

"What's your favourite hymn?"

"...Sorry?"

"When you were in the choir, what was your favourite hymn?"

"Erm...'Dear Lord and Father of Mankind'."

Mohammad kicks off about how Allah is the one true God, until Pulse and Dougie tell him he's about to have his jaw broken.

"Let's sing it now...you and me."

Albie is looking straight at me – direct eye contact.This is a first. "Come on, you and me...I'll start if you like...see how much of it I can remember."

With Albie watching me, transfixed, I launch into the first verse, singing firmly but not too loud, so that he'll feel free to join in. But it doesn't seem to be working. I am already through the first verse and he is just standing, frozen to the spot.

Then, as I begin the line, "Drop thy still dews of quietness", Albie lifts his head and begins to sing. As we complete the next line – "Till all thy strivings cease" – I peter to a halt, because Albie has one of the most beautiful male voices I have ever heard. It's a light, effortless liquid tenor that is slowly filling the room. And he looks like a different person. He's no longer that sickly ghost, he's standing tall, with his chest out, and his face illuminated by expression; he is transported.

He doesn't seem to notice that I'm no longer singing, nor that hardened criminals are staring at him rapt in wonder. Even Gerald is impressed, nodding, with his eyebrows raised in acknowledgement of that talent, pure talent, that makes you feel enriched and inadequate at the same time. As Albie reaches the section about letting sense be dumb and flesh retire, you can feel the electricity in the room. Then he drops to pianissimo for the final couplet of "O still, small voice of calm" and it's as if he is casting a spell.

As the last note is still shimmering through the air, Albie breaks into an awkward little smile. There is an awed silence; grown men, struck dumb.

"Fuck me, Albie," says Dougie, "have you swallowed an angel?"

Albie laughs – genuinely laughs!

"How long since you last sang?" I ask.

"Dunno…long…long time."

Pulse shakes his head. "That's a terrible waste, man. Terrible, terrible waste." Simo steps forward and tries to congratulate Albie, but the emotion scrambles his words and thoughts too much. I hold Albie by both shoulders.

"Has no one ever told you you've got a beautiful voice?"

He shrugs. "When I was little maybe."

"What about at school?"

"Erm…I went to special school…they only seemed bothered about all the things I couldn't do."

"Well take it from me, from us, you've got an exceptional voice, you've got to do something in the show, *please*."

He thinks for a few moments.

"Do I have to do a hymn?"

"You sing whatever you fucking like, fella," Dougie chuckles. "Fucking opera, fucking show tunes…"

Albie stares at the floor for a few moments.

"I…I quite like the Everly Brothers."

"I fucking *love* the Everly Brothers!" exclaims Dougie.

"…my dad used to sing them."

"So did mine!"

"Then do an Everly Brothers song, Albie," I urge him. I'm patting his shoulders now. "That'd be brilliant."

But then he starts to shrink.

"I dunno…me in front of other people, I…" The face-flicking has started again, "Best not, I think."

I can't let him fade away, not now, I hunt for a solution.

"How about a duet?"

The prison psychiatrist remained keen for us to continue our sessions. I had managed to use the Drama Group as an excuse for a couple of weeks, but, in the end, I calculated that I would give less cause for concern if I just bit the bullet and went to see him. Part of me still worried, I suppose, that he might have me down as a psychopath.

The session is very like the others. He asks questions – most of them fatuous – while he plays with his hair. But, gradually, I realise that something has changed. When he runs his fingers through his locks, I am no longer experiencing any inner rage. Previously, I would be directing mental heckles at him all the time, little spits of hatred, but now he isn't getting to me at all. I don't feel warm towards him, but I no longer want to smash his head against the wall. I feel calm, and although his questions seem no more intelligent than before, I find that I'm not so sensitised to them.

"Do you like yourself?" he asks, out of nowhere.

"'Like' myself?"

"Yes, would you say you like yourself?"

"Erm…I…don't 'like' or 'dislike' myself…I just…accept myself as a fact."

He bends down and fiddles with the laces of one of his desert boots.

"As a fact?"

"Yuh."

"Do you see yourself as a good person?"

"No…no, I'm capable of being good…sometimes I am good, or can do good, but I also know that I'm very flawed and weak and unreliable."

"Bad?"

"Sometimes, yes."

"Do you think you're unfeeling?"

I pause to choose my words.

"That's impossible for me to know, without knowing what other people feel. I'd need a comparison."

"That's a careful answer."

"It's an honest one."

"Do you see yourself as an honest person?"

It would be ridiculous for me to answer "yes", he is itching to mention that I'm a perjuror, I can sense it.

"Clearly not," I reply.

"So, you lie."

"Yes."

"To yourself?"

"Probably, but then we all do that to a certain extent, don't we?" For a moment, I am very tempted to point out that his lustrous shock of hair looks like him lying to himself about his age, but then I let it go. There is no point being a smartarse today.

"When was the last time you cried, Kevin?"

I puff my cheeks and try to think back. I had felt moved when Albie started singing, but I hadn't cried tears.

"Actually cried?"

"Actually cried," he repeats.

I had been upset during Sandra's last visit, but I couldn't

remember weeping. When I do finally work out when it was, I let out an involuntary chuckle.

"What's so funny?" he asks.

"Well...erm...the last time I cried actual tears was...um... lying in my bunk, thinking about someone who I barely knew and who I'd always regarded as a pain in the arse."

"Go on."

So, to my surprise, I tell him the whole story about Gavin, his death and how odd it felt to have been so upset.

"Do you think you were crying for someone else?" he asks.

"Probably." I shrug. "It couldn't have been for him, that would make no sense."

He stares out of the window for a few moments.

"Your voice sounds different," he tells me.

"Really?"

"Yes, not the same cut to it. Before, there was always an edge of...of latent aggression...like you wanted to smash my head in."

"Oh, right." I laugh, in a way that I hope sounds relaxed. He laughs as well, but only to be sociable. A glance at his watch and then he hops to his feet.

"I'll leave the date of our next session up to you, Kevin," he announces. "Just make an appointment if and when you feel the need."

"Thank you," I say. "You've been a lot of help."

"Good," he replies.

He couldn't spot a lie if it bit him on the nose.

15

THE GROUP DECISION

It was an inspired idea. I know that sounds smug but I don't care, it was inspired, the duet was the best idea I'd had in God knows how long.

Albie and Dougie's voices combined very well. Dougie's solid, tuneful bass provided a good anchorage in the harmonies, while Albie's voice…well it just kept getting better and better. Over the next few days, his confidence continued to grow.

I managed to borrow a battered upright piano from the staff recreation room and a pianist, Norton, from 'C' Block. The others tell me he used to play for a Shirley Bassey tribute drag act. He doesn't seem to want to talk about it. In fact, he barely talks at all. If the dueting continues to go well I might try to convince Albie he should do a solo.

There are no doubts in my mind that their duet will be a showstopper. The only question is which song to choose. For their own amusement, they keep breaking into Everly Brothers numbers. Their rendition of "Let It Be Me" is outstanding, but Dougie makes it crystal clear that he is not singing any love-songs with another man, onstage, in front of people he will subsequently have to face at meal-times.

"They'll take the piss, I'll lose it, it'll end in fractures." He informs me. "Then they'll chuck me in the box and you could end up with a nutter for a room-mate."

I can see Gerald sniggering with his eyes.

"Any suggestions for a song for Albie and Dougie?" I ask the group.

Gerald suggests "Goldfinger", but only to wind up Norton.

"Du-ets. Think duets."

The suggestions start to come thick and fast.

"'You've Lost That Loving Feeling'."

"'I Know Him So Well'."

"'No True Love Ways'."

"'Close To You'."

"Dougie would prefer something non-romantic," I remind them.

"'Ebony and Ivory'," exclaims Pulse.

Dougie scowls. "Not singing wet stuff about racial harmony. Also, I can't stand McCartney, he held John Lennon back."

"'It's In His Kiss'?" offers Mohammad, but then he spots Dougie's expression. "OK, sorry, no, forgot."

Norton mutters something that I don't quite catch.

"Sorry, Norton, what?"

"'Bridge Over Troubled Water'," he monotones.

"That's not a bad idea. Boys?"

Dougie is pulling a face. "I'm not a muso, but isn't that fucking difficult?"

"Albie will take the top line."

"Yeh, I know but—"

"Albie, you up for that?"

"Erm...yeh, think so."

"It'd make a great finale."

Dougie is still grimacing.

"Tell you what, have a go with Norton, see how you get on. We can always find something else if you're not happy."

I quickly clear out, taking the others to a side-room where we can go through their ideas for the show. To my surprise, Pulse wants to do an excerpt from Shakespeare.

"Weren't expecting that, eh, man?" he laughs. "Now there's a bit of that lib-er-al discomfort going on."

"No, it's great, really great, what bit where you thinking of?"

"Macbeth."

"How much of Macbeth?"

"Just the bit where they've told him that his bitch-wife is dead and he says that life is a story told by an idiot. 'Tomorrow and tomorrow and tomorrow'."

"Why did you choose that?"

"Because it'll sound great in a Jamaican accent."

He's right of course. But I'm still curious.

"It must be more than that."

"I like the way he tells us everything is pointless. We're born, we have our troubles, we die. He nails it."

"OK...um...it's not that long a speech, do you want to do something else? Something more modern maybe, or something you write for yourself?"

"I'll think about it."

Simo tells me, eventually, that he's expanding his dance idea.

"How long's it going to be?" I ask.

His reply is a jerky fusillade of stops and starts, but from what I can gather it involves a polar bear. I decide to wait and see what he comes up with. Mohammad announces that he is writing some poetry that he intends to perform. And then I turn to Gerald, who is looking very pleased with himself. He has already written one piece that he'd like to do, in fact, he's prepared to read it to us now. It turns out to be a twenty-minute dramatic monologue about an embezzler who is judged by his intellectual inferiors. I ask Gerald if he's thinking of editing it down. He looks at me as if I am a curiosity in a museum.

"Edit it down?"

"Yes...just shorten it a bit."

"No, I don't think so, every word is perfect."

* * *

A few days later, with the show slowly beginning to take shape, I find myself back in the governor's office. He seems genuinely thrilled that Albie has found his voice. He congratulates me repeatedly and tries to force-feed me biscuits.

"Had to buy them with my own money. Go on, they're buttery."

"No, I'm fine, honestly."

"Worrying about your figure?"

"Not on prison food."

"We do the best we can for the money."

He reaches across the desk and picks up a letter.

"I got a follow-up today from Going Forward Productions."

I shift in my seat, not this again, I've said no.

"I just wondered if you might have reconsidered at all," he floats.

"There's nothing to reconsider. I'm not prepared to be filmed."

"Ah, right, so it's still all about you then."

That's not getting a response. I know what he's up to. He leans forward, elbows on the desk.

"What about the others? You've got prisoners who are going to recite Shakespeare, read out poems they've written, original work, you've got a virtual mute to sing...these men are making commitments, going out on a limb...backing themselves...don't you feel it'd be good if the world saw that...saw that you don't just give up on people..."

"They'd turn it into a freak show. They'll just treat us as commodities, I know these people, they commodify everything."

"I'm sure we can guard against the freak-show risk in the contract. Insist on final approval, that kind of thing."

I go quiet again, he's working me, I know he is.

"Honestly, Kevin, I don't know why you're so reticent about

letting this achievement be recorded. The Parole Board would chalk it up, I'm sure a programme like this could reflect very well on you."

He's beaming benevolently at me now, like he's some kind of friendly priest, Spencer Tracy maybe.

"It could reflect very well on you too," I counter.

"Yes, all right, you got me, I'd do well out of it too, this place would do well, everybody wins. So, is there really a problem?"

I reiterate that I'm not interested.

"Don't you feel you should at least put it to the group? Don't you owe them that?"

"I don't 'owe' them, or you, or anyone."

And with that, I rise to make a dignified exit, pausing only to take a biscuit. As I head down the stairs, I experience an old, familiar wave of anger against TV types who are too egotistical and infantile to listen.

The ambush came out of nowhere.

Our sessions had been continuing to go well and I had managed to persuade the group that we should do a number from Guys and Dolls – "Sit Down You're Rocking the Boat", which we were going to sing ensemble. The show was beginning to take on a more balanced look, with a mixture of old favourites and experimental material. The most enthusiastic participant by far was Dougie, so I am really not at all prepared when he storms into rehearsals in an extremely aggressive mood.

"I want a fucking word," he begins. "Sit down." He pushes me down into a chair and leans a long way into my personal space, virtually nose to nose.

"Now then, Kev, is there anything you'd like to share with the group?"

I am genuinely bewildered, which comes across as bad acting and incenses Dougie even more.

"Any fucking thing at all?" he shouts, "Cast your mind back."

I'm still at a loss as to how I could have upset him so much.

"You had a letter from some TV people."

How had he heard about that?

"They wanted to make a TV programme about us."

I spend a couple of moments composing myself, controlling my tone and carefully choosing my words.

"Well...with respect, Dougie, the programme would have been about me."

"Oh 'cos we're not interesting enough to make programmes about, is that it?"

"No, no, what I'm saying is they...you know what they're like, they're celebrity-obsessed, it would end up being...y'know... 'Lenny' behind bars. They couldn't give a toss about any drama group."

"So why the secrecy?"

"It wasn't secrecy, the—"

"Why didn't you share it with the group?"

"It was addressed to me, so—"

"But it concerned the group."

"Yes, but—"

"So why not share it with the group?"

"Because it didn't seem relevant to—"

"So now we're irrelevant?"

"No, you— look, I'm sorry if you feel I didn't involve you but I know what these people are like – they're leeches. And the ones who aren't leeches are vultures."

"Man, thank God you were here to protect us," Pulse gets closer too, "protect us from that menagerie."

"The letter was addressed to me."

"Stop fucking saying that."

Dougie takes a deep breath, the way the anger management people told him to. "The thing is, Kevin, you could have relayed the gist of the letter, advised us as to your judgement and that, and then let us take a vote on it."

"Oh, are we a socialist collective now? How jolly."

"Shut your face-hole, Gerald."

I try to take control.

"Listen, the last thing the people in this group need is TV cameras pointing at them." I give a subtle nod in Albie's direction, to try and make Dougie understand. Simo bursts into life. I think he's trying to say that the TV cameras wouldn't bother him. Albie is staring at his old friend, the floor.

"Albie…" He doesn't look up. "Albie, do you want someone filming you?"

Mohammad weighs in. "Well I don't mind being filmed. If it gets my message across to more people."

"And what is your 'message'?" scoffs Gerald. "Don't be a wanker."

Mohammad pushes him in the chest and a scuffle breaks out, until Dougie plucks the two of them apart.

"All right, ladies, let's remain civilised. I say we take a vote on it."

"What's the point? I've said no."

"Oh, Emperor Kevin's said no."

"Well—"

"He outranks us."

"I—"

"I'm not sure I want to be part of something this undemocratic," growls Dougie.

The others mutter their agreement. My mind drifts back to those first nights in the cell, when Dougie would grill me about what it's like to be famous. That's what all this is about. He wants to be on TV. So does Mohammad and Simo and Gerald. They all fancy the attention. But Albie is different. He hates it if one person is looking at him, never mind a million.

"Paul, this is important, would you be happy to have TV cameras come in and film you...film you for millions of people to see?"

Oh no, disaster. He's looking towards Dougie for guidance.

"...only you can answer this", I ask.

"Are you saying it'd be too much for him?" asks Dougie.

"I—"

"Another one underestimating you, don't listen to him, Pauly, you'd be fine."

"Paul-y?" What the fuck is that? Now Dougie has a meaty arm around his new friend's shoulder. "Let's put it to a vote."

"I haven't agreed to a vote yet."

"Let's vote on whether to have a vote. All those in favour." Five arms get raised.

"Carried. And now who wants to do the TV programme, as long as it's uplifting and not sensationalist shit?" The same five arms are raised. Albie looks to Dougie for reassurance. Dougie gives him a piratical smile. Slowly, Albie raises a skeletal arm.

"Six – nil. The Emperor stands alone."

"How did you get to hear about the letter, Dougie?" I ask.

"I can't betray my sources."

"If I duck out, you watch, there'll be no TV show. They won't come."

Dougie gives a wolfish smile. "Well then stop being a selfish prick and don't duck out."

I protest that I'm not being a selfish prick, but this is greeted by laughter, so I storm out. I seem to be doing a lot of that all of a sudden.

I spent the next few hours pondering one of the great philosophical questions. Am I a selfish prick? History would suggest I am. But then isn't the human race just billions of selfish pricks? Or is that just the view of a selfish prick?

To be honest, the rebellion had happened so suddenly that I found it hard to take in. The whole project seemed to disintegrate in a couple of minutes. I had felt I had been achieving something and now that feeling was gone. I was bereft.

But slowly, reluctantly, I began to see what the others were seeing. Perhaps I *was* being egocentric. My assumption that a documentary would be an excuse for the cameras to ghoulishly stare at me was probably way out of date. I had been in prison for a while now. The character of Lenny had long since died in a mysterious fire, off-screen, in Afghanistan. How interesting did I imagine I was any more? Soon, I would just be a nostalgic footnote. Maybe there'd been some honesty behind the bullshit of that letter. Maybe they were looking to make a serious documentary. And if they were, why shouldn't the others get their chance to step into the spotlight and tell their stories? Maybe I'd let my suspicion and arrogance shape my actions. Dougie had a point. Why *did* I have to be so secretive? I could have told them about it. But I've always felt I know best, always, in all my dealings. In my mind, I've always outranked people.

In the end, the decision made itself, it coalesced into a pleasing shape. I would let it go, trust the process, trust in others. I would ask for an appointment to see the governor – an appointment for the whole group.

A few days later I am sitting in Malcolm's office waiting for the others.

"They're always late," I explain. "God knows why, it's not like they have busy diaries."

I decide to get the elephant out of the room.

"Did you tell Dougie about the TV company's approach?"

Malcolm makes piercing eye-contact.

"No. I did not." He maintains the eye-contact. (Is this some kind of technique? Oh for God's sake, I'm doing it again.) "But you know what this place is like for gossip, people are in and out of this office all the time, and various members of my staff would have seen the letter to me...and the follow-up, so...I've no plans to launch an enquiry."

I'm not sure if I believe him, but I decide that it no longer matters. The others are filing in now, Albie sits about as far away from Malcolm's desk as is possible. Malcolm doesn't sit behind his desk, he perches on the edge of it, like one of those teachers who likes you to call them by their first name.

"All right, team, now, as you know, Kevin has some...qualms, um...reservations, understandable reservations, given how the media have treated him...that if we let these cameras in to film the drama group, then the whole thing could turn into a bit of a circus and he – and you – and all of us...could end up getting...um..."

"Royally fucked," says Dougie.

"Yes...that's...pretty much what he's worried about. And I'm concerned too. But I also think there are so many possible positives to be gained, so this is an opportunity for us to air the whole topic. So, the floor is yours. Who'd like to start, any questions?"

Mohammad's arm shoots up. He is wearing his pouty, belligerent face.

"Would we be censored?"

"Well that would depend, I suppose, on the kind of thing you say."

"What if I foretell a global caliphate? Is that OK?"

Malcolm looks unsure.

"Erm...well obviously there are laws about—"

"Laws made by *man*."

"Yes but—"

Gerald intervenes, "I think the legal situation is that you *would* be allowed to 'foretell' a global caliphate, but you wouldn't be allowed to advocate moving towards that caliphate by overthrowing the state and/or killing people."

"Thank you, Gerald. Maybe we shouldn't get bogged down on this, any other questions?"

"Would we get paid?" asks Mohammad.

"I've no idea," Malcolm replies, "that's something that I suppose would get thrashed out in the contract...if we get that far."

Dougie proposes that we stop pussying around and that I should shit or get off the pot.

Malcolm holds his hands up – palms outwards like the Pope – to signify calm.

"Kevin, what are your main concerns?"

"Well two really. One, that there'll be a...um...a focus...a mawkish focus on me and my past – at the expense of the group. And two – and I think this is a very real risk – that once the cameras are here they'll go on a fishing mission, looking for salacious material...and three, how do we stop them distorting things? Once they get into the edit they can make us look however they want. They can make us all look stupid."

I can see the wheels turning inside Dougie and Gerald's heads. They clearly don't relish the prospect of not having control.

"Also, will they handle the material sensitively? For instance, take Paul..." Albie straightens up slightly at the sound of his name. "...he's not great with strangers. Will they treat him seriously? Or will they just treat him as a funny turn, a quirky character?"

I feel a little insensitive talking about Albie this way with him in the room, but I want to spell out the risks. "TV likes to laugh at people. And it doesn't hang around to pick up the pieces."

Malcolm furrows his brow.

"True, very true, Kevin. On the other hand, it can be inspiring and uplifting. Look at that series they did about that school in Yorkshire. Here's an idea," Malcolm stands up, energised, "why don't we get these fellas in and give them the once over, eh? See what we make of them. And if we're minded to proceed, we can lay down some parameters."

Simo doesn't know what parameters are.

"Boundaries. We can tell them that certain things are off-limits. But we'll do it face-to-face. And if we don't like the look of them, fine. On the other hand, if they seem straight enough... well, it'd be a shame for TV audiences not to hear Albie sing, wouldn't it?"

Albie grins sheepishly. Mohammad starts performing one of his poems for Malcolm, but Malcolm's PA sticks her head round the door to remind him he's late for something. She's a very good PA.

We googled "Going Forward Productions" and found that most of their documentaries had titles that ended in exclamation marks. But, when we watched the actual programmes, they weren't that bad. Even the one about annoyingly passive, ludicrously obese people (Fat and Furious!) managed to maintain a reasonably sympathetic tone. So it was agreed that we should proceed with a meeting.

The execs came to see us, Julian and Michelle. The whole group attended, with Malcolm acting as chairman. Julian was affable and articulate, while Michelle said very little, probably because most of the group (apart from me) kept staring at her legs. They were trying desperately hard not to, but somehow that just made the whole situation feel even more embarrassing. I wanted to explain to her that they didn't mean to be intimidating, but I couldn't work out how that explanation would start.

Julian laid out, in broad terms, how they pictured the documentary, which was – guess what – people going on a journey. He saw it as an uplifting piece of television. I itemised my concerns and eventually, after about forty minutes of discussion, Malcolm came up with five conditions which they would have to accept as part of the contract:

1) There would be no detailed reference to the sequence of events that led to my being in prison;

2) I would do no solo pieces to camera;

3) I would be on screen for no more than ten per cent of the programme;

4) They could only film rehearsals when it had been agreed beforehand;

5) We would have final approval on the edited programme.

The fact that they conceded so easily on the last point did make me wonder if they were serious programme-makers, but we had got what I wanted and Malcolm felt any "qualms" had been addressed, so we all shook hands and they said they'd be back to start filming in two weeks.

When they came back, Michelle was wearing a trouser suit.

16

THE OLD FACE

The following weeks were largely uneventful. The show continued to get fleshed out. Gerald wrote a very funny sketch about a rooftop protest which we incorporated into the show and Dougie somehow persuaded Albie he should sing a solo – "I Dreamed A Dream" – a song that I loathe, but I could listen to Albie sing it again and again. Dougie and Albie were forming quite a bond, which seemed the most unlikely of pairings: a bit like a lion befriending a hamster.

There was one unexpected surprise for me: I got a visit from Mac.

"Have you been buggered in the showers yet?" he begins, cackling and wheezing like an old crone.

"Really? Is that the best you can come up with after a couple of hours on a train?"

"I'll take that as a yes."

We then launch into our usual tropes about how everything's been ruined by overpaid wankers. It feels good, like sliding your feet into old slippers. Then he changes the register of our conversation.

"I went to Sandra's wedding."

I aim for nonchalant – and miss.

"Oh…right…how was it? Was it OK?"

"Aye, it was cracking."

He takes out his phone to show me some photos, whether I want to see them or not.

"There she is. Doesn't she look great?"

"Her smile's a little tense."

"Oh…yeh, well I think I'd just said something inappropriate."

"Pete looks like he's won the lottery. What do you make of him?"

"Well…he's…gentle, considerate, solid, reliable."

I can see where this is heading.

"All right, Mac, OK."

"She's married the Anti-Kevin."

"I said OK."

Mac chuckles and slaps me affectionately on the shoulder.

"And she looked happy?" I ask.

"Very happy."

"That's good."

"Yes, it is."

"You can put the phone away now."

"No, no, no, you've got to see this, this is hilarious."

I sit there for a few moments, as he trawls incompetently through YouTube.

"Ah, here it is, clock this."

It's a clip of Derek, on a daytime TV sofa, talking about his autobiography. I don't want to look, but Mac's right, it is hilarious, so I put my revulsion to one side for a moment. Derek is talking about emotional rebirth and the two presenters are trying to move him on to a lighter topic. But Derek won't be stopped. He is now likening himself to a phoenix. He is emerging from the ashes of pain, through the fire of personal discovery. Oh this is wonderfully, fist-bitingly bad. Mac and I are laughing so much that we're getting looks from the other visitors.

Suddenly, one of the presenters manages to stop Derek in

his tracks by asking him about me. For a split second, there's anger behind his eyes. He says he doesn't really want to talk about me because I represent a chapter of his life that caused him considerable distress. Then he's off again, telling the daytime audience how he draws positive energy from the inner sun he's discovered.

Soon the interview descends into farce, as the presenters try to wind up as chirpily as possible while Derek continues talking off-camera about how he was abused as a child.

Mac dries his eyes with the back of his hand before switching off his phone.

"Oh dear, gets me every time, and I've watched it loads of times now. Do you think he was abused as a kid?"

"It's possible, I suppose, God knows. He's such a hall of mirrors."

"He's like, oh, the one who fell in love with his own reflection."

"Narcissus."

"Aye, Narcissus…except this fella would probably try and shag his own reflection."

I can't help smiling to myself. A few months back, I would not have been able to watch that clip. I would have felt a visceral, physical nausea at the sight of Derek's face. But now I had just watched him and found him funny, almost like he was a parrot playing ping-pong or a squirrel trapped in a revolving-door. Mac's forming the same observation.

"You wouldn't have been able to laugh at him last time I visited."

"No, I know."

"That's a step forward from punching him in the face."

"I know."

"You're leaving the little bastard behind, that is genuine progress."

"I know…I'm a phoenix."

We both piss ourselves laughing and the ginger guard, Mr Nethercott, comes over to have words with us.

A few days before the documentary team are due to arrive, as we take a break for over-stewed tea and stale digestives, Dougie has a moment of panic.

"What if they ask us about y'know...the things we've done to end up in here. I'm not sure I want to talk about that stuff. What if my family see it? I don't want them humiliated."

I try to set his mind at rest.

"You're in control, Dougie. You don't have to tell them about anything you don't want to."

"Right...I don't mind telling them about the first post office job, 'cos that was fucking cool. They could make a movie of that."

Dougie begins a game of suggesting actors who could play him in a movie. Albie – more confident now – says Daniel Craig. Pulse says Russell Crowe and Gerald suggests the late Arthur Mullard, which nearly starts a fight.

"I ain't telling them how I got here," Mohammad declares. "That's between me and Allah."

"We all know how you got here, boy," drawls Pulse, "and nobody's going to be at all interested in a fella what stole from old folk."

Mohammad's bottom lip juts out.

"They weren't old. They were...establishment, weren't they."

Gerald says he'll be very happy to talk about both his "crime" and his travesty of a trial. Simo tries to join in the conversation, but he starts to get emotional and his speech crumbles into dust.

"Listen up, everyone," I say, loud and firm. "Nobody, I repeat, no-bo-dy...has to talk about anything they don't want to, is that clear?"

They all seem reassured, but Gerald has got that twinkle in his eye.

"Might be good for people to talk about their misdemeanours. Might be therapeutic. Cathartic. What about you, Albie? Wouldn't you like to share your story?"

Albie looks up, startled, ready to bolt. I try to head Gerald off.

"Gerald, just leave it."

"What is your story, Albie? I'm sure we'd all love to know, you're our man of mystery. What did you do?"

"Back the fuck off, Gerald," says Dougie, spreading his shoulders.

"Perhaps he wants to talk about it?"

"No…no I don't," mutters Albie.

"There are some things one shouldn't bottle up." Gerald is simpering now and part of me wants Dougie to rip his head off, but my main worry is Albie, who has started to tremble.

"*Nobody* has to talk about anything they don't want to…not now, not when the cameras come…not ever." I turn to face Gerald, whose eyes continue to glitter. "This is prison. Secrets are fine here."

Why has Gerald suddenly got on Albie's case? Is it jealousy because Albie looks like he will be the star turn in our show? Or is it just plain sadistic cruelty? Albie's weakness is so plain, maybe Gerald just wants to amuse himself by tormenting him? Either way, I know I will have to keep an eye on Gerald. As I call an end to the tea-break, I can feel him watching me.

The first day of filming arrives and the group, plus a rather fidgety Malcolm, assembles in the games room. Everyone seems to have had a shave and passed a comb through their hair. A cameraman and his assistant lug various bits of kit into the room. Then Julian strolls in.

"Morning all," he breezes, "thank you so much for this. You all remember Michelle, I'm sure…"

The trouser-suited Michelle shuffles a little warily into the room.

"Bonjour, Michelle," beams Pulse, pushing the Jamaican accent for romantic effect.

"And this other young lady is our latest recruit." He holds out an arm, as if to cue her entrance. She comes in, smiling awkwardly.

"Jesus fucking Christ!" I explode. "Is this some kind of sick joke?"

"And hello to you too, Kevin," says Louise.

Everyone looks very thrown by the violence of my reaction, but I don't care.

"For fuck's sake!"

"All right, Kevin, calm down," says Malcolm.

"I don't believe this!"

Julian tries to sound confident.

"Louise is our company's latest acquisition. And we are very excited because she's widely regarded as being the best in the business."

He then introduces her to each member of the group, who shake her by the hand while trying not to look anywhere they shouldn't. I stand watching, beside myself with shock, frustration, rage and lots of indefinable negative emotions stirred by the memories of working under her yoke.

I drag Malcolm outside into the corridor and, as clearly as I possibly can, I try to spell out Louise's character and reputation to him.

"She's a shark, a depraved shark."

Malcolm tells me that, with the greatest respect, he thinks I might be over-reacting. I tell him that she would murder her own grandmother and film it if she thought it would get good ratings. Malcolm points out that, editorially, we have final approval.

"I told you, she's a shark. Sharks don't obey agreements." Now Malcolm feels, still with the greatest respect, that I am being paranoid. I start to tell him stories – most of which I think are true – about how she has fucked various people over. He hears what I am saying, but we have signed a contract. I say we should veto her and he sighs wearily.

"And what the hell is Julian playing at? Eh?" I jab my finger in the direction of the Rehearsal Room. "He must know she was my producer when the whole…when everything kicked off. He must have realised that connection. Why didn't he run it past us? Eh? Why? Tell me that, why?"

"They've only just acquired her, he said."

"Oh come on."

"Why would he lie? And why wouldn't he use her? He obviously feels she's a catch and that she's good at her job. Is she good at her job?"

"Stalin was good at his job."

"Still comparing me to Stalin?" says a familiar voice. Louise has materialised behind me, like she always used to, as if she has her own secret network of tunnels. "I'd have thought you'd have had time to come up with something new."

"I couldn't be bothered."

Malcolm apologises to her for my tone. What the—? Who does he think he is? She gives him her most charming smile. "Malcolm, do you think Kevin and I could borrow your office for a few minutes?"

"I'm not the person you knew," she begins.

I snort with derision.

"What, you don't believe people can change?" she asks.

"A leopard can change its spots, but not by painting over them."

She hesitates. "I'm not sure what that's supposed to mean, Kevin, so I think I'll just press on. It is not my intention to do anything sensationalist with this programme. You have your contract, with all its stipulations, there is no risk. I'm not a producer of soaps any more. From now on, I intend to make documentaries, programmes that I am not too embarrassed to watch."

This sounds very odd. I don't remember her ever criticising the show. She always defended it as "the people's TV"!

"Did you always feel that way?" I ask.

"I came to feel that way. It wore me down. Which is why I left."

"Please tell me you got fired."

"I didn't get fired. I quit. The cast, past and present, made me a lovely farewell tape."

"So sad I wasn't available."

"Very sad."

"Was Derek on it?"

She pauses to gather herself. Have I struck a nerve?

"Unfortunately, Derek is on it, yes."

"I can't believe you cast him like that."

"It was a mistake."

Again, very odd. She never used to admit mistakes.

"But you'll be pleased to know, Kevin, that the mistake is being rectified. He's being written out."

"Does he know?"

"No, the writers have kept it under wraps."

"How's he leaving?"

"In a gas explosion, I think. Or possibly a tram crash, they hadn't made their minds up when I left."

"Was it your decision?"

"Oh yes," she chuckles. "I couldn't take any more. No one could. He's such a pain in the arse. And I've worked with some world-class pains in the arse…" She gives me a little smile. "But he's phenomenal. There's not enough attention in the whole planet to satisfy that boy. By the end, I reckon ninety-five per cent of my time was spent just baby-sitting him. So I rushed off an e-mail telling the writers to kill him. A sort of leaving-present to myself."

I spend an enjoyable moment picturing his reaction.

"He'll be livid."

"Not my problem. I'm out of there."

There's a new lightness to her, which makes me feel a little envious.

"I saw Derek on YouTube," I tell her. "It was so funny. He was promoting his autobiography."

"It's shit."

"You've read it."

"No." We both laugh. "That's just a given."

God, here I am, sharing a laugh with Louise the shark.

"I always liked working with you, Kevin. You made me think. It was nice having someone who liked a fight." That sounds more like the Louise I know.

"You don't have to worry about me here," she continues. "Julian's my Exec, I understand this project, I'm not going to mess with it...or you. I don't want to. I'm a professional."

Is she being straight with me? She was always so hard to fathom.

"You really fucked me over, you do know that, don't you?"

She stiffens slightly.

"It was an unfortunate time...especially for you."

"Yeh...an apology would be nice."

She looks at me long and hard.

"I'm sorry for what you went through, Kevin...but, right or wrong, I was doing my best for the show."

I wait to see if she's going to elaborate.

"That's all you're getting, Kevin."

My conversation in the governor's office with Louise was followed by another hissed conversation with Malcolm in the corridor, where I emphasised how dangerous I thought she was. He listened, and absorbed, and duly noted, and nodded a lot, but after twenty minutes or so he reminded me that we had signed a contract and it didn't include any veto on producers. So, as far as he was concerned, that was the end of the story. But he said I was welcome to keep a watching-brief on Louise, which I told him I fully intended to do.

So, after taking a few moments to compose myself, I re-entered the rehearsal room.

"Oh good," says Louise, "our director is here."

"We don't have a director as such," Gerald informs her, "we're a democracy, aren't we, Kevin?" I so want to punch Gerald. But instead I suggest that we start by rehearsing his sketch.

"Are you planning to film this?" I ask Louise.

"No, we just want to settle in, get a feel of what you're doing. We might shoot some GVs at the end. They'll come in handy at the edit."

"Well, you don't need me here," chirps Julian, "so I'll make myself scarce. Good luck all, and, once again, many thanks for letting us share in this fine enterprise." He pauses by the door to give a friendly wave, and then he's gone. He's the executive producer, so we won't see him again.

Within the first few minutes, I realise that today's rehearsal is going to prove especially difficult. My main problem is that there are two women sitting in the corner of the room, so everyone is showing off like mad. Pulse has upped the lilt in his Jamaican accent to the point where I'm half-expecting him to break into a calypso. Gerald is coming out with snipey little jokes which are his idea of babe-magnet wit, Dougie is flexing his pecs and Simo keeps doing back-flips. They are gymnastically impressive, but sudden and alarming. Only Albie is behaving normally, if that is the right word.

After half an hour of chaos, I get tired of raising my voice, tired of imploring everyone to concentrate, so I call a break for tea and biscuits. In the scrum around the table, Louise pops up next to me.

"That was a bit of a mess, Kevin."

"They'll settle down. It's excitement."

"Who's the one who hardly says anything?"

"That's Paul. The others call him Albie. Short for albino, which he isn't. He's just very fair."

"What's he in for?"

"Is that relevant?"

"Just curious."

I lower my voice. "Well, I can't tell you because I don't know. None of us do."

Louise goes ominously quiet and I realise that I've said too much.

"Leave Albie alone, OK?" I tell her.

I restart the rehearsal and, in an attempt to calm everyone down, I ask Dougie and Albie to give us their rendition of "Bridge Over Troubled Water", which they perform a cappella, as Norton the pianist is in solitary for spitting at a guard.

Everyone sits spellbound as Albie's beautiful voice floats on Dougie's pleasing bass and, as the last note fades, they break into applause.

"That's brilliant, guys," exclaims Louise, "and you'll be doing that in the performance, yes?"

"I think that's going to be the climax of the show," I tell her.

"Well, and of our documentary. There won't be a dry eye in the house."

Again, I feel nervous about how Louise seems to be assuming control. The other producer, Michelle, just sits there like a lemon.

Mohammad asks if he can show the group his latest piece. My heart sinks a bit, but he says he wants feedback, so we give him the floor. What he has come up with is a loud, rhythmic poem (of sorts) entitled "It Ain't Hard, It's the Word of God".

Most of it is lumpen and turgid, then, during a section on

modesty, he suddenly points at the two women producers and addresses them directly:

"So don't flaunt bare shoulders
Or flash your thighs
'Cos you trap men's souls
With your eyes
And the prophet knew that sin
Works through the senses
So cover up them lady-bits
Or face the consequences."

Although Mohammad's doggerel is crass, it feels quite threatening and Michelle the Lemon looks like she's about to run away. But Louise is watching with a wry grin. As Mohammad's ranting rhymes grind to a close there is a general shifting of buttocks in seats.

"OK, guys, feedback, hit me," he says.

Louise asks if they can film the feedback session because she thinks it might be interesting.

"Well, you're wrong," mutters Gerald.

No one expresses any objections to filming, so the operator shoulders his camera as I invite comments on Mohammad's work. Dougie opens with the observation that, in his opinion, it was shit.

"You probably don't understand it," protests Mohammad, trying to appear calm because the camera is pointing at him. "It's about big ideas, innit."

"All ideas look big to you," comments Gerald.

"It's about the word of God." A tiny tremble is creeping into Mohammad's voice. "As told to the prophet. And it's a word you all need to heed because otherwise you'll be destroyed by Allah. Because of your sin, and your blasphemies, and your materialism and, I don't mean to be personal, miss, but you need to wear a longer skirt."

Louise gives a dark chuckle. "Thanks for the tip." Now Mohammad is talking directly into the lens of the camera.

"The prophet says that all people, men and women, should dress modestly."

"Which bit of the Quran mentions skirt-lengths?"

Gerald's question stops Mohammad in his tracks.

"Which surat mentions skirt-lengths?"

"Erm…"

"What is a modest length? Her skirt is knee-length, personally I wouldn't class that as immodest."

"Well…"

"But you seem to find that threatening. Why is that?"

I intervene because I can see that Mohammad is getting very rattled, which was Gerald's objective from the outset.

"Let's not get bogged down on skirt-lengths. Let's widen this. What about the role of religious faith in prison? I've noticed quite a lot of prisoners are religious. Does it help them get through it? Pulse, you wear a crucifix…"

"Yeah, it was my mother's, man."

"Do you believe in God, or a god?"

"On some days, maybe."

"The good days?"

Pulse laughs deep and low. "Hell no, the bad days, that's when you hope someone's looking out for you."

"How about you, Albie? Did Mohammad's…piece…connect with you in any way? Do you believe in God?"

Albie blinks a few times.

"I like Jesus?"

"As a god, or as a person?"

"I don't know…I used to pray to him, but only 'cos my dad made me."

"Gerald, I'm guessing that piece did very little for you."

Gerald straightens in his chair and sighs.

"You're right, many prisoners *are* religious. But which ones? Those who are mentally trapped in adolescence. Religion will always appeal to the adolescent mind because it provides facile certainties. A comfort blanket of simplicity. Complexities are rendered into black or white, pure and simple. But the real world where we grown-ups live is a patchwork of greys."

Part of me agrees with Gerald, but the sneer in his voice is nauseating. The cameraman has pushed in for a profile close-up, because he senses that Gerald cuts an exotic shape and will make good TV. The circus is open for business.

Out of a sense of duty, I ask Simo if he has anything to say. He stutters and stammers for a few moments, then stops. There's a panic behind his eyes.

"OK, let's move on. Pulse, how's your Shakespeare coming along?"

Pulse stands, looking pleased with himself.

"You ready for this, ladies?"

He draws breath to begin, but is interrupted by a deafening crash as Simo backflips into the table.

The Lemon yelps as she's showered with hot tea.

"Like...sorry," mumbles Simo.

We cleaned up the mess and carried on with fitful rehearsals for about two more hours. The showing-off died down a little, as if Simo's pointless backflip had marked a highpoint, and we managed to get some work done. I was surprised at how quickly they all seemed to adapt to the presence of the camera. To begin with, they kept throwing the lens self-conscious glances, but soon they were looking straight past it.

As I bag up the rubbish, Louise comes alongside me with a single polystyrene cup.

"There you go," she says, dropping the cup in the bin-liner.

What's she up to? I can sense her positioning herself.

"I think we've got the makings of a really strong documentary, Kevin. You've assembled a really interesting cast here."

"I didn't assemble them," I correct her, "they chose to attend the group. I'm not their leader."

"Of course, I forgot, this isn't about you. What were the backflips about?"

"Simo's not good with words...so he expresses himself physically...that's why his bit in the show is going to be mostly dance."

"...with backflips?"

"No, that was just him trying to dazzle you."

She laughs. Odd, I don't remember her laughing.

"How did he end up like that?" she asks.

"I've no idea."

"Be interesting to find out though, wouldn't it, why he's like that? And why does Albie say so little? Who filled Mohammad's head with Taliban shit? Did that happen in here? Or was he like that already? These are all questions I think our audience would like answered."

I finish tying up the rubbish bag and hand it to her. "Make yourself useful. Dump this on your way out." She slowly takes it from me.

"Yessir."

A marker needs to be put down.

"Just remember, Louise, I'm going to be watching you like a hawk."

She gives me an inscrutable smile, then turns and strolls towards the door, breezily swinging the rubbish bag, like a young girl contemplating love. She's hatching something. And I'm the only one who can stop her.

17

THE CIRCUS

The following morning, I received a surprise visit. There, waiting for me in the Visitors' Room, and causing a few male heads to turn, sat Nina Patel. She greeted me with a broad smile.

As I sit down opposite her, she reaches into her briefcase.

"I've brought you a present," she says, lifting out a thick manuscript. "It's Derek's autobiography. His publishers sent it to us so we could check it through from a legal standpoint. It's four hundred and thirteen pages long and it's complete and utter vomit-inducing bilge. They'd be mad to publish. It'll be greeted with derision."

So far, nothing she has said could be described as a surprise, so I'm starting to wonder why she has travelled so far to tell me this.

"I had to read every page of it. I may need counselling. *But* the good news...the very good news is that, in several places, Derek gives details which completely contradict evidence he gave in the trial."

"Which trial?"

"The second trial." Her brow furrows for a second. "Actually, and the first trial, come to think of it."

I start to laugh at the sheer inevitability of it. When someone lies in such volume, they forget which lies they've told. Nina Patel's eyes are shining bright with optimism.

"This is an open goal, Kevin. We can prove he told lies in the witness box. That makes your conviction unsound."

"Does it though?"

"Yes, of course."

"But demonstrating he's a liar doesn't prove that I'm *not* a liar, does it? I did commit perjury, that's a fact."

Nina Patel grips my forearm and then withdraws her hand.

"Am I allowed to touch you?"

"Not really, no."

"The thing is – yes, you'd still be guilty of perjury – but we'd be able to show that you were manipulated into committing perjury. We can present you as more of a victim. And we can demonstrate that the prosecution case was built around a fantasist."

A few tables away from us, a young woman visitor is crying very quietly.

I tell Nina Patel that I would not feel comfortable presenting myself as a victim. She exhales in exasperation.

"We can get your sentence reduced, Kevin."

"But only by raking it all up again."

"Well, yes, but—"

"I'm not sure if I'm up for that."

She leans back and swings an arm over the back of her chair.

"Not even if it means doing less time?" she asks.

I shake my head, which makes her laugh.

"Are you enjoying prison, then?"

"I'm in no massive hurry to get out."

She eyes me quizzically.

"Really? Why?"

"I quite like the obscurity."

"Obscurity," she repeats back at me.

"Yuh."

Nina Patel looks me straight in the eyes and keeps looking, as if she's hunting for some tell-tale fleck of meaning.

"What do you do all day?"

"This and that. There's a drama group that I...supervise."

"Ah," she chuckles triumphantly, "you have a project."

"Yeh, it's good."

She leans forward conspiratorially, lowering her voice.

"Kevin, I honestly think we could get you out of here very soon."

A ripple of satisfaction passes through me. After months of distress and confusion, I find that I now know what I want. I don't want my whole story to be told yet again, even if this revision will work in my favour. I want to stay and finish what I've started, see it through.

"I'm very appreciative of the offer," I tell her, "but I think I'd rather just...leave it."

"You'd let Derek go unchallenged?"

Is she trying to goad me into it?

"He'll have told lies about other people. They'll all be going after him."

With a wistful sigh, Nina Patel picks up the manuscript and chucks it into her briefcase.

"I read that entire crapfest for nothing." She looks at me from beneath hooded eyebrows in mock reproach. "You owe me one, Kevin Carver."

Over the next few minutes, we exchange small talk, a little gossip. Graham is thinking about taking early retirement. My barrister, Seymour, has been done for drink-driving. She has taken up flamenco.

As she rises to leave, she tries one last time.

"You're sure you don't want to pursue this?"

"Positive."

"You're looking a lot better than I anticipated," she tells

me. "I'd heard you were a bit of a wreck. But you're looking pretty sharp."

I thank her for the compliment and invite her to come and see our show.

A week passed – three more rehearsals – and Louise made no detectable move. Mostly, she sat and watched from a respectful distance in the corner of the room. The cameraman was discreet and restricted himself mostly to general shots of the group. It all seemed fairly harmless. Occasionally, Louise would ask if she could record some one-on-one interviews during our tea breaks. But I hovered nearby to keep an eye on things. Her questions were serious-minded, never prurient. Although I did wonder what her questions might be like if I wasn't policing her. Her co-producer – the Lemon – mostly sat to one side forcing a smile and trying not to look out of her depth. Then, come the fourth rehearsal, she fails to show.

"Where's your mate?" I ask Louise.

"Off sick."

"What's she got?"

"Nervous exhaustion."

"Oh, right."

"Yeh, I think all that sitting around on her arse has finally taken its toll."

Louise has clearly not lost her dislike of women colleagues.

"What's her production background?"

"She's Julian's shag-bunny. That's her production background."

"Ouch."

"And she owns twenty per cent of Going Forward."

I am enjoying Louise's bitterness. And so's she.

"Still, it suits me, Kevin. I prefer to hunt alone. This session, I was thinking of recording some more autobiographical stuff with the guys, if that's OK."

She spots the alarm in my eyes.

"…with you there, obviously…as their guardian."

The date for the performance was finalised as August 3rd – three weeks away – in the chapel, to an audience of invited guests and specially-selected inmates. Malcolm clearly wanted to make sure there would be no boisterousness or heckling.

Temperatures had started to climb into the high 70s Fahrenheit and life in an old prison with no air-conditioning was starting to get uncomfortable. So, there I am, lying on my bunk, headphones on, listening to the "Test Match Special", trying to ignore the stickiness of the air, when I hear Dougie turn a page of his newspaper and groan.

"Oh fuck me, no."

"What?"

"They're saying next week's going to be the start of a proper hot spell. Ninety degrees. As hot as fucking Kuwait. Jesus wept. Everything will start to stink, the drains, the people, prisoners start getting grumpy over the tiniest things, so do the screws, someone does something stupid and then it all kicks off. You mark my fucking words, Kev-boy, I've seen it happen. If it hits ninety, this place will go up like a fucking firework."

I turn the cricket up a little and try not to worry about Dougie's grim prediction.

"Fucking global warming. And yet those posh restaurants with outside bits are allowed to have fucking great heaters to warm up the open air. How is that legal, eh? Answer me that."

I don't bother answering. I'm saving energy, listening to Geoffrey Boycott fulminating about how his granny could bat on this wicket with a stick of rhubarb. Then the springs above me start to bounce, Dougie is laughing.

"Hey, Kevin, your mate's in the papers again. And he's not happy."

"Is this Derek?"

"Yeh, his publishers have binned his autobiography...and now, his character's been axed from your show. He's talking about suing them for unfair dismissal."

Poor Derek. And he said I wasn't any good at dealing with rejection.

"He says he's the victim of a 'malicious secret agenda'. Do you want to read it?"

"Nah."

"Says he's not going to take it lying down."

"He'll probably throw himself in front of the queen's horse."

Dougie chucks the newspaper down to me.

"I said I don't want to read it."

"Clock the photo. Looks like he's chewing a wasp."

Dougie's description is pretty accurate. Derek's face, normally so forgettable, looks thunderously resentful. Despite my indifference, I find myself reading the news article. There is a diplomatic quote from the network, thanking Derek for his work but explaining that they had to make room for exciting new characters aimed at younger audiences. Derek won't like that. But he's their problem now, they brought it on themselves.

A bluebottle is dozily circling the light. Boycott thinks the bowlers are banging it in too short. It's a Saturday. And nothing in the newspapers is going to bother me ever again.

Louise, her camera operator and a sound man continued coming to our rehearsals and, to be honest, it was not nearly as intrusive or destructive as I had feared. She was consistently polite, always asking permission before she started filming and always respectful if we asked her to stop. This unsettled me still further. Again, this was not the woman I remembered.

The group seemed to quite like her and she seemed genuinely interested in all of them; but especially interested in two. One, obviously, was Albie, because he was such a mystery. Also, on camera, his translucence made him look like – to quote Louise – a spectre. The other was Gerald. My suspicion was that she had spotted a kindred spirit, someone else who – when bored – liked to push people's buttons.

The performance is about ten days away when Gerald announces that he's been working on a comedy stand-up routine that he would like to be included in the running order.

"What if it's shit?" asks Dougie.

Gerald looks him squarely in the eye. "It's not shit," he informs him.

And he is right. From the first gag, Gerald is funny, often vicious, but funny. His act is a satirical tableau of prison life, mocking everything and everyone. He does a very well-observed parody of the governor's liberal jargon and some brutal impersonations of some of the guards, the prison chaplain and the prison psychiatrist who loves his lustrous hair so much. Then he turns his attention to the inmates.

People start shifting a little uneasily in their seats. Most of his characters are types – macho, old-school gang-bosses, gay opportunists, weasel-like black marketeers – but some are identifiable as particular individuals. And now he is doing Dougie, doing him very accurately, as a comic mixture of thuggishness and sentimentality. I find myself watching Dougie intently and inching ever so slightly towards the red panic button on the wall.

But Dougie is laughing, laughing and nodding in recognition. Even when Gerald's version of him talks about building himself an extra testicle because he's run out of body-space for his tattoos, Dougie is laughing, dabbing at his eyes with the back of his meaty wrist.

Next it's my turn. I am portrayed as a rather effete luvvie, slumming it with the lowlife. He gives me a catchphrase – "this isn't about me" – which everyone seems to find hilarious. He's a bit unfair, but I feel obliged to laugh along with them. Also, I can feel the camera is trained on me, looking for reactions. As Gerald moves on to his next creation I catch a glimpse of Louise grinning like a cat in a bird-house.

The next few characters are types, a junkie, a God-squad type and then a failed suicide bomber who is writing a letter of complaint to Semtex. As he reaches a section where he is lamenting about all the virgins who will "not now be deflowered as faulty equipment prevented his scheduled arrival in Paradise", Mohammad jolts to his feet and starts yelling.

"Shame on you! Shame on you! Do not mock the martyrs, my friend, they are the messengers of Allah! Allah sees everything! He is all-powerful! The martyrs will smite the enemies of Allah!"

"Well if he's all-powerful, why does he need to employ middlemen?" retorts Gerald, instantly.

Mohammad rocks back for a moment.

"You show some respect!"

"Do I have to respect mumbo-jumbo?"

At this, Mohammad bursts towards Gerald who does not retreat one millimetre, but Dougie and Pulse intervene and push the two of them apart.

"Alright...put the handbags down," says Dougie.

"Just ree-lax," adds Pulse.

Now Mohammad is pacing in crazy circles around the room, his eye filling with tears.

"I'm not standing for this, man, no way, this is bullshit, man, being disrespected, no fucking way, this is total bullshit."

He punches the wall in frustration. I indicate to Louise that she should stop filming, but she pretends not to have seen me.

"Are you going to allow him to disrespect my religion like that?"

Slowly, I realise this question is being directed at me.

"Well…um…it's not really a question of my 'allowing' or 'not allowing'."

Gerald interrupts "It's not about him. That's right, isn't it, Kevin?Decisions are taken by the group." There is a savage light in his eye, he is relishing every second of this.

"Well that's right, and if the group feels that—"

"Oh fuck the group."

"Mohammad, listen…"

"Fuck the group! Fuck the lot of you! Fuck right off to Hell! I'm out!"

The door slams behind him, rattling in its frame.

"I don't know," mutters Gerald, "you just can't have a laugh with some people."

Albie and Simo are both looking a little shaken, so I call a coffee break and make an immediate bee-line for Louise.

"I signalled for you to stop filming."

"Oh, did you? I didn't see, sorry."

"Well that's got to come out."

"Sorry?"

"That's got to be edited out."

"What?"

"That's got to be edited out of the final programme."

"Really? Why's that?"

"Because…it's not fair on Mohammad. He wasn't in control of his emotions, he was upset, all over the place."

She furrows her brow in fake puzzlement.

"And…" I jab a finger in her face, "you were specifically requested to switch the camera off."

"By you."

"Yes."

"Not the group."

She wants to smirk, I can tell, but she hides it behind a wide-eyed mask.

"Well here's another thing, Louise, you'll have to get Mohammad to sign off on that and he's going to say no."

"Well, let's see."

"I'm telling you, he'll say no."

"Oh loosen up, Kevin, all we filmed is a good, old-fashioned piece of human conflict. It'd be an interesting element. What we saw was a microcosm of what's happening in society at large. Free speech versus extreme Islam, Liberalism versus intolerant religiosity. Gerald's like a cross between Richard Dawkins and..."

"A hyena."

"He's a very watchable character."

"Well he certainly needs watching, he's a total—"

"It was great TV."

"Look, Louise, Mohammad is young and very vulnerable and—"

"You're his protector, I know."

"This isn't about me," I snap. Oh shit, I said it. She giggles at the catchphrase Gerald gave me.

"Look." I pause to steady myself. "Look, you agreed, Going Forward Productions agreed, that we would have editorial approval and I, for one, wouldn't be happy to see that go out on TV and I don't suppose, for one moment, that the prison governor would be prepared to let that go out either."

She has that challenge in her eyes; the look of someone who needs to win, always.

"Well why don't we all go away and have a little think about it?" she breezes. "Let's mull it over."

I watch her as she walks away to chat with her technicians. What is it about her? Why does she always get a reaction out of me? Maybe I've become sensitised to her, like an allergy.

We resume rehearsals as if nothing had happened.

"Is Mohammad coming back?" asks Albie, quietly.

"I don't know, Paul."

And then Simo tells us he has some new dance moves he would like to show us, so we clear some space.

It was somewhere around this time that I got a letter from Mac who was touring across Europe with yet another theatre company that nobody had ever heard of. It was a few pages long, full of gossip and salacious stories, but tucked away on the last page was the news that Sandra was pregnant.

I was genuinely taken aback. Although I don't know why I felt that way, because it was hardly an extraordinary plot-twist. She had made it crystal clear that she would be trying for a baby, so how come I was so shocked? Was it just plain egotism? Maybe, because I was also surprised that she hadn't written to tell me the news herself. But then again, why should she? I was a finished chapter, it was none of my business. Perhaps she was still angry with me. My conciliatory letter had not prompted a reply. Perhaps she had given up on me, I could hardly blame her.

Ah, what the hell.

There had been a period, towards the end of our relationship, when we had tried for a baby, probably for the wrong reasons – a last roll of the dice, an attempt to see if two people could bind themselves together by creating a third person. Well, it didn't work. She gave up coffee and alcohol and we had lots of sex at propitious times but, deep down, my heart wasn't in it. Perhaps that was a factor in why she failed to conceive. Perhaps my sperm were demoralised. Mum always used to say "Nature Knows Best". I can hear her saying it now. I am not sure she was right, because Nature presents all sorts of abominations, but perhaps there is an unseen timing to life. Sandra was ready for a baby, at the right time, in the right place, and now one was on its way. If she and I had had a child, it would have been a disaster. I'm far too selfish to be responsible for another human being. Acknowledging that makes me feel sad, because I wonder what I'm missing, but I'm comfortable that I understand the limitations of my personality. I'm tumbleweed.

I did debate whether to drop her a line of congratulation. But somehow that felt like a presumption, so instead I accepted myself as an irrelevance and tried not to think about her any more. I did wonder what she would think about my work with the drama group. She would approve, I felt sure. That was a comfort, to know she would be proud of me, if she knew what I was doing. Isn't that odd? Fifty-three years old and looking for approval.

I did once have a fantastically intense dream where I was a dad, one of those dreams that is so vivid that when you wake up your brain spends several moments refusing to accept that the world you've left wasn't real. I had a son, named Christopher, he looked about five or six years old and he had black hair, blue eyes and an infectious, gurgling laugh. We were hunting crabs in a series of sparkling rock pools. But then I lost him in a department store which, for some reason, was staffed entirely by people with one arm. So I woke up feeling bereft and ashamed. So many of my dreams end in failure. Is that normal?

Well, I know it is probably too late for me to be a dad now. I have reached an age where I often sit down to pee. Even if I met the perfect Mrs Carver tomorrow, which is highly improbable, I would be one of those fathers who is always mistaken for a grandad.

I can't remember what I did with that letter from Mac. I think I must have thrown it away.

Mohammad made it crystal clear that he would not be rejoining the group and, in addition, he filed a complaint that he had been subjected to racist abuse, which means that I end up in the governor's office, staring at the many colour-coded charts on his wall.

"It does feel a little like you let this get out of hand," muses Malcolm, as he scans the text of the complaint.

"Well, first off, I don't see how it's down to me, I'm not their leader, or carer, or whatever, and second, what was I supposed to do? Shut Gerald up the moment he started doing a Muslim character? Censor him? He was just doing jokes – I mean yes, it was black-ish humour, it was Gerald, but they were clearly jokes. Mohammad over-reacted. He lost control of his emotions, everyone knows what he's like."

"He's alleging there was racially offensive content. Biscuit?"

He pushes a plate of Hobnobs my way.

"Well, I don't remember any."

"It mentions hate-speech here."

"I didn't hear any hate-speech, whatever that might be."

Malcolm doesn't respond, but continues reading.

"Well…this is a bit of a bummer…I'll have to do something… otherwise they'll send me on another course on Diversity and Ethnicity." He gives a Harry Secombe chuckle. "I don't want two days in Hastings."

"It's all down on tape."

"Is it?"

"Yeh, they filmed the whole thing, Gerald doing his stand-up routine, the fight, well, it wasn't actually a proper fight, just a—"

"So I could present that as evidence?"

"Suppose so."

He chomps pensively on his biscuit for a few seconds. "What was Gerald's stand-up like?"

"It was a sort of…satire on prison life."

The chomping quickens. "I don't like the sound of that." Now he starts texting someone. "I'd better ask Louise for a copy."

"Incidentally, when the…dust-up was brewing, I did ask Louise to stop filming and she refused."

He keeps texting.

"Said she didn't see me signalling her. I thought it was a bit opportunist...and I thought what she was filming might give a rather negative impression of the prison."

Now I've got his attention.

"Negative? In what way, negative?"

"Well, it could make this place look like a bit of a...a cauldron of sort of racial-slash-religious tension."

He starts drumming his fingers on the desk.

"We have editorial approval," he says, as if confirming it for his own peace of mind.

"I know, but...well, you know my feelings about this whole process. I think the camera just stirs people up, I just sense trouble ahead."

The fingers stop drumming.

"I share your concern, Kevin."

"Good."

"But I still feel that, provided it's handled properly, the programme could be a valuable social document."

Where's he going with this? He seems uncomfortable.

"I'll raise these concerns with Louise tomorrow. She's... um...she's coming in to record some interviews with me in the office here."

"Oh, right."

"Yes, she says that she thinks my, um...observations will provide the narrative spine of the piece."

"Right."

"But no, I will raise the...I'm of a mind to say she can't use the footage of Mohammad's...upset."

"I think that'd be best."

"And if she disagrees then..."

"We pull the plug on the whole thing."

"Absolutely, Kevin. That's our back-stop position."

He starts flicking through the pages of the complaint again.

"I'll have to follow this up somehow. His Imam's coming to see me tomorrow."

"Best check those biscuits are halal then."

Not a flicker.

"Definitely no racial abuse, you reckon?"

"Watch the tape," I say.

I presume he must have watched the footage because a few days later he stops me cheerily in the corridor and tells me that, after due consideration, he feels that the confrontation between Gerald and Mohammad should be included in the documentary, as it's an interesting microcosm of what's happening in society at large. Louise has got to him.

I trudge back to the sapping heat of my cell, certain that what I feared from the very beginning is now playing out before me. We are being turned into screen-fodder. It's happening. Just as I predicted.

Circus time.

18

THE AMBITIONS

The next day, in the canteen, I told the others my concerns about the group being exploited for cheap sensationalist TV. I recommended that we abort the whole thing but they were having none of it. To a man, they felt I was over-dramatising, Dougie slapped me playfully around the back of the head and told me to stop being such a queen. Even Albie, normally so quiet, said that it would be a shame to stop now. So I was stymied. I would just have to get on with it.

The general attitude towards Mohammad was that if he wanted to throw a strop, let him. Good riddance. Word had gone around that he had made a formal complaint about racial abuse, so now pretty much the whole canteen was subjecting him to racial abuse. Some of the Muslim inmates started shouting in his defence and soon bits of food were flying through the air, until the prison officers stepped in. Luckily for Malcolm, no cameras were there to witness it.

The heatwave was strengthening its hold now. The air seemed to smother you like a blanket and I found myself recalling Dougie's dark predictions. What would I do if there was a riot? What was the etiquette? Was hiding frowned upon? Riot-etiquette struck me as a funny idea, so I gave it to Gerald and he developed it in his stand-up.

Louise had clearly sensed my suspicion because she definitely backed off for a couple of days. Rehearsals carried on in a reasonable atmosphere, despite the pervading smell of stale sweat.

The TV crew stayed as uninvasive as possible, but in my gloomy state of mind, it felt like the still, quiet dawn before a great battle.

Then, halfway through a tea-break, Louise takes the floor.

"If it's OK with everyone, I had a little idea for a section of the programme. Um…it's basically each of you talking about when you were a kid. What you wanted to be when you grew up, y'know, childhood ambitions. Is everyone happy to do that?"

A ripple of shrugs goes around the room, so they set up the camera, point it at a chair and first on to the chair is Pulse.

Louise sits down behind the cameraman's shoulder.

"So, Pulse, tell us your childhood ambition."

"Well, Louise, I—"

"Can you answer without saying 'Louise'?"

"Oh…right…sure…well, my childhood ambition was simple. I wanted to be Viv Richards."

Louise looks blank.

"He's a cricketer," I tell her.

"Just Pulse on his own, if you don't mind. Sorry, Pulse, could you start that again."

He clears his throat. "My childhood ambition was to be like Viv Richards…the cricketer." He laughs to himself. "And when I say the cricketer, I mean *the* cricketer, 'cos there ain't ever been anyone like him, and there never will be."

Louise asks him what made Richards so special.

"Everything!" exclaims Pulse, clapping his hands in delight at the memory. "Ev-er-y-thing. Everything about him was so cool. I wanted to be him, I wanted to look like him, I wanted to bat like him, but most of all, I wanted to walk like him. Man, he could strut. When he came out to bat he'd walk out of that pavilion like a King – King Viv – he'd walk out with his sleeves rolled up like he was on a day out, his chest sticking out, whirling that bat of his through the air like it was a sword and, man, you could see the blood draining from the faces of the other opponent fellas when they saw him coming. They knew he was destruction in human form, and so did he. That's why he swaggered, he knew he was destruction. When he walked out that stadium would shrink, it belonged to him and once he start batting – boom! Boom! That ball's a-flying to all four corners, boom! Out of the ground! He was *it*. He was proof that a black man could be king. And loved. A loved king. And *that's* who I wanted to be."

Pulse leans back in his chair and breaks into laughter. "Sadly, I was crap at cricket."

Laughter all round. Next on the chair is Simo who, to no one's great surprise, wanted to be the next Jackie Chan. Louise soon gets bored with him and invites Gerald to take the chair.

"As a child," he begins a little wearily, "I wanted to be Viceroy of India."

We all laugh, who wouldn't?

"I mean it," he continues. "Viceroy of India, that's what I wanted to be. I'd read about Viceroys in a book."

Louise leans forward.

"But when you were young, there *was* no Viceroy of India. Hadn't been one for decades."

"No, I know. But nonetheless that is what I wanted to be. Viceroy of India. Or failing that, emperor of somewhere."

Everyone laughs again, because they think Gerald is laughing at the child-version of himself, but I'm not sure. There is a half-smile there, but it's inscrutable.

"So, Viceroy, or Emperor…anything a little more…mundane perhaps…more achievable?"

Gerald ponders her question for a few moments. "Forensics expert, possibly. I liked Sherlock Holmes. Or an explorer perhaps, discovering lost tribes, that kind of thing. Cricketer as well. Scientist. To be honest, there was nothing that I felt I couldn't do."

After a few more questions which reveal Gerald as a terrifyingly certain little boy, Louise turns to me.

"I suppose there's no point asking you to take the chair."

The others jeer at me like schoolkids, so reluctantly I plonk myself in the chair.

"So, Kevin, did you always want to be an actor?"

"No, originally I wanted to be a footballer. When I was six I wrote to Arsenal asking for a trial."

"Did they reply?"

"They wrote saying I was too young. So I switched to supporting Chelsea."

"And you're still Chelsea?"

"Nah, I don't support anyone now. Pointless. Been ruined by the money."

"And how old were you when you realised you wanted to be an actor?"

"I dunno, fifteen, sixteen."

I'm waiting for the next question, but it doesn't come, so I fill the silence.

"I was at home, watching The Great Escape and…well, it was Steve McQueen. He got me hooked. My reaction to Steve McQueen was…similar to Pulse's about Viv Richards. Steve McQueen was cool."

"And when you became a professional actor, what did you most enjoy about it?"

She's using the past tense. Is she winding me up?

"Was it the chance to lose yourself inside the character, to become someone else? To stop being you?"

Right, that's it, that's her lot.

"I thought this was supposed to be about our childhood ambitions."

"Yes, it—"

"Well, I've told you mine." And I rise out of the chair.

She pushes her tongue into her cheek as she tries to control her reaction. I've annoyed her. Excellent.

"Well, thank you for sharing, Kevin. Who's next?"

Dougie virtually throws himself into the chair and starts talking about his early dreams. The stuff pours out of him, how he wanted to be a Grand Prix driver and then a boxer like Barry McGuigan and then a popstar and, before that, a human cannonball.

"A human cannonball?" she echoes.

"Yeh. Someone who gets fired out of a cannon."

"Why were you so keen on that?"

Dougie looks at her in bewilderment.

"What young boy doesn't dream of being fired out of a cannon?"

He thinks about what he's just said. "Actually, I'd still quite like to be fired out of a cannon."

Pulse laughs in his deepest bass. "He'd do it as well, he's one mad human being."

Louise is a little thrown, so she changes direction.

"You said popstar. Was music a big thing for you as a kid? You have a very good voice."

"I was in the church choir."

I get a fleeting image of a tiny Dougie wearing a ruff and a cassock and covered in tattoos.

"A church choir?"

"Yeh, I didn't listen to the religious shit. I just liked the hymns. I love a good song, me. My dad was a good singer. When he was pissed he'd sing. Well, in the early phase of being pissed, y'know…then he'd sing, but later…when he hit the nasty phase, he'd get that look about him – then the singing would stop."

Dougie tails off and stares at the floor with a bleak expression.

Nobody quite knows what to do. I can hear the whining of the camera. Is she hoping he'll spill his guts for her?

"Let's take a break, shall we, Louise?" She shoots me a look. "It's very hot in here."

"Damn right," says Pulse.

"Of course." She smiles. "Kevin's right."

Around the drinks table, Dougie soon regains his composure, but he tells Louise he doesn't want to spend any more time in the chair.

"Sometimes looking back's not so helpful for me, y'see, I can get a bit unmanageable."

Louise would clearly love to find out more, but she knows better than to force it now.

"That just leaves you, Paul," she says.

Albie looks hesitant, to put it mildly.

"You don't have to if you don't want to," I tell him.

"It's OK," he mumbles.

"You're happy to do it?"

He nods and puts down his drink. The operator shoulders the camera while Albie approaches the chair as if it is electrified.

"You can stop whenever you want," Louise reassures him. "Like Kevin did."

Another little nod from Albie, then he settles slowly into the chair. The camera starts to turn. Louise softens her voice.

"So, when you were little…what did you want to be?"

He looks as small and as hunted as I can remember.

"I…erm…well…it's odd."

"Odd?"

"Yeh…I've been thinking and, um…" He shifts his weight in the chair. "…I, er…I can't remember wanting to be anything."

His next sentence fades off to a mumbled whisper.

"Sorry, Paul, what was the last bit? Didn't catch that," she asks.

He raises the volume to barely audible.

"Erm...I don't think there was anything."

"As a child," she presses, "there was nothing you wanted to be?"

"...No."

"Why do you suppose that was?"

Albie shrugs.

"You have a beautiful voice, did it not occur to you that you could be, say, a singer?"

Now Albie is staring at the floor, like Dougie was, as if it is screening his past.

"I didn't sing if people were around."

Again, his voice thins to nothing. Louise edges closer to him.

"That's quite unusual, Paul...for a boy to have no ideas about what he might like to be when he grows up."

Albie looks up, paler than ever, the light seems to be shining through him.

"I know," he mutters. And then the muttering starts to fade again.

"Sorry, Paul, louder."

"I suppose I...I just never thought that I *could* be anything."

Albie's words are still hanging in the air when, from the corner of the room, we hear a sharp-edged drawl.

"Oh p-lease! Are we going to have to listen to much more of this shit?"

Louise gestures to Gerald to be quiet, but he is walking forward now.

"Oh, come on, this whole little-me routine of his is sick-making! I don't believe a word of it. Ooh, I'm so pale, I'm so sad..." Now he is mimicking Albie's expression. "I'm a startled fawn, give me a fucking break."

What's he up to? Is he jealous of the attention Albie is getting? I decide to take control.

"Gerald, this is Albie's turn, just sit back down and——"

"He's an act, all mysterious and enigmatic like some pathetic bloody sphinx, how come he's the only one who we don't know what he's in for, eh? How come? He won't tell us, no one will tell us. What's all that about? Why's he getting special treatment?"

So, it is jealousy.

"What did you do, Albie, eh, why are you here?"

Albie is sitting, frozen with terror in the chair, his knuckles white as he grips the plastic, grips it hard.

"Come on, Albie!" Gerald is shouting now, his shirt darkened with sweat. "Spill the beans!"

Dougie steps forward, with great purpose.

"Shut it, Gerald."

"Yeh, mind your own bis-ness," calls Pulse.

"Ignore him, Albie," adds Simo.

I feel sure Gerald is playing up for the cameras, because somehow he manages to skip around Dougie to taunt his prey.

"How old are you, Albie? How much time you done?"

Dougie grips Gerald firmly by the shoulder.

"What's it all about, eh?"

Suddenly, Gerald is singing, loud and grating.

"What's it all a-bout, Al-bie?"

The last note is cut short, when Dougie's hand clutches Gerald by the throat and tosses him dismissively across the room. I am poised to hit the alarm button, but then I realise that there is not going to be a fight, Gerald is bent double, coughing and choking.

"Is he OK?" asks the camera operator.

"He'll be fine," says Dougie, like a man who knows about throat injuries. Then he turns to Louise with a warm smile. "I'd rather you didn't include that last bit, Louise, only it could lose me some privileges."

She nods vigorously. It's the first time I've ever seen her looking truly scared. In a few minutes she's witnessed both sides of Dougie, the innocence and the capacity for sudden violence. She knows she's stepped into someone else's world, somewhere beyond controls. The cameraman is already packing his kit away and the rehearsal breaks up in virtual silence, apart from Gerald's strangled splutters as he curls up against the base of the wall.

There was a bit of an atmosphere after that. Gerald knew better than to make a complaint of assault against Dougie – nobody likes a snitch – but every now and then he would give him a venomous glance. Dougie, on the other hand, seemed totally unaffected, as if the whole episode had never happened. Albie, I noticed, started giving Gerald a very wide berth, but seemed to relax a little whenever we were rehearsing music.

Our rehearsals made steady progress. We had found ourselves a new accompanist, Mrs Braddock from the Administration Office. She wasn't as good a pianist as the previous one, but she was less likely to end up in solitary. She thumped the keys gleefully through the numbers and looked transported whenever Albie started to sing. More pieces to camera were recorded but, though I watched her like a hawk, Louise did not put a foot wrong. Nothing she did was cheap or exploitative. There was still time, I told myself.

Gerald's stand-up routine got slicker each day, although I managed to persuade him to take out his impersonation of Dougie – which I thought might be a risk too far. Malcolm sat in on one rehearsal and laughed all the way through Gerald's portrait of a prison governor. Was he really that happy to laugh at himself? Or did he want to look like a good sport?

Everything seems to be going moderately smoothly, until, with a few days to go to the performance, Albie doesn't appear at rehearsals.

19

THE FINAL REHEARSAL

"Where the fuck is he?" yells Dougie, in an uncharacteristic panic. "We've got no show without him. No one's seen him. He's the star turn. What the fuck's happened?"

Then the rumours start to ping around the room. Simo's heard that Albie's in hospital, possibly with AIDS. Pulse has heard that he's in solitary for stabbing someone.

"Albie? Stabbing someone?" I query.

"What I heard, man."

"Who did he stab?"

"I dunno, some fella."

The door opens as a guard shows in Louise and her cameraman. Dougie tries to tap the officer for information about Albie, but his questions go unanswered. I ask Louise if she knows anything.

"First I've heard of it."

"Christ, we need to know," hisses Dougie.

"Perhaps he's had some sort of breakdown," drawls Gerald. "Let's face it, mentally he's a car-crash."

Dougie advances to within a few inches of Gerald's face.

"If anything of that nature has occurred, Gerald, I shall be holding you personally responsible."

"I think that's absurd," flutes Gerald, on his toes, ready to move.

"You stressed the boy out, you arrogant fucker." At this moment, Mrs Braddock enters, to be met by a barrage of questions about Albie. She says she's not sure if she's allowed to tell us what's happened and scuttles off to check with the governor.

About twenty minutes later, I get a message to go see Malcolm.

His office has two fans running, but the air still hangs limp and heavy.

"I'm so sorry Kevin," he begins, "I would have given you a heads-up about Paul, but the situation emerged without any warning."

"Is he sick?"

"No, no, nothing of that nature, no, he's on release for a couple of days for...compassionate reasons."

"Why, what's happened?"

"Well, I can't tell you that, I'm afraid. Don't want to breach a confidence."

"When will he be back?"

"Well...hopefully by show day."

One of the fans starts to make a clicking sound as it half-rotates. Malcolm stares at it for a few moments, preoccupied.

"He...um...when he comes back...Paul may...may be a little...fragile."

Where's he going with this?

"Fragile?"

"Yes..."

"Too fragile to do the show?"

"Hard to say. You'll have to keep an eye on him, y'know, use your judgement as to whether the pressure will be...containable for him..."

"Perhaps we should just cancel the whole thing. Perhaps it's just too much pressure all round. Everyone's getting very tense and—"

He stops me, holding his palms towards me, like I'm traffic.

"Whoa, whoa, there. Let's not jump the gun. Paul will probably be fine. And I think the show is looking great. You've done a brilliant job and I think everyone is going to get a lot out of it. Just keep an eye out, that's all I'm saying."

He winks at me. Nobody winks any more, what does he think he's doing? Nobody's winked at me since my Uncle Ralph, who turned out to be a pervert.

"I know I can rely on you," he says, with no basis whatsoever.

I leave his office confused and apprehensive. One of the few pluses of prison life had been the complete absence of responsibility. But now it seems that is over. Somehow I have been cast as the officer on the bridge. How the fuck did that happen?

I go back to the room and we rehearse what little we can without Albie. Pulse demonstrates that he has really mastered his Shakespeare soliloquy, but Simo's chaotic beat-box dancing seems to have got even more crazed.

"You look like an epileptic. No offence," offers Dougie.

The group agrees that we will continue to rehearse as much as we can on the basis that Albie will be back in time to do the show. As we are packing up, Louise comes across to tell me not to worry and that she has a good feeling. Slowly I begin to recognise the anxiety I am experiencing: pre-performance nerves. How long had it been since I cared enough to have those?

Come the day of the performance, at two in the afternoon, with just five hours to go, Albie walked through the door of the rehearsal room to ironic cheers and a bear-hug from Dougie. He seemed very disconcerted; although it probably didn't help that everyone kept staring at him, trying to assess his state of mind. He received many offers of cups of tea etcetera and, with the obvious exception of Gerald, everyone made a real fuss of him.

After about ten minutes of this, I clap my hands to start the rehearsal. Louise sits down, her cameraman gets in position and

Mrs Braddock attacks the piano as we practise our new finale – "Sit Down You're Rocking the Boat".

I am standing next to Albie and his voice is clear and confident. Maybe he's pleased to be back with us. Seems Malcolm's concerns were unwarranted.

We sing the finale four or five times, then we spend some time going over "Hey Jude", which is still a bit ragged. Gerald is not quite committing to it and, at one point, I catch him rolling his eyes. But morale seems reasonably high when we stop for our first break and I am pouring Simo some tea when I hear the sudden shuffle of feet behind me and I turn to find Albie, his eyes fluttering, being cradled in Dougie's arms as he is lowered towards a chair.

"It's OK, son," Dougie is saying, "I've got you."

"The fella fainted," explains Pulse.

"You're all right, aren't you, let's sit you down."

I hear movement to my right, which I know is the cameraman picking up his camera. I am about to pick a fight about it, but then Albie starts to groan like a stricken animal.

"Is – is he – the – he's—"

"OK, Simo, stay calm, it's under control," I say, as Dougie and Pulse gently persuade Albie to put his head between his legs.

"Shall I fetch a medic?" asks Mrs Braddock.

"No…I'll be OK." Albie is starting to lift his head now. "Just give me a sec."

"Can't we open more windows?" asks Louise. She moves towards the windows, but realises they're designed to only open a few degrees. "Sorry, silly question."

Simo flails his arms around, trying to vent his anger at the heat in choked-off sentences, until Mrs Braddock volunteers that there is a fan in her office and bustles off to fetch it.

Albie's breathing starts to become slower, less shallow, and he straightens up in the chair.

"Sorry about that," he sighs. He receives a friendly volley of reassurances.

"When did you last eat?" I ask.

"Erm..." He screws up his eyes, thinking back. "I, um...I had some crisps...just after the funeral."

"And when was the funeral? Yesterday?"

"Erm...yeah."

"Was it someone close?"

"Yeh...pretty close...her name was Carol."

Pulse squeezes his shoulder. "You don't have to talk about it if you don't want to, fella."

"No," he replies, bold and loud, lifting his head. "No... that's fine...I want to talk about her...tell her story." He looks, fleetingly, at the camera. "No one else will."

"I don't think we need to film this, Louise," I say.

"Hear, hear," adds Gerald.

Albie starts to shake his head. "No, let them film, I don't care...she should be remembered."

Full of apologies, Mrs Braddock enters and plugs in the electric fan. It has little effect, other than to shunt warm air around. Albie breathes through his nose, hard, several times, as if he's steeling himself against pain.

"You don't have to tell us now," I whisper.

"Yes, I do. Before I chicken out...This happened, like...a *long* time ago," he begins. "Long time, see...I'm a lot older than people think...been in prison...er, lots of prisons, long time now...they try to put me out but, like...I keep doing stuff to get back inside."

"Yah, we know, in-sti-tu-tion-al-ised," says Pulse, trying to be supportive.

"Yeh...um, anyway...before prison, y'know...um, they sent me to a special school...'cos I was backward...they don't call it that now...and Carol, she was there an' all, although I don't think she was...well, she was clever, she knew stuff...but she, like...she

got...bit panicky, y'know, around people...so we were different...
but we were the same...and she liked me."

He clears his throat. He pauses, before looking up.

"She was the first person who I felt really liked me...y'know...
who wasn't my mum."

Simo hands him a paper cup with water in.

"Thanks...anyway, her dad was gone...like mine...and her
mum was a bit sort of...mental...so she and me would hang
out...y'know, just hang out, just chatting and stuff...she was
nice...it felt nice...safe..."

"How old were you?" asks Louise.

"Erm...fifteen...then sixteen...we got engaged..." He smiles
at the memory. "No one took us seriously...until..."

An awful premonition pops into my mind a moment before
he confirms it.

"...until Carol finds out she's having a baby...we don't mean
to, it just happened...loads of people told her to get rid of it,
but Carol...she wasn't having that...she said no, she was keeping
it...and I wanted to stand by her, y'know...because I...because
she had no one else, we just had each other...well, and my
mum...when she was sober...the Council kept saying, y'know,
that the baby would have to be given away, like, but Carol just
kept fighting...she said we'd take care of the baby...my mum
said she'd help...so the Council gave us a flat, high up in a tower
block, tiny, it was...and damp, but it was home, our home...and
Carol had the baby, little boy, we named him Sean...and so there
was three of us, me, Carol, and our little bundle, Sean, for us to
look after and love."

His face breaks into a smile as he stares into the crackling fire
of his memory.

"He was lovely...well, no, he...well he was lovely, but..."
His expression clouds a little and his speech gets a little faster.
"Anyway, it didn't turn out well, me and Carol, we...we went

different ways and that's – I haven't seen her since – yesterday that was the first time since – yesterday, lying in that box...my Carol, only not my Carol...old-looking and...her liver packed up, they said...just drank and drank...all 'cos of me...'cos of me."

His hands are visibly trembling now. Mrs Braddock throws me an anxious look. She leans towards me.

"I think I'll go fetch a medic," she says, before creeping quietly towards the door.

"It wasn't 'cos of you, we all make our own choices," says Dougie. "She chose to drink."

"Hardly anyone was there to say goodbye...just me and three others."

"Was your son there?" asks Louise, softly.

Albie runs a shaking hand through his hair. There is a painful little catch in his voice now, like the words are snagging on something.

"No...no, he wasn't, no...Sean had something wrong with him...in his tummy...it wasn't joined up right...so he got a lot of pain...and you can't explain things to a baby, can you...so he just got pain...and the pain would frighten him, so he'd cry...so me and Carol were up and down the hospital all the time, y'know, in those first weeks...and then Mum...died...sudden it was...fell down dead in the Post Office and the Social Services lady said maybe we wouldn't be able to manage Sean, but Carol said he was our son and we'd look after him, but he kept crying and crying...and when he cried...it was like the pain went through you, through your body...we weren't sleeping, none of us, and then...then Carol got down...really down...post..."

"Post-natal depression," prompts Louise.

"Yeh, only she won't talk to anyone 'cos she reckons they'll take Sean away and, like, when the Social Services lady comes, she puts on an act, so do I...we smile and say it's all fine, but it's not fine, it's not, it's really not."

His voice seems to have gone up a few semitones now and every word is quavered as he gallops towards the end of the story and part of me wants to step in and stop him, but I dare not. I am transfixed, like everyone else in the room.

"And I'm not sleeping and Sean's just crying every second of every day and Carol's crying all the time and drinking, and there's neighbours starts thumping on the wall and it was too much, so one night, he's screaming, he's purple, his face, purple, been screaming, she's hysterical, I feel like...like my mind is going to explode, explode through my head and she's yelling horrible things at me, and I can't think, can't *think*, she's yelling that she hates me, she wishes she'd never met me, and he's screaming even louder, and she yells louder, she's screaming she wishes he'd never been born and I can go to Hell and she can't take any more and I can't think, and he's still screaming and I just want to make it all stop and she's beating the floor with her fists asking God to kill her and before I can think, I don't think, I can't think, I'm in a rage, he's screaming, she's screaming and I pick up Sean and I throw him out of the window."

I hear a gasp behind me. Then utter silence. I can see Pulse's jaw hanging down. Simo has his hand over his mouth. Horror. Horror is filling the room, like nerve gas. And Albie is standing before us with his hands tearing at his hair.

"I never meant to hurt him! It happened before I could think! A split-second! My little boy!"

Dougie is the first to speak, slow and deliberate.

"You...murdered a baby."

Albie's eyes are hollow with terror.

"I know...I'm an animal. I must be, mustn't I?"

"We..." continues Dougie, "...have been eating biscuits...and drinking tea...with a baby-killer."

Suddenly Pulse stands and hurls his chair across the room, it clatters against the wall and the floor.

"I never meant to," Albie wails. "And I killed Carol."

And then something bursts inside him and he collapses sobbing into the floor. We all freeze, paralysed by the intensity of his torment – except for Dougie. Dougie attacks him. He starts kicking him hard, in the head, in the ribs, and, from what I can remember, Albie's not trying to protect himself, he's not curling up into a ball, not shielding himself with his arms, he is a rag doll for Dougie to kick and kick and after that it is a blur of arms and legs and curses. Prison officers, three, four of them are knocking Dougie to the ground, and pinning his arms behind him, pushing his face to the floor. The medic rushes in and crouches over Albie, as Dougie is dragged towards the door screaming that Albie is vermin and how you should kill vermin and, as they try to drag him out through the doorway, his blazing eyes fix on me.

"And you…you fucking knew, didn't you, eh?"

Stupidly, even though I am guilty of nothing, I try to justify myself.

"No…I knew there was a secret, but I didn't know what it was."

It sounds so limp, I wouldn't believe it if I was him either.

"You're a liar, the whole world knows you as a liar." I go to reply but suddenly he has broken free and is surging towards me. Two of the guards rugby-tackle him a few inches in front of me.

"Yeh, you fucking knew…you're halfway up the governor's arse, you knew! And you didn't tell us! You're a fucking traitor!"

As they finally succeed in squeezing him through the door, he begins shouting that he is going to kill me. The threats continue, fading slowly, as they bump and haul him down the corridor.

The medic is on his walkie-talkie, asking for assistance, Albie is going to need a stretcher. There is no whimpering, no pain, no noise of any kind, he is staring blankly into nothingness. He looks anaesthetised, purged of feeling.

I sense movement behind me and turn to confront Louise.

"All this has to be wiped, do you hear? Not one second of this is to be includ—"

I stop in mid-shout. There is a tear rolling down her cheek and her eyes are blurred with more.

"What…?" Her voice cracks, her chin is trembling. "What kind of monster do you think I am?"

The camera operator is packing up. He throws me a perfunctory glance.

"She told me to stop filming ten minutes ago."

20

THE LONG NIGHT

An hour later, I am summoned by Malcolm. But I have to sit outside his office while he finishes a phone call. Is he making a point by keeping me waiting? Who cares? Mrs Braddock gives me the occasional supportive smile.

There is a pile of magazines on a table and I find myself leafing through a copy of the New Scientist. My eye is drawn to an article titled "How Real is Reality?" It is written by a neuro-scientist to explain what science does and doesn't understand about perception. The section about vision is quite interesting. Basically it says that what we think of as vision is mostly virtual. Only the central section of the rectangle of our field of vision is actually recorded by the optic nerve. The rest of the picture – the periphery – is modelled by the brain, like a computerised simulation. In the final paragraph, the writer challenges how much of our view of the world can be defined as real. He argues that we only see what we *think* we see. Or what our brain thinks we want to see.

"My life in a nutshell," I mutter. Mrs Braddock looks up from her computer screen to give me another wan smile. I smile back.

"You can never see the full picture, can you?"

She keeps smiling, even though she is bewildered.

Then the door flies open and Malcolm tells me, briskly, to step inside. There are no biscuits. His tone is distant, detached.

He tells me that he is disappointed in me, he expected me to manage things a little better.

I protest that my various warnings had gone unheeded. Also, I point out, I might have been able to manage things better if I had known Albie was a time-bomb. He lapses into jargon about trust, confidentiality, duty of care and boundaries. By the end, I have stopped listening. I feel nauseated, probably from delayed shock. I don't want to be sick, I loathe it, but as a precaution, I inch closer to the waste-paper bin.

"How's Albie?" I ask.

"Broken ribs, fractured jaw."

"But...he'll be OK?"

"Physically, maybe."

"Will he be coming back?"

"I think he'll need to go to a special unit."

"And Dougie?"

"Solitary. Three weeks. Then we'll see."

He calls up an e-mail on his laptop.

"You're getting a new cell-mate. He's Lithuanian, Vilnis."

"What's he in for?"

Malcolm ignores the question and waves a copy of an email at me.

"I just got this. From Louise. 'Due to recent events', blah-di-blah-di-blah…'and as the performance will clearly no longer be taking place, we feel that the documentary would have no climax. We do have some dramatically interesting footage, but I feel that it would be inappropriate to broadcast. Thank you for all your help, we are sorry that this experiment has not worked out as we might all have hoped. We will, of course, honour any contractual financial obligations thus far. Yours, Louise'."

He swivels his chair around to look out of the window at the gun-grey sky.

"Well, that makes sense," I say, to his back. "I…um…I think

I may have been a little harsh on Louise...y'know, perhaps I um...obsessed about her a bit, y'know...drew too heavily on previous experience."

"This is a setback for the prison," says Malcolm's back. "If we'd been showcased, well...we might have attracted more funding, but now...?"

He swivels back round to face me, circles of darkness beneath the armpits.

"You let us down, Kevin."

"I'm sorry your vanity project went tits up, Malcolm."

He giggles nervously – not the Goonish laugh – and closes his laptop. Shouts can be heard in some distant corridor.

"I looked out for you, Kevin...I won't be doing that any more."

A prison officer enters with an "excuse me" and informs the governor that there is a riot in C block. Malcolm orders a lockdown and I am escorted, through the wet, warm air, back to my cell.

The next few days were quiet, virtually silent in fact, because none of the inmates would speak to me. I was being sent to Coventry. It took me a little while to piece together why this was happening. The riot had seriously blackened the mood inside the prison, several people – prisoners and prison-officers – had been hospitalised and, according to one of the warders, the trouble had started when Dougie had somehow got hold of a plank of wood.

The rage in Dougie had triggered the riot and, because of the riot, prisoners had lost all privileges. Furthermore, Dougie's rage was being laid at my door. I was the traitor who – in collusion with the governor – had kept from them all the filthy secret that there had been a baby-killer in their midst. So I was now a pariah, an outcast.

My new cell-mate, Vilnis, anxious not to get involved, communicated with me only in grunts and nods. But at least the heatwave was easing off and, to be honest, the silent treatment didn't really bother me. I was in no mood to talk to anyone. I felt numb from the shock of that final rehearsal. The speed with which the explosions had happened felt impossible to take in. One moment Albie had been receiving support and sympathy, the next...

Silence was fine by me. There was nothing more to say. True, it was obscene and unfair to blame me for Albie's secret, or Dougie's insane reaction, but there was little point my trying to set the record straight. No one was going to listen, not when the lies and the rumours were more attractive. People need scapegoats. That's how we make sense of things going wrong. Prison is like society, only more so.

I would be lying if I said that I had not considered the possibility of being attacked. But, although I had spotted many contemptuous glances, no actual threats had been made. After a while, I began to think if anything was going to happen, it would have happened by now. If the silence was the worst I could expect, then, fuck it, I could handle that. What did that matter compared with the carnage of that last rehearsal?

Then the silence was broken.

I am in the prison garden, on my knees, weeding, when Gerald quietly kneels down beside me and pretends to be weeding too.

"How's things?" he asks, extremely quietly.

"Quiet", I whisper.

"Yeh." He gives a soft, mischievous chuckle. "This time it really *is* about you."

"Should you be talking to me? I'm the leper, aren't I?"

"Too right...all sorts of rumours circulating about you..."

"I don't care, I'm not interested."

My instinct is not to give Gerald the satisfaction of rattling me.

"Shame about the show," he sighs. "I'd worked up all that material."

"That's showbiz."

He glances over his shoulder, then edges slightly closer.

"I can get you a knife."

It takes a few moments for what he has said to sink in.

"What?"

"I can get you a knife."

"Why the f—" I pause to get control and lower my voice. "Why the fuck would I want a knife?"

Gerald looks at me as if I'm an amusing oddity.

"You'd want a knife if you found yourself with someone else who has a knife."

He waits to see the penny drop. He is creating his own entertainment.

"That's bollocks," I tell him, "no one cares enough about me to stab me."

"That might have been true, but not now. The rumours have changed that. New rumours."

"What new rumours?"

"What do you care? You're not interested."

He is wearing that simpering grin of his. I don't want to play his twisted little game, but I need to know.

"What new rumours?"

"Word is…you're one of these 'establishment' paedos."

"What?! How the…?!"

"That's the rumour, courtesy of Dougie."

"He's in solitary."

Gerald gives me a pained look. "What? You can't start a rumour from solitary? Come on Kevin, you know what this place is like. Stuff passes clean through the walls…"

For a moment, I wonder if Gerald is making all this up, just for the recreational value of frightening me. But can I risk ignoring him?

"I hate gardening," he says, "it's what average people do." He pulls up some clover. "Three leaves. Has there ever been such a thing as a four-leafed clover? Or is that just a con?"

There is a pumping inside my forehead now.

"I am not a paedophile."

"That's irrelevant, I'm afraid. So do you want the knife or not?"

"Come on, Gerald, you know I'm not a—"

"Well, strictly speaking, I don't."

"Is no one prepared to stick up for me?" I ask, aware that it sounds pathetic. "What about the group? Pulse, Simo...?"

"Have they spoken to you at all?"

"No."

"Well, there's your answer."

In his repellent, cold way, Gerald is driving it home to me that I am abandoned and without allies. Hence the knife.

"Apparently, Dougie has commissioned some associates to do the deed...soon."

This fills me with unspeakable sadness. The man with whom I had shared all those rambling nocturnal conversations, all that trench humour – that same man now wants me dead. And for what? Some infantile, warped, synthetic sense of betrayal.

"This makes no sense," I mutter.

"He's a madman," says Gerald, casually. "Now, do you want the knife?"

"Why are you looking out for me?" I ask.

Gerald giggles. "I'm not looking out for you. I'm selling it to you. I'm not a charity shop."

Well, I didn't buy Gerald's knife. I decided to put my faith in the system. I went straight to the nearest prison officer and told him I had reason to believe my life was under threat. He did not seem particularly bothered. He said he would report my concerns to his superior. I told him that was not good enough and asked to see the governor, Malcolm.

"He's not the governor any more," I am told.

"Really?"

"No. He's gone on gardening leave. There's a new man now. Interim."

I feel no sympathy for Malcolm. He, more than anyone, set these events in motion. The prison officer repeats that he will record my anxieties in his file notes for the next shift and that a review procedure will be set in motion. The abstract tone of his words is terrifying, set against the physical reality of a prisoner – somewhere close – who has a knife and orders from Dougie.

I return to my cell with a sense of leaden dread. Perhaps I should have bought the knife. Or perhaps Gerald was making it all up. For some reason, a song, an ear-worm, is burrowing into my brain.

"I've grown accustomed to her face..."

How the hell did that get there? When I have such serious matters to worry about, how has some banal lyric sneaked into my head?

Is this really all Malcolm's fault? Is it anyone's fault? Where does the chain start? With Albie's alcoholic mother? Dougie's brutal father? Or his father's father? The man who might be coming for me has a father.

Gerald could have been lying. He was definitely enjoying himself.

It was after midnight when they came for me. Not that I had been sleeping, I had been staring at the blank, answerless ceiling with Albie's horrifying words echoing through my head. I had been replaying Louise's tears and Dougie's animal snarl and Gerald's insidious offer, so I didn't register the approaching feet.

Suddenly, two officers, Henderson and Bluntstone, were shaking my bunk. My cellmate, Vilnis, pretended to be asleep as they ordered me to get dressed, now, immediately, and not ask any smartarse questions. I knew better than to remonstrate with Bluntstone, he had a reputation for sly violence. I got dressed as fast as I could to a backing of affected snores from Vilnis, then they marched me out of my cell, through the neon whiteness of many corridors, to a side-exit that I never knew existed and into the yard, where a prison van was waiting, headlights on, engine ticking over. As they push me through the cold night air towards the back of the van, the fear kicks in.

"Where are you taking me?" I ask, as I'm steered through the doors.

"Don't piss me off with lots of questions," says Bluntstone. "Night-shift's supposed to involve watching porn, not driving low-life around."

"Where are you taking me?"

The front doors slam and the engine is revved into life.

"I have a right to know where you're taking me."

Through the grill I can glimpse the prison gates opening and, as we edge into the dark outside world, the fear intensifies.

"Where the fuck are you taking me?"

"Don't bang on the grill, Carver," Henderson sighs. "Just sit back and enjoy the excursion."

I repeat the same question, two, three times, but am ignored. Now we're driving through some suburbs, I can see loft extensions, trimmed hedges, my temples are drumming as my mind clicks through the possibilities.

A transfer? Is that it? They've decided I won't be safe in the same prison as Dougie, so they're moving me out of harm's way. The prison authorities don't want some ex-soapstar being found with his throat slit, so they're shifting me. Yes, that makes sense. But why now? Why the early hours of the morning? Why all this melodrama?

"Am I being transferred?"

Henderson lets out a grim chuckle.

"Tell you what, Carver, I'll cut you a deal," says Bluntstone casually over his shoulder. "You don't ask any more questions and in return I don't come back there and kick your goolies into fine goolie-dust, how's that?"

I fall quiet, but as we trundle out of the speed-bumped avenues into the black emptiness of the country roads, my fear ratchets up another few notches.

I decide to ask again, very, very politely.

"Listen, Carver, we can't answer your questions, 'cos we don't know, all right? Now shut up."

Henderson sounds sincere, but is that believable?

"You've no idea?"

"I think someone wants to have a chat with you," says Bluntstone, mischievously.

A chat? I start spinning through some more sinister possibilities. Are they taking me to some woods to administer a beating? Why? They could have given me a clandestine beating back at the prison. Could it be Dougie? Are they in cahoots with Dougie? Has Dougie arranged for me to be whisked away to some secret location where some of his underworld mates can dispatch me and bury my body? Could that be it?

"Is this officially sanctioned by the governor?"

"You'll find out," Bluntstone answers, enjoying his power.

For what seems like hours, we bounce and rattle through the night and, sitting in the gloom, the notion that I will be met by Dougie's associates takes a grip on my racing thoughts.

We come to a halt.

I feel some sick in my mouth. Am I going to vomit? The back doors fly open and it is with some relief that I see a dozen or so policemen in high-vis jackets. Some have guns. A couple of them help me out of the back of the van. One of them, older, steps forward.

"Sorry to drag you out like this, Mr Carver, but we've hit a bit of a dead end."

"Sorry?" I am momentarily dazzled by the headlights of an arriving police car.

"Has nobody explained the situation to you?"

"No."

He looks at the two prison officers.

"We were just told to bring him here."

The senior policeman shakes his head.

"So sorry, Mr Carver. Communications 'air-gap'."

My eyes are starting to adjust now. We appear to be on the edge of a dark-filled wood and a cordon of about six police cars is forming a kind of barrier. Beyond the cars, there seems to be a field, sloping slightly uphill, and from somewhere out in the middle of that field I can hear the indistinct sound of a shouting voice.

"He's said he'll only talk to you."

The voice is fast and manic, pitched high with adrenalin. It takes a moment for me to realise.

It is Derek's voice.

"He seems very upset and he's got a gun. His only demand, so far, is that he speaks with you."

I start to laugh, without wanting to, and the senior policeman looks bewildered.

"Says you're a friend of his."

"No, that's not true," I reply, trying to stifle the nervous laughter, "in fact, I hate his guts."

"Oh...oh, I see...um...well, the thing is...we've got three armed response boys here obviously...y'know, as a last resort, but ideally I don't want to have to go down that road...that'll probably mean another enquiry...but if someone like yourself could just talk him down then...my colleague, Cliff Barham, has been conducting the negotiation so far...he's out there with him now – but Cliff's view was that you'd have a better chance of calming him down, given that he's asked for you."

I take a few moments to try and take in the absurdity of the situation.

"Obviously, Mr Carver, it's entirely your choice."

"This man is *not* my responsibility."

"I appreciate that, Mr Carver, I'm asking you as a citizen."

A citizen? When did I become a citizen?

"It is your decision," he continues, "and I appreciate your misgivings, I really do, but we would hide a microphone on you. And if we deem you to be in danger then a marksman will take him down."

"Take him down? What...? Shoot him in the kneecaps, that sort of..."

"No, Mr Carver, that only happens in the movies. If someone's in danger, we always shoot to kill."

In the distance, I hear Derek yelling something about the Illuminati. More nervous laughter from me. How did I end up here? In a field, in the middle of the night, being guided towards a shouting, gun-waving wanker.

"I know we're asking a lot, Mr Carver." He studies my face intently. "But it's our best hope of a satisfactory outcome." He pauses, still waiting for me. "And it would probably play very well, um...with the parole board."

His idea of an incentive makes me giggle. "Right."

Behind us, an owl screeches and makes one of the marksmen jump.

"Give me one good reason why I should say yes."

He considers for a few beats. "To stop anyone getting hurt."

21

THE SIEGE

I have often wondered why I said yes. It's a decision I'll never fully understand, but I think it took shape somewhere in the zone between me being myself and me observing myself. Vanity, as ever, played its part. Normally, I am not the kind of man to walk towards the possibility of gunfire, but so many people had now written me off as worthless that I wanted to defy expectations. I guess I had grown tired of disappointing people – especially myself.

The only truth that I know for certain is that, at that precise moment, I had stopped caring about what might happen to me. Life had become a sick joke. The project that had been restoring a vestige of meaning to my life now lay in ruins. The unlikely friendships that had begun to reanimate me were over, destroyed by Albie's secret. Sandra was married and happy. Eventually, I would be released from prison, but to what? Days of sidelong glances and unreturned phone calls. I would be poison, I had nothing to lose.

There was one other important factor. I had come to regard Derek as a ridiculous individual, so I found it hard to believe that he would ever fire a gun. To me, he was someone playing at being armed and dangerous. To the police, he was a life-threatening situation, an unknown factor brandishing a weapon and shouting in the darkness; they had to take him seriously. But I couldn't.

And, needless to say, I thought I knew best. History is littered with absurd little men who no one took seriously. I'd have done well to remember that.

The policemen in high-vis jackets take me behind the police van and start helping me put on a bulletproof vest. It's a little big and so it's not easy to button my shirt over it. The senior officer is nervously jangling some change in his pocket.

"We really appreciate this, Kevin," he says, not for the first time. "I mean we could sit it out, but, um, the Chief Constable..." He tails off, realising that whatever he was about to say was not information that should be shared with an outsider.

"I'm doing this on one condition," I tell him.

"Fine, what is it?"

"No press. No cameras. No journalists. No one filming anything on their phone. Nothing."

A sergeant, standing behind the officer's shoulder, pulls an embarrassed face.

"Erm..."

"What is it, sergeant?"

"Well, sir...there is a local TV crew already here. I've tucked them over behind the vehicles."

"What?" shouts the officer, before reducing his voice to a whisper. "Who the hell tipped them off? Whoever it was, he is toast, is that clear? Who rang them, eh?"

The sergeant nods in the direction of the sloping field.

"I think it might have been him, sir."

Of course it was. Derek wouldn't initiate a siege-situation without summoning the cameras first.

"Move them too far away to see anything," I say. "Otherwise I'm not going anywhere."

The sergeant sighs and turns away, muttering something about transparency. Then a tall man in plain clothes, mostly denim, walks out of the gloom.

"This is Cliff, our trained negotiator," explains the senior officer.

Cliff extends his hand towards me. His handshake is self-consciously manly. As they hide a microphone under my collar, he starts to brief me in a slow, carefully measured tone which is really quite irritating – surely a handicap in his line of work.

"Alrighty, Kevin...Derek has indicated to me that he would be prepared to talk to you. I've been trying to talk him down for an hour but...well, he got very angry at the beginning when I didn't recognise him...and we've struggled a bit after that so...he's a hard man to get a handle on."

"I know...there's no centre to him."

Cliff looks impressed. "Yeh, yeh that's...that's sort of it, I think. Now, these are the things I need you to remember, Kevin. One, don't get closer than ten yards. He might feel threatened. Also, you'll create a problem for the marksmen. Two. Talk soft and calm, like I am talking to you now. Can you do that?"

God, this man is patronising. It's a miracle some maniac hasn't shot him by now.

"Three. Try and find out what he wants. But don't hit him with too many questions. Four, offer him hope. Tell him that, whatever his problem is, we can all work it out. In my experience, people in his situation are looking for an opportunity to give themselves up, provided that it doesn't involve a loss of face. Five, once you feel he's calm enough, ask him to put down the gun. Don't ask too early, the gun gives him his sense of control. So get him calmer first. OK, Kevin? Shall I recap?"

I tell him that I've got all that, but he recaps regardless.

"One. No closer than ten yards. Two, soft and calm. Three. Find out what he wants. Four, hope. Five, the gun, but don't rush it."

Suddenly, out of the murk, comes Derek's voice, louder and more shrill than before, yelling incoherent threats.

Cliff puts his hand on my shoulder. "From what you know of him, Kevin, does he have a propensity for violence?"

"No, no, no, all this stuff is just bluster. He's a fantasist. I can't imagine him using a gun. I bet he doesn't even know how to use it."

Cliff looks a little perplexed.

"Well...he's already used it."

"...I'm sorry, what?"

"He's already used the gun. Has no one told you this?"

A coldness seeps through my insides.

"...No...no, that hadn't been mentioned."

Cliff gives the senior officer a look that says "What the fuck...?" The officer shrugs and jangles some more change. Then he steps towards me.

"I do apologise, Kevin. I thought I'd told you, sorry, there's been a lot going on. Derek shot a couple of sheep. Then the farmer called us out."

I struggle to put the sequence of events together. Derek has shot some sheep in order to get himself surrounded by police? That's a calculated, cold act of mindless violence. With a firearm. That doesn't fit with my picture of him at all, and it changes everything. Do I still want to be the man in the white hat?

"Listen, we fully understand if you want to back out," says Cliff. "Totally understandable."

The microphone has been fitted now. They want me to say something to test it.

Still disorientated, I mumble: "Testing."

Cliff asks me if I'm OK.

Derek is still shouting, out there, in the night, with the dead sheep. Lots of half-lit faces are turned towards me. Am I brave enough to face this sheep-killing version of Derek? Is that really me?

A voice asks me to test the mic again.

"Testing, 2, 3, 4."

I have often relived that walk through the gloom towards the outline of Derek and his gun. The soft swish of the wet grass against my trousers. The cool breeze caressing my face. But most of all I remember the contradiction; because even though I was walking towards an unknown danger, I felt a sense of icy, inner calm, almost a suspended state, as if the clocks had stopped ticking for me. It was a feeling I had experienced once before, with Sandra, when a van had knocked our car out of the fast lane at eighty miles per hour and we had bounced, in tantalising slow-motion, across the central reservation and into the restraining barrier, which had punched rivets and joints through our doors, the metal scraping and screaming, till we came to a juddering halt. And as we stepped out of the wreck of that car, with barely a scratch on us, I remember being blanketed in that same stillness and clarity, as if I understood everything, as if I was part of everything.

That was the feeling that had returned to me, and was now slowing my pulse as I walked towards the hardening shape of Derek.

When I got to within about thirty yards, I could make out two small hummocks on each side of him, which I slowly realised were the corpses of the sheep.

"Is that you, Kevin?"

I stop. "Yes, Derek."

"Come a little closer."

I move forward to within fifteen yards. He peers at me through the gloom.

"Well, well, old friend," he begins, "thank you for coming."

I search for a response that won't sound preposterous.

"I'm here to help."

"This is like old times, eh, you and me, together, riding against the law."

Oh God, he's got us down as Butch Cassidy and the Sundance Kid.

"How can I help, Derek?" I ask, in a voice that, to my surprise, sounds completely relaxed.

"I just needed to see you, Kevin, that's all. Last time we met, it went so badly, I hated that. You punched me in the face."

"I'm sorry about that, Derek. I was under a lot of pressure."

His voice turns a little tinny. "*You* were under pressure? My God!"

I find myself staring at the gun. It's a revolver, which he is holding in his left hand while gesturing expansively.

"Pressure? My whole life is pressure. God. I tell you, Kevin, no one has any idea...they...they..."

As he shakes his head, ransacking his mind for words, I consider asking him to put down the gun. But then he suddenly jabs it in front of his face for emphasis.

"They've...they've done for me, Kevin, just like they did for her."

"...Her?"

"Princess Diana." He cocks his head to one side, like a bird, puzzled and a little offended that I hadn't made the connection. "Her emotional honesty threatened the establishment. And so does mine. So they just hunt you down."

In normal circumstances, I would have felt nauseated by the self-obsession, but my brain seems to have shut down all emotions, or anything that might get in the way of the job at hand. The gun is down by his side. I'll try hope.

"Listen Derek, whatever your...um...understandable grievances are, I'm sure everyone can sit down and talk through them constructively with you, but to do that we're going to need you to put the gun on the ground. Will you do that for me?"

Derek steps back half a yard. Have I spooked him? His shoulders droop.

"I shot these sheep," he wheedles, in a small, cracked voice. "I shot them dead. And I've never hurt a living thing in my life. That's what they've done to me."

I realise that I am going to have to let this stuff pour out of him for a while, he's too unstable to force anything. His paranoia seems to be growing and his voice keeps changing in volume and character.

"They've fired me off the show. Can you believe that? The fans are furious, you should see some of the tweets. I know they were ordered to get rid of me by someone high up. It's a shame Louise left. She'd have stood up to them, she liked me."

Now he is cuddling the gun against his chest with both hands, like it's a teddy bear.

"I've tried all the usual channels to try and make them realise their error. I got told to stop being – and I quote – 'a pest'."

He lets the word hang in the air. I am clearly expected to comment.

"Right…that's…not a nice word."

"No, it's not. Rats are a pest…bedlice are a pest."

The gun is lowered to his side again. For a moment, he seems intolerably weary.

"These people…" he mutters, "…they've dogged me all my life." Perhaps this represents some kind of opening.

"Listen, Derek…the police have asked me to find out exactly what you want, y'know…what are your demands?"

Suddenly, he looks skywards, as if he's searching for inspiration. The awful thought occurs to me that he has engineered this whole opera without the faintest thought why. Maybe the opera *is* the why?

"Tell me what you want, Derek," I say, in the smooth voice I once used to advertise cars. "Take your time, I'm not going anywhere."

"No, I know," he chuckles, with a faint spark of malice. For the first time, I notice my pulse quicken.

"There's lots of things I want, Kevin...lots of them..."

"All right then...let's make the list."

"OK then." He starts to spin the revolver in his hand, like a gunslinger.

"Can you not do that, Derek? I'm worried there might be an accident."

He stops spinning it. "Good point, Kevin. Health and safety."

I wonder, for a moment, if he's made a joke to relieve the tension, but then he continues. "Too many people are cavalier about it. That's how I got a broken toe in the scene with the cow. I had mentioned my concerns but, guess what, I wasn't listened to."

The hiss of anger has crept back into his voice.

"Al-righty, the first thing that I want, Kevin, is an acknowledgement."

He pauses for effect, so I play along.

"An acknowledgement?"

"From you."

"What kind of acknowledgement, Derek?"

"I want you to acknowledge...that we are friends."

Is he setting some kind of trap? If I say we are friends, will he accuse me of insincerity?

"Why is that important for you, Derek?" (Am I overusing his name?)

"It's important for both of us," he replies. "I need you to accept that, despite everything, the punch, everything, despite all that, there is still a bond of friendship between us that transcends all that, a friendship that dates back to that day you poured that cup of tea for me, when I was a supporting artist in that queue at the catering van, a friendship that was consolidated when I tried to save you in your moment of need. I need you to acknowledge that friendship, I need you to say, loud and clear, that the friendship between us is *real*."

All through the acceleration of that outburst, his expression has grown more and more alarming and now he is fixing me with a beady intensity that makes him look like a different person. The only sensible course of action would be to appease him with a lie. But, for some reason, the lie won't come. My lie-duct is blocked. So I look for something soft and conciliatory.

"Well...I'm here, aren't I?"

"Ex-actly! Exactly, Kevin." He bounces on his feet with excitement. "You having come here is living proof of our friendship. You couldn't pass by on the other side. Our story has come full circle. I was there for you when you needed someone to rescue you from malignant forces and now you are here to rescue me. That's proof, isn't it?"

"Yes...yes, I suppose it is."

"But I need you to say it out loud."

I glance back at the police, huddled behind the flaring headlights. One more lie is all that is required of me. One more moment of expediency in a life that has been full of them. And if ever one would be justified it would be now. The man has a gun. But a bone-weariness is descending on me. Appeasement is pointless. Derek has moved to a new level now, he is building himself an even larger cathedral of fantasy. Well, I want out. I will be free of this man crouching in the gloom. So, very calmly, I say what needs to be said.

"It is true, Derek, that there was once, briefly, a bizarre connection between us, born of my desperation and your delusions of grandeur."

He starts shaking his head, but I carry on, still composed and clear-headed.

"But that was not friendship. We are not friends. We never were."

He considers for a moment, then laughs bitterly to himself.

"Well, how stupid of me. How stupid to raise the subject of friendship with a man who has no feelings."

"You may have a point there, Derek. Perhaps I don't experience enough feelings…but you binge on them…you manufacture them to feed your addiction."

He is straightening up now, but the gun is still hanging at his side.

"Did they tell you to say this garbage? To rattle me? Hm?" He raises the gun and waggles it angrily in the direction of the police vehicles. "Is that their game?"

I take a deep, quiet breath and concentrate hard on keeping the relaxation in my voice.

"This was about power. Well, you've achieved what you wanted. You got them here, you got me here, but now it's over. So, put down the gun. You're not a killer, Derek."

There is a tremble in his voice now. "I'm not, I'm really not."

"I know, now put the gun on the ground."

"I'm a victim of injustice."

"You're a victim of victimhood. Your grievances are manufactured as well."

He steps forward, one pace, two, three. I went too far, always the smartarse.

"I *am* a victim of injustice," he repeats. "And you are going to tell the press why I'm here, why I've got the gun, how those bastards have—"

"I sent the press away, Derek."

It is an instinctive interruption, to try to calm his growing agitation, but suddenly the gun is being jabbed in my direction. And his voice has changed again, this time to a low growl.

"You had no right to do that, Kevin." He drops his head for a moment and stares at the earth. I hear a scrabbling movement behind the police vehicles. "You've let me down. I reached out to you, a fellow human being in pain, who—"

Again, the interruption leaps out of my mouth.

"Derek, a few days ago I saw someone in more pain than you,

or I, or anyone, could ever begin to imagine, and which, frankly, makes this whole…pantomime seem rather ludicrous."

He takes another couple of steps forward, he's just a few feet from me now and I can see that his sandy hair is plastered to his head with sweat.

"Pantomime?" he growls. "I'm a pantomime?"

The gun is pointing directly at my chest, but I look him straight in the eye.

"Derek…I am really sorry that you seem trapped in the person you are…but my presence here is achieving nothing…so I am going to leave now."

"Don't you dare!" he hisses, thrusting the gun forward.

I turn away from him, with a firm smoothness that surprises me in the circumstances.

"Don't you *dare* leave me!"

I start to walk away, slowly but steadily. I know I'm taking a risk in turning my back on him, but in a life that has an impressive tally of poor choices, this feels like the best decision I have ever made. As I walk through the wet grass, back towards the lights of the police vehicles, my step feels light, my thoughts are lucid and I feel like the young man I once was, back when the world was mine, back before I so carelessly lost Sandra, before I fell out of love with my craft, before I started coasting, before the big shutdown. So, even though the trees are ringing to the rants and shouts of an enraged Derek, and even though the gun is probably being pointed at me, my fear is outbalanced by elation because I am unshackled. I have taken control. He can cast no shadow over me now, nor squat in some dingy corner of my mind. He is history and this is the beginning of – crack! crack! Something knocks my legs from under me. What the— what just happe— have I been shot? Has he sho—? Wha—? There's some pain, an ache, in my— my God he has! The little fucker's shot me! The pain is deepening now, jagged, like a knife being dragged backwards, through my stomach— hard to— crack!!

Has he shot me again? Is he finishing me off?

I can hear screaming – a blood-curdling, long shriek, like an animal in a slaughterhouse. Then the scream shapes into words:

"You fucking bastards! My knee! My kneeee! You bastards!"

There's shouting now and a thumping. Running feet, feet running towards me, faces, faces looking down at me, faces with mouths saying foggy words, calling my name, the knife is twisting inside me and the pain makes me feel sick, I'm going to throw up, please God no, I hate throwing up.

There's panic on the faces, they're scared, they're looking at me and they're scared, why are they scared?

Is this it then?

After all that.

You prick, Kevin. What a stupid way to go. In a field, shot by a nobody.

Really hard to breathe now. Want to sleep.

In a field, God knows where.

I've grown accustomed to her…

Need to sleep. In a cave. For nine months.

…like breathing out and breathing in.

Rea-lly sleepy.

Who'll come to my funeral?

Got to sleep.

Sandra, Mac. Maybe Nina Patel.

Getting cold now. I'm in mid-air? Why am I in mid-air?

And the people all said sit down.

Now I'm floating.

Sit down, you're rocking the boat.

Feeling so sleepy, flashing lights, white and shiny. Why is "ambulance" written backwards? Everything shiny-shiny.

Sandra, Mac. Who else?

Got to sleep.
Who else?
Go to sleep.
Who?
Sleepity-sleep.
...I should have done more.

22

THE DATE

I had been in hospital for a few days before I learnt the truth. Inevitably, my picture of events turned out to be completely wrong. Derek had not shot me. He had probably been about to shoot me – or at least, that was the police interpretation – so a marksman had decided to down him. Unfortunately I had – again, according to the police – "strayed into the line of fire" and had taken a bullet at the top of my left thigh, just below the bullet-proof vest. A second marksman had then shot Derek, in the knee. Whether that was through incompetence or design was unclear. I learnt all this from Nina Patel, who was my first visitor. She was wearing black tights and every time she crossed her legs there was a soft, swishing whisper. It felt odd to have a libido again. I had almost forgotten my old friend.

"Stop staring at my legs," she says.

"I'm not staring, they just happen to be in my eyeline."

"Then close your eyes, I need you to pay attention."

I lever myself up a little, but get my drip-lead tangled. She leans forward to help. She's wearing perfume.

"Do I need all this rubbish sticking out of me?"

"Yes, you lost quite a lot of blood. Does it hurt much?"

"Bit sore, achey."

"They've been giving you something for the pain."

I find myself seized by an uncontrollable fit of the

giggles, can't stop myself, even though it causes me pain in several places.

Nina Patel looks puzzled.

"What? What is it?" She starts to giggle.

"Sorry, it's just...I just got to thinking what a mental farce it all was...Derek in that field, with his gun, and his dead sheep... those useless policemen...that idiot of a negotiator...and me playing the Jimmy Stewart part...what a prick." I wait for the giggles to die away. "Sorry, just got to me."

"We could be talking quite a lot of compensation."

"Eh?" I dab at my eyes with a corner of the sheet.

She hands me a tissue.

"It's a national news story. The police are keeping it as vague as possible at the moment. You 'were wounded'; they're using the passive quite a lot. They're launching an internal investigation. But they know there was incompetence, so you've got a good case if you want to pursue it."

"Oh I dunno...I'm not sure I can be bothered...it'd just keep the whole story going, wouldn't it?"

She has a lovely smile, it lights up the room.

"Well, I think you might be right. But don't say I said that. A lawyer who advised against legal action, my colleagues would string me up."

I laugh, till the pain stops me.

"So what's happening to Derek?"

"Well there's a rumour that he might be crippled."

"Oh, he'll love that."

"I mean he's looking at, well...five years' jail minimum, I'd say...there'll be a psychiatric assessment of some kind."

"That'll take decades."

"Are the jokes to stop you getting angry?"

She has stopped me in my tracks. I pause to consider her question properly.

"No." A wave of relaxation passes through me. "No...not at all...isn't that weird? I *was* angry with him obviously, with all of it...but, I dunno...now it just all seems so...negligible. When I'm up on my feet...y'know...and a free man, do you fancy a trip to the theatre, or having dinner or something?"

She looks at me without blinking for several seconds.

"What's the 'or something'?"

"I mean if you don't—"

"Yes, Kevin, dinner would be nice."

"I mean don't worry if—"

"I just said yes."

"Oh right, great...thanks."

There is a flicker of embarrassment between us. What is wrong with me? Why does she make me feel so gauche? She rises out of her chair and kisses me softly on the forehead. Did I let out a tiny yearning groan then? Oh God. She pretends not to notice.

"They said not to wear you out." She pauses by the door, "If you change your mind about suing the arse off them, let me know."

"OK."

Then she gives a surprisingly girlish wave and she is gone.

I lie there, still and small, listening to the laughter of nurses in the corridor, and wondering if I will be allowed to eat proper food today.

Within a week, I was home, with daily visits from the District Nurse to check on my dressing. The remaining time on my sentence, I was informed, was under review, but Nina said she was totally confident that I would not be going back to prison, although I would probably have to do some form of community service. So effectively Derek's little nocturnal melodrama had freed me.

We made an agreement with the police that I would only talk to their internal investigators and not the press. In return, they agreed to make a donation – the size to be negotiated – to the charity of my choice. I chose the Prisoners' Education Trust.

I asked Nina if she could make enquiries about what had happened to Paul, sometimes known as Albie. She did her best, but it appeared that the new regime at the prison was not very forthcoming. I told her the full story of Albie's shattering secret and she offered to keep looking for him, but I decided to drop the matter. What difference would it make if I found out what happened to Albie? He was probably in some special isolation block somewhere, along with all the narks, nonces and anyone else who would be at risk in an understaffed prison. Or perhaps they'd moved him to the other end of the country, where his secret would have less chance of following him. I felt sad when I thought about Albie, but I had been just one catalyst among many that had triggered the latest explosion in his life. If Malcolm had not insisted that I start the drama group; if Dougie had not grown so fond of him; if his childhood sweetheart had not died. There were so many factors. I was only one of them, anyone could see that.

As for Dougie, well, I knew what had happened to him because it was in the newspapers. He had been so violent in the riot, assaulting several prison officers, that his sentence had been extended by five years. It was hard to imagine him as a threat any more. The others, I presumed, were carrying on as before, counting down their time, their lives describing the same small circles.

One morning, as the nurse is applying some stinging stuff to my bullet wound I hear a long, insistent, familiar ring of the doorbell. She answers the door and heavy feet come charging up the hall.

"There he is! Fuck me, look at that hole, that's an impressive wound, yer old bastard."

Mac leans forward to embrace me, but the nurse tells him he'll have to make do with a handshake.

"OK, nurse knows best."

"This is Malgosia. She's Polish. She's cleaning this up for me."

"Good, 'cos it looks revolting."

"It's better than it was."

"So fill me in, I've been in Romania touring with a modern opera about Ceaucescu."

"Oh right. When's that coming to the West End?"

"Am I allowed to punch him?"

"Not for two fortnights," replies Malgosia sternly.

"What the h-ell were you thinking of? Is it true the tosser had a shotgun?"

"No, it was a revolver."

"He actually shot you with a revolver?"

"Well no, he…" I wonder if I should give Mac all the details. He would enjoy the farcical aspects and I trust him like a brother – an indiscreet, mouthy brother.

"It's…I sort of got caught in the crossfire…it's all a little unclear…the police are launching an enquiry."

"Aye, well they'll probably conclude you shot yourself."

He grasps my hand and squeezes it affectionately.

"Well, I'm impressed, I'm also bewildered and furious. You could have got yourself killed…" He studies my face intently. "Or is that what you were after? Was that it? You were hoping he'd take you out?"

It upsets me to hear the crack of emotion in his voice, but Malgosia is packing away her things, so I shrug and switch the topic to football. We have a brief conversation about how any player who prays before kick-off should be immediately red-carded, and then put up against a wall and shot. There's a call of "cheeribye" from Malgosia. Mac calls "cheeribye" back, before he comes at me again.

"So, *were* you trying to get yourself killed?"

"I…I honestly don't know."

"You stupid bast—"

"At that moment, I dunno, nothing seemed to matter much any more." I tell him a shortened version of the final rehearsal. By the time I have finished, he is staring into the distance, slowly shaking his head.

"Jesus H. Christ. How could anyone throw a baby out of a window?Je-sus…"

"He was beside himself…desperate…"

"Moment of madness."

"Yeh."

Mac stretches back in his chair and blows hard.

"Life's a bitch, isn't it?"

The banality of this rips a laugh out of me, a painful laugh.

"Yes…yes it is."

We fall into silence for a while. He looks older, his face more care-worn.

"How's the love-life?" I ask.

"Oh, y'know…mixed…I met a lovely wee girl in Bucharest but her boyfriend turned out to be a gangster so…well, let's just say I can't go back to Bucharest again…and you?"

"Not sure…looking up, I think…possibly, very early days."

"So the trouser department's firing up again, then?" And he's off. Chuckling and cackling at the idea of his friend getting an erection.

"How old are you?"

"Thirteen and a half," he replies triumphantly. "That's the secret of my charm."

We settle into discussions around the usual topics for ten minutes or so and then, out of the blue, he asks me:

"Have you heard from Sandra?"

"Yeh…yeh, I have." I pause for a tiny moment to swallow. "Yeh, yeh, she sent me a lovely letter a couple of days ago…really lovely letter, saying she hoped I was OK and that she was sorry about my getting shot and –" Mac snorts with laughter. "– I'm paraphrasing here, obviously. And she said she can't visit me quite yet, y'know, on account of her just having had the baby."

"I've got a photo of little Eleanor on my phone." He gets out his mobile and swears at it for a few moments as he tries to locate the picture.

"Ah, gotcha. There, look, isn't she a cracker?"

The newborn baby looks like a newborn baby, but I make the right noises.

"And here's one of the proud mum."

Sandra's face is illuminated with joy. She looks fantastic.

"I'm thrilled for her."

"Are you sure?" asks Mac.

"Yes. It's brilliant for her, because that's what she wanted, and that's what she deserves."

It's such a relief for me to be talking this way about Sandra and to know, for once, that it isn't bullshit. Mac is nodding in admiration.

"You should get shot more often. It's improved you no end. Have you worked out what you're going to do?"

"Nope. Something new, I hope. Some sort of adventure."

We take another couple of spins around everything that is wrong with this world and then Mac gets up to leave. As he opens the door he turns and salutes.

"Keep up the good work. We like this new Kevin…he reminds us of someone."

I'm lucky to have Mac, amidst all the flux he's been a constant; chaotic, erratic, but constant.

There is not much left to tell. We are virtually up to date now.

The wound took a couple of months to heal properly, but once I felt my old self again I began to throw myself into new projects. I hired a tutor and started to learn Chinese. I got my camera out from the back of a drawer and started photographing the birds in the garden. I even tried to write poetry. I'm still trying. I'll probably never show it to anybody.

One final postscript. A few mornings ago, I am sitting in the garden doing some translation exercises when Jade's voice comes on the radio. She is plugging a play about the Suffragettes that she is appearing in at the Young Vic. She sounds at ease, self-confident. It feels strange hearing her voice after everything that has happened. It was stupid of me to be so cruel with her that night in the restaurant.

As she talks about how excited she is to be working in live theatre, I find myself replaying our fateful argument in my mind. She was so upset and the scuffle we had is still a bit of a blur, but maybe, on reflection, I gave her a bit more of a shove than I was prepared to admit to myself at the time.

Still, she sounds fine now. And so am I. I drank the puffin blood and I got rescued. A robin lands on the lawn and gives me a jaunty look. I know this bird well now, he is quite bold, so I go inside to fetch my camera. As I enter the kitchen, the doorbell rings. I answer the door straight away – I no longer look out the window to check who it is – and standing on the doorstep is an eager-looking man in his late twenties.

"Hi, Kevin," he says. "Sorry to ambush you like this."

He thrusts out a hand towards me, which I shake hesitantly.

"It's Brett."

I know I know him, but I can't put the face into a context. "We worked together on the show."

Brett? Oh of course, yes, Brett, the runner – the annoyingly pushy runner.

"Can I come in?" he asks, as he comes in.

I make tea and we go through to the garden. Brett informs me that he is now a producer on the show and that he is envisaging lots of changes.

"We've been stagnating," he says. "You can't afford to stagnate in this new environment. The audiences are too nomadic."

Then he shows me some colour-coded audience research on his laptop. Apparently it charts a slow but steady decline in the figures since Lenny was written out.

"The show lost its heartbeat once Lenny was gone. These numbers speak to that."

What? "Speak to"? I hate that.

"The core audience love Lenny, so let's give them Lenny back, give them what they want."

It takes a few moments for me to realise what he is proposing.

"But Lenny's dead," I point out.

Brett waves his hand around dismissively.

"He can have faked his own death. The writers are already working on it."

He starts to enthuse about possible plotlines, but there is so much meaningless gush that I soon start to tune him out.

"Isn't it a problem…that I've been convicted of perjury?" I ask.

"You're making a new start – just like Lenny. That will chime with the audience."

Now he is talking about resonance and meta-narrative and even post-modernism. I pour the tea and steady my thoughts. Then he starts talking money. Big money. He is offering me my old life back, all that fakery and vanity and bogus prestige. He is offering a return to the days when I never had to pay for anything and any restaurant could find a table for me at a moment's notice. He wants me to reset the clock, turn it back a couple of years, he wants me to regard everything that has happened to me as no more than a sidestep.

"Well," he concludes, his eyes bright with expectation. "What do you say?"

I finish pouring the tea and then I tell him that I'll think about it.

SUPPORTERS

Unbound is a new kind of publishing house. Our books are funded directly by readers. This was a very popular idea during the late eighteenth and early nineteenth centuries. Now we have revived it for the internet age. It allows authors to write the books they really want to write and readers to support the writing they would most like to see published.

The names listed below are of readers who have pledged their support and made this book happen. If you'd like to join them, visit: www.unbound.co.uk.

Tania Ackroyd
Alison Adams
Geoff Adams
Keith Adsley
Anthony Allen
Richard Allen
Sandra Anderson
Tom Anderson
Nicholas Andrews
Steve Angell
Phillip Ansell de Percy
Lucy Armitage
Philippa Arthan
Jamie Asher
Claire Atcheson
Michael Atkinson
Julia Attwood &
   Tim Joy
Simon Axford
Clare Axton

Carrie Baide-Pugh
Eve Baker
Sam Baker
Derren Ball
Jason Ballinger
Paco Banos
Keith Barnes
Katherine Barr
Alex Batchelor
Ian Beaumont
Sarah and
   Simon Bedwell
Adrian Belcher
Saurabh Belsare
Nicole Benjamin-Ma
Julian Benton
Terry Bergin
Ray Bewick
Morag BFP
Jessie Bicknell

Richard &
   Evelyn Billett
Emily Bird
John Birtles
Kat Blair
Paul Blanchard
Nathan Bloomfield
Lee Boardman
Colin Bodley
John Bohan
Gilly Bolton
Charles Boot
Carole Booth
Tom Bowles
Claire Bradley
Alan Bradshaw
Lisa and Bill Brannan
Janey Brant
Richard W H Bray
Sophie Bridge

David Briers
Jon Briggs
David &
  Sally Brokenshaw
Ian Brooks
Emma Brown
Margaret JC Brown
MC Brown
Norma Brown
Anne Brown-Robins
Nick and Jane Bryan
PJ Bryant
Louise Buckley
Catherine Bull
Valerie Ann Bull
Simon Bullett
Adrian Bulley
Alison Burns
Sally Burrows
Sheila Bushell
Marcus Butcher
Sue Byrne
Tom Byrne
T C
Jo Cameron
Dave Campbell
Jane Campbell
Andrew Campling
Victoria Cargill-James
Anne Carlin
Barry Carpenter
Jonathan Carr
Micah Carr-Hill

Neil Carruthers
David Catley
Dawn Cavendish
Rick Challener
David Challis
Allen Chaperlin
Paul Charlton
Jill Chatt
Tim Clark
Stephen Clay
James Clelland
Louise Clover
Thom Clutterbuck
Alastair Cobb
Stevyn Colgan
Peter Constable
Nigel Cook
Simon & Sarah Cook
Julia L Cottrell
Richard Courtice
Peter Courtney-Green
Bev Cox
Gillian Craigie
Kevin Crane
John Crawford
Andrew Croker
Heather Culpin
Dave Dalton
Ivo Stormonth Darling
Dave (hedgecutter.
  com)
Clive Davey
Nick Davey

Stuart Davidson
Tracey Davidson
Lewis Davie
Clare Davies
Harriet Fear Davies
Bernadette Davis
Ian Davis
Andy Davison
Jonathan Davison
Steve Day
Graham Debenham
Paul Dembina
JF Derry
Brian Diamond
Dr Alison Diaper
Simon Dicketts
Miranda Dickinson
Ian Dickson
Max Dighton
Martin Docherty
Michelle Donlan
Christopher Dottie
Abbie Douet
John Dowie
Bob Dowling
Lawrence T Doyle
Rhian Drinkwater
Robert Dumelow
Keith Dunbar
Celina Dunlop
Neil Dutton
Dave Eagle
Nicky Edmonds

Nick Efford

Greg Erskine

J Evans

Udall Evans

Simon Everett

Peter Faulkner

Káit Feeney

Ginny Felton

Mark Finch

Anthony Fincham

Christine Fisher

Anne Fox-Smythe

Pat Fraser

Mark French

Paul Fulcher

Keith Gale

Paul Gallagher

Ina Gallo

Natalie Galustian

Amro Gebreel

Christopher Giavotto

Rob Gibson

David Giles

Aileen Gill

David Gillborn

Dorn Gillborn

Paul Godden

Jake Godfrey

Eleanor Goldsmith

Sophie Goldsworthy

Kevin Goodall

Chris 'Chairs' Gough

Keith Grady

Mark Graham

Heather Grant

Lucille Grant

Paul Grant

Mark Gray

Mark Greaves

Fenella Greenfield

David Griffiths

Heather Griffiths

Paul Groom

Stuart Guy

Owen & Liz Gwynne

Ben Hall

Keith Bryan Hall

Steve Hall

Tracey Hall

Gretel Hallett

Andrew Harding

Andrew & Dorte

   Bille Harding

Dorte Bille Harding

Alan Hardy

Jeremy Hardy

Pat Harkin

Simon Harper

Bridget Harris and

   Ivan Furness

Jo Hart & Nick Dean

Tony Hatherall

Christopher Haywood

Rebecca Haywood

Caroline Hearne

Nick Helweg-Larsen

Richard Hemming

David Hemmings

Charlotte Henwood

Adrian Hickford

E O Higgins

Jilly Hilton

Robert Hinchliffe

Jon Hobbs

Elizabeth Hogg

Christopher E Holden

Wendy Holland

Antonia Honeywell

Helen Hooker

Sir Deian Hopkin

Phil Houston

Ginny Howard

John Howard

Matt Huggins

David Hughes

David Hughes

Tim & Alison Hunt

Nik Hurrell

Florence Hyde

George Stanley Irving

Johari Ismail

Ian Jack

Barbara Jackson

Judith Jackson

Helen James

Gavin Jamie

Marjorie Johns

Mike Johnson

Jonathan

Chris F Jones

Claire Jones

Nick Jones

Peter Jordan

Tim Lund Jørgensen

Julie Kay

John Kelly

Tricia Kelly

William Kelly

Alistair Kemp

Michael Keohane

Kevin Kevane

Kevin Kieran

Patrick Kincaid

Mike King

Simon Kingston

Tim Knight

Shreena Kotecha

Samuel Labib

Evelyn Laing

John Latham

Jimmy Leach

Jane Learner

David Leddy

Caroline Lee

Jonathan Lee

Max Lehmann

Daniel Lennox

John Leonard

John Leonard

Paul Levy

Rupert Lewis

Margaret Lewisohn

Mark Lilley

Daisy Line

Nicole Loutan

Shirley Lowe

Martin Loxston-Beed

Rhian Luke

Duncan Lumsden

Anne Macdonald

Cara Macdonald

George and
    Angela Mackay

Yvonne Maddox

Mike Manger

Frances Marshall

Jane Marshall

Ros Martin

David Martindale

Chris Maryon

Guy Mason

Matt, Terri, Joseph
    & Clara

Nikola Matthews

Aidan McCann

Beth Mcgowan

John A C McGowan

Sean Mckay

Mark McKean

Gavin McKeown

Sheena McKerrell

Philip Meehan

Lynne Mendoza

Daniela Menezes

Ellie Middleton

Miggi

Peter Milburn

Stuart Millar

Anne Miller

Ben Miller

Andrew Mills

Brian Mills

Ann Mills-Duggan

Margo Milne

Claire Minett

L Mitchell

John Mitchinson

James Moakes

Mark Moncreaff

Loveyou More

Adrian Morris

Andrew Morris

Much Ado Books

Lauren G L Mulville

Gary Murrell

Jon Naismith

Craig Naples

Carlo Navato

Richard Neath

Rog Newman

Simon Newman

Al Nicholson

Ann Patricia Nicoll

Chris Nicolson

Anya Noakes

Thomas Nolan

Vaun Earl Norman

Alex Norton

Bryony &
Peter Nowell
Jan O'Malley
Chatrina O'Mara
Desmond O'Neill
Susan O'Reilly
Adrian Oates
Gail Ollis
Paul Johan Omar
Erwin Oosterhoorn
Dave Overall
Alison Owen
Jennifer Pahnke
Julia Parker
Angela Paskins
Chris Payne
Rob Peaker
Neil Pearson
Bella Pender
Thomas Perry
Dan Peters
David Petts
Stephen Phelps
Gary Phillips
Laven Pillay
Philip Pinnell
Lynne Pointer
Justin Pollard
Andy Porter
Howard Posner
Daniel Potter
Wendy Potter
Stephen Powell

Louise Preston
Janet Pretty
Neil Pretty
Rhian Heulwen Price
Tim Prollins
Jenny Pryer
Francis and
Maise Pryor
Graham Pughe
Jude & Philip Pullman
Huan Quayle
Brent Quigley
Andy Randle
Tiny Tina Rashbrook
Manoj Rathod
Colette Reap
Lesley Reeves
Troy Gordon Rich
Philip Richards
Christopher
Richardson
Liam Riley
Graham Ring
Jennie Ritchie
Andrew Roberts
Wyn Roberts
Martin Robertson
Andy Robinson
Elizabeth Robson
Phil Robson
Stian Rødland
Tony Roe
Alan Roebuck

Ben Rogers
David Rose
Hilary Rose
Chana Rochel Ross
Dominic Rushforth
Roy Russell
Dominic Salles
Charly and
Ben Salvesen
Rosemary Sandars
Michalis Sarigiannidis
Tony Sawford
AJE Sawyer
Dawn Schultz
Marianne Scobie
Suzanne Scott
Dr David A Seager
Matthew Searle
Owen Seddon
John Sheehan
Tamsin Shelton
Jodi Shields
Robert Shooter
Caroline Shutter
Glen Simmers
Laurence Simpson,
'According to The
Daily Mail'
Adam Siviter
Keith Sleight
Michael Smeeth
Alan Smith
Andy Smith

Bob Smith
Lewis Smith
Mathew Smith
Nic Smith
Nigel Smith
Richard Smith
Ross Smith
Stephen Smith
Stuart Smith
Stuart Snaith
Jeremy Snead
Eulalie Soeurs
David Somers
Richard Soundy
Chris Spath
Andrea Speed
Lorna Speirs
Jason Spencer
Martin Spencer-
    Whitton
Joe Trevor Spivey
Janice Staines
Robert E. Stephenson
Michael Stevens
Adrian Stewart
Martin Stewart
Rachel Stockdale
John Stokoe
Katie Stowell
Katie Sutcliffe
Stephen Swindley
@tanjastweets
Greg Fenby Taylor

Heather Taylor-
    Nicholson
Jane Teather and
    John Henderson
Jayne Thomas
Rhys Thompson
Mike Scott Thomson
Tristan Thorpe
Catherine Tily
Mike Totham
Fiona Turnbull
Cara Usher
Mark Vent
David Verey
Paul Vincent
Paul (Vini) Vincent
Mike Wade
Kris Waite
Philip Walberg
Stephen Walker
Steve Walker
Nick Walpole
Kate Ward
Stephen R Ward
Adam Warn
Phil Watkins
Andrew Weaver
Anne Wheelhouse
Richard Whitehead
Nigel Williams
Peter J E Williams
Sean Williamson
Derek Wilson

Joan Wilson
Nathan Wilson
Tanawat Wongwiwat
Kevin Wood
Lionel Woodcock
Kim Woods
Daniel 'not quite
    Scumspawn/
    Thomas Crimp'
    Wright
David Wright
Ian Wright
Phil Yates
Heather Zytynska